Praise

Love BITES

New York Times bestselling author Lori Foster

"A sexy, believable roller coaster of action and romance."
—*Kirkus Reviews* on *Run the Risk*

"Intense, edgy and hot. Lori Foster delivers everything
you're looking for in a romance."
—Jayne Ann Krentz, *New York Times* bestselling author

New York Times bestselling author Brenda Jackson

"Jackson's trademark ability to weave multiple characters
and side stories together makes shocking truths
all the more exciting."
—*Publishers Weekly*

"Jackson's characters are wonderful, strong,
colorful and hot enough to burn the pages."
—*RT Book Reviews* on *Westmoreland's Way*

Love
BITES

NEW YORK TIMES BESTSELLING AUTHORS
LORI FOSTER
BRENDA JACKSON

USA TODAY BESTSELLING AUTHOR
CATHERINE MANN
VIRNA DePAUL * JULES BENNETT

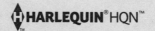
HARLEQUIN® HQN™

ISBN-13: 978-0-373-77781-5

LOVE BITES

Copyright © 2012 by Harlequin Books S.A.

The publisher acknowledges the copyright holders of the individual works as follows:

LOVE UNLEASHED
Copyright © 2012 by Lori Foster

SMOOKIE AND THE BANDIT
Copyright © 2012 by Brenda Streater Jackson

MOLLY WANTS A HERO
Copyright © 2012 by Virna DePaul

DOG TAGS
Copyright © 2012 by Catherine Mann

MANE HAVEN
Copyright © 2012 by Jules Bennett

Recycling programs for this product may not exist in your area.

Printed in U.S.A.

HARLEQUIN®
www.Harlequin.com

CONTENTS

LOVE UNLEASHED 7
Lori Foster

SMOOKIE AND THE BANDIT 81
Brenda Jackson

MOLLY WANTS A HERO 171
Virna DePaul

DOG TAGS 249
Catherine Mann

MANE HAVEN 315
Jules Bennett

LOVE UNLEASHED

Lori Foster

CHAPTER ONE

SITTING ON THE sofa in front the television with his brother, his best friend, his cat and his neighbor's dog, Evan Carlisle stared at the screen—but his thoughts were well away from sporting events, and smack dab on the neighbor.

Cinder Bratt. Mid-twenties blonde bombshell. Friendly and familiar. Cuddly but…sexually elusive.

Hot, with a capital *H*—not that Cinder seemed to realize it.

Idly he stroked her dog, Doug, while his calico cat, Cate, purred beside him. Yeah, he and Cinder had come up with the names together after a trip to the shelter almost a year ago—only a few months after meeting each other and hitting it off.

As friends.

She'd wanted a dog, so he'd gone along, but Cinder wasn't the only one to come home with a pet that day.

She and Doug had bonded, just as he and Cate had.

And Cate and Doug had already been best friends, so…it had all worked out.

He'd once teased Cinder, saying they should get a house together and adopt a horse that they'd name… Horace.

She'd laughed, swatted at him—and totally missed

the implied interest in his suggestion. Cinder missed all his clues, and never gave any of her own.

She was a pal, and it drove him nuts, a little more so every day.

Suddenly Doug's ears perked up and his head lifted, alerting Evan to Cinder's early arrival. Her big German shepherd never missed a thing, especially where it concerned Cinder. He was the most vigilant dog Evan had ever known, but also gentle and loving.

Even to his cat, Cate.

The animals got along great, hung together like best friends and had created an unbreakable bond between Evan and Cinder.

Cinder didn't acknowledge that bond. Yet.

But he was working on it.

Doug's ears twitched, then went flat, and he whined. His reaction also alerted Cate, and both animals leaped from the sofa to race for the door.

Evan checked his watch. She was more than two hours early. Because the televised sporting event would go late, he'd planned to use it as an excuse to wait up for her.

Doug barked at the door, more fretful than usual.

Before Cinder had a chance to come in, he joined the animals and opened the door for her.

"Hey." Despite the dark of evening, she wore sunglasses with her requisite nurse's uniform. Head down, posture tired, she trudged in, her bouncy blond hair a little wind whipped from the recent storm.

As comfortable in his apartment as she was in her own, she kicked off muddy shoes on the entry mat and, face averted, tugged off her windbreaker.

"You're off early." Cinder's hair wasn't the only

bouncy thing. Evan watched her breasts as she shed the jacket. She had a body that no guy could dismiss. Big breasts, full hips, round thighs…

And thinking that brought his gaze around to his older brother, Brick, and Brick's best friend, Jesse. Wearing small smiles and looks of masculine awareness, the men stared at her.

When Brick noticed Evan glaring at him, he grinned. Like big brothers everywhere, Brick took great pleasure in being annoying, especially when it concerned Cinder.

"Women in uniform are so sexy."

Jesse nodded. "Cinder in uniform, more so than most."

"Yeah," Cinder said, "rubber-soled white shoes and blousy smocks are such a turn-on."

On her…they were.

Cinder hung her jacket on the coat tree and knelt to the animals.

Still in her sunglasses.

Suspicion sparked. "Cinder?"

"Hello, kiddos," she said to the animals. Ears still flat, Doug nuzzled her neck and chewed on a curl. He was the funniest dog ever, doing things Evan had never before seen a dog do.

Right now he looked far too fretful.

Cinder hugged him. "You learned that from Cate, didn't you, big boy?" On her other side, the cat crawled up to poke her little pink nose into Cinder's hair, making her grin. "You're both so silly."

Feeling very on edge for reasons he didn't yet understand, Evan suggested, "Maybe it's your shampoo." He took her arm, hauled her upright and did his own nuzzling. "Mmm. Smells good."

Predictably, Cinder froze. "It's unscented."

"Huh." Because he already knew that, he just shrugged.

She ducked her face more.

Brick sat forward in his own show of suspicion. Making a play off her last name, he asked, "What's up, Bratt?"

"Nothing."

"Baloney," Jesse said. He looked her over, too. "We know you too well, so fess up."

They did. For over a year now, they'd all hung out together during their free time, mostly at Evan's apartment. They were a *group*, and that was all well and good.

Except that he also wanted to see Cinder alone. On a date. Or better still, in a bed. His or hers, he didn't care. Hell, the couch would work. Or even the floor.

Maybe the kitchen counter…

Pushing those thoughts aside for the moment, Evan said, "Jesse's right. What are you hiding?"

She stuck her tongue out at Jesse, and he laughed, saying, "Suggestions like that will get you in trouble."

For them, she didn't blush, or falter, or care even a little when they dropped sexual innuendos. She took them as jokes, and reacted in kind. "You wish." She gave her dog another pat. "Did you bums leave any dinner? I'm starved."

And just like that, she tried to sidle into the kitchen. Still in those ridiculous sunglasses.

Oh, hell no. "Cinder." Evan gently clasped her arm to draw her around. She reluctantly let him.

Staring at his feet, she muttered, "It is *not* a big deal."

Alarm started a slow crawl up his spine. "What isn't?"

With an exaggerated sigh, a heartbeat of hesitation, she took off the sunglasses.

What she revealed hit him as an emotional sucker-punch to the gut. "Son of a bitch," he whispered.

"Evan…" she complained at his reaction.

"Shhh." Her left eye was badly bruised, swollen, her cheekbone cut and abraded. By morning, she'd have one hell of a black eye.

Something hot and lethal settled like lead in his chest.

Both Brick and Jesse slowly approached, the paused sports show now forgotten.

"It's nothing," she insisted, giving them each a quick but fractious glance.

It was something, all right. "What happened?"

"An idiot patient who got out of control, that's all."

Evan cupped her chin and lifted her face. Her hair fell back, exposing a cut on her forehead, too. A neat row of tiny stitches marred her fair skin near her hairline.

His stomach clenched and his shoulders stiffened. *"Who?"*

She rolled her eyes. Or rather, she tried to, but with her left eye so swollen and discolored, she didn't get much effect. "I don't remember his name. He was waiting to be seen, but then he flipped out—"

"On you?"

"On everyone, really, but yeah, I was…closest at hand." She wrapped her arms around herself and tried to look impervious. "He was high on something, I guess. He decided it took us too long to get to him, and then he sort of...blew, raging on everyone." She let out a breath and forced a smile that wouldn't fool anyone. "When the guards showed up, he ran off without doing too much damage."

"Looks to me like he did plenty of damage." Evan could barely speak around the commingling emotions of rage, concern, protectiveness....

"Superficial stuff, that's all." She patted him—as if to comfort him! "You know how easily I bruise."

From playing, sure. Not from violence.

Brick lifted her wrist to examine another mark. "He grabbed you?"

"My arm, yes." She eased away from his hold. "It all happened really fast, but now it's over, and I'd as soon not talk it into the ground, so let's move on."

Everyone ignored that request.

Jesse asked, "Did the police get him?"

"They have the name he used when he signed in at the hospital, and we all saw the snake tattoo on his neck." She shrugged. "Last I heard, they were still looking."

"Snake tattoo?" Evan asked.

"It sort of wrapped around his neck and went down somewhere on his chest." She cleared her throat. "Very colorful."

Doug whined, so she began stroking him again.

Brick looked her over. "Did you get hurt anywhere else?"

"No."

"Are you sure?"

She glared at him for doubting her. "I'm a nurse, remember? I'd know if I was hurt." Focusing on Evan again, she said, "Can't the rest of the inquisition wait?

I'm starved, I need caffeine and I desperately want to change clothes."

He moved closer to her, speaking softly, drawing her in. "You promise you're okay?"

She nodded too fast. "Cross my heart."

Hands on his hips, Jesse searched her face. "You don't have to be stoic with us, you know."

That wrought a genuine laugh. "So I should do what? Look pathetic? Maybe shed some tears? That'd make you guys feel better?"

Both Brick and Jesse blanched, saying together, "God, no!"

Evan shook his head. "She's not going to cry." At least, he hoped not. "Are you?"

He watched her shoulders go back, her mouth firm, and he wanted to kiss her. All over. Every place that she might have been hurt, and in all the places where she hadn't been.

"Definitely not."

"Good. If you did, those two would fall apart."

Brick grinned around his remaining concern. "I seriously can't handle crying women."

"It's devastating," Jesse agreed. "Turns me to mush."

Relief took the tension out of her shoulders. "Well, we can't have that, now, can we?" She sniffed the air. "I hope you guys have something good left over from dinner."

This time when she walked off, Evan let her go. Doug loped along beside her, and Cate followed behind the dog like a feline caboose.

After watching her retreat, Brick whispered, "Despite the bravado, she shouldn't be alone."

Evan agreed. "I got it." He knew Brick and Jesse

cared about her, but not in the same way. Tamping down the automatic rage at seeing her hurt, Evan went into the kitchen and found her in front of the sink, staring out the apartment window at the parking lot. Security lights reflected off wet pavement, and wind whistled by.

She looked a little lost, but rallied when he joined her. "I think it's going to rain again."

Evan wanted to pull her into his arms, hold her close. But she had Don't Touch signs all over her. "We grilled before the storm hit, and we saved you a piece of chicken and a baked potato. I can heat that up for you if you want."

"Sounds heavenly. Thank you."

"No problem." Tenderness put a stranglehold on him. God, he wanted…so many things, all of them oddly amplified by seeing her this way. "If you want something to drink, help yourself."

"Okay." She opened his fridge and found a Coke. After popping the tab, she leaned back on the counter and upended the can for a long swallow. "Honest to God, I'm dead on my feet."

Working twelve-hour shifts was rough enough without brutality thrown in. "Should you maybe get checked?"

She held the can to her bruised cheekbone, sighing at the touch of the cold aluminum. "I work at a hospital, Evan. Believe me, I've been checked and rechecked."

He winced for her. "Right."

Her smile didn't quite reach her eyes. "If you want the truth, that was the worst part of it all—being seen like that by the people I work with."

She hadn't wanted to talk to the others, but with him,

she volunteered her feelings. He appreciated the significance of that. "When did this all happen?"

"A few hours ago. But there was a little…blood."

"Damn." He cupped the back of her neck to encourage her to talk, to comfort her. To connect with her.

"Head wounds, you know? They can be messy. After we got that under control, I had to talk to the cops and see the doctor and all that." She stared off at nothing in particular. "One of the other nurses helped me to clean up. There was blood in my hair, on my shirt…."

Unable to stop himself, Evan touched a gentle kiss to her forehead. "Go sit down. Put your feet up. I'll have the food ready in a few minutes."

"If it's okay, I'll run next door to change first." She held out the hem of her smock. "Like I said, I got blood on the top I wore to work. This is a spare I leave in my locker, but it's pretty old and not all that comfortable."

Usually he couldn't stop thinking how damned cute she looked in her colorful uniforms. Brick hadn't lied; with her curves, she gave the shapeless cotton nursing scrubs a fetish edge.

But tonight, after what she'd been through, he could only think about protecting her.

"You want company?"

Her eyebrows lifted. "To change my clothes?"

"No." Yes. What the hell was he thinking? He shook his head. "Just to be there with you, I mean."

She watched him with big, dark eyes.

Jesus. "C'mon, Cinder. Give over. You have to be a little nervous. No one would blame you if you didn't want to be alone right now."

Dark lashes swept down to hide her eyes. "I'm not that fragile, Evan. Seriously. I'll be fine."

He didn't want to let her out of his sight, but he didn't know what to do about it. "All right, then, if you're sure."

She set down the half-empty Coke and walked off in haste. He heard her say to the others, "Be right back," and then, as if she was the Pied Piper, both the dog and the cat followed her out his door and across the hall to her own apartment.

Glad that she'd taken Doug along, but still with thoughts churning, Evan turned to microwave her food.

Jesse and Brick abandoned the TV and joined him in the kitchen. Jesse pulled out a chair, turned it around and straddled the seat. "She's shook up."

"I know." Evan scrubbed a hand over his face, wondering how many more bruises she had on her body, bruises hidden by her clothes. "But she'll be okay." Cinder was one of the strongest women he knew.

Brick, aptly named for his hardheaded attitude, cursed low. "Who could ever hurt a sweetheart like her?"

She *was* a sweetheart. Gentle, loving, happy and giving. He tensed even more.

Jesse eyed him. "Tonight might be the perfect time to make a move."

Rather than pretend he didn't understand, Evan gave him a killing glare. "She's hurt, you ass."

"I didn't say to molest her. Just let her know how you feel."

As long as they both accepted that she was off-limits, Evan could tolerate the ribbing. "I don't know."

Brick shook his head in mock pity. "He's usually not so chicken shit with women."

"He's just been timing things," Jesse said in Evan's defense. "Waiting for his opportunity to strike."

Bull. He'd "struck" several times, but Cinder wasn't reciprocating. The last thing he wanted to do was run her off by overstepping the boundaries she'd set, especially now that she was hurt and in need of a friend. "She's not exactly giving off signals, ya know."

Jesse looked taken aback, then said in an aside to Brick, "Yeah, maybe you're right. Total chicken shit."

Ignoring the continued insults, Evan checked the clock. How long before she returned? "If she ever seems willing, I'll be all over it."

"And by then," Brick said, "some other dude might've swept in and stolen the opportunity."

That idea got him pacing the tiny kitchen. What was taking so long?

"She is surrounded by doctors," Jesse pointed out. "You know, guys with pedigreed backgrounds and plenty of money to spend."

And he was an elementary math and gym teacher—but he knew Cinder didn't care about that. He checked the time again. "She doesn't even date, damn it."

"No," Jesse said, "she just hangs out here—with you."

"With all of us."

"For *you*," Brick stressed.

"Because Doug likes me. You know we pet sit for each other."

"Damn, brother, you're being so obtuse, it's embarrassing." Brick gave him a shove. "Pet sitting isn't the only thing on her mind."

Were they right? And if so, then why didn't Cinder show some interest?

It was as if Jesse read his mind. "She's shy, you know."

"Cinder?" Evan snorted. "She is not."

"Not when it comes to patients, or to caring for her dog, or helping neighbors—no, she's not. For that stuff, she's friendly and outgoing and funny. But anything sexual…she's supershy."

Mmmm…possibly. Cinder never hesitated to approach a new neighbor. She was open and welcoming to everyone. But whenever one of the men in their apartment building flirted—and most of them did—she shied away, or didn't notice.

Brick added, "Why else would she hide that killer body?"

Food for thought. Contrary to most sexy women, Cinder did tend to cover up and dress down. He spoke his thoughts aloud. "It's almost like she has no clue how sexy she is."

"So tell her," Jesse suggested.

"Then go from there." Brick thought about that before shaking his head. "But go easy tonight. I mean, she's a little beat up—"

This time Evan shoved him. "Like I need you two giving me advice?" No, he wouldn't pressure Cinder tonight, but he would love to reassure her, to comfort her. "When was the last time you had a significant other?"

"Never," Brick said. "Thank God."

"You know he likes playing the field," Jesse added. "As do I."

"I thought you and Lisa were going strong."

"Nope. That's over."

"What happened?"

Jesse shrugged. "Nothing." And then: "I only went

out with her four times, Evan. Don't make it sound like we were engaged."

"Four times is two times too many, far as I'm concerned." Brick shuddered. "It gives women ideas."

"You're both Neanderthals," Evan accused. "Why is it you're all set to stay single, but you want me to hook up?"

They said together, "Cinder is different."

Amen. Very different. "I can't argue that."

"So do something about it already." Jesse toasted him with his cola. "Before it's too late."

"While you stew on it, I think we'll go watch the rest of the fights." Brick elbowed his way out of the tiny kitchen, and Jesse went with him.

Evan heard them take the TiVo off pause, and then the raucous noise of a competition filled the apartment.

Because Cinder liked to watch the fights, too, Evan always recorded them for her. She'd missed the first two fights already.

Maybe he'd convince her to hang around after the guys left. Maybe, given what she'd been through, he'd convince her to stay the night.

With him.

Nothing sexual, not with what had happened today. But to hold her all night…

His front door opened without a knock. Neither of them stood on ceremony when visiting. If either of them had anything private going on, for instance, when Cinder showered, the door was locked.

Wearing a big, loose white sweatshirt with jeans that fit her voluptuous shape like a second skin, her feet bare, she led in the dog and the cat.

She'd washed the rest of the ruined makeup from her

face and left her blond curls loose. Given the movement of her heavy breasts under that sweatshirt, she wasn't wearing a bra.

For any guy with a pulse, she'd be a lush, sweet fantasy come to life.

"Is the food ready?"

Evan drew his gaze from her chest to her face. Heat pulsed beneath his skin and his muscles felt twitchy. "Take a seat. I'll bring it to you."

She graced him with a teasing smile. "You're too good to me." Then she parked her pretty rear on the corner of the couch. Doug immediately sat on the floor by her feet and laid his head over her knee. Cate got on the back of the couch to curl up near her shoulder.

After giving her a long look, Jesse said, "You're just in time. The third fight is about to begin."

She pulled a throw pillow into her lap. "Were the other fights good?"

Brick spoke quickly. "Don't tell her a thing."

"Ohhh," she said, a little peppier now that she knew the guys wouldn't continue questioning and pampering her. "They must've been good. I can't wait."

Evan set her Coke on the end table and handed her the plate of food on a tray. She balanced it on the pillow.

Near her ear, Evan spoke quietly so the others wouldn't hear. "You're up to watching the fights?"

Just as quietly, she said, "It's a good distraction."

Because he couldn't help himself, he brushed a thick curl behind her ear, then cupped her cheek. "All right. But if you need anything, tell me."

For a brief moment, she leaned her shoulder into his, a familiar and comfortable gesture. "For right now,

this—all of it—is enough." She tucked into her food
and gave her attention to the big-screen TV.

Even with the black eye, she looked precious to him.
This—all of it—is enough. What did she mean by that?
The camaraderie? The food?

The closeness?

An hour later, he still didn't know. She'd eaten all
her food and insisted on putting her own dishes away.
He heard her get an OTC pain med while she was in
the kitchen, and it left him rigid with concern. When
she returned, this time with a bottle of water for each
of them, she sat a little nearer to him, almost as though
she needed the contact.

Trying to guess her thoughts kept him so distracted,
Evan missed more of the fights than he saw.

Doug stayed especially close to her side, no doubt
sensing her upset. He didn't demand her attention, but
he was there, protective and attentive.

Maybe, Evan thought, he should do the same.

And since when did he start taking his cues from
a dog? But as she hugged Doug several times, he decided it was the right thing to do. Somehow he'd convince her to stay near to him—and eventually she'd
enjoy being there.

CHAPTER TWO

THE DREAD BUILT as Cinder watched the last fight. Now the guys would leave, and…she'd have to go back to her own apartment.

Alone.

But she wouldn't be a sissy. She wouldn't be a burden. She had Doug. Everything would be fine.

The guys were animated, yelling suggestions to the last two fighters, cheering, groaning and cursing a little. Tonight, being distracted, Cinder watched them more than she watched the fights.

Brick looked a lot like Evan, with his dark hair and eyes, his height over six feet. Less than two years separated them, but Brick seemed older. Maybe more jaded.

He might share a resemblance with Evan, but his demeanor was darker, edgier. He played harder, cursed more and dated endlessly. It seemed to her that Brick went from one woman to another, while Evan…well, she'd rarely seen him date much. Or if he did, he didn't tell her about it.

Probably a good thing, given how tough it would be for her to know the intimate details of his social life. That is, whatever social life he had when she wasn't around. Couldn't be much of one, between work and the time he spent at the apartment…with her.

"No!" Jesse sat forward, disgruntled over the turn in

the fight. He was tall, too, but unlike Evan and Brick, he had dark blond hair and vivid green eyes that sometimes looked right through a person, into her soul. He was a serial dater like Brick, but maybe more romantic. When he dated, anyone could see that he made a woman feel special.

Brick, apparently, just made the ladies hot. For certain, he never wanted for female attention.

When the fight suddenly ended with a knockout, everyone yelled. Doug jumped up with an energetic bark, his tail thumping in excitement. Disgruntled, Cate curled tighter and put her tail over her little face.

Cinder tried to join in the discussion of the fight, but it was futile. Instead, she gathered up the empty cans and bowls of chip crumbs and carried them to the kitchen. She was rinsing out cans when arms came around her.

Brick.

Smiling, she put her head back on his boulder-hard shoulder. "Ready to leave?"

"Yup." He kissed her temple. "Keep me posted, okay? Let me know if they catch the bastard who hurt you."

She patted the hands laced around her waist. "I'm sure they will."

Brick released her and, as she turned, Jesse drew her in for a hug. He carefully lifted her right off her feet. "Take it easy, okay? Maybe consider letting Evan coddle you a little."

She'd been smiling over the embrace—until he mentioned Evan. Looking toward Evan, she saw him standing back, arms crossed, gaze attentive.

And damn it, she blushed.

"I keep telling you guys, I'm fine." She pushed away from Jesse with a frown. "I don't need to be coddled."

"He doesn't mind, do you, Evan?"

"Be my pleasure," Evan said in a low, suggestive voice that sent her pulse skittering into overdrive.

Her face went hotter still. Lord, now they were all three scrutinizing her, but she did not want to be forced on Evan. "You're all a bunch of old ladies." She shooed them away. "Go home. But drive carefully. It's storming again."

There was another round of hugs, and then she stood alone with Evan. Doug watched her, waiting to see if they would leave or stay.

Evan remained near the kitchen doorway, arms still crossed, his attention burning.

What did that mean? Was that hot stare out of concern, or something more? "I'm going to help pick up before I go." She straightened a cushion, turned off a lamp, went back to the kitchen—passing close by Evan.

He didn't move. If it was one of the other guys, she'd give a hip bump or a playful push, maybe even make kissing noises at him.

But with Evan, given her hidden feelings, she always felt awkward and obvious and sort of exposed. So she squeezed past him without a word—and he let her.

After she went to the sink, Evan came up beside her. She froze as he reached around her…and took a doggy treat from the container on his counter.

Her breath escaped in a sigh.

"Here you go, boy." Evan handed the treat to Doug.

Until then, she hadn't realized Doug was dogging her heels so closely. She turned and gave him a pat.

"My shadow," she teased. "I should have realized you were there."

"He's worried about you."

She did not want to feel guilty for making her dog worry. "He always follows me."

"Not like this." Evan again touched her hair. "He's probably picking up on things you want to hide."

"What do you mean?" She knew exactly what he meant. "I'm not hiding anything." *Such a big fib.*

Evan stood so much taller than her that when he stared down at her that way, she felt small, and incredibly…feminine.

In truth, she was neither. She was far too chubby, a tomboy who preferred sweats to skirts for everyday life.

"Cinder," he chided, and his hand curved around her jaw.

He had such big, warm hands that her toes curled. "Hmm?"

"There's no one here but us now."

She was all too aware of that. "I know."

"We're good friends, right?"

Sadly, yes, they were only good friends. She nodded.

His mouth quirked at the way her hair bounced around. He smoothed it before continuing. "I don't expect you to fall apart, because that's not you. Hell, the world could start coming down around you, and you'd take charge."

"Thanks." That made her sound sort of…bossy. And cold. "I think."

"But you were attacked. No way will I believe you're blowing that off."

He knew her too well—except he didn't know that she'd fallen hopelessly in love with him only days after meeting him. "Okay, so I'm a little jittery. No big deal. I'll be fine."

"'Course you will. But with me, you don't have to put on a front." His other hand lifted to her face, too, so that now he held her caught in his gaze. "Okay?"

He had such a piercing, sexy expression that she felt herself swaying toward him. Doug leaned into her side, breaking the impact of that awesome stare.

To cover her reaction, she laughed a little too loud. "Sure, okay. No problem."

Given the way he watched her, he wasn't fooled. "When do you return to work?"

Because it made her look wimpy, she gave the admission defensively. "The hospital offered me time off, and I took it. I don't have to go back until Wednesday."

"Good." His thumb brushed her cheek once, twice, and he dropped his hands. "It'll reassure Doug and me both to keep you within reach for a few days."

Within reach? "Umm…"

"You might be indomitable," he teased her, "but I'm as shaken as Doug is."

She gave him the smile he expected over the outrageous comment. As a gym teacher who partook in physical activity every day, Evan was in primo shape. Tall, muscular, lean. Only a few years older than her, with black hair and mellow brown eyes shades lighter than her own.

He was downright dreamy—and she was his *pal*.

Turning away, she busied herself by rinsing dishes. He took them from her and dried. It was always like that. They worked as a friendly team.

It sucked.

After she wiped off the counter, she returned the

dishrag to the sink, turned to Evan and prepared to force herself to say goodbye.

Before the first whisper of sound left her mouth, Evan said, "Stay."

She drew a blank. "Stay?"

"Here with me."

She looked at Doug, but he didn't seem to find anything amiss in the invitation. In fact, he thumped his tail as if in encouragement.

"You mean…to watch the first fights I missed?"

"If you want."

That left her totally confused. "What do *you* want?"

"For you to stay here with me."

Well, that cleared up…nothing. To buy herself some time, Cinder said, "I was going to take a nice, long shower." She wrinkled her nose. "You're right that I'm a little tense still. I figured the hot water would help relax me before I head to bed."

"You're tired?"

It seemed as good an excuse as any to escape the awkwardness of lusting wildly after a guy friend. "A little, yeah."

His expression warmed. "Go ahead, then." He fingered the sleeve of her sweatshirt. "But when you're done, change into your pj's and come back over."

"But…"

"You can sleep here."

Her eyes rounded and heat rolled through her. She squeaked, "Here?"

Amused at her reaction, his smile spread. "You've dozed on my couch before."

Oh Lord, oh Lord. Once, after a long shift with overtime, she'd come over to get her dog, sat down to talk and all but passed out. She was still embarrassed about it—especially since he'd been sitting there looking at her when she'd awoken. "Not on purpose!"

All too serious, he asked, "Would you rather have my bed?"

While the bottom fell out of her stomach, he continued.

"I'd actually prefer that. But, honest to God, honey, I'd like to keep you close. At least for tonight." He held her upper arms. "You can give me that, can't you?"

Oh, she wanted that so badly. But was this a misguided come-on? And if it was…wouldn't he end up disappointed?

And would his disappointment end the friendship she cherished so much?

Evan put his forehead to hers. "Stop thinking and just go indulge in your shower." After a quick kiss to her brow, he led her to the door. "I'll be here when you're done."

Feeling more than a little numb, she retreated across the hall to her own place again. She let herself in, and Doug came in behind her. Before she shut the door, Cate shot through, too.

It was endlessly amusing how Cate followed Doug, and vice versa. Back and forth from her apartment to Evan's and back again. Wherever one animal went, so went the other. Even when Doug did his business outside, Cate would follow. She didn't need a leash, because she didn't wander away from his side.

Evan still stood in his doorway, one shoulder propped against the frame, watching her.

"I'll bring them both back with me in just a little bit."

"Take your time, honey. I'm not in a rush."

No, he wasn't in a rush. And despite the fancy of her imagination, he wasn't interested. Not in *that* way.

Not in the way she most wanted.

Hadn't she learned the hard way her lesson on the preferences of big gorgeous men?

But then he added, "And, Cinder? After you're done showering, I think I'll show you a few other ways to relax."

LEAVING HIS DOOR unlocked, Evan rushed through his own warm shower. Driven by heated anticipation, he shaved and brushed his teeth in record time. While thinking of Cinder, of having her with him all night, he dressed in boxers and jeans, with a plain white T-shirt.

Then he paced.

And tormented himself with images of her in the shower, her curvaceous body soapy and wet....

In the middle of a groan, he heard a noise in the hallway near his front door. Thinking it'd be Cinder, wondering why she didn't just come in, he smiled and strode to open the door.

With a high-pitched, startling screech, Cate shot in, her fur fluffed out, her tail so full she resembled a raccoon. Doug jumped up against his body, uncharacteristically anxious, whining and barking at almost the same time.

"What's wrong, Doug?"

Now that he had Evan's attention, Doug ran to Cinder's door and back again.

"What the...?" Evan looked up and down the hall, but didn't see her. No way would she have let Doug out alone.

The dog jumped at her door, snarling, and somehow, Evan just knew.

The fine hairs on the back of his neck stood up. Heart racing, he tried her front door and found it locked. Of course, with her in the shower, it would be. He could get the key, but with Doug turning panicked circles, Evan wasted no more time. Doug had gotten out somehow— and that's how Evan would get in.

He snapped his door shut to keep Cate confined, and while calling Brick, he jogged out and around to Cinder's patio door.

Still snarling, Doug ran with him.

Brick answered with, "I thought you'd be busy, brother. You disappoint me."

The patio slider wasn't locked. In fact, it wasn't even closed all the way. Evan said simply, "Send the cops to Cinder's apartment. Now."

"Shit." No longer teasing, Brick said, "On the way."

Disconnecting the call, Evan slid the door open farther and crept in. With the bathroom door standing open, he could hear the shower, a radio turned up, and Cinder singing. Loudly. She didn't sound troubled.

Hackles raised, Doug shot forward, past the bathroom and into…Cinder's bedroom. A raucous barking started.

Someone let out a shout.

Evan strode forward. When he reached the open bathroom door, he leaned in to say, "You have an intruder."

From behind the shower curtain, she shrieked. "Evan! What in the world?"

No time to pander to her delicate sensibilities. He

spoke up to be heard over the blaring radio. "I'm locking your door. Leave it that way until the cops get here."

He hit the lock, pulled the door shut and turned in time to nearly collide with a big bruiser wearing a black ski mask and black leather gloves. The guy was wet, his jeans soaked to his knees, the ski mask smelling of wet wool.

Enraged, the guy stumbled back, swatting wildly at the dog as he snapped and roared and tried to find a way to get hold of the masked man.

He had a gun in his right hand. Evan's blood ran cold when the bastard aimed that weapon at Doug.

Hell, no.

Reacting on pure protective instinct, Evan launched himself at the thug. He managed to grab his gun hand and hold on as they crashed hard to the floor in a tangle of limbs and rage. A table overturned. A lamp shattered.

Evan cracked his head on something and felt warm blood run down his temple.

Doug went berserk, lunging in and out of the fray, teeth bared, growl feral. The guy pulled his head back to avoid sharp teeth, and it displaced the mask enough for Evan to see…a snake tattoo on his neck!

Son of a bitch.

Trying to keep that gun hand suppressed and dodging fists and kicks, Evan had his hands full. The big man wasn't a wimp, and he wasn't about to give up. A fist the size of a lunch box clipped Evan in the chin, and he saw stars.

But no way would he release his hold.

Furious, he twisted the wrist hard and, with a bellow, the man's fingers loosened until the gun fell free. Taking advantage of that, Evan landed a few blows of his own, two to the face, one to the gut. Managing to daze the guy, Evan felt him go limp, and then suddenly...

No fucking way.

Wearing only a skimpy, damp towel, her body still glistening wet, her blond hair piled up atop her head, Cinder darted close to grab for the gun.

For a single instant, seeing her like that, Evan went stupid—and got slugged for it. He fell back, Doug leaped in, and the intruder tried to get to the gun before Cinder could.

In the struggle, she lost her towel.

Even the intruder went stupid that time.

Doug, the only one not affected by her nudity, got hold of the leering bastard's calf and sank his teeth in.

The man howled in searing pain, wrestled his way to his feet and tried to kick free of the dog. Doug shook his head, mangling the guy's leg, hanging on with tenacity.

Taking advantage of that, Evan dove forward and snatched up the gun. He didn't dare take aim, not with Cinder standing there and Doug so close at hand. If a bullet ricocheted or the gun misfired...

Anxious to escape, the intruder dragged toward the door. Doug did his best to hold him back, teeth clamped tight, paws digging in, haunches quivering.

Evan stepped in front of Cinder, the guy got outside the patio door, closed it on Doug, and just as he disappeared from sight, limping badly, lights from a police cruiser lit up the night.

Holy shit.

Evan couldn't get enough air into his lungs. His heart popped so hard in his chest, it racked him with each sucking breath. Still frenzied, denied his ultimate victory, Doug whined at the door, scratching, trying to find a way to give chase.

And the police would come in any second.

Very slowly, his head pounding and his vision narrowed, Evan turned and looked at Cinder. He used a forearm to swipe the blood from his gaze. Her eyes were wide, her lips pale, her body…luscious enough to distract him from the danger they'd just encountered.

He didn't want to be a jackass, but he couldn't stop himself from soaking up the sight of her. All of her. Top to toes and everywhere in between.

Especially the places in between.

She stood frozen, trembling, one arm crossed over her abundant breasts, a hand tucked over the notch of her thighs. If she hoped to conceal herself, she did an inadequate job of it.

A boner, right now, at this particular moment, would be impossible.

Knowing he had to get it together, Evan dragged the back of one finger over the top of her left breast. *So silky soft.* "You don't have enough hands for that. And under any other circumstance, I wouldn't say this. But right here, right now…don't you think you ought to go get some clothes on?"

Her jaw loosened, closed again when she gasped, then she turned and literally ran.

Wow.

The bathroom door slammed. And locked.

The blaring radio finally shut off.

Even with the blood from his head wound in his eyes, he'd seen plenty. Enough to tighten his muscles and spike his temperature and make him determined—*more than determined*—to win her over. Tonight.

To hell with the drama unfolding—he needed her, sooner rather than later.

Placing the gun on the chair behind him, Evan went to the patio doors. He took hold of Doug's collar to ensure he wouldn't run off and opened the door to flag in the cops.

The second they reached him, he backed into the apartment and started explaining. "I live next door. The guy who broke in just took off. That's his gun, not mine. Those are his muddy footprints everywhere. He was wearing a ski mask and black leather gloves, but I saw a snake tattoo on his neck, and he'll have a bad bite on his left calf. He was limping when he got away." He drew a breath. "My neighbor…my female neighbor… is in the bathroom. Naked."

From the bathroom, he heard Cinder shriek again.

She was unharmed—*this time*—he had to remind himself.

Adrenaline continued to pump through his veins, and now, with the danger over, it surged into a riot of conflicting reactions—the uppermost being rage. "He's the same bastard who attacked her at the hospital today. He must have followed her home." Realizing that sickened Evan. He shouldn't have let the guy get away. "She was in the shower when he broke in here. Her dog came to tell me."

After that rambling explanation, the smaller of the two officers lifted a brow, saying only, "Her dog?"

As if he understood, Doug sat down and stared at the cops with sincerity. He swallowed some slobber, let his tongue drop back out and panted from the excitement.

Evan scratched the dog's neck to let him know he'd done well.

The disbelieving officer watched Doug while giving some orders through a radio.

The other cop took the gun off the chair and nodded at Evan's head. "You're okay?"

"Yes."

Cinder stepped out. Shy. Still damp. Flustered. Now, thankfully, dressed in pajama pants and a dark T-shirt. But he'd already seen her, and now knew firsthand all the secrets of her amazing body.

She could have been wearing armor and it wouldn't have mattered to his throbbing interest.

Ignoring everyone else, she carried a towel and came to Evan's side. "Sit down."

"Do you need an ambulance?" one officer asked.

"No." Evan dropped into the seat. Doug leaned into his side, still twitchy. Evan continued to give him firm pats. "You did good, Doug. You're a brave dog."

Leaning close enough for him to breathe in her scent, Cinder tipped his head toward her, parted his hair and checked his injury. "It's not too bad. I don't think he needs stitches."

Evan said to the cops, "She's a nurse." And he slipped his free arm around her waist.

She went stiff as a board, but only for a second. Then she lurched away. "Cate!"

"Who?" the cops asked. They looked around as if expecting more trouble.

"My cat," Evan explained. He pulled Cinder close again. "She was with Doug when he came to tell me what was happening. I closed her into my place."

"Oh, that poor thing!" Rushing past the officers, Cinder went out the front door and across the hall to retrieve the cat.

Just like Cinder, to think of everyone and everything other than herself. Evan smiled at the cops. "My cat. Her dog." He shrugged. "They're close."

To prove that, Doug anxiously met her at the door when she returned. She set Cate down, and the two animals greeted each other as if they'd been separated for a year. Cate pranced on her tiptoes, rubbing her arched back along Doug's muzzle. Ears forward, he lowered his head and snuffled her small body in excitement.

Bemused, the cops watched until Doug urged the cat to his favorite spot in front of a window. Cate stretched out beside him. Doug put his face on his front paws and watched them.

Just to add to the confusion, Brick and Jesse both showed up. Brick took one look at the cops and went straight to Cinder to embrace her. Jesse waited for his turn.

Despite Evan's bloody head, they both ignored him— thank God. He felt asinine enough for getting hurt. He could usually handle himself without a screwup, but it had left Evan clumsy—the combination of Cinder in the shower and a masked, armed intruder undoubtedly bent on hurting her, Doug, or both.

Avoiding injury had been far from his mind—he'd thought only of protecting them.

For the next hour, chaos reigned.

Brick made coffee for everyone. Jesse cleaned up the mess in Cinder's apartment, including the muddy footprints, once the cops said it was okay. After bandaging Evan's head, she stayed at his side, answering questions about the break-in while judiciously omitting any mention of losing her towel.

Evan sure as hell wasn't going to share that with anyone.

The cops noticed her blackening eye and the bruise on her cheek. "You get that tonight, in the scuffle?"

"No." Because it was important, Cinder gave them the details about the incident at the hospital.

The bruise on her arm had also darkened, but Evan had seen her naked, and hadn't noticed any other injuries.

Not that he'd been looking for injuries. Mostly he'd just stared…and absorbed.

Other officers searched the area for the intruder.

They didn't find him.

Everyone assumed it had to be the same guy who'd attacked her at the hospital. It didn't take an investigative genius to see that he'd broken the lock on the patio door to get in.

Cinder explained that both the dog and the cat had been lounging in the bathroom with her, so the guy must have gone straight to her bedroom. She remembered Doug barking and running off, but she'd thought nothing of it.

Whenever she showered, Doug stayed extra vigilant, barking at cars in the lot, tenants coming or going, every leaf that blew by. She'd had no reason to think anything unusual had happened.

"Why did you have the radio turned up so loud?" Evan asked.

Her face went hot pink. "Singing helps keep me from thinking too much."

His heart softened. "You were fretting about what happened at the hospital?"

She had that deer-caught-in-the-headlights look about her before she shrugged. "Okay."

What the hell did that mean? If it wasn't the incident from the hospital, then what hadn't she wanted to think about?

One cop looked up from a notebook. "With what you've told us, he must have followed you, scoped out the place, and after you left the apartment, he decided to wait around until you returned."

Alone. With that realization, Evan felt sick. She'd been a specific target for a lunatic. He shared a look with his brother and friend.

"Given the disarray of your closet," the other officer added, "I think he planned to hide in there."

The hot color leeched from her face. "My closet? But...why?"

"He probably figured you'd make too much of a fuss if he tried to take you from the shower. Close as these apartments are, someone might have heard you."

"Or more likely," Brick added, scowling at both cops for scaring her more, "he went past the bathroom when he saw Doug coming after him."

"Good thing you had him with you," Jesse agreed.

What if she'd left Doug behind while she'd showered? Granted, Doug wouldn't have liked that idea. But if the dog had thought she was going to work, he wouldn't have kicked up a lot of fuss.

Looking at her now, sensing her disquiet, Evan knew she would never again ignore the dog's bark. The events of the day had irrevocably changed her. What would it take to make her feel safe and secure once again?

He'd damn well figure it out, one way or another.

Pulling his gaze away from Cinder, Evan addressed

the cops. "Are we all done here?" He wanted to be alone with her. Now.

"Since there's not much else we can do, I guess so. But I would recommend you get that door fixed right away. Until we catch him, there's no guarantee he won't be back."

Evan wasn't the only guy to tense over that, especially when Cinder wrapped her arms around herself.

Brick said, "I'll take care of fixing the door. I'll change the lock, but I'll also make a brace that she can use, so even if someone tampers with the lock, they won't be able to get the door open."

Brick ran the family hardware store. Jesse was a carpenter. Together they'd no doubt make her door impenetrable.

"You have what you need?" Evan asked.

"Yeah, piece of cake. Don't give it a thought."

Jesse said, "It's going to take a few hours, at least. Cinder should stay with Evan tonight."

The cop nodded. "Not a bad idea, all things considered."

Cinder looked at each of them in turn, her expression annoyed. Then she shook it off. "Brick, thank you. I appreciate the help."

"No problem, hon."

"Jesse, you should not throw Evan under the bus like that." Before Evan could protest, she turned those big eyes on him. "But I really wouldn't mind camping out with you tonight, if that's okay?"

Camping out with me. And she thought he might mind?

The two male cops, Jesse and Brick all stared at her with indulgent expressions. He knew exactly what they were thinking, something macho and sex inspired about a woman in distress and a guy being the big, protective hero.

Cinder would never play the role of damsel in distress, but he was relieved to know she trusted him enough to admit she wanted the company.

Right now, given the expression on her face, she didn't have a clue where all the male minds had wandered.

Damn, he adored her. "I would have asked if Jesse had given me a chance."

"I'm relieved, thanks." Her gaze skittered away from his, and she cleared her throat. "Maybe you could put a brace in your own door as well, just to be extra cautious?"

"All right." Whatever it took to make her feel secure. "Soon as we get over there, I'll rig it somehow. Tomorrow, Brick can make me something more permanent."

"Sure thing," Brick agreed.

"So that's settled, then." As hospitably as possible, Cinder showed the cops to the door. They promised to call if they found out anything new, and for the rest of the night, they'd be sure to drive past the apartment complex while on duty. She thanked them with great sincerity, closed the door and then just stood there with her back to Evan, almost undecided on what to do next, when she was never undecided.

It bothered him.

He had a feeling her mood had more to do with him seeing her naked than with any ominous danger.

Gently, without approaching her, he asked, "Do you need to get anything together?"

She turned, bit her lip and shook her head. "No. I

don't think so." Grabbing up her purse and pulling the strap over her shoulder, she made her preference for leaving the apartment clear. "I already showered and brushed my teeth."

"Time for us to go, then." Reminding himself over and over again that she needed comfort, not a sexual pursuit, Evan took her spare set of keys off the wall and handed them to Brick. "Lock up when you leave."

"Will do." He dropped his voice. "But get her out of here. She looks ready to jump out of her skin."

Because he'd seen her naked. Not that he'd share that with his brother.

"Right." Evan called to Doug, and as the dog came to him, Cate followed. "Let's go, guys. Time to settle down for the night." Together they crossed the hall to Evan's apartment.

"It's been like musical chairs today," Cinder said. "Except we're playing with apartments."

Unable to take his eyes off her, Evan got her inside and locked the door. Doug made a beeline to his usual spot in front of the couch. He circled twice, tightening with each turn, then plopped down with a relieved sigh, his nose very close to his rump. Cate sprawled on her back next to him, pawed his muzzle lazily and closed her eyes.

"Looks like they're exhausted," Evan said.

Cinder smiled. "And so precious."

She was precious, too. Keeping his hands to himself wasn't easy. "They love each other."

"I know." She dropped her purse and went to sit on the couch. Head back, legs straight out in front of her, arms flopped at her sides, she let out a long breath. "God, what a day."

With any luck, Evan would help her have a much more peaceful night. Whatever it took…he just had to keep reminding himself that tonight was for reassurance.

Tomorrow…tomorrow he could start an earnest pursuit.

CHAPTER THREE

AFTER BETTER CLEANING the blood off his face, and then blocking his patio door with a broom handle, Evan sat down beside Cinder. At his nearness, she felt her face heating once more. It didn't help that he kept staring at her so intently, making her feel naked all over again.

Even while wedging that broom into place, he kept looking back at her. Since seeing her buck-ass, she doubted ten seconds had passed without his gaze roaming over her.

"What's it to be?" He took her hand, ran his thumb over her knuckles.

Such a simple touch, not any different from the way he'd touched her many times.

But that was before she'd lost a towel in front of him.

"Bed," he asked low, "or a little TV so you can unwind?"

Ho boy. She had a preference, all right, but she didn't dare share it. It took all her concentration not to curl up as close to him as Cate had to Doug. "Maybe a little TV?"

"Okay." He used the remote to turn on the set. "Anything in particular?"

Noise. That's all she needed. Some way to block the memory of losing that towel, the image of his hot gaze roving over her in shock.

Her throat tightened. "Doesn't matter."

"Ooookay," he said again, this time stretching out the word. He turned on an old movie and, still holding her hand, slouched back comfortably on the couch.

Not once did he look away from her. She became far too jittery.

"Cinder?"

"Hmmm?" Oh geez, that sounded way too loud, with forced cheerfulness. She cleared her throat. "Yes?"

"I told you to stay locked in the bathroom."

She snorted before she could think better of it. "It was my apartment." Someone had come into her home. Someone with nefarious intent. She barely contained a shiver of dread over what might had happened. "I couldn't just hide."

"You could have stayed safe." His voice dropped to a rasp, his attention like a warm caress. "You didn't have to jump into the middle of things."

"I wanted to get that gun so he couldn't use it." There'd been no time to think. She'd taken one look at Evan tussling on the floor, blood on his head, Doug far too vulnerable, and she'd known she had to do something. Fast. "I didn't want to take a chance on him shooting you or Doug."

He lifted her hand to his mouth and pressed a warm kiss to her knuckles. His mouth lingered, his breath hot, soft. "It was a brave thing to do."

She felt a tingle clear down to her toes. "*You* were brave. I just sort of went blank and reacted on instinct."

"Mmm." His mouth moved over her knuckles again. "And lost your towel."

Was that supposed to be news to her? She pulled

her hand away and frowned at him. "You keep staring at me."

"And you keep trying to ignore that I'm staring at you." He caught her hand again, tugged her closer and into his side. "But that pretty blush tells me you're plenty aware of me."

Her face got hotter still.

"Why are you embarrassed?"

She tipped her head back to give him a disbelieving glare. "Seriously, Evan? After all that, you have to ask?"

He frowned now too, but more with determination than annoyance. "I want to give you plenty of time. The rest of the night, and all of tomorrow too, if you need it. But you might as well understand right now, there's no going back."

Some special meaning infused those words, stealing her breath. "What is that supposed to mean?"

"We've been friends a long time."

"I know." Her heart thundered. She cherished every day with him and didn't want to lose their closeness. "So?"

"So now I've seen you naked, honey. I can't just go on pretending you're only a friend to me."

Only a friend? Relief tried to take over, but he wasn't done.

"Just as I can't pretend I don't want you."

The bottom fell out of her world. Jubilation mixed with mortifying memories, swamping her, tightening her chest, burning the backs of her eyes.

How could he say something like that?

He touched her hair, letting his hand trail down a thick curl. He paused at her bruised cheek, staring so intently that she felt his concern. "I'm not pressuring you, you know. No reason to look so spooked. You can have all the time you need to get used to the idea."

"Uh...thanks?" She would *never* get used to that idea. Sure, most women had body issues. She'd always wished to be a few pounds lighter, a little more athletic, less...rounded. But after her last lover, well, she'd had her body issues driven home in a big way.

"Thanks?" He kept touching her in small ways, as if doing so gave him pleasure. He put a barely-there kiss to her bruised cheek, then another just below her eye. "What kind of reaction is that?"

"I don't know." He was so close, she could see the striations in his honey-colored eyes. "You've taken me by surprise, that's all." She knew Evan was a nice guy, so he'd never insult her—not the way she'd been insulted. And with Evan being as male as the next guy—maybe more so, at least in her opinion—a naked woman equaled thoughts of lust.

Except that she cared too much for him to blow their relationship with a quick fling. She wished it was different, because, holy smokes, she'd wanted him a long time. Sometimes she couldn't sleep for thinking about how it'd be....

But she wasn't the type of woman who would ever keep him for long—except as a friend. And she wasn't about to give up that friendship for a night or two of sex.

No matter how mind-blowing it might be.

Misunderstanding her lengthy silence, Evan reassured her. "For tonight at least, you can trust that I'll keep my hands to myself."

Bummer.

"I just thought it was important for you to know how I feel."

Yeah, she got it: he felt momentarily turned on. The rush of the danger, the intimacy of seeing her nude, had affected him, as it would affect almost any guy.

But he wasn't just any guy, not to her.

"Evan…" How did she clarify things? "You did see me, right?"

"Oh yeah."

The way he said that… "And?"

His eyes went heavy. "You have a great body."

Such a nice guy. "But?" she said, encouraging him to honesty.

"There's a but?"

Her face pinched. "You know there is."

For the longest time, he studied her. Finally he seemed to come to some decision. He sat back, putting distance between them and breaking her heart just a little.

"*But,*" he said, stressing the word, "your body would look even better—"

Here it comes. She braced herself to hear him say: *If you lost weight. If you did some cardio. If your figure wasn't so overblown—*

"—under mine."

That bombshell turned her spine into a noodle, and she slumped against him. "What?"

"Or over mine." He warmed to the subject. "Your naked body could only look better if it was against my naked body." He reached for her. "In fact, naked or not, I want your body closer."

He pulled her right up and into his lap.

Surprised, she let him arrange her comfortably, almost as if she was a tiny person instead of a full-figured, grown woman. "Evan?"

"You have a totally kicking body. Smoking hot. No 'but' to it." He kissed her hard and fast, sort of annoyed but also determined. "How could you not know that?"

"I'm…" No way would she insult herself, so what could she say? "I'm not slim."

"No, thank God."

Was he being obtuse on purpose? "You know women are expected—"

"To be sexy," he interrupted. "And you are." He tunneled a hand into her hair, careful not to hurt her stitches. He lifted her face to his. "In your clothes, you're hot enough to drive me nuts. But without clothes…Damn, Cinder, that's not something I'm ever going to forget."

She blinked at him. "You mean—"

"I want to see you again. At my leisure. While I have permission to touch as well as look."

He sounded so sincere. "Touch as well as…?"

"Look. Oh, and taste." He used his pinkie to brush back one curl. "I really want to taste you, too."

This time the heat flooding her body wasn't embarrassment. And if he truly enjoyed her figure, then that changed everything, didn't it?

He shook his head at her disconcerted look. "News flash, Cinder. I want you. I've wanted you since the first day we met."

She drew back to better see him. "No way."

"What am I, blind? Of course I did. Like I said, you're hot. But you're also adorably funny and smart and caring."

"You never said anything!"

"You didn't seem receptive, so I've tried to be noble."

The idea of so much wasted time choked her. *"Noble?"*

He nodded with grave sincerity. "Lots of sleepless nights on my end. But like I said, seeing you in the raw—now all bets are off. If you hadn't been through hell today, I'd be giving it my best shot to get you into bed. Or laid out on this couch."

That sounded pretty awesome to her.

"But you need some time."

Was he nuts? "No I don't," she rushed to assure him.

The corner of his mouth kicked up. "No?"

She shook her head hard and fast. "I'm fine." All hot and bothered, but otherwise, no problem. "I swear."

"You're bruised. You have stitches." He lifted her arm to kiss the marks there, too. "You've had an upset."

Her mouth opened twice with nothing coming out. What could she say? Screw the stitches and the bruises, she wanted him? Maybe. "I don't care about any of that."

"You're not sore?"

Heck no. The second he'd gotten her into his lap, every ache and pain had ceased to exist. "No." She put a hand to his solid chest. "Not anymore."

He grinned outright. "So you want me, too?"

"Of course."

His grin slipped. Suspicion darkened his eyes. "Why do you say it like that?"

"Pfft." She caressed his chest, over that rock-solid shoulder. It hadn't escaped her notice that he wore only jeans and a white T-shirt. She loved how the cotton shirt hugged his chest and shoulders, the way it fit across his back. "Not only are you smart and funny and so incredibly nice, the nicest guy I've ever known, but *look* at you." She barely repressed a sigh. "What woman wouldn't want you?"

A frown crept over his brow. "I could say the same about men wanting you." It wasn't her shoulder he reached for.

His big, hot hand curved over her breast.

She went still on the outside, all aflutter on the inside. "*Evan.*"

"I'm asking again, honey." His thumb brushed over her nipple. "How come you don't realize how beautiful you are?"

He actually expected her to talk while he did that? Not easy. "Because…I'm not dumb." Throwing his words back at him, she added, "Or blind."

"Meaning?"

She swallowed back a groan. "I know I'm not the standard size."

"Hate to break it to you, honey, but women don't have a standard size." His thumb continued to play with her. "And men appreciate the variety."

That was exactly how she'd always felt! "Maybe. But they appreciate skinnier women more."

"Who says?" He reached down and slipped his hand up under her shirt, so that now he touched bare skin.

Oh wow. Her eyes closed as his fingers stroked over her. His palm was so hot, a little rough.

"Cinder?"

"I don't know. Society?"

"But I'm the only one here." He stroked down to her waist, back and over her hip. "And I'm not keen on all of society ever seeing you in the buff."

"I didn't mean that."

"Thank God." He hugged her close, tucking her head under his chin. "So someone has made you feel less than perfect? Tell me who."

"No one is perfect."

"You are. So tell me who said otherwise."

What did it matter now? "Just an ex." She breathed in his scent and wanted to eat him alive. "It was shortly before I met you." And she hadn't dated since.

Evan was silent a moment. "You're still hung up on him?"

"No!" Shuddering with revulsion, she said, "Not even close."

He tangled his fingers in her hair again to gently massage her scalp. "Then what does it matter what he thought?"

She couldn't believe him. "You really want to talk about this *now?*" A wiggle against his erection made her meaning clear.

"Yeah, I do. I've been thinking about getting you in bed so long that, once we hit the sheets, I don't want you to be shy." He held her tighter. "So sit still, stop tormenting me and tell me what the bozo said that was enough to derail all the interest I've shown."

"I didn't know you were showing that kind of interest."

"My point, exactly." He palmed her rear. "Now, give over, so we can get to the bed part of this disclosure."

Far as encouragement went, that was a doozy. "Okay, fine. He was…cruel." She did not want to give details. "That's all."

"That's all?" He tipped her back. "Tell me."

Reliving that awful day wasn't easy, but she supposed Evan deserved an explanation—albeit a shortened version. "We'd dated for a few months, mostly hanging out at my place or his."

He scowled. "Sort of like what you and I do?"

"I'm low-key, I guess. I enjoying hanging out at home."

Disgruntled, he said, "Me too." And then, "But I hope that's where the resemblance ends."

"Believe me, it is." She put her head on his shoulder so she wouldn't have to look at him. "I thought things were going along great. Then one night I went out to dinner with a lot of people from the hospital. We ran into him all cozy and intimate in a bar with another woman."

Evan grunted. "Jerk."

"It was so embarrassing. He'd been drinking, so maybe that's part of why he was so nasty about things. But he broke it off by telling his current date that I was just…" Her words trailed off.

Evan kissed her, not so hard and definitely not as fast as before. She curled her fingers into his shirt and held on.

When he lifted his mouth, he breathed deep. "What did he say?"

"He said a lot, and I won't repeat it word for word." She would never voice the awful litany of insults. "But the gist of it was that a woman my size was desperate and made it easy on him…you know, to get laid. He said he assumed I knew he wouldn't be interested in a cow like me, not for anything…public." She tucked herself in closer to Evan. "Because he didn't want to be seen with me."

Evan's arms tightened around her. "You know I wouldn't mind demolishing him a little for you."

She shook her head. Evan was not a bully, and he didn't pick fights with idiots. She knew he'd said it only as a way to soothe the memory of the insult. "Everyone stared at me. And sure, some of them protested that, saying he was an abusive drunk. But they also... felt sorry for me."

"Because he'd deliberately embarrassed you, not because anything he said was true."

In her heart, she knew that. Her associates at work were good people who genuinely liked her. But the humiliation had struck deep.

Standing, Evan took her hands and pulled her from the couch. "Come on."

"Where?"

"To my bedroom." He looked her over. "To my bed."

"Oh." 'Bout damn time. She'd rather do that than rehash old hurts any day. "Okay."

As she stepped over Doug, he lifted his head, as always aware of her and what she did.

"Just a second." She knelt down to the dog. "Stay, okay?" She scratched his neck, rubbed an ear. "I promise I won't be far away. You can rest now."

He looked at Evan, his furry expression somehow worried, then reassured. He let out a doggy sigh and went back to sleep. Cinder stroked his neck, gave Cate a pet and stood again. The animals trusted Evan, with everything.

With her.

How could she not do the same?

CHAPTER FOUR

IN THE BEDROOM, Evan closed the door so they wouldn't get a surprise visit from one of the animals. He said to Cinder, "Now that we're here, I don't want any interruptions."

"Okay." She remained by the door, her small, bare feet together, her hands clasped behind her, her hair hanging in sexy disarray around her beautiful face. "Your head feels okay?"

She had more injuries than he did. Did she really think he'd complain when she didn't? Or that he could even feel discomfort when she stood in his bedroom, ready to get intimate with him? He'd waited so long to be with her, loving her for what felt like forever, that not much could have slowed him down now. She wanted him. That was all he needed to know. "I'm fine. Great."

"Me too."

Urgency kept his blood thrumming, but he knew he had to do this right. He wanted more than just the here and now. He wanted an eternity. "Understand something, Cinder." Hungry for the sight of her again, he turned on the bedside lamp, then walked toward the window to close the blinds. "I'm not talking about one night. I'm going to feel the same in the morning, and the morning after that."

Probably a few times during the night as well. But

she needed some rest, and he didn't want to be too greedy.

She searched his face, nodded. "Okay."

She kept agreeing to everything—but he wanted more than agreement. He wanted full participation.

"What you're wearing." He nodded at her big, loose pajama pants paired with an even bigger T-shirt. "Is that a choice for comfort, or because you want to hide?"

She looked down at her shirt as if confused. "I was getting ready for bed."

Tonight, she'd sleep in the nude—but he saw no reason to tell her that yet. "Earlier, you wore a sweatshirt two sizes too big."

"You don't like my clothes?"

"I like *you*. Everything about you." With them now sealed off in his room, their privacy assured, Evan approached her again. "Sometimes the stuff you wear is almost a tease, hiding more than it shows. And now that I know what it's hiding, it'll be especially provocative."

Realization dawned in her big, dark eyes. "You want to make sure I'm not being insecure?" She smiled up at him. "That's so sweet."

At the moment, with a straining hard-on, he felt far from sweet. "Are you?"

She put a hand to his chest to give him a tentative stroke. It seemed she enjoyed touching him almost as much as he enjoyed touching her.

"After wearing a uniform all day, I like to get comfortable in easy clothes, that's all. But like most women, I enjoy dressing up every now and then."

"I've never seen you dressed up."

"Probably because I haven't dated since…well, you

know." She shrugged her shoulders. "Not since the jerk."

Damn, but he'd love to see her in a skirt, her shapely legs in heels. He'd make it happen, and soon—after he took the edge off with a few days of endless sex. He'd take her out to dinner, the movies, maybe get her to a club and show her off.

Yeah, he liked that idea—especially knowing what her ex had said to her. The bastard. Evan hadn't been kidding when he'd said he'd take the guy apart. But he also saw no reason for her to waste even a second more thinking about a guy now in her past—where he'd stay.

"Let's forget him, okay?" He took her mouth, hot and slow and deep. She went on tiptoes to get more, her hands clenching on his shoulders, her lush breasts pressed against his chest.

Filling his hands with her incredible backside, he lifted her more so that her soft belly aligned with his erection. He shifted against her, stroking himself and her both.

When she groaned, he said, "How about we lose the shirt for now?" Going slow, giving her time to protest, he caught the hem and eased it up.

Breathing fast, Cinder raised her arms to help him. He tossed it aside, and then just looked at her. The loose-waisted pajama pants hung down on her hips, leaving her midsection bared. He devoured the sight of her softly rounded belly, the small navel, how her rib cage expanded with each hungry breath.

That incredible rack.

"Damn." Using both hands, he traced the flare of her hips, the indentation of her waist, up to her heavy breasts. She was a stacked handful and then some. Firm and full. Her pink nipples puckered tight, and he had to bend down to taste her.

Against her flesh, he murmured, "Beautiful."

She sucked in three deep breaths, and said on a sigh, "I'm so glad you think so."

Damn it, but he couldn't let her shortchange herself. He raised his head up again to stare at her. "You realize both Jesse and Brick think you're hot, too."

That threw her. "They don't!"

"So did those cops."

Her face colored. "No way."

Evan braced one hand on the wall beside her head and used the other hand to delve down into her pajama pants. Now more than ever he appreciated her preference for loose, comfortable clothing.

She shivered, gasped, then dropped back to the wall.

While he touched her silky skin, he spoke to her. "It's kind of cute how oblivious you are to this stuff." He traced the sweet contours of her ass, then around a hipbone to her lower belly. He met her gaze. "I'm not oblivious, though. When you said you'd like to camp out with me, they all shared a look. Know what that look was?"

She shook her head.

"Envy." He let his hand drift lower, over her pubic curls. "Brick knows I've been hot on your tail for a while. He's heckled me endlessly for not making a move before this."

She opened her mouth to say something, but he pressed a finger into her and she ended up gasping.

"We all noticed how comfortable you are with Brick and Jesse, but you treat me with more caution."

"Evan." Her fingers dug into his shoulders. "Can't we talk about this later?"

Smiling to himself, he kissed the fragrant skin of her throat, her stubborn jaw, that awful bruise on her cheek. "They told me if I didn't quit dragging my feet—" he pressed a second finger into her "—some rich doctor would steal you away."

Knotting her hands in his shirt, she pulled him closer. "I don't care about any doctors, so hush it and kiss me."

"Yes ma'am." He took her mouth hotly, his tongue delving just as his fingers delved—until he felt her hand on the front of his jeans. Even that, a curious brush of her fingers through the thick denim of his jeans, had him on the ragged edge. "Cinder…"

Almost in slow motion, her eyes staring into his, she opened the snap and eased his zipper down. "I want you naked too, you know."

He locked his knees, drew a deep breath. "Fair enough." Before she could actually get hold of him—which would probably be the end of him—he put a little space between them and peeled his shirt off over his head.

"I love looking at you."

The breathless way she said that seduced him as surely as a touch. "I'm glad." He pushed her pajama pants down, taking her panties with them. "Step out."

With no show of uncertainty, she bared herself again.

Seeing her naked at the worst of times was one thing. Seeing her naked now, in his bedroom, knowing he'd soon have her, was something altogether different. The impact nearly leveled him.

He reached for her.

She held out a hand and laughed. "Off with the

jeans." She went past him to the bed. "I've waited long enough."

Red-hot lust smoldered, but it was her emotional effect that took him to a fevered pitch. He watched her climb up to the middle of his bed, her smile coy, her eyes bright with desire, and he knew he wanted to see her there, looking at him just like that, for the rest of his life.

But first things first: he shed the jeans with haste.

"Wow." Cinder stared at him so hotly, his erection flexed in reaction. "Evan?"

"Yeah?"

"Hurry up."

It was almost enough to make him laugh, but not quite. He got three condoms from his dresser drawer and dropped two on the nightstand. As he tore open the third, he said, "I'd like to promise this will be perfect, but I'm so far gone, I just don't know."

In an innocently seductive pose, she rested back on her elbows, her legs shifting restlessly. "I don't need perfection, Evan. I just need you." She held her arms open to him, and he was a goner.

Protection in place, he came down over her, gathered her up close to his heart and kissed her the way he'd wanted to for far too long. So many times he'd thought of having her here. He'd always planned to go slow, to overwhelm her with pleasure and passion.

But as he settled into the enticing cradle of her parted thighs, he knew he'd seriously overestimated his control. Her hands were all over him, his all over her. He licked her nipples, sucked, greedier by the second.

Moaning, she hooked one leg over his and arched up. Evan felt the wetness of her, heard her small sounds

of need, breathed in her aroused scent. Reaching between her thighs, he parted her slick lips, opened her
and thrust in.

For a heartbeat, they both stilled, suspended on the
sharp pleasure as he filled her. He felt their heartbeats
sync up. He felt her fingers tighten on his shoulders.

Cinder broke first on a long, vibrating groan. She
rolled her hips, taking more of him, urging him to start
the rhythm they both needed. He took her mouth while
thrusting hard and deep. She anchored herself by locking her ankles at the small of his back.

All too soon he felt her tightening, and it both
amazed him and turned him on more. She freed her
mouth to cry out, her neck arching, her blond hair spilling out around her head.

There wasn't a single shy or reserved thing about
the way she came, and it pushed him into pleasurable
oblivion with her. He stiffened his arms, put his head
back and growled out a mind-numbing release.

Seconds, maybe minutes later, little aftershocks of
pleasure continued to ripple through Cinder. Evan became aware of her kissing his shoulder, and of the dog
scratching at the door.

"Doug's worried about you," he murmured, and he
nuzzled her throat, relishing the feel of her, all soft and
warm around him, under him.

With him.

"He's not used to hearing me…" The words fell off.

Was she back to being shy? "Come?"

She bit him again, not as softly this time, then sucked
at the small sting.

Evan shuddered. "It's okay, Doug," he managed to
call to the dog. "She'll be out in a minute."

Doug barked.

Her tongue moved over his neck one last time. "Okay, okay," she said so Doug would hear her voice. "I'm on my way." She tried to move out from under Evan.

"You're not going anywhere." Evan came up to his elbows. "Doug can join us in here if you want, but you'll be sleeping next to me."

"Sleeping, huh?"

Such a sexy tease. "At least for an hour or so."

Trailing a hand down his back, she sighed. "I can accept that, I guess."

He looked into her sated eyes, down to her pale shoulders and her now softened nipples, and whispered, "Then again, might not take a whole hour at all."

She tried to say, "Good," but the word tangled with a big yawn.

The evidence of her exhaustion caught Evan, and he could do no more than hug her tightly for a few moments. "You need some sleep."

"We all do." She returned his hug just as fiercely. "Doug prefers to sleep on the floor, not the bed, but he's used to being in the room with me."

"Not a problem." Sitting up beside her, he said, "I'll take him out one more time first. Make use of my bathroom if you like. Do…whatever it is you do before bed. I'll be right back."

"Evan, wait." Looking well tumbled, she sat up. Her gaze went from him to the window and back again. "Be careful, okay?"

After finally making love to Cinder Bratt, it'd be so easy for him to concentrate on the wonderful parts of the day instead of how she'd been frightened, her life threatened.

The bruises she'd sustained.

One look at her face and he knew it was again uppermost in her mind.

"I'll take my keys and lock the door behind me. Give me five minutes and I'll be back, okay?"

As if she felt foolish, she ducked her face. "Okay."

Evan tipped up her chin to kiss her. "No hiding from me, remember? Not your body, not your thoughts."

"I'm not." She let out an uneasy breath. "It's just that, for a little while there, I forgot all about it."

He was glad. "Five minutes. And, Cinder?"

"Hmmm?"

"Don't bother getting dressed again."

CHAPTER FIVE

BRIGHT SECURITY LIGHTS illuminated the parking lot and the surrounding grassy area that the tenants' pets used. The rain had passed, but dark clouds still concealed the moon. Evan held Cate in one arm and Doug's leash with the other. Since the dog went about his business without a care, Evan knew he didn't need to worry about the intruder being anywhere near.

The building was mostly silent, with only the sounds of cars passing by on the street to break the peacefulness of the humid night. Consumed in pleasurable thoughts—all of them centered around Cinder—he stood silent until he noticed Jesse and Brick coming out of the building, talking quietly to each other.

They saw him right off, gave him a quick, speculative once-over and grinned while walking toward him.

"Shut up," Evan said as soon as they got close.

Jesse took Cate from him. "Is she sleeping?"

"Probably not yet." Given her worry, she wouldn't let herself fall asleep until he returned. "But soon."

Brick nodded at his neck. "I suppose I shouldn't comment on that love bite."

Thinking of how she'd kissed him, he touched his neck. So she'd marked him? He kind of liked that. "Best that you don't." Cinder was off-limits for a whole lot of things, and Brick understood that. Not that it stopped him.

"Can I just say—"

"No."

"—that I'm glad." He squeezed Evan's shoulder. "That you two hooked up, I mean."

Evan measured his brother's lack of jesting, saw he was totally sincere, and nodded. In all things important, Brick backed him up. Cinder was important. The most important person in his life.

"I like her," Brick added. "A lot."

Jesse nodded. "Same here. It's like she's been part of the family for a while, you know?"

Damn. They were marrying him off when he'd only just gotten her into bed. "You aren't family," Evan told Jesse.

"Just like."

True enough. But he wasn't going to go into anything that heavy tonight. Cinder didn't need Jesse or Brick steamrolling her. "Her place is all locked up?"

Brick grinned, nudged Jesse and grinned some more. "Notice how he dodged things there?"

"Jumped topics real quick," Jesse agreed. "Maybe his brain is sluggish from satisfaction."

Not even close. His brain, his body, were both still buzzing. "I told her you two thought she was hot."

The most comical looks came over their faces.

Jesse handed Cate back to him. "How the hell did that come up?"

Now that he had the control again, Evan grinned. He wasn't about to share Cinder's private history with anyone else. That'd be up to her if she chose to do so. "Just letting you know where things stand."

"Why?"

"Because she'll be staying with me."

A slow grin came over Jesse's face. "For how long?"

If he had his way...forever. But he wasn't there yet. He and Cinder had a whole lot of talking to do before he could spring that on her. "I don't know. But until her attacker is found, I can use that excuse to keep her close."

"And after he's caught?" Brick asked.

"I'll figure out something."

Doug finished, kicked around a little dirt, and started leading him back into the apartment. The big dog really did want to turn in.

Evan tossed a doggy pickup bag at Brick. "Do the honors, will you?"

Appalled, Brick looked at the bag, then the ground. "For *Cinder.*" He scowled. "But just this once."

"I'll let her know how special she is." Evan laughed. "Thanks for hanging around, guys. Appreciate it." He propped Cate on his shoulder, opened the door and re-entered the building. Cinder opened his apartment door for him when he reached it. She wore her T-shirt, but nothing else.

When she unleashed Doug, Evan got a few peeks of her behind. Amazingly enough, he felt himself stirring. She needed her sleep, so he ignored the reaction of his body and instead concentrated on getting her back to bed.

Together, they settled the animals and locked up the apartment. Cate chose to sleep by Doug, both of them on the floor at the foot of the bed.

Evan didn't mention the T-shirt, but Cinder surprised him by stripping it off before crawling under the covers with him.

With the naturalness of a longstanding relationship, she cuddled up close, her arm over his chest, her head on his shoulder.

"Evan?"

He kissed the top of her head. "Hmmm?"

"I'm very glad to be here with you."

A nice start—and a perfect opening. The room was dark, quiet, intimate. "Will you stay here with me?"

Uncertainty throbbed in the air. "You mean...tonight?"

Forever. "Until they catch the guy who broke in."

Her fingers played over his chest. "That could be awhile."

"It's not a problem for me."

She shifted, looking up at him in the darkness. He touched her mouth, grazed his fingertips over her bruised cheek.

"Stay with me, Cinder. Please."

Two heartbeats passed before she snuggled back into his side. With emotion thick in her voice, she said, "Thank you. I'd love that."

Now that they had that settled, she yawned.

Evan said, "Go to sleep, honey. I'll be right here."

And just like that, she did.

CINDER CAME IN from an early shift to find Jesse, Brick and Evan all in the apartment. They were in the kitchen talking, laughing. It wasn't uncommon for them to be around, usually on the weekends, but occasionally during the week, too.

She'd been with Evan for three weeks now and still they hadn't caught the guy who'd come after her. It was a scary thought, but she was almost resigned to the fact that they might never find him.

And if they didn't, then what? She couldn't just stay with Evan indefinitely. Not that he seemed in a hurry for her to leave. But it felt like a torturous type of limbo, to be unsure of when her situation might change.

Doug, the only one to hear her come in, greeted her with barking enthusiasm. *He* certainly loved staying with Evan and Cate. In no time at all, he'd acclimated, and now Cinder was just using her apartment as a big closet for her clothes and furniture. They rarely went there—and yet, she hadn't mentioned giving it up.

Setting aside her purse and keys, Cinder sat on the foyer floor so Doug could drape himself across her lap. Cate crawled up to her shoulder, her face in Cinder's hair. "Such a warm greeting," she teased the animals, while giving them each the attention they wanted.

All three men emerged from the kitchen, already smiling toward her, their expressions accepting, indulgent.

Such great guys.

Given they were here now, she assumed they'd have a night in, and she was glad. Not that she hadn't enjoyed the "dates" Evan had insisted on. Mostly she preferred the long walks in the park with the animals, or just hanging at the apartment with friends. But dancing at the club on occasion was nice too, especially with the way Evan looked at her when she wore heels and a skirt. He was always so complimentary, he left her blushing.

But then, he looked at her the same when she wore jeans. Or pajamas.

Or nothing at all.

She thought he probably wanted to prove he wasn't

like her ex. Not that he needed to. She loved him—she knew the difference.

"Everything okay?" Jesse asked her.

Realizing that she'd been lost in thought, Cinder grinned. "Oh, yeah. I'm great." And she was. Tired, but oh so happy. She stretched. "It was a long day, that's all." But how could any day go wrong when it ended with her at Evan's apartment? With Evan. She gave a sappy sigh.

Watching her in that concentrating way of his, Evan walked over and offered her a hand up. She let him haul her back to her feet—and into his arms for a proper greeting.

"I'm glad you're home," he said against her mouth, and kissed her again.

Home. His home, not really hers.

Maybe she should just come right out and ask him if the arrangements were permanent.

Brick rubbed his hands together. "Now that you two have the smooching out of the way, I hope you're hungry. I brought over steaks."

Yeah…she'd talk to him about their living arrangements—after they were alone. "I'm starving. We were so busy today, I didn't get much time for lunch."

"The grill's already hot," Brick told her. "You've probably got fifteen minutes before we eat."

Doug barked at the door, whined.

"Perfect timing." She took his leash off the wall. "I'll take him out, then change clothes before we join you."

But as she opened the door, Doug lunged forward, almost yanking her off her feet. Cinder held him tighter, confused—and suddenly Evan was there. In one smooth move he handed her Cate and relieved her of the leash.

Brick stood with him. Both men looked like thunder-clouds.

Cate sank her claws into Cinder's arm, hissing in upset at the way Doug behaved.

Jesse took her elbow. "Come back inside, hon."

"But what…?" Doug continued with an awful racket, barking and snarling—and suddenly it hit her. The intruder. "Oh my God."

While holding her with one hand, Jesse used his other to make a call on his cell.

Evan's gaze met hers. "Wait with Jesse."

"*No.*"

As if they had it all planned out, each with an assigned role, the men moved in an orchestrated manner. Jesse nudged her back into the doorway, Brick tried to block her. And Evan…Evan allowed Doug to lead him down the hallway toward the front door.

Oh, no, no, no. She watched in horror as Doug yanked at the leash, doing his utmost to get free.

"Wait!" She pulled away from Jesse. When Evan glanced back at her, he wore such an unyielding scowl that she didn't bother trying to deter him with reason. Instead, she cuddled Cate closer and squared her shoulders. "I won't have my dog hurt."

"He won't be," Brick told her. "Look at the lot. It's daylight still. People are out and about. But someone is lurking, and Doug knows it. Let him do his thing, Cinder."

She said, "Doug," in pleading tones, but he paid her no attention. He wanted to be free to attack.

Brick stepped in front of her, and with some male-inspired meaning, said, "Let Evan do his thing, too. Okay?"

What in the world was *his thing?*

"The cops are on the way," Jesse announced.

That did little to ease her reservations. "What if he still has a gun?" What if, this time, he used that gun?

"We can't let him get away," Evan told her. The force of his determination showed in every rigid line of his body. "Not this time."

"Oh God." What to do, Cinder wondered. Jesse continued to hold her arm, but she wasn't dumb. If they were hell-bent on a showdown, she wasn't going to race out and get in the way. However, she did turn in a rush and race to the patio doors to look out.

Jesse secured the front door and joined her. Together, their ears touching near the glass, they watched as Evan and Brick strode out. The men refrained from talking, almost as if they didn't know each other. Evan pulled a resistant Doug to the grassy area, but Doug had no intention of doing his business. Not right now.

Brick circled around to his truck and got behind the wheel.

"What are they doing?" Cinder asked.

"Thanks to Doug, they know right where he's at, but they don't want him to know they're on to him yet."

She looked at her dog, at how he strained toward an old white station wagon parked farther down the lot. "Oh."

"Don't worry, honey. They won't let Doug get hurt—but they also won't let the guy get away."

"Okay." Now it sort of made sense…a little.

In amazement, Cinder watched as Brick pulled his big truck around—and stopped in front of the car with his passenger side nearly touching the hood, blocking it in. He turned off the truck and got out, but stayed behind the cab.

Evan and Doug joined him, and now that he had gotten his way, Doug showed more manners. He stopped the awful racket, but kept the leash taut. Evan said something to him, patted his flank, and Doug sat beside him.

Huh. When had he taught Doug that trick?

"Smart dog," Jesse told her. "Now all they have to do is wait. Cops should be here any minute."

Pride filled her. She stroked a fractious Cate. "Hear that, baby? Doug is a hero." Cate nestled closer to her neck, and Cinder sympathized. She knew just how the cat felt.

Police sirens sounded, and a second later, two cruisers pulled into the lot.

Suddenly the driver of the car caught on. A little panicked, knowing he couldn't drive away, he opened his door and tried to run. Even from the distance, she saw that remarkable snake tattoo on his neck.

Cinder almost panicked herself—until she saw the officers giving chase, not Doug. Evan continued to hold the dog back.

Protecting him—which she should have realized was his intent. Evan loved Doug.

Did he love her, too?

Another police car showed up on the other side of the fleeing intruder.

Cornered, he reached into his pocket, possibly for a gun—and got hit with a Taser that wrung a guttural scream from his throat, bowed his back and then dropped him flat.

Wide-eyed, Cinder stared in horror at the big man now on the ground. "Wow."

With her attacker now subdued, Jesse asked, "Want to go check it out?"

Not really, but she could tell that *he* did. "I guess." With grave uncertainty, she put Cate on the couch, tucked between some pillows so she'd feel secure. She followed Jesse, who grinned ear to ear as he strode out to the lot. Men.

Doug had his ears up in an alert, fascinated way, watching as the man was handcuffed and lifted back to his feet. Everyone could see the tattoo, which for Cinder was proof enough. But the attentive officer also fished a wallet from his pocket. "It's him."

"The same guy from the hospital?" Evan asked.

"According to his ID, yeah."

The dog suddenly turned, saw Cinder standing there, and loped over to greet her. Evan followed.

Her stomach was still in knots, and a crazy shakiness had invaded her limbs.

Evan pulled her in close. "It's over."

Yes…she feared it was. All of it.

With her head resting against his chest, she said, "I guess it's safe for me to use my own apartment now."

He went still, but not for long. "Come on. We need to talk." They reached the patio doors before Cinder realized that both Brick and Jesse had followed, too.

Jesse opened the door and waited for her to enter. Doug leaped ahead, met by Cate. Evan unleashed him. "It's amazing how they communicate."

"They love each other," Cinder said, then bit her lip because that *L* word landed like a thunderclap in the otherwise quiet apartment.

Brick closed the door, then stood there, arms crossed as if barring escape. "Yeah, they do."

Unsure what else to do, Cinder went to the couch, but sat on the floor in front of it. She scooped up Cate, and Doug crawled across her lap.

Evan dropped down to sit beside her. "I couldn't stand the idea of that creep still out there, possibly showing up again."

"Always a threat." She swallowed hard. "I know."

"He's gone now, though." Evan touched her hair, brushed it back behind her ear. "So yeah, you don't need to stay here to be safe."

Blast. It wasn't easy fashioning a smile past her regret, but she got her lips to move. "Thanks to you guys."

"Thanks to Doug," Evan corrected.

Brick stepped forward. "Cate and Doug are used to being together now."

Evan said, "They see each other daily anyway." He brought her face around to his. "You don't need to live with me for the animals to stay together."

"Very true." With her heart aching, she looked down at his mouth rather than meet his steady gaze. "They were together long before we brought them home."

Jesse stood alongside Brick. "You guys aren't just friends anymore."

"No, we aren't." Evan slid his hand around and into her hair, his thumb brushing her jaw. "But she doesn't need to live with me for us to keep dating."

"You more than *date*, damn it."

Why did Brick and Jesse sound so angry? She glanced at them both, and frowned at their identical expressions. "You guys could give us some privacy, you know."

Brick snorted.

Jesse said, "I thought you were happy living here."

Now even Doug and Cate looked at her, and she felt like a spectacle. "I haven't actually moved in." Sure, she slept with Evan every night and woke with him in the morning. They had amazing sexual chemistry together. They shared meals and they shared responsibilities.

But that wasn't the same as actually living with him. It wasn't a...commitment.

"I still have my apartment, filled with my belongings," she pointed out. "Most of what I own is just across the hall at my place."

Evan tipped up her chin so she had to meet his gaze. "You love them both."

His mood, as with his statement, confused her. "Doug and Cate? Or do you mean Jesse and Brick?"

He looked comical for a moment, then determined. "All of them."

Softening, she nodded. "I really do."

Jesse and Brick held themselves silent and very still. Evan's breath came out. "And what about me?"

Whoa. He'd just dropped that out there like it was nothing. And now he watched her in that deep concentration, his gaze boring into hers as if he could read her thoughts before she voiced them.

She curled her fingers into his shirt and felt the furious pounding of his heart. Hers immediately matched it. "Yes."

The tension lifted from his expression. His dark eyes brightened. "You love me?"

She wouldn't lie to him, ever. "Hopelessly. Madly. Forever."

He put his arms around her, and since she held the dog and cat, they got encompassed as well. "I love you, too."

"So," Brick said, his tone gruff, "guess I can go ahead and put on those steaks to cook."

Softly, almost with reverence, Jesse said, "I'll help."

Doug stuck his head up between Cinder and Evan, pelting them both with doggy breath before stepping away to join Brick and Jesse in the kitchen. As always, Cate crawled up and out of the huddle to follow him.

With Cinder still locked close to his chest, Evan said, "You'll give up the lease on your apartment?"

"Yes."

He put his forehead to hers. "And will you marry me?"

Her heart felt so full, she thought she might burst. "I would love to."

Around a satisfied smile, he said, "I'm probably rushing you, but how would you feel about us getting a house together? Maybe one with a nice, big backyard for Doug and Cate to play in."

"That sounds wonderful." Then, harking back to a comment he'd made long ago, she smiled up at him. "On one condition."

Unconcerned, Evan pulled her up and into his lap. "And what's that?"

"I love Doug and Cate. I love Jesse and Brick. And I most especially love you." She gave him a quick kiss. "But we will not be adopting a horse to name Horace." And because she knew anything with Evan would be perfection, she added, "At least, not anytime too soon."

Their combined laughter filled the apartment, and

though neither of them noticed, both Jesse and Brick, along with Cate and Doug, stood in the doorway, watching them, smiling, and very satisfied with the outcome.

* * * * *

LORI FOSTER is a Waldenbooks, *USA TODAY*, *Publishers Weekly* and *New York Times* bestselling author with books from a variety of publishers, including Berkley/Jove, Kensington, St. Martin's, Harlequin and Silhouette. Lori has been a recipient of the prestigious *RT Book Reviews* Career Achievement Award for Series Romantic Fantasy, and for Contemporary Romance. She's had top-selling books for Amazon, Waldenbooks and the BGI Group. For more about Lori, visit her Web site at www.lorifoster.com. And look for *Bare It All*, the second book in her new Love Undercover series, coming soon from Harlequin HQN!

SMOOKIE AND THE BANDIT

Brenda Jackson

To everyone who enjoys reading a good romance story where the sexual chemistry is oozing all over the place, this one is for you.

Happy is the man that findeth wisdom,
and the man that getteth understanding.
—*Proverbs* 3:13

CHAPTER ONE

"YES, MAY I HELP YOU?"

Raquel Capers swallowed as she gazed into the face of the man who leaned in the doorway. She'd heard that Quest Newman was a hottie, eye candy of the third degree. However, in light of why she was there, she'd shoved the information aside.

"Miss?"

She blinked. "Yes?"

"I asked if I can help you? However, if you're here soliciting, this complex has a policy against it."

Raquel stiffened her spine. "I'm Raquel Capers and that's not why I'm here."

"Then how can I help you?" Quest asked. She was a looker, and he could definitely come up with a few good ideas if she couldn't. But unfortunately, he didn't have the time. He was best man in his twin brother's wedding and the rehearsal dinner was tonight, so he was in a hurry. Then, later, it was guys' night out with a huge party planned. The last one his brother, Quincy, would enjoy as a single man.

"I'm here because of your dog."

The woman's words, spoken in a deep, sultry voice, reclaimed his attention. "Bandit?"

"If that's what you call him."

He straightened and placed his hands in the pockets of his jeans. "I do. What about Bandit?"

"My dog is Smookie."

Quest lifted a brow, wondering why she felt that information was somehow vital to the conversation. "And?"

She crossed her arms over her chest, and his gaze automatically went to the uplifting of her breasts. Pressed against her pretty pink blouse, he could tell they were a nice, full and firm pair.

"*And* it seems your Bandit is about to be a father."

He frowned, pretty damn certain he hadn't heard her correctly. "Excuse me?"

"Let me spell it out for you, Mr. Newman. Your Bandit has knocked up my Smookie."

"He did what!"

Quest Newman definitely had a good set of lungs, Raquel thought. And the shocked look on his face would have made her laugh outright if the business at hand wasn't so darn serious. But she didn't have time for amusement.

"That's not possible."

Raquel lifted her chin and glared at the man. "Trust me, it is."

Quest sighed, getting annoyed. "Look, like I said, that's not possible. I don't know you or your Smookie, but I do know that whenever Bandit is out, he's on a leash with me or my dog sitter."

"Well, on this particular day, he wasn't with your dog sitter."

He narrowed his gaze. "And what particular day are you talking about, Ms. Capers?"

"Friday, May tenth."

Quest knew immediately where he'd been that day. He'd gone camping with a couple of his frat brothers from college and had left Bandit, his Yorkie, with his nineteen-year-old cousin Tawny, who would dog sit whenever he traveled. While he was gone, it was customary for Tawny to move into one of his guest rooms to take care of all Bandit's needs, which included walking him on a leash—at least three times a day.

"What do you mean he wasn't with my sitter?"

"Just what I said. I was out of town at the time and left Smookie with my elderly neighbor, Ms. Albright. Well, it seems on this particular day while Ms. Albright was at the doggy park, your sitter approached her and asked for a favor. She said an emergency had come up."

Quest's eyebrows lifted. "What sort of an emergency?"

"She claimed that one of her aunts had passed away and she needed to leave town immediately."

Since he and Tawny shared the same aunts and all of them were alive and accounted for, he knew that wasn't true. "And?"

"And she asked Ms. Albright if she would watch your dog for a couple of days while she left town to attend the funeral. Being the Christian woman that she is, and since Ms. Albright had seen your sitter at the park on more than one occasion, she agreed. And when questioned, your sitter assured Ms. Albright that your Bandit was fixed."

Quest knew that part was far from the truth. He had meant to get it done but kept putting it off, mainly because he felt a pain between his own legs whenever he thought about it. "Bandit *isn't* fixed."

"Ms. Albright found that out later when she walked

in on them. My Smookie and your Bandit. Needless to say, she was horrified."

"I bet she was."

"She told me what happened the moment I returned to town. I called the vet and she said there was nothing that could be done, but for me to watch for any signs that my Smookie was pregnant. I did. She is. And it's your Bandit's fault."

Quest heard a sound and glanced over his shoulder. His Yorkie, who had finished his supper in the kitchen, strolled into the living room. Quest did recall that Bandit had been in a damn good mood when he'd returned from that camping trip. Now he knew why. Too bad there wasn't such a thing as a doggy condom. And as far as Tawny was concerned, he'd seen her several times since then and not once had she mentioned anything about leaving his dog with anyone else while he'd been gone.

He glanced back at his visitor. "Look, Ms. Capers, I have no proof what you're claiming is true. I will speak with the person responsible for taking care of my dog at that time."

"Yes, you do that, Mr. Newman. And when she verifies my story, then you can give me a call." She all but shoved a business card into his hand. "I think it's only fair that you share the cost of Smookie's vet expenses associated with this pregnancy."

"Share the cost?"

"Yes, share the cost. After all, it was your dog who was someplace he shouldn't have been," she said, moving to get in his face.

"And if your story is true, it was *your* Ms. Albright who accepted the responsibility," he said, moving closer to get in hers. He was so close he could see her hazel eyes clearly and thought they were beautiful.

"Need I remind you that if your sitter hadn't lied, none of this would have happened."

She had a point there, but at the moment he wouldn't agree to it. "Like I said, that has yet to be proven."

He took a step back. His mouth was too damn close to hers, and temptation was too high. It wouldn't take much for him to be pushed to cop a taste.

Quest checked his watch. He needed to leave now if he wanted to be on time for the rehearsal dinner. Tawny was one of the bridesmaids, so he would talk to her then. He shoved the business card into his pocket. "I'll get to the bottom of this and call you."

"Yes, you do that."

She turned and walked away. It was then he saw the full picture. Her cute little outfit consisted of a low-cut pink blouse, snug-fitting black miniskirt and a pair of black polka-dotted stilettos that could probably kill. And speaking of *kill*, her legs were a killer pair. And that voice of hers…he could get a boner just from hearing it. She had sounded good even when her words came out stinging.

He heard a doggy yawn and turned, catching Bandit in the act as he stretched across the floor, looking well fed and as if he didn't have a care in the world. Little did the mutt know, all of that might be coming to an end. When you played, you had to pay.

"So Bandit, I understand you've been keeping secrets," he said, closing the door and walking into the room. The dog, with his short tail wagging, moved toward him for the pat on the head he knew was coming

"You might have gotten laid that week, but in the

end it might cost you…or should I say, cost *me*. If I end up getting stuck with puppy support payments, that's a few less dog bones for you, my friend." The dog, with his tongue lolling out, merely looked up at him with a silly dog grin.

Quest shook his head and moved toward the table to get his keys. He intended to see Ms. Capers again, even if it wasn't for any purpose other than to tell her she had his mutt mixed up with another.

He glanced down at her business card. *Raquel Capers. Actress.* He really wasn't surprised. She had the looks and the body for one, but what kind of work would an actress find in Talladega, Alabama? There was the Ritz Theater, which put on live shows on occasion, but was that enough for full-time work? And would it enable someone to afford a condo in Gresham Falls?

Umm, Ms. Capers was getting more interesting by the minute.

CHAPTER TWO

RAQUEL LEANED BACK in her chair, propped her feet on the desk and adjusted Smookie's position in her lap while she talked on the phone. Tonight's caller was over-the-top, but if he was willing to pay twenty-five bucks an hour just to have sex talk with her, then she wouldn't complain.

She knew the picture he had pulled up on his computer screen wasn't her, and she would never, ever on this planet do any of the things she was suggesting in this call. But she was an actress and it paid the bills.

She stroked Smookie's fur and smiled. "Oh, Robbie, I just love it when you talk to me that way," she said, referring to him by the first name he was using. "You keep it up and I'll be coming soon. I won't be able to hold it back," she said with a bated breath, sounding like a woman on the verge of having an orgasm any minute.

"Then I'm going to give you multiples."

Yeah, right, she thought, rolling her eyes. He'd had her on the phone forty-five minutes already and had even hinted at calling 906-HOT-WIRE for an additional hour. Little did he know that chances were when he did call back, he wouldn't get her. This was her last call for tonight.

"You know, before this call ends, sweetheart," he was

rasping into the phone, "you can give me your address, and I can come over and continue things."

She rolled her eyes again. *Not on your best night, bud.* Besides, he'd already let it slip he lived somewhere in Iowa. Did he really assume she was the girl next door from his hometown? Seriously? In that case he'd probably be pretty darn shocked to know she lived thousands of miles away in Alabama. On top of that, instead of wearing the skimpy white negligee she'd claimed, she was in her shorts, T-shirt and flip-flops. Definitely nothing sexy about her tonight.

"You know our policies, Robbie," she said, not caring if he knew them or not. By the time midnight rolled around, she would have made an easy thousand or more. Not bad, when on a given day she could move around her condo and clean up while making all kind of lewd and lascivious noises. She could understand why Smookie looked at her strangely sometimes.

Smookie.

She glanced down at the one thing she held most precious. The last birthday gift her brother, Jordan, had given her before he'd died two years ago in a car accident. It had been her twenty-fifth birthday and Jordan had dropped by her apartment to surprise her. At first she'd been upset, since he'd known she wasn't into pets. They required too much time and way too much attention.

However, once she'd looked in the box at the snow-white toy poodle puppy staring back at her, she'd been smitten. And now, almost two years later, she truly didn't know what she would do without her Smookie. The dog was everything Raquel had needed after Jordan's death. Smookie was her baby.

Moving her hand to gently caress Smookie's soft belly, which showed signs of protruding, Raquel thought, *My baby is about to have a baby*. Possibly more than one. According to Dr. Jones, a toy poodle Smookie's size and age could have up to four.

That thought made her think of Quest Newman and his Bandit. She frowned. Just like a male to make a hit and then run. But if he thought he was going to get away with it, he had another thought coming. "I have to believe he's going to do what's right," she muttered aloud.

"Precious, what did you say? It feels right?"

Raquel blinked, remembering she still had Robbie on the phone and she was supposed to be rubbing her hand over her breasts. "Yes, Robbie, it feels right," she purred.

She glanced over at the clock. Less than ten minutes to go. She hoped she could last that long, since she was getting sleepy. She would never forget when her best friend, Whitney Frazier, had come up with the idea of starting what she'd called Companionship Plus. Whitney had purchased one of those 900 hotlines and gone into business. She had talked Raquel into being her first phone actress and, within less than six months, Raquel had made enough money to quit her day job as a claims adjuster for an insurance company.

Then Whitney began throwing the what-ifs out there, and suggested that with Raquel's voice—one that a lot of guys described as sultry—they could start the hot wire, a special line just for Raquel. The callers would pay a premium because they would feel they were getting exclusive services. It had worked. Raquel's income had nearly tripled.

Although the sex conversations could get rather explicit and graphic at times, she still couldn't believe how much money men would pay for such foolishness. Now, almost a year later, she considered herself an actress, because acting was what she did. Her role as Precious was to make men happy by fulfilling a fantasy.

Overall, being a phone actress had definite perks. Including being able to work in the comfort of her own home, and speaking to a lot of interesting guys who just wanted to talk and needed someone to listen. Most wanted to fulfill their fantasies over the phone, fantasies they felt they couldn't share with their wife or significant other.

And now Companionship Plus, in which she was a silent partner, employed more than two hundred other women across the country, providing most of them with extra incomes earned from the privacy of their own homes, working schedules that were ideal for them. Most handled the hotline, but twenty had advanced and, like her, worked the hot wire exclusively. She preferred letting Whitney run the business while she worked with the staff on the phones.

The beep sounded, letting Robbie know he had only a minute left. "I enjoyed talking to you tonight, Precious. Who knows, maybe we'll meet up in person one of these days."

She frowned, thinking she definitely hoped not. "Yes, maybe we will. It was nice talking to you."

Moments later she hung up the phone and stood, cuddling Smookie in her arms. "That was the last call for the night, Smookie. Thank goodness. Time for us to get ready for bed."

After taking a shower, she moved around her condo, cutting off lights and making sure all the doors were secured. It was on nights like this that she missed Jordan something awful. It had not been unusual for him to drop by her place after one of his late-night poker games. In fact, he'd been on his way to a poker game when a drunk driver had lost control of his car and plowed into Jordan's.

Her baby brother. Her only brother, who'd been only two years younger than her, had lost his life instantly. Leaving her all alone with no other relatives close by. Her parents were living in England. After retiring from the military seven years ago, they had decided to make Europe their home.

Less than an hour later, Raquel was cuddled beneath the covers with Smookie lying on top of them beside her. Raquel couldn't stop her thoughts from drifting to when she'd confronted Quest Newman earlier that day. All the talk she'd heard from the women out walking their dogs was true. He was good-looking, well built, sexy and just all-around luscious. But her business with him took top billing over all that. She would see if he kept his word and followed up with her.

What if his dog sitter lied? Then it would be her word against the sitter's. She wondered if they could run DNA testing on dogs. She rolled her eyes, not believing she would consider taking things that far. If Quest Newman didn't believe her and refused any responsibility, then she would take care of Smookie's expenses herself. She could certainly afford to do so. It was just the principle of the thing.

Yes, she thought as she closed her eyes and drifted off to sleep. It was the principle of the thing.

QUEST STARED AT HIS COUSIN, trying to get a grip before he opened his mouth to speak. "So you're telling me that everything Raquel Capers said is true?"

Tawny shrugged, trying to keep the *"Busted!"* look off her face. "Well, I can't validate her claim that Bandit actually copped some off her doggy, since I wasn't there to see it for myself," she said. "But then, knowing Bandit like I do, I don't doubt it. You know what they say, 'Like owner, like doggy.'"

He frowned. "And what do you mean by that?"

She rolled her eyes. "Come on, Quest. You know what I mean. You're a Newman. You and your brothers like females, and evidently so does your dog. Besides, Bandit's a male—four years old—which is a lot of years in human years. He needed a woman. All men do."

Quest rolled his eyes. "We're talking about a dog, Tawny."

"Yes, we are. So you should have gotten him fixed years ago like I suggested. So in a way, it's all your fault."

He couldn't believe she'd said that. "My fault? Is it my fault that I trusted you to keep my dog? I paid you to do it, and the first chance you got you dumped him on a stranger."

"The old lady wasn't a stranger. I used to see her in the park all the time. She was nice. I could tell. And once I told her about my emergency, she understood."

He crossed his arms over his chest. "And that's another thing—there wasn't an emergency."

She lifted her chin. "There was to me. Okay, I shouldn't have lied and said someone had died, but when Roy called and said he had a weekend pass from the marine base and asked me to meet him in Vegas, and there was a paid ticket waiting on me at the airport, what was I to say?"

"That you had responsibilities you needed to fulfill and that you'd gotten paid to do them."

Aggravated, he rubbed his hands over his head. "And why did you tell that woman Bandit was fixed?"

"I was desperate," she said, with a pitiful look on her face that she evidently figured would get her some slack. "Besides, I didn't know the other dog was in heat," she implored. "Bandit wasn't paying that dog any attention. How was I to know he was just being cool and nonchalant until he got her behind closed doors?"

Quest released a deep breath, wondering why he'd even initiated this conversation with Tawny. But he had needed to know the truth and now that he did, he had to contemplate his next step. One thing was certain: he definitely owed Ms. Capers an apology.

"And why wasn't her dog fixed?"

Tawny's question barged into his thoughts. "Don't you dare try placing the blame on Raquel Capers. The point is that you knew Bandit wasn't fixed, yet you lied and said that he was."

Tawny shrugged. "Why are you getting so uptight about it? It's not like she can take you to court to make you pay puppy support." She snickered as if she found the very thought amusing.

He didn't see anything funny. She might not take her responsibilities seriously, but he did. Bandit was his dog and he would take full responsibility for his actions and behavior. "Don't count on ever keeping Bandit again, Tawny."

"Hey, that's not fair, Quest. Bandit likes me. If I don't keep him, who will? Your parents don't have the time, Quincy isn't into dogs and Brett's in Atlanta. That leaves just me," she said, smiling.

He glared. "No, that doesn't leave just you. There are other dog sitters out there. The person I leave Bandit with has to be responsible."

"But—but I need the extra money for my classes at the university. What about my hair, my nails, my music?"

"Then I suggest you get a real job." He walked off.

CHAPTER THREE

THE DOOR OPENED and Quest felt his mouth lift into an easy smile. He knew that he had done the right thing by coming here. "Thanks for agreeing to see me, Ms. Capers."

Maybe it was the cool look on her face that had him wondering if, although she had agreed to this meeting when he'd talked to her on the phone, perhaps she wished it wasn't taking place.

Instead of saying anything, she moved aside and allowed him to enter her home. He turned and she closed the door behind him. "Would you like something to drink, Mr. Newman?"

At least she was being hospitable. "Yes."

She nodded. "Beer? Wine? Soda?"

"Beer is fine. Thanks."

She pushed back off the door. "I'll be back in a minute."

He watched her leave, once again getting a backside view that he could appreciate. She was in a pair of jeans with a cute pullover blouse. Blue. He'd seen her twice, and both times he'd liked her blouse. This one showed enough cleavage to make him want to see more. And her body was real tight, firm, which made him believe she worked out a lot.

He glanced around and thought she had a nice place,

spacious, with appealing contemporary furniture. He appreciated fine things and could tell she did as well. Only difference was she had somehow made all of her nice things appear like a home instead of a museum. He liked that.

He felt a movement at his leg and glanced down, smiling at the white toy poodle staring up at him. He had never seen such a beautiful dog—and she looked so girlie with the pink bow in her head and the polished pink toes.

On instinct, Quest leaned down and picked her up in his arms, thinking about how fluffy she felt. "So you're Smookie. No wonder my Bandit liked you. You're a pretty little thing and would turn any male head." *Just like your owner*, he thought, remembering Raquel Caper's exit from the room and how he had enjoyed watching it.

He continued to pat the dog's head. Smookie was friendly, and he bet she had a good temperament. Bandit could be a handful on his I-don't-want-to-be-bothered days and was moody at times. Quest glanced up when he heard Raquel return carrying a bottle of beer and a glass.

"I wasn't sure if you wanted to drink out of the bottle," she said, placing both down on the coffee table.

"Thanks."

She reached for Smookie and the dog went straight to her. It was easy to see Raquel and Smookie had strong affections for each other, just like he and Bandit.

"I prefer straight out of the bottle and this is my favorite brand," he said, taking a huge swig.

"Figures."

He glanced over at her. "Why 'figures'?"

"That was my ex's favorite brand as well. That's the only reason I still have it."

He lifted a brow. "Ex, as in husband or boyfriend?"

"Ex as in boyfriend."

Quest lifted the bottle to his gaze as if searching for an expiration date, knowing that for beer there wasn't one. "How long ago?"

"How long ago?"

He lowered the bottle and held her gaze. "Yes. How long ago did the two of you split?"

There was something about the way Quest was looking at her that made Raquel suddenly feel funny inside. It definitely hadn't helped matters when he had walked into her home with a sexy stride that made her pulse flutter. It had been hard to school her expression and not show female appreciation at seeing him in a soft yellow button-down polo shirt and a pair of relaxed-fit jeans that emphasized strong, masculine thighs.

He also had a gorgeous pair of eyes. She'd noticed them the last time but had been too pissed off to appreciate them until now. Then there were his features, sharp and handsome. The creamy cocoa color of his smooth skin made her want to lick him all over. Boy, was it tempting.

She blinked, realizing they were just standing there staring at each other, and that the question he'd asked still hung in the air between them. She nervously licked her lips, and her stomach clenched upon seeing how his gaze followed the movement of her tongue.

"Derrick and I broke up over eight months ago."

He nodded slowly. "But you still have his favorite brand of beer in your refrigerator?"

What was in her refrigerator was really none of his business. She lifted her chin. "And what if I do?"

"Then I have to assume you're hoping he's coming back."

Raquel narrowed her eyes. *Not hardly.* "Excuse me, but what business is it of yours, Mr. Newman? If I recall, you're here to discuss your dog's inability to keep all his body parts to himself."

He smiled, and she hated admitting it, but he looked even yummier when he smiled. "His body parts?"

"Yes."

He chuckled. "We're discussing dogs. Animals. They live to eat and breed. My mistake, which I will admit to, is not taking that to heart and making sure Bandit was fixed. I erroneously thought that as long as I kept him away from female dogs in heat, things would be okay. My vet suggested neutering him years ago, but I didn't. Wish I had. Like I said, my mistake."

Good, Quest thought. They were talking about the issue that had brought him here, and not about her ex. The last man who'd probably held her, kissed her, made love to her. Some part of him was superglad she was no longer attached to anyone. Why that was of monumental significance, he didn't know.

"Please have a seat, Mr. Newman. I'm getting a neck ache looking up at you."

He sat down on the sofa and watched as she eased into the chair across from him. "And I think under the circumstances you can call me Quest. And I hope you don't mind if I call you Raquel."

She shook her head. "No, not at all."

"Pretty name, by the way."

"Thanks."

Just as pretty as she was, he thought. And was that heat he felt seeping through his body from just looking at her? "I had a chance to talk to my cousin Tawny," he decided to speak up to say. "She was dog sitting Bandit the week in question. I had gone camping with friends. Anyway, she admitted things were just as you said."

Raquel lifted her chin, and he thought it was a strong one. Perfect for the set of lips right above it. "Glad for you to know that I don't lie."

He could tell that was a sore spot with her. "I wanted to verify things first, Raquel. I think, under the circumstances, most people would."

She sighed. He was right. If the roles had been reversed, she wouldn't have believed him, either. People were good at running all sorts of scams these days, and she knew who he was. Former NFL star. Current CEO of a chain of stores that sold sporting equipment. He was pretty well-off financially, which would make him a target. And quite possibly there were a few women out there who would stoop low enough to come after him through their dog…but she wasn't one of them.

She placed Smookie on the floor, and the canine proceeded to stretch out beside her chair. "And since you're here, and your cousin has verified my story… what do you want to do?"

He leaned back in his chair, smiled and said, "You tell me, Raquel. What do you want me to do?"

At that moment, she had a feeling he wasn't talking about the issue at hand, and no matter how tempting this new topic was, she intended to keep them on track. "Well, for starters," she said, "I talked to the vet and she thinks Smookie will probably have more than one puppy. We should split them up."

He took another swig of his drink before saying, "You can have them all. I have no need for another dog or dogs."

She shook her head. "Neither do I. Yorkie-Poos are popular, so we can give them away to a family or friends who might inquire. But only if they're deserving and responsible."

Quest agreed. "What about the cost of your dog's medical bills? I have no problem splitting it."

"I appreciate that. My costs will be slightly higher to include Smookie's spaying. I don't want to go through this again."

He understood. Neither did he. "I already made Bandit an appointment with the vet this week. He'll be taken care of. Is there anything else we need to cover?"

"Umm, the vet did say it would he helpful if she had a copy of Bandit's medical records."

He nodded. "I'll make sure she gets them. Who's your vet?"

She told him, watched him key the information into his iPhone and then asked, "Have you had Bandit long?"

He glanced back at her and smiled. She drew in a deep breath and tried to downplay the fact that her pulse was hammering away. "Since the day he was born. His parents are owned by a friend, a guy I played ball with."

Quest paused. There was no need to tell her that Bandit had been there for him when he'd gotten cut from the NFL, and then during a more joyous time when his firm had made its first million. Whoever had said a dog was a man's best friend knew what he was talking about.

He glanced down at Smookie. "How is she doing so far?"

Raquel smiled. "Other than getting fat, she's okay.

No weird cravings yet. The vet said she'll probably deliver in a month, give or take a few days. In a way, I'm getting excited. I've never been a grandmother before."

He laughed. "And I've never been a grandfather. We're a little too young, don't you think?"

She joined in his laughter. "Evidently not, thanks to our babies."

"Yes, I guess you're right, although they aren't babies anymore." He took another sip of his beer and then said, "Your business card says you're an actress."

"Yes, I am." She shifted in her seat. Why did he have such a penetrating gaze, and why did watching him sip his beer turn her on? And was she imagining things, or was heat actually radiating off them both? She might be imagining it, but her thighs seemed to be quivering inside her jeans. She had been in the presence of a good-looking man before. No biggie. Then why was her body trying to make it one?

"Have you starred in anything I might have seen?"

She shook her head. "No, I'm not that kind of actress."

"Oh, what kind are you?"

Raquel thought over his question. There was no reason for her to answer it, since what she did for a living wasn't any of his business. And very few people knew her profession anyway. It wasn't that she was ashamed of what she did, but people had a tendency to pass judgment when it came to unorthodox occupations.

But for some reason, she had no problem admitting to him what had made her a rather wealthy woman. She decided to be honest about it. "I'm a phone actress."

He lifted brow. "A phone actress?"

"Yes."

She watched and was aware when the full scope of what she did for a living dawned on him. He looked at her and said, "Oh."

She chuckled. He truly seemed surprised...but not scandalized. "Umm, that's all you have to say?"

He chuckled as well. "No, sounds interesting. I guess you get to dress up in all kinds of interesting outfits."

"No, I just have to pretend. In other words, although you get a real person to talk to, your fantasy is only playacting on my part."

He looked crestfallen. "No sexy lingerie? No adult toys?"

"Sorry. No. Most of the time for me it's cutoff jeans with a T-shirt, flip-flops and bad hair, while moving around the house cleaning with a Bluetooth in my ear. I own plenty of adult toys just in case someone calls me out for a description of one. It's rather easy. All you need to know is how to act, along with a sense of humor and a good listening ear."

"A good listening ear?"

She nodded. "Yes. Believe it or not, most men who call aren't calling to talk sex. A number of them just want to hear a feminine voice. One who knows how to listen. They tell me how their day was at work, the trouble they're having with their girlfriend, family or friends. They talk about their dreams, disappointments and problems."

She paused a moment and said, "I actually talked someone out of committing suicide once."

His brow lifted. "You did?"

"Yes, I really did," she said, proud of herself. "That was one time my psychology degree came in handy."

"You have a psychology degree?"

"Yes, from the University of Alabama. Instead of going into that field after college, I took a management position at a bank. Hated it. But it paid well. Then when Wall Street came tumbling down, so did my position. A girlfriend and I were in the same rut and she came up with the phone-entertainment idea."

She shifted in her seat to a more relaxing position. For some reason, she felt comfortable talking to him. "Whitney created Companionship Plus and hired me as her first phone actress. Now she employs over two hundred other women across the country."

"A success story."

"So is yours." At the lifting of his brow this time, she said, "I know you own a slew of sporting shops."

Quest nodded and eased to his feet. "Well, I'm glad we've had this time to talk. I'll get Bandit's medical records to your vet in a few days."

She stood as well. "Thanks. And if you run into a problem faxing them to her, you can just drop them off here," she offered.

Quest wasn't sure seeing her again anytime soon was such a good idea. He was attracted to her, way too attracted for his peace of mind. "It shouldn't be a problem. If it is, I'll let you know. When would be the best time to reach you?"

"I work from home, so I'm here the majority of the time," she said, leading him toward the door.

Mentioning her work made him want to see her in action. "If I wanted to try my luck at calling you one night on your hotline, just to see how good an actress you are, how can I reach you?"

Raquel smiled. "Oh, I think I'm pretty good, but

if you would like to see for yourself, you can call the main number."

She rattled off the 900 number. "But keep in mind that there's no guarantee you'll get me. Like I said, we have over two hundred women working for the company now." She decided not to mention anything about the Hot Wire where she had her own private number. That was reserved for exclusive clients.

"I'll take my chances. Maybe I'll luck out and get you."

There was no need to tell him that that was a big maybe. "Yes, I guess there is that possibility." Why did the thought of talking on the phone to him in an intimate conversation send rushes of heat through her body? Tempting her to slide her hand beneath his shirt to rub his chest?

"I enjoyed my visit, Raquel. And I'm glad we straightened things out regarding our pooches."

She was glad for his intrusion into her thoughts. No telling what she would have thought of next. "So am I, Quest."

She glanced down at the poodle that had followed her to the door. Raquel leaned down and picked her up, cuddling her close to her face. "Smookie means a lot to me. She's the last birthday gift from my brother before he was killed in a car accident."

"I'm sorry."

She felt his sincere sympathy. "Thanks. That was a couple of years ago. Time heals all wounds."

"Yes, but you're never fully rid of them, are you? We don't forget the scars left behind. Goodbye, Raquel."

"Goodbye, Quest."

He opened the door and left. She closed the door behind him and released a rush of breath she hadn't been
aware she'd been holding.

CHAPTER FOUR

"SO TELL ME ALL ABOUT Quest Newman."

Whitney was on Raquel's Bluetooth as she moved around the kitchen preparing brownies for Ms. Albright's bridge party that night. "Not much to tell. He was in a way better mood than the last time, and of course he still looked like eye candy. Not that I'd expected his looks to change or anything. But sometimes an improvement in attitude can also improve your looks."

"I know what you mean. So he's willing to share the cost of Smookie's expenses? He didn't ask for proof or anything, like DNA?" Whitney asked, chuckling.

"Nope. And I have to admit I enjoyed his visit."

"What woman wouldn't? Not only is the man gorgeous, but he's well-off. I followed his career when he played for the Broncos and even later when he was traded to the Colts. He got two Super Bowl rings before getting hurt."

Raquel slid the tray into the oven. "There's something he said before leaving that gave me pause, though."

"What?"

"I mentioned Smookie had been a gift from Jordan and that he'd gotten killed in a car accident. He said something about, although time healed all wounds, there would always be a scar."

"Umm, I can understand him saying that," Whitney said softly.

Raquel lifted a brow. "Why?"

"You're not into football, so you probably don't remember the scandal."

"What scandal?" Raquel asked, leaning back against the counter. She glanced over at Smookie, who was entertaining herself with a stuffed toy Raquel had surprised her with yesterday.

"He walked in on his girlfriend making out with one of his teammates."

"Wow, that sucks!"

"I know. That was two years ago. Now I hear that, although he dates, he won't let another woman get close. I read in the papers last weekend that his twin brother got married."

"He has a twin?" Raquel asked, surprised. There was definitely a lot about Quest Newman that she didn't know.

"Yes, not identical though."

Raquel nodded. She couldn't imagine there being two men with Quest Newman's looks out there. "Well, I don't expect to see or hear from him again for a while. He's agreed to be fair with Smookie's expenses, and that's all I wanted. It's not that I couldn't pay for them, but it's the principle of the thing. Males, even dogs, need to own up to their responsibilities."

"You're thinking about what an ass Derrick was."

"Umm, I guess I am." Her ex-boyfriend had always been considerate…at least, he had in the beginning. But then when she began making money as a phone actress, he hadn't felt the need to do practically anything…including work. He thought it would be okay to live off her income and do whatever the hell he wanted…which was to play golf all day. He'd gotten to the place where he hadn't wanted to take out the trash.

She figured he had been shocked as hell when he'd come home one day from a golf game to find she had packed his things and had them waiting for him on the doorstep, with the locks to her doors changed. She had pretty much decided that her relationship with him had been a year of her life wasted.

"Any calls scheduled for tonight?" Whitney asked, reclaiming her attention.

"No, I need time to study." She had decided to pursue an MBA from the University of Alabama in Birmingham. Although school didn't start until the fall, she'd chosen to get a head start by taking a few summer classes.

After her phone call with Whitney ended, Raquel pretty much settled down for the evening with a quantitative analysis book, but she couldn't help but replay in her mind Quest's visit. Her condo was rather spacious, yet he had almost appeared bigger than life standing in the middle of her living room. And the man was so darn handsome and fine. But what she liked most of all was that, once he'd acknowledged his dog sitter's lack of responsibility, he'd agreed to do right by her Smookie.

She took a sip of coffee, opened her book and decided to push any thoughts of Quest from her mind for now.

"I JUST SENT YOU the information you wanted on Raquel Capers, Quest."

Quest smiled. "Thanks, Brett."

He'd known his brother would not fail him. After

all, Brett was computer savvy, a bona fide technical expert who worked as a private investigator in Atlanta for the Peachtree Private Investigative Firm. All you had to do was give him a name and he could research just about anything on that individual. The good, the bad and the ugly.

"Any reason you're so interested in Ms. Capers?"

Quest tossed aside a report he'd been reading as he adjusted his cell phone to his ear. "Yes, Bandit knocked up her poodle."

"What! How in the hell did you let that happen? I warned you that would happen one day, but you wouldn't listen to me."

Quest rolled his eyes. His brother was the main one who'd strongly recommend getting Bandit fixed, if for nothing more than health reasons, not to mention the issue of overpopulation. "It was during one of those times I left him with Tawny." He then told Brett what Tawny had told him.

"For Pete's sake, I warned you about leaving Bandit with Tawny. She's our cousin and I love her to death, but she is one spacey chick. You should have taken my advice on both counts."

"Well, okay, I didn't, and it is what it is."

"What kind of dog does Raquel Capers have?" Brett asked. "And I wonder how many pups she'll have."

Like you're interested in taking one, he wanted to say. He knew his brother, who was a couple of years older, had no time on his hands to care for a dog. "She has a toy poodle. White. A beauty."

"Evidently so is the owner, since you want to know everything about her. She's a phone actress, I see."

"Yes, that's what she says."

"It seems to be a rather good occupation financially, and the business is operated differently from some of those sleazy ones. They have a high-end clientele, and if anyone gets out of line they are dropped. So I guess you can say Companionship Plus could be considered the cream of the crop. Classy and all of that. But still, there's no telling what kind of conversations these guys are engaging her in. What one person might consider *clean* doesn't necessarily mean someone else will."

Quest twirled a pen between his fingers while listening to his brother give him a personal summation of what he'd uncovered in his investigation. "Anything else?"

"Yes. Although she's a partner in the business, she evidently likes being a phone actress and leaves the running of the business to her partner. She made close to a million as an actress the first year. Kind of makes you wonder what she's saying to the clients to make them call back."

It was probably her voice, Quest concluded, remembering how good she sounded during their conversations.

"She's so popular, she was given her own private call-in line. Now the only calls she gets are through what's called the Hot Wire. The callers pay more to talk longer. Trust me, the rates aren't cheap. And some of the restrictions as to what they can say or ask for are toned down somewhat."

Quest rubbed his chin. "Umm, I bet things can get pretty kinky then."

Brett chuckled. "Probably. But I have to say, your Ms. Capers is pretty smart, and so is her business partner, Whitney Frazier. The latter has an MBA, and your

Ms. Capers is presently working on hers. She's even taking summer classes. She's scheduled to finish in another year."

Quest heard Brett take a sip of something, probably a beer or soda, before he continued. "Her father is retired military, and he and her mother chose to remain in Europe to live. She had a brother—two years younger—who was killed in an auto accident a few years ago when a drunk driver ran a stop sign. Since then, she visits her parents during the anniversary of his death and usually stays a month, as she did earlier this year."

Which is when her dog got pregnant, Quest thought to himself.

"She had a boyfriend who didn't seem to want to be employed. She took it for a while and then dumped him."

Quest couldn't help wondering how his brother had gotten all this information. This was some real personal stuff; it gave him the creeps to know someone's life history could be pulled from computer data banks. Maybe he ought to feel guilty for wanting to know so much about her, but he didn't.

"What about the phone number to her private line? Were you able to get it?" he asked.

"Yes, but it wasn't easy."

Deciding it was time to get his brother off the phone, he said, "You know where to send the bill."

"It's already been sent."

Quest chuckled as he hung up the phone. He quickly turned to his computer to download the information Brett had sent him.

CHAPTER FIVE

"HELLO, THIS IS PRECIOUS."

"Hello, Precious, how are you doing?"

"Fine, and who am I talking to?"

The person paused a second and then said, "Renaldo, but you can call me Ren."

Ren was a new caller. Raquel didn't recall ever talking to him before and wondered how he'd come through the hot wire. "So what can I do for you, Ren?"

"Plenty."

She chuckled. "Okay, what's for starters?"

"Say my name."

"Renaldo," she said in a sultry voice.

"You sound good. I love the way you say it."

Raquel settled back against the sofa cushions while thinking he sounded pretty good himself. He had a deep, sexy baritone voice. Something about it was oddly familiar, but she pushed the thought to the back of her mind. Because talking on the phone was her line of business, it was no surprise some voices seemed recognizable.

She usually enjoyed the hot wire calls because she never knew what to expect with some of them. Once in a while, she would have to end the conversation because the caller got too graphic and explicit, but seldom was that the case. The majority of the time the men were respectful.

"What else can I do for you tonight, Ren?"

"Tell me what you're wearing."

Raquel glanced down at her skimpy shorts and T-shirt. "I'm in a red teddy," she lied, wanting to set the mood.

"I love red but I want you to take it off. I want to give rub you down."

"Do you?"

"Yes."

"You sure you don't want me to give *you* one?" she asked, grabbing a magazine off the table to flip through and wondering how long he would keep her on the phone.

"No, I want to take care of you tonight."

She couldn't help but smile at that. Most of her callers had a list of what she could do for them, but this one had the opposite in mind. He wanted to take care of her as he thought he really could. How sweet. This should be interesting. Okay, she would get into the mood right along with him by removing her shirt, at least. And she might as well remove her bra. "Okay, I'm naked," she said. She wasn't totally naked, but at least her body above the waist was bare.

"Good. Now go get your favorite body lotion. I want to rub it all over you."

Getting up and crossing the room, she padded on bare feet into her bedroom and grabbed the lotion in question. With her Bluetooth in her ear, she said, "I got it."

"What fragrance?" he asked her.

"Warm mango."

"Sounds delicious."

His voice sounded so darn sensual, so blatantly erotic, that a rush of heat flowed through her. That reaction surprised her since she'd talked to hundreds of men in the past, and she fought back that pulsing heat. But the throaty timbre of this voice had an alluring effect.

Deciding that since she was in her bedroom, she might as well stay there, she asked, "Now what?"

"Stretch out on your bed and squeeze some lotion in your hands so I can rub you down. And I want you to close your eyes and concentrate."

With that voice enticing her to do whatever he asked, she moved toward the bed and tossed the covers aside. She sat on the side and squirted some lotion into her hand before stretching out on the soft sheets.

"Go ahead. Close your eyes and think of me, Precious."

She thought his request was odd, given that she didn't know him, nor did he know her. So instead of imagining her mystery caller as the invisible man in her bed, she focused on a man she did know, one who had been in her thoughts a lot lately. Quest Newman.

Why on earth Bandit's owner had begun lurking in her mind when she'd only seen him twice was beyond her. The only reason she could come up with was that he was so pleasing to the eyes she couldn't help herself. And although she tried to downplay it, she had been physically attracted to him from the start. What woman wouldn't be?

"Your eyes are closed?"

"Yes." She smiled and closed them as she spoke.

"Good. Now take your hand and use your fingertips

to slowly stroke up and down your throat. I want you to think about me and get familiar with my touch."

Doing as he instructed, Raquel stroked her throat and thought about Quest. She remembered how he had appeared in his doorway, looking sexy and annoyed—the combination was mind-blowing and had the throat she was stroking feeling tight. And then she recalled last week when he'd come to her place, wearing a pair of relaxed-fit jeans, a soft yellow button-down polo shirt with tan boat-shoes and no socks. She had known the moment she opened the door and found him standing there that she would have to keep her senses under control.

Just thinking about him had her heart pounding, and then she began fantasizing that the hands touching her were strong, firm hands belonging to Quest.

"Now move them lower to the center of your chest and stroke there. Already I can feel the way your heart rate has increased."

She wondered if he really could, because he was right—her heart rate had increased and her breathing and pulse right along with it.

"I love the way you feel, Precious," he whispered in a husky voice. "Soft, gentle. All woman. And I like the way you smell as well. Warm mango. The scent on you is so seductive. My hands are on you, moving across your shoulders, under your neck, working my way toward your breasts. Oh, I like the way they feel. Full and firm. The tips are hard beneath my fingertips."

She didn't want to admit it, but they were hard. She couldn't ever recall a caller luring her into his fantasy.

"And I like how your belly button looks, all sweet

and sexy. Cute as a button. I think I'll put a little extra lotion around there as well," he added.

Knowing she was still wearing her shorts, but curious to see how much of her body he intended to cover, she lifted her hips and, with eyes still closed, she tugged down her shorts and tossed them aside, leaving her completely naked.

As if he knew exactly what she'd done, he said, "The area between your legs is beautiful. Looks good enough to eat, and I intend to do so after I lotion you down some more. I want to touch you everywhere, and then I intend to lick you all over, especially there."

He paused a moment, then said, "I intend to tell you just what I'm doing every step of the way, and I want you to concentrate, okay?"

"Okay," she responded in a voice she barely recognized as her own. His words were doing a number on her, and she felt herself getting heated all over.

"I'm kissing your stomach, licking around your navel. Umm, I like the taste of your skin."

His words caused blood to rush through her veins while heat sizzled in her pores. She was concentrating hard and, in the deep recesses of her imaginative mind, she could smell his masculine scent, could feel the tip of his tongue as it moved over her.

"And while my tongue is all over your stomach, my hand has moved between your legs. Oh, it feels so good down there. You're hot and wet."

Raquel felt her womanhood throb. Sensations were moving through her and settling at the apex of her thighs. "Ohhh," she moaned and wondered how something imaginary could feel so real.

"I'm slipping my fingers inside your heat, inside your

wetness. Oh baby, your scent is driving me crazy. Your juices have mingled with warm mango and it smells heavenly."

For the next few minutes, he kept it up and with his sexy baritone voice, he told her what his fingers were doing inside her. Somehow in the back of her subconscious mind, she could envision herself with him—this sexy-sounding client whom she pictured as Quest. And whose hands had touched her all over, but were now busy between her legs while he whispered in her ear some of the hottest, naughtiest and most erotic words she'd ever heard. And those words were making a slow, steady thrumming sensation take her all over. What he was doing defied all logic and pushed her to want more.

"Please."

Raquel could barely keep her hips level with the mattress. She could feel him, actually feel him, and she bit down on her bottom lip to keep from crying out.

"Let it go, baby, while my fingers work you this way. Just let it go. I'm right here. Let your juices flow."

As if his voice had the ability to command her actions, she jerked when sensations exploded within her. They were feelings she hadn't felt in almost a year, and never to this extent, this magnitude or to this extreme.

She snatched her eyes open, not believing what had just happened. Evidently, he'd heard her intense moans, because he said, "Baby, you sound beautiful when you come. Listening to you makes me want to start all over again, but this time take you hard, penetrate deep. Maybe next time. I'll be ending our call now."

She sucked in a deep breath. Pulling herself up in bed, she sucked in another and then asked, "You will call back?"

"Yes."

She couldn't believe she had asked that. She had definitely lost control, because she sounded downright needy. Somehow their roles had gotten reversed, and she had become the client and he the one dishing out pleasure. A part of her felt it had been a deliberate move on his part. Hadn't he said at the beginning of the call that he would take care of her? He'd certainly done that and more. Who was this guy, and how did he have the ability to verbally seduce her this way? Having an orgasm during one of her calls was definitely out of character for her.

"Good night, Precious."

"Wait!"

"Yes?"

She thought of what she wanted to say, but decided there was no way she could voice it. He'd said he would call back, and she had to believe that he would. "Nothing. Good night, Ren. I hope you enjoyed our conversation." She gave him the closing statement she gave all her callers.

"What I enjoyed, baby, was touching you and licking all over your breasts and belly. Trust me. Your mango scent will be with me for a while. Good night."

"Good night."

The call was disconnected, and Raquel drew in a deep breath and shifted in bed. Too weak to move just yet, she stared up at the ceiling wondering just what she had gotten herself into.

QUEST STEPPED INTO the shower. A cold one. His sex talk with Raquel had gotten out of hand, affected him right below the gut in every possible way. His groin was still throbbing, needing the release she'd gotten.

And the thought that she'd actually come. He had heard her on the phone, and there was no way he would believe it had been an act. It had been too perfect, the timing just right, her moans and groans on cue and believable. But then, he should know, because the sounds had aroused him to the point where he'd had to hold himself in check. This cold shower was a damn lousy way to end the evening.

No wonder men called her on the hot wire. She had the sexiest phone voice and had gone along with everything he'd asked. And like he'd told her, he would be calling her back.

But what if she'd only been acting? Hell, then she had done a damn good job of it. In his bedroom, he had actually gotten into the thick of things to the extent that he was convinced his nostrils were still filled with the sweet scent of warm mango.

And when he had told her he had been fingering her, he had honestly imagined doing just that to the point he had sucked his fingers when the call had ended. Her taste, the one he imagined, was simply delicious— mouthwateringly good.

A few moments later he got out of the shower and dried off. In his subconscious mind, he could swear the scent of mango was in his room, still lodged in his nostrils. Yes, he would be calling her again, but not too soon. For now, he wanted both of them to savor the memory of tonight.

IT HAD BEEN A WEEK. He hadn't called back and a part of Raquel wondered if he would. Maybe not calling was a good thing. But if she really thought that, then why had she been in a bad mood for the past few days?

"Okay, Raquel, what's wrong? Your concentration hasn't been the best lately."

She was pulled back into her phone conversation with Whitney. They had been discussing the need to hire more women—ten at least—to handle the increase in phone calls. She had informed Whitney that in a few months she would need to come off the call list for a while. She needed to put in more study time with her classes. Plus the responsibility of taking care of Smookie and her pups would be a job in itself.

Thinking of Smookie's pregnancy made her think of Quest. Her vet had called to say they'd received Bandit's medical history and were pleased with the care Quest had given his dog.

And later that day, Quest himself had called to check on Smookie. He had a sexy phone voice, and there had been something about his voice that reminded her so much of Ren. But then she knew why she thought there was a similarity. That night during her phone call with Ren, when she'd closed her eyes it might have been Ren's voice, but it was Quest she'd fantasized was the one touching her while saying all those naughty things to her.

"Raquel!"

"What?"

"Okay, that does it. Time out. What is going on? Is all that studying getting the best of you? Is something wrong with Smookie? Your parents? What? You need to get laid?"

Raquel couldn't help but laugh, because with the latter her best friend had hit the nail right on the head. Oh yes, she needed to get laid and all because of Ren. She had talked to the man once, and her hormones seemed to ooze all over the place whenever she remembered that episode.

"It's probably your fault," she told Whitney.

"My fault?"

"Yes. Who is Renaldo and how did he get special privileges to call the hot wire?"

"Renaldo?"

"Yes, but he prefers to be called Ren. He called my direct number. He has a real sexy voice and, needless to say, he reminded me of just how long it's been since I slept with a man."

"He sounded that good?"

"It wasn't just the sound of his voice, it was what he said. He called once but hasn't called back, although he said he would."

"And he probably will, but you know I have no way of checking on anything, especially the identity of the clients who call the hot wire, and most will give fictitious names to protect their privacy. All we can track is the amount of time they spend on the call to make sure we're getting paid."

"Well, he certainly made my night. I hope he calls back."

"Umm, I've never heard you this eager to hear from a caller before."

"I know, and in a way it's kind of scary. It was as if he was really here with me and we were doing everything he said on the phone."

"Wow! Maybe he'll call tonight."

"Maybe."

Later that evening, after she had taken three calls

on the hot wire, Raquel was about to opt out of taking another when, around ten-thirty, she decided to take just one more.

"Hello, this is Precious."

"Precious, this is Ren. I've missed you."

Sensations swirled in the pit of her stomach, and the area between her legs clenched in response to the sound of his voice. "And I've missed you, too, Ren," she said, knowing she shouldn't admit such a thing. He probably didn't believe her anyway and only assumed she was playacting.

"Nice to be missed and I'm going to make up for it, because tonight I plan to make a meal out of you, baby. In other words, I plan on eating you alive."

DAMN, HE *HAD* MISSED talking to her, Quest thought, leaning back in the recliner in his family room. All the lights were off, except for a lamp burning in a small corner. The television was on, but the sound was muted. Instead, Usher's "Lay You Down" was playing low on his stereo system, and the sound was vibrating through the house.

The mood was set, and already his groin was throbbing in anticipation of their talk. He had tried not to think about her over the past week, but had done so anyway. And doing so had filled him with a degree of animal lust he hadn't been aware he possessed.

More than once he'd thought of coming clean, calling her and revealing his true identity. But then he would talk himself out of it. He was a paying customer like any of the other callers she spoke to. So didn't he deserve to enjoy himself? And hadn't he made sure she enjoyed herself as well?

His imagination had run wild that night. He'd actually imagined touching her hardened nipples, feeling his fingers working inside her, stroking her clit. It had been throbbing as he gave it the attention it deserved, then held her when she climaxed. And when it was over, he'd tasted her on his fingers.

And all in his imagination.

"Ren?"

Her saying his name brought his mind back to the present. "Yes?"

"What do you want tonight?"

Her question was asked in a ragged breath, and he wanted to think she'd looked forward to this call as much as he had. "I told you, baby. I plan to eat you alive, lick you all over and swallow you whole."

She didn't say anything, but he felt it, all the way across the mobile network. An electrical charge that connected them with smoldering intensity. It couldn't be helped. He didn't know her excuse, but for him there wasn't one. He found her attractive and desirable. Extremely so. From the first time he saw her.

"Ren, are you still there?"

"Yes, I'm here. And I want you to strip. Take if all off and talk to me while doing so."

He could hear the rustling of her clothing. "Okay," she said. "I'm shimmying out of my skirt and kicking it out of the way."

In his mind he could imagine her doing that, and the thought had his mind bristling with heated lust. "What are you doing now?"

"Removing my panties."

His groin stirred and his erection throbbed. "I like

that color on you," he said, knowing he hadn't a clue what color they were but hoping she would tell him.

"Thanks, I prefer black to colors. Always have."

So she was wearing black panties. He bet they looked sexy on her brown flesh.

"Now I'm taking off my shirt, pulling it over my head. Oops, my hair just got caught." A few seconds later, she said, "There, I got it now. It's all off. I'm naked."

His erection continued to throb mercilessly. "What about your bra?"

"I wasn't wearing one."

He drew in a shaky breath, closing his eyes and imagining her standing in the middle of her bedroom with her clothes scattered around her naked body. He could picture that body—long neck, beautiful shoulders, uplifted breasts, flat tummy, shapely hips, firm ass and a pair of gorgeous legs.

"Okay, what's next?"

He kept his eyes closed when he said, "Cut off the lights and go to the bed. I'm joining you."

He swore he could hear the sound of her feet moving across the floor, and his stomach tightened in desire and an intense need filled him to capacity. He knew the moment she had gotten into bed by the sound of her body rustling the sheets.

After a few moments, she asked in a whisper, "Where are you?"

And he responded, "I'm here, not far. Close your eyes and listen…and enjoy."

He began speaking, talking softly and in a low voice, not even trying to hide the urgency, need and hunger in his tone. First he stroked her cheeks tenderly, needing to reacquaint himself with her soft skin, before moving his hands upward to run his fingers through the silky strands of her hair. It carried the scent of cherry vanilla to his nostrils.

And then he straddled her body, lowered his mouth to her neck. He placed a passion mark there before licking his way down to her breasts. He didn't need the lights on to see they were full and ripe. They felt that way underneath his mouth. His hands palmed the twin globes, loving the feel of them, before drawing a nipple toward his mouth to lick, suck and nibble at the hardened tip. He heard her moans while he told her what he was doing and how he was doing it.

He felt her move under his mouth, in pleasure and in torture. He could imagine her gripping the bedcovers, but he couldn't stop devouring her breasts like a madman.

At that moment he had to do something he hadn't done yet, which was to kiss her…even if it was only in his mind. He leaned forward and went straight for her mouth, sliding his tongue between parted lips. And in his mind, he kissed her the way he'd been dying to do for days, the way he'd done in his dreams. He felt it all the way to his groin, where it sent electrical shocks up and down his body.

And when she took hold of his tongue and began mating with it the same way he was mating with hers, he let out a guttural groan. He broke off the kiss and drew in a deep breath and growled out his need. It was then that he lifted her hips and lowered his head between her legs, letting his tongue slide between the slit of her womanly folds.

She cried out when he found her clit and began lapping it with a hunger he'd never felt before. Desire slammed into him, almost knocking him out his chair. "Yes, baby, feel what I'm doing to you, what my tongue is doing to you. You taste good and I have every intention of eating you alive as I told you I would."

And then his mind went to work, eating away at her like a madman, like a man who needed her taste then, there and now. "Wrap your legs over my shoulders."

He could actually feel her doing so, her scent continuing to take him over as he sucked the swollen clit between his teeth, holding it hostage while his tongue licked it like crazy. He felt his erection press hard against his jeans and moaned at the torture.

And when she began to tremble the moment he did, and her hips quivered beneath his mouth, he knew what was happening to the both of them as his tongue continued to explore her with deep, sensual strokes.

He breathed out a deep breath when the last eruption passed through him, and was glad he had thought to wear a condom during this phone call. Otherwise he would have exploded in his jeans. The sensations he felt had been spectacular. And they had shared the climax together during a phone conversation over the hot wire.

"You okay?" he asked when his breathing was back to normal.

"Yes. What about you?" she asked in a choppy voice.

He chuckled softly, satisfied. "Yeah, I'm okay, but it has me wanting more. Call me a greedy ass, but I can't help it. The next time I'll want more."

"More?"

"Yes, more."

There, he'd said it but wasn't sure exactly how he could get it. Maybe he ought to be concerned as to whether or not sharing phone sex with her would be enough.

For some reason, he had a feeling that it wouldn't.

CHAPTER SIX

"Raquel, you got a minute?"

"Sure, Whit. What's up?"

"We've been hacked."

Raquel raised a brow. "Hacked?"

"Someone has your direct hot wire number and is calling you without coming through the proper channels."

A frown settled on Raquel's face. "But how, and who is it?"

"I'm suspecting it's that guy named Renaldo. Is he still calling you?"

"Yes."

"When was the last time?"

That was easy enough for her to remember, since she still had dreams about that particular call. "Four days ago."

"Aha! He's our man. Do you have any idea who he might be?"

"No, I assumed he was a client." She nervously began nibbling on her bottom lip. "Should we call in security?"

"Umm, not yet, because we've also received an anonymous cashier's check in the mail with no return address that equals the amount of time for the calls. So although he didn't come through proper channels, he's honest enough to pay for the calls."

"How did he get my phone number?"

"I don't know."

Raquel's forehead furrowed. "That doesn't make sense. My number isn't listed anyplace. The only people who know it are us and the phone company."

"True. The only thing I can figure is that someone has managed to hack into our system for the hot wire."

"Then why didn't we go through the phone company and trace his phone number?"

"Because evidently he wants to keep his identity hidden. I talked to our attorney and she said we could find out his identity, but in the end we would spend more money trying to find out who he is than what he paid for the calls. She feels we should count our blessings that he's being honest and not worry about it."

Not worry about it?

"Unless he becomes a nuisance. Has he?" Whitney asked.

Raquel licked her lips. No, he hadn't been a nuisance, unless you called him revving up her hormones a nuisance. Ren had a way with words, and it was amazing how her body would react to them. The man could get her fired up in an instant, when it should be the other way around. It was as if he was servicing her instead of her servicing him.

"Well, has he been a nuisance?"

Raquel blinked, realizing Whitney was waiting for her answer. "No. And like I told you, I enjoy his calls."

"Umm, I wonder why."

She knew her best friend was teasing her, since she'd told her before how much Ren's call turned her on. "You know why, and if that's all you want to know, I need to go out for a few errands."

"You go do your errands. I think I'll check out a few things."

"A few things like what?"

"Oh, nothing important. I'll chat with you later."

Raquel ended the call thinking Whitney had too much free time on her hands.

"SORRY IF MY happiness is making you ill, Quest," Quincy said, smiling to his twin as he eased into the chair across from him.

Quest rolled his eyes. His brother had just returned from his honeymoon and dropped by his place to aggravate him. "It's not making me ill. I'm just surprised you and Kandi have finally allowed each other space. I was beginning to think you were joined at the hip."

"Funny. Make your jokes now, but your day is coming."

"Hardly."

"And what's this I hear about Bandit being an expectant father?" Quincy asked.

Quest had figured the news would reach Quincy soon enough. He took a sip of his beer and then asked, "What of it?"

"Well, if you're giving the puppies away, Kandi and I want one."

Quest stared at his brother. He had to be kidding. If he recalled correctly, Quincy was the one who'd tried to talk him out of owning a dog, saying they weren't anything but time and trouble. "You want to take on dog ownership?"

Quincy took a swig of his beer and leaned back

against the sofa. "Hell, if you can do it, then certainly I can. Whatever you can do, I can do better. And I definitely won't make the mistake of hiring Tawny as a sitter. And you better believe I'll get my dog fixed as soon as the vet recommends it can be done. It's called being a *responsible* owner."

"Okay, I dropped the ball. Bite me." He checked his watch. He hoped he'd timed it right to take Bandit out for a walk at the same time Raquel would be walking Smookie. He wondered why they never ran into each other at the doggy park and figured she liked walking Smookie midmornings and early evenings, whereas he preferred early morning and late afternoons. The puppy park tended to be less crowded during those times. However, he would make today an exception.

"How long do you plan to visit?" he asked Quincy.

"I was waiting for Kandi to finish her hair appointment, then I'm picking her up. The salon isn't far from here."

He checked his watch again. "What's wrong with her car?"

"Nothing."

"Then why are you using one vehicle?"

"I love having her around."

Quest simply sat there and stared at his brother, wondering how one woman could take a man from a player to being whipped. But then he thought about Raquel, the hot-wire conversations they'd had over the past week, and he knew it was possible. Kandi was an attractive woman who had captured Quincy's attention from the first.

Like Raquel had captured his.

"You're welcome to hang around, Quin, but I need

to take Bandit out for his walk. I might be gone for a while."

"You're going a little earlier than usual, aren't you?" Quincy asked, eyeing him speculatively.

"Yes, but when you got to go, you got to go."

"RAQUEL, WE NEED TO TALK."

This was the second time Whitney had called her that day. "Okay. I was about to take Smookie out for her walk. What's up?"

"You and that caller name Ren. I know what our attorney said about not wasting our money trying to find out his identity unless he becomes a nuisance and all, but I was getting worried. What if he was someone who knew you? A stalker or something?"

Raquel drew in a deep breath. It wasn't like Whitney to introduce drama when there shouldn't be any, so she knew her best friend was really concerned. "I'm sure that wasn't the case, Whit."

"Possibly. But I wanted to make sure you were safe, so I—"

"Please don't tell me you did what our attorney suggested you not do."

"Well, I'd think you would want to know who your Ren is."

"I don't have to know."

"Maybe you should. And you not wanting to know bothers me."

A part of her knew Whitney was right—maybe she should want to know. And probably the main reason she'd avoided finding out was because Ren had become her fantasy man, and finding out his identity might ruin things. What if he was one of the guys from school who had a receding hairline and potbelly waist?

She paused a second and then said, "So, okay, who is he?"

"You might want to sit down for this."

Now she was curious, so she pulled out a chair from the kitchen table and sat down and crossed her legs. "Okay, tell me."

Whitney hesitated only briefly and then said, "Quest Newman. Or should I say, Quest Renaldo Newman."

Oh, crap!

CHAPTER SEVEN

A HALF HOUR LATER, Raquel drew in a deep breath as she leaned down to hook the leash into Smookie's harness. Her head was still reeling from the information Whitney had doused her with a few moments ago. She probably would still be sitting at the table in shock if Smookie's bark hadn't reminded her it was time to go. And her doggy *had* to go.

Quest was actually her Ren?

She shook her head remembering how, after talking to Quest that time when he'd called to check on Smookie, she'd thought that he had a sexy voice just like Ren. Now she knew why. They were one and the same.

A part of her wanted to feel tricked, used and taken advantage of. But in all honesty, she couldn't. That day, before leaving, he had expressed an interest in talking to her on the hot wire. At no time had she assumed he would actually call her, and definitely not that he would go to the trouble of getting her direct number. And how had he managed to get it, anyway?

She quickly moved out the back door and locked it behind her. It was a beautiful June day, and she was glad for this time to get out and think. How would she handle her next call from him now that she knew his identity? And that call was scheduled for later that night.

She continued walking, keeping up with Smookie,

who was moving at a brisk pace toward the doggy park. What she really liked most about the park was the separate fenced-in area for small dogs, the beautiful water fountains and several pieces of agility equipment. There were also benches under shaded trees where you could sit while watching your pet romp around in a free and safe environment. And for her that was good, since she definitely needed to think about the recent turn of events with Quest Renaldo Newman.

She unhooked the leash, and Smookie took off running toward one of the huge decorative boulders, to sniff away and do her business. Raquel couldn't help but smile as she watched other dogs join Smookie and they began to play tag.

Sitting down on a bench so she could keep an eye on Smookie, she started to pull out her cell phone to call Whitney back, just to make sure her best friend hadn't made a mistake. But deep down, Raquel knew she hadn't. It all made perfect sense now. Whether or not she'd wanted to admit it, she had been attracted to Quest from the first, but had convinced herself that dealing with him was strictly business, involving Smookie.

Her mind drifted back to her last phone call with Ren...or Quest. It seemed real, and even now the memory had her stomach muscles quivering as sensuous stirrings began running through her. The things they had done together that night had probably scorched the sheets and...

Suddenly, a shadow crossed directly in front of her and she felt increased stirrings in the pit of her stomach. She knew even before she glanced up who was standing there. But her breath was snatched from her lungs anyway when she looked up.

"Raquel," he said in a deep, husky and throaty voice. "It's nice seeing you here."

It took a minute before she was finally able to respond. "Quest, it's nice seeing you here as well."

"Mind if I join you?"

She glanced around. "Where is Bandit?"

"Over in the park. You didn't see when I unleashed him?"

"No," she said, scooting over to make room on the bench when he made a move to sit down.

"I'm surprised. You were staring in that direction when he made a mad dash to Smookie. I assumed you saw us."

Raquel knew she might have been staring in that direction, but her mind had been a million miles away. "I guess I was absorbed in other thoughts." She bit back saying, *Thoughts of my last hot-wire conversation with you and how I can't get you or the memory out of my mind.*

He had slid down on the seat beside her. Close. He smelled good. Fresh. Robust and manly. Like her, he was wearing a pair of shorts and a T-shirt, and he was looking comfortable yet sexy all at the same time.

"I'm sorry if I interrupted your thoughts, Raquel."

"No big deal." She twisted slightly toward him. "So what brings you here this time of day? This is my usual time and I've never run into you before."

He smiled and glanced over to where Smookie and Bandit were playing together in harmony.

"I know. I came home early from work and thought it was a nice day to take Bandit out."

Like Quest, she watched their dogs playing. "They get along well together, considering…"

He looked over at her. "Considering what?"

She met his gaze. "Considering he got what he wanted from her and left, leaving her carrying the load, or the litter, in this case."

He shook his head. "They're dogs. They don't have a sense of responsibility, and they don't act on emotions when it comes to mating. They do it on instinct. If a female is in heat, the male goes for it."

Pretty much like a typical man, Raquel thought. "Yes, I guess you're right."

"Trust me, I am."

She dragged her gaze away from him and toward Smookie and Bandit, who were playing a game of hide-and-seek. She then glanced back at Quest. "About the male just going for it, what if the female's not in the mood?"

He chuckled. "Doesn't matter. However, if he was a man and not a dog, then it would matter, especially if she says no. And if the man was smart, he would put her in the mood. But then a female in heat is usually in the mood."

She didn't really have anything to say to that. Besides, he would know, since he'd certainly put her in the mood a couple of nights.

"When do you take Smookie back for her checkup?"

"In two weeks. Why?"

"I'd like to go with you when you do."

That surprised her. "Why?" she repeated.

"Because I'm interested in how she's doing. She's so small and all."

Raquel nodded. "So is Bandit. But he's such a cutie. I bet they've made beautiful puppies."

An aircraft flew overhead, and she looked up to see

a sign trailing behind a small plane. Quest glanced up as well as she read the sign. "'I'm Sorry, Becky.' Looks like someone had to take to the skies in seeking Becky's forgiveness. I hope she looks up and sees his apology."

"Yeah, me too," he said, staring up as well. A moment passed and then he asked, "What happened between you and your boyfriend?"

She shifted her gaze to his mouth, a mouth that—in her fantasies—had done a lot of things to her, stirred her in places she hadn't known could be stimulated. "Any reason you want to know?"

"Curious as to why a beautiful woman isn't in a serious relationship."

She leaned back and smiled over at him. "There are a lot of beautiful women who are not in serious relationships…and thanks for the compliment, by the way. So tell me, Quest. Are you in a serious relationship?"

Raquel saw him wince, although his smile remained intact. "No, I haven't been in one for a number of years now."

She could guess why. His fiancée's infidelity. All too late, she recalled what Whitney had told her about it. She chimed in, "My ex, Derrick, was an ass."

He cleared his throat. "Well, that's certainly not sugarcoating words."

She couldn't help but smile. "No. And I don't when it comes to him. He was selfish and thought only of himself. As soon as I became successful as a phone actress, he decided he shouldn't be required to lift a finger. Claimed he was going through some sort of emotional meltdown and just wanted to be left alone—to eat my food, spend my money and do as he pleased. Now, tell me. Do I look like the kind of woman whose mother raised a fool?"

No, she most certainly didn't, Quest thought. What she resembled was a woman any man would appreciate saying was his. "No, you don't look that way at all," he said. "So I can safely assume the two of you won't be getting back together anytime soon?" he asked.

She snorted and it wasn't all that ladylike. "Anytime *ever.*"

"You sound certain of that."

She twisted her body around on the bench, getting in a comfortable position. "I am so positive anything negative won't come my way."

He looked at her. "Okay. Any questions for me?"

She cocked her head, tempted to ask why he was Quest by day and Ren by night. But then she thought, why knock it when she was definitely enjoying both. So she decided to play it safe and asked, "Will you tell me about your family?"

He chuckled. "No reason why I can't, although I'm going to warn you, the Newmans are a pretty boring group."

He stretched his legs out, leaned against the back of the bench and said, "My parents, both doctors, had three sons. My older brother, Brett, lives in Atlanta and is a private investigator. My twin, Quincy, recently got married and just returned from his honeymoon. He's so much in love it's sickening."

Raquel's mouth twitched in a smile. "It's usually that way when two people are in love and marry, Quest."

"I guess."

"You don't sound convinced."

Instead of responding, he shrugged his shoulders.

Moments later he asked, "What about you and your family? I know you said you lost your brother."

She nodded. "Yes. He was my only sibling. I'm an air-force brat. My father was stationed in England when I was in my teens. He and my mom loved it there and always said they would return to live out the rest of their days after Dad retired."

Over the next half hour while their dogs played together nearby, Raquel and Quest shared conversation, exchanging tidbits about their childhood, their siblings and what they thought of the upcoming election and the candidates. She told him about her travels abroad and how her favorite country had been Germany, where she had lived for four years with her parents and brother.

And she talked about Jordan. She felt herself open up as she conversed with Quest, sharing with him the times she'd spent with her brother and what a close relationship they'd had. She also shared that, had she known he would be taken away from her, she would have spent even more time with him.

"Every year on his birthday, I take a moment to recall the good times. It's those times when I wish I could have been a better older sister and tolerated his mischievousness a lot more than I did. I regret not doing so."

Quest could hear the tremble in her voice and saw a glimmer of tears in her eyes. Instinctively, he reached out and captured her hand in his. "But that's just it, Raquel. We never know what life has in store for us—the good or the bad. I'm sure your brother didn't expect you to act any differently. And I'm certain if he were here and I asked, he would say you were a great sister."

At that instant Raquel knew that, although there was a lot she didn't know about Quest, the one thing she did know was that he had a way of making her feel special. His words had been thoughtful, comforting and had touched her deeply.

They sat there and stared at each other, not saying anything. But she was fully aware he was still holding her hand. She was also aware of the frisson of heat that was slowly building between them.

And then she felt herself leaning toward him as he simultaneously leaned toward her. And when their mouths were merely inches apart, he reached out and stroked the side of her face with his fingertips and whispered in that deep, husky voice that was Ren's, "Come closer."

And she did, leaning in closer. And he swooped down on her lips in an openmouthed kiss that snatched the breath from her lungs.

QUEST COULD ACTUALLY taste her desire, as well as his own, in this kiss. It was strong, sharp and keen. They were sitting on a park bench, for heaven's sake, out in public, but for the life of him he couldn't let go of her tongue. The same tongue he dreamed about, and had devoured in their phone talks. Now he was actually tasting it. He'd meant for it to be a brief kiss, but brevity was the last thing on his mind at the moment. She had been temptation from the beginning, and now she was the promise of heated bliss.

A dog barking made them unlock lips, but because he couldn't resist, he brushed another quick kiss across her mouth.

She stared at him, not saying anything, which propelled him to ask, "What's going on in that pretty little head of yours, Raquel?"

A gentle breeze floated through the air, and Raquel picked up his scent as it was easily drawn into her nostrils. "What's going on in yours?"

Quest wasn't sure she would be able to handle his bluntness, especially after that kiss. Sitting beside her on this bench, he could see how gorgeous she really was. Granted, he had seen and met women just as beautiful, but there was something about her that was so knockdown, drag-out feminine and ultrasexy, that he was getting more aroused by the second. No woman had aroused him to this degree, either on or off the phone.

And speaking of phone…

They had a conversation scheduled tonight on the hot wire, and he couldn't wait.

"What's wrong, Quest? Cat got your tongue?"

He smiled, tempted to tell her that if the cat did have it, he would eagerly take it away and give it to her again. Deciding what the hell, he would leave her something to think about, he leaned close to her and whispered, "Why, you want it back?"

He saw how her eyes darkened and could hear the sound of her heart thumping in her chest. He watched as she eased to her feet. "I better not touch that one, Quest."

"Umm, I wish you would."

Raquel wished she would, too. That kiss had left her pretty dizzy. She broke eye contact with him and glanced over to where the dogs had evidently tired themselves out and lay stretched out under a shade tree.

Not bothering to comment on what Quest had said, she spoke. "I think it's time for me to get Smookie home. I stayed out longer than usual and it's past her dinnertime."

He then stood as well. "I enjoyed your company, Raquel."

"And I yours."

She moved toward the fenced area, and he took her hand as they walked beside each other. Tiny flutters danced in her stomach at his touch.

"How's school going?"

She glanced up at him. "How did you know I was in school?"

He shrugged. "I don't know. I guess at some point in time you mentioned it."

She nodded, knowing for certain that she hadn't. "Yes, I must have."

They gathered their doggies and, when Smookie pulled on the leash as if she wanted to follow Quest and Bandit, Raquel jokingly said, "Come on, girl. Haven't you learned your lesson by now?"

Quest chuckled. "Hey, don't try teaching her to be a hater."

They walked away from the doggy park in silence and, when they got to where he would go his way and she would go hers, he said softly, "I would like to take you out sometime, Raquel."

She tilted her head back to look up at him. "Why?"

"Mmm, why would any guy want to take a pretty girl out?"

"I don't know, you tell me."

He held her gaze. "To get to know her better. And personally, I like being with you."

Good answer, Raquel thought. He'd said it in an intimate way, as if he had been out with her before and they'd spent time doing more than sharing a bench and a kiss. "I'd like that."

"Okay, what about this weekend? I have a small boat that I take out on Coleman Lake."

"How small?"

He grinned. "It won't turn over, if that's what you're worried about."

She hugged her arms around herself and asked, "Can we bring our doggies along? I don't like leaving Smookie by herself too much these days."

He smiled. "Sure. I've taken Bandit out with me several times before. He likes it and I'm sure Smookie will, too."

She returned the smile while thinking she was certain that Smookie's owner would like it as well.

CHAPTER EIGHT

LATER THAT NIGHT, Raquel moved around the house checking everything before she entered her bedroom. Tonight would be different and she intended to make it so. She and Ren might be having off-the-charts phone sex, but tonight she wanted to set the mood with the lit candles she'd placed around her bedroom.

She glanced at the clock on her nightstand. He would be calling in twenty minutes and already her pulse was beating something fierce, and that wasn't a good thing. She was supposed to be in control of the conversation, but Quest had pretty much taken that control away during the first call.

She touched her lips, still feeling a sharp tingling sensation there. The man definitely knew how to kiss. It was a good thing she'd already been sitting down, or else her knees would have buckled beneath her. He had sucked on her tongue as if he had every right to do so, and she'd let him as though he did.

Raquel eased the robe off her body and slid naked beneath the covers. She couldn't help remembering how earlier he had almost given himself away when he'd mentioned her attending school. She could have called him out then, but chose not to. A part of her was curious to see how long he would play the game. But as long as she was one up on him, she would wait it out and see.

She glanced over at the clock again. She had less than fifteen minutes, and a part of her wished things were different. She wished that he was here with her in the flesh, in the bed with her...just as naked as she was. She could imagine them snuggled up close, skin to skin, with his muscled chest resting against her back in the spoon position. That would also mean that his groin would be pressing hard against her butt.

Raquel drew in a deep breath and tried taking her mind off the phone call that she was waiting for. She glanced around and thought the candles looked beautiful the way they were placed around the room.

Romantic.

Enticing passion.

At first she had felt silly when she'd gone around lighting them, but then decided she had no reason to feel that way. Men called her all the time to play out their fantasies, and now it was time that she play out hers.

It had rained earlier, not long after she had returned from the doggy park, and she could still hear the steady drip of water falling off the roof. A wry grin touched her lips. What would Quest think to know she was fully aware he was her Ren? Maybe it was time to let him know she knew his identity. It was just a matter of time before one of them would give something away. Besides, why were they playing this game anyway?

She glanced over at the clock again, thinking she was playing the waiting game, but she had a feeling it would be well worth it tonight.

QUEST MOVED AROUND his condo, trying to convince himself he wasn't counting the minutes before it was time to call in to the hot wire. He had taken care of Bandit for the night. Usually the dog slept on the floor next to his bed, but tonight Quest didn't want anyone, not even his dog, listening to his conversation with Raquel. He knew it was crazy, since Bandit wouldn't understand a word he said anyway, but it didn't matter. He wanted total privacy.

He couldn't help but recall their time together at the doggy park and, although they'd tried ignoring it, there had been a primitive magnetism between them while sitting together on the bench. And he enjoyed listening to her talk, with that sultry voice of hers that put plenty of ideas into his head. More than once he'd been tempted to reach up and slide his fingers through her hair and pull her mouth closer to his.

He thought her mouth was perfect and her taste delicious. Even now he wanted to kiss her again, plenty of times. But he didn't want to stop with just one kiss. He wanted to do all those things with his mouth they'd pretended to do during their phone talks.

He'd almost given something away when he'd mentioned her going to school. She'd never mentioned anything about taking classes to him. It had come directly from the report Brett had provided.

Turning off all the lights, he headed toward his bedroom. Usually he would sit in a chair in the office with his legs stretched out in a comfortable position during their calls. But tonight he wanted Raquel in her bedroom, and he intended to be in his.

His house was quiet, almost too quiet. Not that he was complaining, but he was realizing he'd lived a pretty lonely life since Monica's betrayal. It wasn't that he wasn't over her; it was because he was. And as his brothers had told him, it was better to learn now what type of woman she was than to do so later. And just to think he had pretty much decided to ask her to be his wife. So finding out the truth had been a blessing.

Today Raquel had looked good in her white cuffed shorts and blue-paisley halter top. The memory of just how good she looked was burned inside his brain, branding his senses in a way no other attraction to a woman had ever done.

He glanced at the clock again. Less than ten minutes and he could feel a stirring in his groin. He was definitely looking forward to that phone call he was about to make.

RAQUEL WAS ABOUT to shift to another position in bed when the phone rang. She glanced over at the clock. Ren was five minutes early. Was he just as anxious for their phone talk to begin as she was?

With her pulse skipping all over the place, she reached out and clicked the Bluetooth in her ear. "You're early."

"I couldn't wait," was the husky reply. "Where are you?"

"In bed."

"Under the covers?" he asked her.

"Yes, I'm under the covers."

"What are you wearing?" The raspiness in his voice sent tremors through her body.

"Nothing."

There was a silence on the phone, which made the sound of dripping raindrops off the roof become more noticeable. "Can I slide into bed with you?"

She felt a moment's pause with his question. This would be their third phone conversation, and if things were hotter tonight than they had been before, she wasn't sure she would be able to stand it. "Umm, I was hoping you would," she said.

"All right, I'm sliding into bed with you. The sheets are warm from your heat."

She closed her eyes, imagining he was actually making good on his words. "Do you like the candles burning?" she asked, knowing he couldn't see them.

"Candles? Ahh, sure. Yes, they're as beautiful as you are. I plan on getting lost inside you tonight," he said in a husky note. "But first I want to lick my way all over your body. I became addicted to your taste from the last time."

She breathed in deeply and could envision his lips trailing a path from the center of her neck to her collarbone. In her mind she could actually feel those thick, long lashes caressing her skin. And just the thought that his sensual lips were coming in contact with her flesh made her moan.

"You feel soft and smell good."

Her lips moved into a smile. "Do I?"

"Yes. I have my hands all over you."

And as if he willed it to be so, willed her to feel him touch her, she did. Sensations started at the bottom of her feet, a prickling of electrical charge that was surging slowly upward, settling at the juncture of her legs.

"Imagine my fingers there," he whispered, and the sound of his voice had her heart thumping hard in her chest.

She slowly opened her eyes, knowing what she wanted tonight. The hot wire would not be enough and it was time to bring their game to an end. She wanted him, not in her fantasy but in reality.

"Open your legs, baby."

She shook her head and whispered, "No."

"No?"

"No. I don't want to pretend anymore. I want the real thing. I want you here with me in the flesh."

There was a pause and then he asked, "How am I supposed to do that?"

She pulled up in bed, sat on the side and pushed her hair away from her face. "I think you know the answer to that…and Ren?"

"Yes?"

"You know where I live. I'll be waiting."

THE PHONE CONVERSATION ended with a resounding click in his ear, letting Quest know two things. Raquel had ended the call and she knew his identity. He couldn't help wondering what had given him away. Did it matter?

No, he thought, quickly easing off the bed and grabbing his jeans and shirt off the chair. Aroused anticipation took over his senses as he slipped into his shoes. No woman had ever had him wanting her this much. And to play it safe, he shoved a bunch of condoms into his back pocket. Shivers had begun running down his spine in an adrenaline rush, and in no time at all he was almost running for the front door. His libido was in an uncontrollable state and his erection throbbed mercilessly against the zipper of his jeans. She had him wired up to the point of no return.

He hesitated a moment before grabbing his key off the table. It was a short walk, but he wouldn't do so tonight. He needed to kill as much time as he could. He hoped she knew what she'd done because there was no turning back now.

CHAPTER NINE

RAQUEL'S HEART NEARLY stopped beating the moment she heard the knock at her door. She tightened the sash around the waist of her bathrobe and took a long, deep breath before opening the door.

And then she and Quest just stood there and looked at each other. Their eyes held for one heat-blazing moment. She thought he couldn't look any sexier than he did standing in her doorway in a T-shirt and pair of Levi's that looked so good on him. His eyes were deep and penetrating, and there was a sharp edge of intrinsic masculinity about him that sent her hormones into a state of excessive activity. And had desire exploding into a thousand pieces within her body.

She wasn't sure who moved first, but within seconds he was there, slamming his lips down on hers at the same moment that he swept her off her feet into big, strong arms. He closed the door with the heel of his shoe, not breaking contact with her mouth, while she threw her arms around his neck to hold on. His tongue penetrated deep, exploring her mouth in sensual strokes that had her moaning.

He slowly pulled back, broke off the kiss to stare down at her with those mesmerizing dark eyes, and simply said in a low drawl, "I'm here."

Yes, she thought, he definitely was. She could certainly see that. And she had a feeling that before the night was over she would be seeing a whole lot more. She swallowed hard, nodding. "I'm glad you came."

He didn't say anything. Instead he lowered his mouth again and took her mouth in another hot, scorching kiss. She felt him moving, carrying her somewhere, and she knew just where when her bottom came into contact with the hard edge of her dining-room table.

And then he broke off the kiss. "Where's your bedroom?"

She tilted her head. "Down the hall that way."

He smiled down at her and her heart thudded heavily in her chest. "I can't wait to take you there and get you naked."

Her nipples hardened with his words and her belly began quivering. It wouldn't take much for him to do that, given she was naked beneath her robe anyway. He swept her back into his arms and began moving in long, powerful strides.

When he reached her bedroom, he glanced around at the candles before turning his full attention back to her. He then lowered her to the floor, letting her slide her body down his masculine build in the process. And then he just stood there and stared at her for a second, while heat settled everywhere within her, especially in the area between her thighs.

Nervously, she bit her lower lip. "Why are you staring at me like that?"

He smiled, reached out and brushed a few strands of hair back from her face. "I'm trying to get control, sweetheart. Otherwise, I'll make love to you, right now, right here, standing up, without making it to the bed."

His voice had lowered, dropped an octave, and she

could feel his words brush across her skin and her pulse rate increase. And then, without any warning or preamble, he reached out and pulled her toward him and lowered his mouth to hers.

Some men kissed you. Others devoured you. Then there were those, like Quest Renaldo Newman, who gobbled you up whole. The thrust of his tongue into her mouth immediately sent a heated rush through her body as blood raced through her veins. And then in a dominant way, he moved that tongue around, conquering everything in its path, sending shivers through her body and absorbing every inch of her mouth into his.

And she felt his hands moving all over her body and the hard, erect front pressed against her middle. He was aroused in a big way and the thought of that escalated her need tenfold.

He broke off the kiss, and she heard his uneven breathing as he reached out and undid the sash at her waist and pushed the robe off her shoulders. She watched his penetrating gaze rake all over her naked body, covering it inch by inch. She drew in a deep breath when she felt that heated gaze linger at the juncture of her thighs. And the male intent in his eyes should have warned her to take a step back. Instead, she tempted him further by readjusting her stance to widen her legs in a way that let him see it all.

She watched him lick his lips, and the sight of his tongue—the same one she had imagined doing all kinds of naughty things to her over the hot wire—had her body trembling in anticipation.

Her breath caught when he reached out and with the tip of his finger trailed a path across her shoulder and down her arm, before zigzagging across to her breasts.

She barely heard him murmur the word "beautiful" before his fingertips circled around a hardened nipple. Pleasure points shot out to every part of her body and she knew if he kept this up she would eventually lose her mind.

"I imagined how you would look, but this is far more than my expectations, Raquel. You are truly a beautiful woman."

She couldn't help but smile at the compliment. Tilting her head, she said, "You don't look so bad yourself, even in clothes. When do you plan to take yours off?"

He held her gaze and the mischievous glint in his dark eyes told her he would be taking them off soon enough. But first he planned to enjoy her for a while. She was proven right when his hand drifted low and gently caressed her belly, fanning desire all through her.

"Tonight, I plan to do everything we did on the hot wire, as well as other things I wished we could have pretended to do," he said in a deep, husky voice as his fingertips moved around her belly button, causing sensations to spark to life there.

Other things? She could barely handle what he was doing to her now. Suddenly, she sucked in a deep breath when his hand moved lower, between her legs to gently cup her sex.

"Damn, you're hot."

Had he honestly thought she wouldn't respond to what he was doing to her? Fat chance.

"Would you like to explode with me tonight, Raquel?" He leaned close to whisper the question in her ear. "Hell, I hope so, because I plan on making us come all over the place."

At that moment the fire that was already blazing

within her suddenly began raging out of control. Boldly she reached out and cupped him through his jeans, felt his erection—long and thick—and said, "Yes, I'd like that."

He smiled and the curve of his lips almost made her swoon. And before she could catch her next breath, he knelt between her legs.

QUEST GRABBED HOLD of Raquel's hips just moments before shoving his tongue inside of her. Then he began feasting on her with a greed that made his erection press hard against his zipper.

Her taste was just as he thought it would be and he intended to lap her up completely. She was sweet with a flavor that was uniquely hers. He wanted to slow down, keep his hunger under control, but the moment he took her clit between his lips to lap up more of her exquisite-tasting juices, he was a goner. The sound of her moans was enough to push him over the edge.

And then he tightened his hold on her hips as he plunged his tongue deeper inside of her, determined to taste every inch of her this way. She tried pushing his head away but he wasn't going anywhere. Pretty soon she gave up and began grinding her sex hard against his mouth, letting him know she wanted more.

He gave her more by deepening the intimate kiss to her pulsing core. He felt her beginning to quake all over and within seconds, her body exploded in his mouth. She screamed but he didn't let up. Instead he held her tight while increasing the strokes of his tongue inside of her. When the last strangled cry had left her mouth, he released her and leaned back on his haunches to smile up at her. He wanted her to know just how much he had enjoyed savoring her that way.

Disoriented, Raquel swayed and would have fallen flat on her face if Quest hadn't stood up and pulled her into his strong arms. Every nerve ending in her body was on fire and she could barely catch her breath.

"Now to get you in the bed," he said, seconds before he swept her into his arms and carried her over to the bed. He moved back and she watched as he removed all his clothes, piece by piece. First came his T-shirt to reveal powerfully built shoulders, a beautiful, sculpted chest with tight abs. Next he lowered his jeans and his briefs right along with them. Air was suddenly snatched from her lungs and her sex throbbed upon seeing the thick erection he uncovered. It looked bold, daring and confident as hell.

The thick veins running along the head of his shaft were enough to make her swoon again. But instead of swooning, her clit tingled in anticipation. She was oh so ready for this. And she wanted to taste him the way he'd tasted her moments ago.

"Come closer." She said the same words to him that he'd said to her earlier in the park.

When he was within reach, she took him into her hand and began stroking him, moving her fingers up and down, liking the feel of his thick shaft in her hands. She curled her fingertips around the hard muscles while imagining something so big and powerful buried deep inside of her.

That thought made her lean forward to lick the tip of his engorged shaft while she continued to move her hand up and down, pumping it. She swirled her tongue all around it, as if taking its measure, and when he groaned her name at the same time she tasted his salty-sweet release spilling out, she opened wide to slide him into her mouth.

Using her lips, she locked him in and began working her tongue, deliberately rippling across nerve endings, tunneling across veins and stretching her mouth wide while she felt his stomach muscles quiver.

His response aroused her more and her mouth increased its pressure and nearly gobbled him down her throat.

"Raquel!"

She looked up and the penetrating look in his eyes was filled with a degree of lust that almost singed her lips. "No more, baby," he said reaching down to use both hands to pull himself from her mouth. "I can't take any more." He quickly reached for his jeans and pulled out a condom packet. She watched as he ripped it with his teeth and hurriedly put it on.

And before she could finish licking her lips to savor his taste, he reached out and pulled her halfway off the bed to where her legs extended over the side. He then moved between them.

"I need you. I need this," he said in a guttural groan just seconds before thrusting inside of her. Automatically she arched to him, feeling his erection thicken even more inside of her. A whimpering moan tore from her throat when he began moving in and out of her with rapid precision. She was pinned between him and the mattress and he was giving her one hell of a workout as he plowed her body with deep, powerful thrusts. They were so forceful, the bedsprings protested and the sound echoed throughout the room.

None of what they'd ever shared over the hot wire

had prepared her for this. He was taking her with such hunger and need that her bed was rocking. She kept up with his rhythm and closed her eyes as sensations began taking over and her stomach began convulsing.

"Look at me."

At his command, she opened her eyes and looked right into his as he tilted her hips and drove harder, touching what had to be her g-spot, because that's when her body exploded in an orgasm that ripped all through her and made her holler. She discovered at that moment there was a big difference between a scream and a holler.

This was a holler, and her lungs could barely take the pressure. She clenched down on her jaw to keep from hollering again when another forceful orgasm tore through her. Never had she felt so vulnerable and sexy all at the same time. She could actually feel her toes curl.

And then the sound of him shouting her name filled her with satisfaction in knowing she had given him the same degree of pleasure that she was feeling.

Moments later he collapsed on her and then pulled them both up to the middle of the bed. With their limbs entwined, their bodies sweaty, he pulled the covers over them while they both fought to get their breathing under control. No words were spoken. None were needed.

He leaned down and brushed a kiss across her lips before pulling her deeper into his arms. "Sleep now."

Raquel sighed contentedly and smiled as she settled into him and closed her eyes to peaceful slumber.

Hours later, right before the crack of dawn, Quest tilted Raquel's chin up so that her gaze could meet his. "How did you know I was Ren?"

She smiled up at him, reached out to caress his un-shaven jaw. "My business partner discovered your identity and told me, less than an hour before I saw you today at the park."

"Yet you didn't say anything."

She shrugged. "No. I recalled the last time you were here and you expressed an interest in talking to me. I didn't take you seriously and figured you just wanted to see if I could really act. After finding out who you were, I didn't think you were trying to take advantage of me or anything. After all, you were a paying customer so I couldn't complain."

Her gaze dropped for a second and then she glanced back up at him and asked in a quiet tone, "I was right, wasn't I? You weren't trying to take advantage of me."

His hand shifted from her chin as he gently reached out and stroked her cheek. "Yes, you were right. I wasn't trying to take advantage of you."

He shifted their positions in bed, bringing her closer into his arms, and said, "That day I was here and I mentioned talking to you on the hot wire, I was letting you know I was interested in a relationship with you beyond Smookie and Bandit. I couldn't resist calling you, but figured my chances of getting you on that 900 line were pretty damn slim. So I hired my brother to get your personal hot-wire number."

"Your brother?"

"Yes, Brett. The one I told you was a private investigator living in Atlanta."

"And he investigated me?"

"I only wanted the number to your private line. But Brett, being Brett, took things further. He probably knew I was interested in you and decided to make sure you were okay."

She raised a brow. "He's a little overprotective, don't you think?"

Quest nodded. "Yes, but he's still on a guilt trip since he's the one who introduced me to the last woman I was serious about."

Raquel nodded, knowing who that woman had been. "The woman who betrayed you?" she asked, deciding to let him know she knew the story.

"Yes, that one."

"Well, after going to all that trouble, I hope your brother likes me."

He chuckled. "Doesn't matter. I like you. After our phone talk the first night, when you came apart while I was talking to you, I knew then that you had to be one of the most sensuous women I've ever met."

She grinned. "How do you know I wasn't faking it? I am an actress, you know."

"Yeah, I thought about that possibility, but dismissed the idea after replaying everything in my mind. And then, after that second time, I knew without a doubt you were for real. You weren't acting. And that kiss today in the park cinched it."

No, she hadn't been playacting. She had gotten into their phone talks so much that she'd actually thought she could feel him in the room with her, touching her, tasting her. And when he had kissed her today at the park, she had gotten an erotic glimpse of just how it would be between them if they ever took things further. Now she knew and couldn't help wondering if this was one and done, a one-night stand.

As if he'd read her mind, he reached out, touched her

chin and lifted it for their gazes to meet. "We're still on for this weekend, right?"

She nodded. "If you want."

He smiled. "Yes, I want. And you know what else I want?"

"No."

"I want more dates with you. We're practically family anyway."

She lifted a brow. "We are?"

"Yes. Your Smookie is having my Bandit's babies."

She chuckled. "Yes, we can't forget that. After all, that's how we officially met."

He pulled her closer into his arms and kissed her hard and, at that moment, their pooches became the last things on her mind. Raquel had a feeling that tonight would be the start of something very special.

EPILOGUE

"ARE YOU SURE she's okay, Quest?"

Raquel continued to stroke Smookie as she glanced up at Quest when he knelt beside her. It was time and Smookie would be delivering her puppies any minute. Dad Bandit was across the room, stretched out on the floor as if he preferred not being a part of the excitement. Typical male. Poor Smookie was doing all the work. At least Quest had gotten Bandit neutered, so he wouldn't be responsible for any other female dog going through this.

A couple of days ago, they had made Smookie a delivery nest in an empty closet in one of the guest bedrooms, with plenty of towels and blankets. Her temperature had dropped to 98 degrees that morning, which according to the vet meant she would deliver within twenty-four hours.

Raquel was trying to make Smookie as comfortable as possible. Due to the amount of weight Smookie had gained, the vet had warned them to expect a full litter of four puppies.

"She's fine, sweetheart. Things are progressing just as the vet said they would," Quest said.

Raquel nodded. She was glad Quest was here with her. But then, over the past four weeks he hadn't been too far away. After the night they'd spent together it had become a foregone conclusion they were dating exclusively. He no longer called the hot wire; he received special treatment whenever he showed up at her place.

She had met his family at a Fourth of July barbecue at his parents' home and thought everyone was extremely kind. They had made her feel right at home. His twin brother was a riot, and she thought his wife Kandi was superfriendly. She and Kandi had formed a friendship and gone shopping together a number of times. And his brother Brett, who had come in from Atlanta, was definitely a hottie. She admired the close relationship among Quest, his brothers and parents.

"Have you taken her temperature lately?" Quest asked her, reclaiming her attention. He was shirtless, in his bare feet and wearing jeans riding low on his hips. He looked sexy and so much at home. It was no surprise he was now spending more time over at her place than his own. But then, she had stayed over at his place a number of nights as well.

"Yes and it's still holding at ninety-eight."

Raquel's gaze dropped back to the little dog that meant so much to her, and she nervously bit on her bottom lip. She glanced back over at Quest. "What if she can't do this on her own? What if something goes wrong? What if—"

Quest reached out and placed a finger to trembling lips. "Shh, she'll be fine, babe. And if there is trouble, Dr. Martin is just a phone call away. We've made Smookie comfortable and it's up to her to do the rest... with our help if needed."

He chuckled and glanced over at Bandit. Calling out to his dog, he said, "You better get a good look at this,

Bandit, because this will be the only time you'll have any offspring, now that you've been fixed."

Bandit lifted his ears as if he was listening and then, deciding he didn't want to hear what Quest had to say any longer, he lowered his ears and yawned before looking away.

Raquel had to press her lips together to keep from laughing. "I think he's still upset with you about it."

Quest grinned back at her. "Trust me, I felt his pain."

When Smookie let out a doggy moan, they looked at her and Raquel threw her hand to her mouth. "Oh, Quest, the babies are coming. Look!"

"I see."

It took less than fifteen minutes for Smookie to deliver all four puppies. Quest and Raquel helped by using a nasal aspirator to eliminate secretions in the puppies' mouths and noses so it would be easier for them to breathe on their own.

"They're so tiny and beautiful," Raquel said in awe, placing the puppies next to Smookie's belly and watching as they grabbed their mother's nipples.

"Yes, they are, and they are ours," he said, hugging her close.

Raquel nodded and smiled. "Yes, they are." They had decided to keep one and give the other three away. One would go to Quest's twin brother, another to Whitney and another to the family of four who lived downstairs. Only good homes for Smookie's babies.

Quest stood and reached out to help Raquel to her feet. "I think it's time to leave Mom and babies alone. It's bonding time."

Bandit had the decency to move from his spot to

stroll over to see Smookie and the puppies. Then he went back to his spot on the other side of the room.

Taking Raquel's hand, Quest led her toward the living room and to the sofa. He sat down and pulled her down into his lap. "We've been dating seriously for a while, and with our growing family, I think we should make some decisions."

Wrapping her arms around his neck, she asked, "Decisions about what?"

"Us."

Raquel's heart nearly stopped. Yes, they had been dating exclusively longer than a month, and yes, their time together had been wonderful, fantastic, totally unbelievable. But she'd never allowed herself to hope that maybe, quite possibly, they were an "us". And now…

She swallowed. "Us?"

He chuckled. "Yes, us. Me, you, Smookie, Bandit and the puppy yet to be named."

She nervously licked her lips. "So what do you have in mind?"

"An engagement that I hope will lead to marriage before the end of the year. So, Raquel Capers, will you marry me?"

She felt the tears flowing down her cheeks. There was no way she had known, when she had decided to go over to Quest's place to confront him about Bandit that day, that things would lead to this. He was everything Derrick hadn't been. He was sweet, kind, giving, attentive and a fabulous lover. Everything she could want in a man.

"Yes, I'll marry you. Does that mean you won't be calling the hot wire anymore?" she asked, leaning down and placing kisses around his mouth.

"I'll have my own personal hot wire."

She smiled. "Good. And I've been thinking about giving up my career as a phone actress to finish up the hours I need for my MBA. What do you think of that?"

He smiled. "I think that's a wonderful idea." A serious expression touched his lips. "I love you."

She returned his smile. "And I love you, too."

She leaned down to his mouth and he crushed hers in a kiss that had her moaning upon impact. And she knew without any doubt that their love affair was one dreams and fantasies were made of, and had come about because of Smookie and the Bandit.

* * * * *

New York Times and *USA TODAY* bestselling author **BRENDA JACKSON** lives in the city where she was born—Jacksonville, Florida. She has a bachelor of science degree in business administration from Jacksonville University.

Brenda is a retiree who worked for thirty-seven years in management at a major insurance company. She divides her time between family, writing and traveling. She loves writing connecting stories and happily admits that she is a die "heart" romantic who married her childhood sweetheart, and still wears the ring he gave her when she was fifteen. Brenda and Gerald have been married forty years and are the proud parents of two sons, Gerald Jr. and Brandon.

Brenda has more than ninety novels in print. You can visit her at www.brendajackson.net. And look for her newest novel, *Bachelor Unclaimed*, available now from Harlequin Kimani!

MOLLY WANTS A HERO

Virna DePaul

I'm so thrilled to be included in this anthology.
My deepest thanks to Lori Foster, whose incredible talent
inspired me to become a writer; to Margo Lipschultz,
who's helping me become a better one;
and to Cyndi Faria, Amy King, Susan Hatler
and Karin Tabke, dear friends who helped
bring Wade, Molly and Gator together.

CHAPTER ONE

"GO AHEAD."

Crisis counselor Molly Peterson smiled at the words that drifted from the small room behind her. She waited two beats for the punch line.

Sure enough, the strident voice immediately continued, "Make my day." *Squawk*. "Make my day."

"I'll sure try, buddy," she called. "As soon as our shift's over, I'll get you home and set you up with your favorite things, okay? I just need a few more hours. Nick will be here at midnight to relieve us."

Gator, the green macaw Molly had inherited from her grandparents—along with their little carriage house in downtown Charleston—didn't answer her. She bet if she peeked under his cage cover she'd find the parrot asleep, his little head tucked into his wing feathers. It wasn't unusual for Gator to channel Clint Eastwood while awake, but in the past two months, his sleep talking had become more frequent.

In fact, that was the whole reason he was now at work with her. Gator's increased sleep chatter appeared to be a traumatic side effect of losing his owners. Understandable, as she was still feeling the loss of her grandparents, too. As a counselor, she couldn't help wondering if a grieving parrot could benefit from some type of therapy, and she wasn't taking any chances with the mental health of her grandparents' beloved pet.

Molly had actually been on her way to the vet with Gator when Jenny, her supervisor, had called her cell, begging her to sub in for another shift on the hotline. Forget the fact that she'd just finished her own twelve-hour shift. But Jenny had been desperate and no one else had been available. The hotline calls didn't come often, but when they did, it was imperative that a trained professional be there to answer. Still, after almost twenty-four hours of isolation in the quiet medical office, Molly was happy to have Gator's company—even if that included his sleep talking.

"You asleep, Gator?" she crooned.

Sure enough, the office remained eerily quiet except for the low music she was playing on the radio and the occasional click of the minute hand on the ancient analog clock. When the phone finally rang about thirty minutes later and Molly answered, the first words she heard were, "I'm naked."

Molly smiled. Despite the importance of her job and the heartache often associated with it, it was vital she keep her sense of humor. Eventually, she'd probably burn out. Until then, calls like this made it easier to keep going. They kept things manageable but interesting. Zero to sixty in under two seconds.

Without missing a beat, she picked up her pen and jotted down the phone number on the caller-ID screen. It was purely precautionary. Barring illegality or imminent danger to human life, the people who called the clinic hotline were guaranteed anonymity, but because a call could turn urgent on a dime, the smallest details could be needed to stop a crime or a suicide in progress.

As a result, Molly always took notes. Most of the time, she just ended up shredding the notes at the end of her shift, but it was always best to be prepared.

Since she'd immediately recognized the caller's voice, she wrote *Boyd* in neat block print. "Hi, Boyd," she said as she jotted down more notes. *Recurring caller. Likes to shock or titillate to begin conversation.*

"Hi, is this Molly? I'm naked."

Boyd was generally naked whenever he called, so Molly merely said, "Is that so?"

"I'm naked and I'm standing on my porch."

"Are you sure you should be doing that, Boyd? Your neighbors might not want to see you naked." In her mind, Boyd was rather pasty-skinned and spindly legged, with freckles and a gap between his two front teeth. A grown-up version of Opie Taylor, awkward yet endearing. Well, except, she assumed, when he was nude on the front porch.

"Nah. They don't mind. But I've been having thoughts."

"What kind of thoughts, Boyd?" she asked, even though she already knew.

For the next hour she listened to him and offered what help she could. Boyd had been depressed ever since his young wife had died four years ago. Since Molly had started working at the clinic, he'd called a handful of times to discuss how lonely he was. And how he wasn't sure he wanted to go on.

Molly stayed on the phone with him until he abruptly said, "Thanks. I'm gonna get dressed now. Bye, Molly."

"Bye, Boyd," she replied and gently hung up the phone. A feeling of satisfaction thrummed through her. An hour of her time and Boyd was feeling better. More optimistic about life. She didn't care what her father said—she might not be raking in the bucks or seeing her name in the paper, but she made a difference, and that's what kept her working at the hotline despite the times she felt weighed down by the urgency and desperation of the crisis calls.

She tapped her pen against the desk, then moved the sheet of paper with Boyd's information to the pile of notes she'd made earlier. When she heard what sounded like flapping coming from the other room, she rose to check on Gator.

But then the phone rang again. Molly resettled in her seat before picking up. "Charleston Mental Health Hotline. How can I help you?"

"This is Officer Wade King with the Charleston Police Department."

This time, Molly's response to hearing a male voice on the other end of the line was far from blasé or amused. Warmth infused her and her insides literally clenched. It was as surprising as it was electrifying. And completely inappropriate.

Given her reaction to the man's smooth, husky voice, he might as well have been smoking-hot, ripped and gorgeous, standing in front of her, and whispering, "I want to cover you with honey and then lap it all up."

Clearly, two years of celibacy had finally taken their toll.

Despite the fact that she was alone, Molly's face heated with embarrassment. Straightening in her chair, she struggled for the right professional response. She routinely talked to cops as part of her job. This cop, the one she immediately dubbed Officer Hottie, had called for a reason, and it wasn't to turn her on.

"What have you got for me this evening, Officer King?"

"A possible 1096," he said, referring to the police code for a citizen exhibiting mental-health issues. "And your name?" he asked in that way cops had, polite but clearly expecting deference.

"Molly Peterson."

"Well, Molly, here's the thing. I've responded to a domestic situation and now I have a twenty-two-year-old suspect in custody. Dispatch received several 911 calls from the suspect's father requesting assistance with his son, who was acting 'crazy.' But upon my arrival, the suspect seemed calm. Able to follow directions."

"Did you talk to his father?" Molly asked.

"I did. And to a neighbor. The father thought his son was drunk but smelled no alcohol on him. I've confirmed no outward signs of intoxication. The neighbor said he saw the suspect sitting outside on the curb before he got up, walked onto the lawn, collapsed to his knees and started crying. Then he'd laugh and dance. Then cry again."

"Has the neighbor seen the suspect exhibit this kind of behavior before?"

"Not specifically, but he's witnessed other behavior that's made him think he suffers from a mental illness. Only I'm not seeing signs of it myself right now, which is why I'm calling."

"Is this your first 1096 call?" she guessed, figuring he was new since they'd never talked before.

"The first one that doesn't present an obvious answer. I've been in patrol for a couple of years, but I'm new to the tactical response squad."

She nodded, liking the fact he didn't try to hide his

relative inexperience. Liking even more that he'd called for a second opinion. Many cops wouldn't have called on the off chance it made them look weak. "Just the fact you're entertaining a doubt is enough. Given the neighbor's statement and previous observations, bring the suspect to an E.R. It's not uncommon for someone to slip into and out of visible psychosis, and that unpredictability is actually quite dangerous. You did the right thing by calling, Officer."

"Okay," he said slowly, his voice losing some of its professional edge. "Uh, great. We're pulling up to the E.R. now." He laughed softly, his voice sheepish. Endearing. "I just wanted to double-check before I actually walked him in."

"Wonderful," Molly said, then hesitated. He didn't hang up. Neither did she. For some reason, she was reluctant to end the call. It had been completely routine. Two colleagues discussing a case. She received several such check-ins on any given night. Yet this was the first time she'd ever been tempted to turn a routine crisis call into something more—something personal—-even if it was only to ask how long Officer King had been a cop. Or why he'd become one. Or whether he looked anything like he sounded, and if he did, how he could possibly function with women doubtlessly following him around all day and throwing themselves at his feet.

"Are you still there, Molly?"

Molly jerked at the low male voice in her ear. "Uh, yes, Officer King, I am." She picked up her pen again. "Did you have another question?"

"Please, call me Wade. And actually, yes, I do have another question. But I need to escort my in-custody

into the E.R. first. Can I call you right back? Will someone else answer the phone or will you...?"

"No, I'm the only one manning the hotline. There's
twenty-four-hour medical staff here, but they're on the
other side of the building. If you call this number again,
you'll get me." Her unintentionally provocative words
made her blush. "I mean—"

"Good. Because you're the one I want. That is—I
like the sound of your voice. I'll call back in a few."

She hung up. Good, he'd said. And he'd definitely
sounded pleased at the prospect of talking to her again.
Her in particular. But that couldn't be, could it?

It wasn't the celibacy that was getting to her, it was
the double shifts and lack of sleep. Why else was she
responding so foolishly to a routine call?

Nonetheless, several minutes later, when the phone
rang again and she picked it up, the caller seemed to
breathe a sigh of relief before saying, "Hi, Molly. It's
Officer King—*Wade*."

Amazing how she almost breathed a sigh of relief
herself. "Hi again."

"Hi." He cleared his throat, as if gathering his courage. "I wanted to pose a hypothetical question. Is that
all right?"

"The phone lines are clear, so sure." She bit her lip,
curious and slightly apprehensive. Hypothetical questions almost always came from someone seeking advice for himself or herself.

"Say I know someone who's acting...Oh, how should
I say it...a little off. Like...let's say this hypothetical
someone has taken a sudden liking to hunting ducks."

An odd sense of disappointment filled her. Okay, so
this was just another crisis call, albeit one more personal

to him. Unless "hunting ducks" was a euphemism for something kinky, which she seriously doubted.

Rolling her eyes, she shook her head. *Concentrate, Molly.* "Go ahead," she said softly. "Is it this hypothetical person, the ducks, or someone else you're worried about?" The part about the ducks just popped out. She wasn't a hunter. Didn't understand people who were. But even her grandfather had hunted game when he was younger, which, considering how close he'd been to Gator, seemed quite ironic.

Officer King remained silent for several seconds before saying, "You a yank, darlin'?"

Pure sex, she thought again. That slow southern drawl was tinged with humor. Low and deep. Masculine with a hint of sweetness and spice. After several months in Charleston, she should be immune to the unique strains of southern dialect, both male and female, but this man's voice was different. Mesmerizing.

"I'm a yank through and through," she confirmed. "But I'm here to help. Who is it you're concerned about?"

"Actually, it's my grandfather," he said, and she felt an immediate rush of relief. Far better to reconcile that virile, tempting voice with a concerned grandson rather than with a man—and a cop, at that—personally on the emotional or mental edge. Either way, she was suddenly glad she'd been asked to extend her shift and was here to answer this man's call.

It wasn't simply that he had a sexy voice. Somehow she knew the voice belonged to someone who didn't ask for help, at least of the personal variety, very often. She didn't know how she knew it, she just did. Her desire to heal and nurture welled inside her. Her job was about

helping others get their emotional bearings back, but too
often she only encountered people when they were in
pain, whether it was personal or the pain of witnessing
someone they loved suffering, and then she mostly evaluated them and referred them elsewhere. Despite this
man's attempts at humor—an obvious defense mecha-
nism—he sounded genuinely concerned for his elderly
relative. It reminded her of the close relationship she'd
had with her own grandparents. It made her miss them
even more. And it made her feel less alone in her mis-
sion to aid others.

"So why is it you're worried about your grandfather,
and what does duck hunting have to do with it?"

He laughed, the sound both amused and frustrated,
and it shivered through her, traveling straight to every
erogenous zone in her body. Lord, the man's voice was
lethal.

"You haven't been in the south very long, have you?"

"What makes you say that?" Her muscles relaxed
slightly and she sank a little deeper into her chair. The
situation clearly wasn't an emergency, given Officer
King's casual questions. Still, she needed to get the
conversation back on track.

"Any self-respecting southerner knows that duck-
hunting season ended over a month ago."

Ah, she thought. Right. "So how does his desire to
go duck hunting equate to a psychiatric problem? I'm
not sure I follow."

"Well, it just so happens my grandfather hates duck
hunting. And he hasn't been any kind of hunting in over
thirty years. Plus, now he has two ticked-off neighbors
who no longer have mailboxes."

"Sorry, but again, I'm not sure I follow. Did he leave

to go duck hunting and mow down the mailboxes? Does he still have his driver's license?"

"Molly, I don't think you're understanding me. He didn't take out the mailboxes by sideswiping them with his fifty-seven Buick. He used a Smith and Wesson."

"Excuse me? Oh." She winced slightly. "Ohhhh yeah, that could be a problem."

"Yes. Thankfully, he lives on a remote farm and doesn't seem to mistake humans for fowl. But he keeps talking about his successful hunt."

"How old is your grandfather?"

"Seventy-five."

"Has he been exhibiting signs of senility? Alzheimer's?"

"No. In the past year, he's gotten a bit more forgetful, but nothing like this. The duck-hunting thing has been coming and going for about a week, and seems to be worse in the late afternoons and evening. He's fine during the day, and when I ask him about duck hunting then…well, he looks at me like *I'm* crazy."

"Any other signs of confusion?" she asked.

"No…not really."

She wondered if it could be sundowning, a symptom that often occurred in people with dementia. "Has he ever had these types of incidents before? Any recent stressors?"

"No and no."

"Has he been ill?"

"He did say he felt a little warm, but I figured it was just a change in the weather, as they say."

"Change in the weather, huh? I'm guessing that's not something I'm going to find in the American medical journal."

"Na," he drawled. "Probably not. It's an old-timer's term for sinusitis."

"Okay. Well, there are a few different possibilities, but I wouldn't be able to say for sure unless he was properly evaluated."

"Hmm," he sighed. "That's what I was afraid of." The line was silent for a few seconds before he said, "My grandpa isn't what you would call a fan of shrinks, but I bet I could get him to come in to see a pretty lady for a physical."

Pretty lady, huh? For all he knew, she was a troll. But she was betting that voice of his was matched by dreamy eyes and a lazy smile. His charm probably worked on every woman he ever came across.

"You can have him stop by the clinic. We can run a standard psych exam, a few memory-skills tests and some basic labs."

"Labs? What kinda labs?"

"Just a met panel and urinalysis. You can always take him to his primary-care physician, of course."

"We've made an appointment. But to be honest, I drive right by your clinic almost every night and I've seen the sign advertising complete confidentiality. I mean, in theory, the results of any doctor's visit would be confidential, but…" He sighed. "My grandfather's proud and—well, his standing in the community is an issue. I don't want word getting around that he's…ill… if I have no cause to worry."

Ah, she thought. So the charming voice went with an upper-class background and a need for discretion. Instantly, she felt a part of herself close up. She knew it was happening, but she couldn't stop it. Her own father, who'd made his money in the dot-com boom, was a perfect example of how the wealthy generally equated fairness with favoritism. With entitlement. As if that hadn't been enough of an example, the last well-off man she'd dated had been genuinely perplexed when she'd broken things off with him after several dates; it had taken only a few angry comments and some rough handling from him before she'd finally understood why—he couldn't believe someone *like her* (read humbly middle class) wasn't genuflecting with gratitude at the chance to date a man *like him* (read arrogantly loaded).

Please. As if being rich and well-connected outweighed that the guy had sweaty palms, bad breath and left her completely cold.

When he'd put his hands on her, she'd taught him just how truly uninterested she was. He'd been walking funny when he left. Needless to say, she hadn't been moved to break her bout of celibacy with or since him.

Abruptly aware that she hadn't responded to the officer's last statements, she reassured him, "You're certainly right, you know. Everything you say to me, and anything your grandfather might say to me, is confidential."

"Thank you."

His obvious gratitude seemed so genuine, she relaxed. She jotted down a few notes next to the incoming phone number on her sheet of paper.

Duck hunting = shot mailboxes. Wants discretion. Social standing. Grandson caring and HOT....

She stared at the last word she'd written and shook her head. She'd circled "hot" several times. What was wrong with her? Throwing down her pen, she spoke more crisply.

"So...what do you mean by increasing forgetfulness?

And is your grandfather being supervised? Have you locked up his gun?"

"Mailboxes aside, he's not dangerous. But yes, I have confiscated his shotgun. And he's forgetful in the way many of us can be, although he's never been so in the past. Misplaces his keys. Walks into his room and forgets why."

"Does he live alone?"

"Yes. He has ever since my grandmother died three years ago. But he has a full-time assistant, and I try to stop by as often as I can."

"So, what do you say? Will you consider bringing him into the clinic for an evaluation?"

"Would you be the one to evaluate him?"

She sensed more than concern and curiosity in his tone. She sensed…hope? Anticipation? "Our medical techs would run the labs. As for the psych evaluation itself, I wouldn't necessarily—"

"Because that's what I'd want. I'd certainly be grateful to you, ma'am, if you can make time for him."

To a "Yankee" like her, being called ma'am would normally have been an insult, given she wasn't quite yet thirty, but the way this man said it…

"Why do you want *me* to see him?"

"I'm a good judge of character, and I feel like I can trust you with him. With this situation. Can you see him later today?"

Since it was just after ten p.m., later today would mean early in the morning. When she'd be sleeping. Then again, he'd said his grandfather's psychosis had only presented itself later in the day. "I'm afraid after working two shifts, I won't be back until tomorrow night, but the staff here is—"

"What time does your next shift start?"

She hesitated then said, "Nine p.m. tomorrow."

"That should be perfect. How about I see you tomorrow, Molly? When I introduce you to my granddaddy."

She was suddenly anxious for the opportunity to meet him. To see if his face and body matched his voice. To see if he really cared for his grandfather as much as he seemed to. "If you're sure you don't want to bring him in earlier," she said slowly, "that'll be fine."

"I'm sure. Thanks for talking to me, Molly. Sweet dreams."

Sweet dreams? With that voice running in her head, they would be sweet indeed. But first she had to finish the rest of her shift.

It was almost two hours later when Nick, Molly's replacement, finally showed up. By then, she was running on exhaust and anxious to get home. After gathering her things, including Gator's round cage, she walked into the main clinic lobby and passed by the guard's station, frowning when she saw he was gone, likely making his rounds. Danny was a quiet young man who appreciated the brownies she sometimes baked for him and the rest of the staff at the clinic. It had been awkward when he'd asked her out last month, but he'd taken her gentle refusal in stride and things had gotten back to normal after he'd started dating a girl he'd met at church. She'd been hoping Danny would walk her to her car, as he usually did on late evenings, but who knew how long he'd be gone. And though there were a handful of employees working graveyard throughout the building, Molly certainly didn't want to bug them. Even so, despite being bone-deep tired, with the lure of a soft bed calling to her, the thought of walking outside alone unnerved her.

She'd been a victim of a carjacking a few years ago when her grandparents had still lived in Los Angeles. The guy, a man named Luther Jones, had knocked her around. After she'd testified at his trial, he'd yelled that he was going to hunt her down as soon as he got out of prison. It had taken years for her to start to feel safe again, but self-defense classes had helped. She'd felt secure enough that she'd even started dating again— until Elliott Rich-and-Stuck-on-Himself had proven once again that some men didn't know how to control themselves. Despite growing up with a father who'd smacked her mother around, logically she knew all men weren't violent. Still, she was beginning to believe that, when it came to dating, at least, it was better to be safe than sorry.

She walked to the outer door and peeked out.

Her car was about halfway down the near-empty parking lot, not more than two hundred feet away. She took out her keys and held them between her fingers the way she'd been taught in self-defense class. Then she stepped out, Gator's cage in hand.

She walked quickly.

"My little friend," Gator chirped suddenly.

"Yes, *say hello* to my little friend," Molly said with a smile. Gator and her grandfather had loved watching the same type of shoot-'em-up action movies that her grandfather had once acted in and directed. Gator could quote Arnold, Clint and Bruce. With Al, Gator had never managed to say the entire line from *Scarface*, but Molly hadn't given up hope yet.

Her steps slowed slightly as she relaxed. "You were

such a good bird today, Gator. Maybe I can convince Jenny to let me bring you—"

She was almost to her car when a voice sounded from just behind her.

"Mawwwwwwlleeeeeeeee," it singsonged.

Involuntarily, she screamed and dropped Gator's cage, which tipped over on its side. Dimly, she heard Gator's piercing shrieks as the cage rolled away. She jerked around and caught a flash of movement out of the corner of her eye. Instinctively, she tried to turn, but it was too late. The hooded figure was almost on top of her.

Strong fingers dug into her arms.

Under the dim parking-lot lights, most of what she saw was black. Black clothes. Black ski mask over her attacker's face. But she also saw two tiny patches of white where his eyes shone through the mask's eye-holes. Terror seized her, but then her previous self-defense training clicked in. "You bastard! Let go of me!"

He jerked her closer. "Shut up!" he muttered, the strong odor on his breath escaping from the mouth hole in his mask. For a second, the distinct scent made her freeze, but then she continued to struggle.

"You damn—" But his words choked off when she kicked out, catching him in the groin. She'd hoped his grip would loosen, but it tightened instead. She fought to wrestle away, but a second later she felt a stunning blow to the side of her head.

Through her dizziness, she lunged forward, trying to bite the man's neck or chest, anything she could reach, but he grabbed a hank of her hair, yanked her head back and punched her in the face. Her body slumped and she almost blacked out. Dimly, she was aware of Gator shrieking and her feet dragging against the asphalt as the man hauled her away from her car.

Suddenly, light blazed directly in her face, blinding her. She heard the heavy, panicked breaths of her attacker just before he cursed and shoved her forward. She fell face first toward the ground, scraping her palms where she caught herself, but her torso and head hit with painful thuds anyway.

She heard the pounding of running feet. A deep, masculine voice just over her head shouting for backup to apprehend a fleeing suspect while he checked on a victim. Then gentle hands touched her shoulder.

"Shhh. You're okay, darlin'. He's gone."

When she whimpered and flinched back from the hands touching her, they retreated. A victim, he'd called her, when she'd never wanted to be a victim again.

She lay there for a few seconds, the newcomer crouched down next to her, his hands deliberately hanging between his knees where she could see them, as if he wanted her to know he wasn't a threat. Her eyes wandered upward until she could take in his dark blue police uniform. In the background, blue lights flashed, and she registered it was from his patrol car.

"Are you okay?"

Groaning, she forced herself to move and slowly brought her knees under her. It was harder than she would have expected. She raised a shaky hand to her temple, wincing as the raw scrape on her palm met her tender eye and cheek. "Is he gone?"

"Yes, you're safe, ma'am. He was wearing a mask. Did he say anything? Any idea who he was?"

"N-no. I mean, he said my name. Told me to shut up. But he used a weird tone. I didn't recognize his voice."

"Okay, so it wasn't a random attack. He knew who you were. Do you work here?"

She nodded.

"What's your name?"

"I'm Molly— Molly Peterson."

"Molly, it's me. Officer Wade King. We talked earlier, remember? You're safe now, don't worry."

She stared at him. Despite the trauma she'd just suffered, she wasn't too far gone to notice he was just as gorgeous as she'd imagined. Sandy-blond hair. Brown eyes—dark, deep orbs that reminded her of mink. A firm, square jaw, a full bottom lip and a slightly cleft chin. The first word that popped into her head was *yum*.

But despite all that, it was really his voice she focused on.

That voice. She recognized that voice.

"Molly, I said you're safe. Did you hear me?"

"Yes, yes. I'm safe. And you're—you're hot."

CHAPTER TWO

BEMUSED, WADE STARED at Molly Peterson, who brought a hand to her forehead as if she'd suddenly gotten dizzy. "What I mean is, of course I remember you. You called earlier. About your grandfather and the ducks. I recognize your voice."

Wade said, "That's right," even as he forced his expression to remain impassive.

Molly thought he was "hot," but Wade didn't smile for three reasons. First, her face was red where the bastard had hit her, and his adrenaline was still rushing through his veins at the close call she'd suffered. Two, he was keenly aware of the flush of embarrassment that washed across Molly's face and he didn't want to contribute to her embarrassment even more. And three, he was too busy trying to regain his equilibrium, not just because of the attack he'd seen, but because of the intense response he was having to the woman in front of him.

Ten minutes ago, he'd been doing his nightly patrol down Broad Street when he'd had the strong urge to swing by the nearby clinic's parking lot again. Maybe it was because he'd talked to the woman named Molly on the phone earlier and knew she'd be leaving work late, or maybe it was because he'd continued to think about her long after he'd hung up, picturing a sultry brunette with kissable, lickable and caressable, pale skin. Whatever the reason, something had led him here. Only the clinic had been quiet, no signs of trouble anywhere.

He'd moved on to the lot across the street when he'd seen a woman exit the medical-clinic building. He'd stared at her, wondering if the pretty brunette with—yes, it certainly looked like she had smooth, milky skin just waiting to be properly appreciated—could possibly be the Yankee he'd talked with. That woman's voice had been kind, but at the same time all crisp with sharp edges. It had made him think of a buttoned-up schoolmarm and her ruler and all the fun things she could do with it.

Yet, despite his curiosity and slightly kinky thoughts—or maybe because of them—he hadn't planned on approaching her. It hadn't seemed appropriate. Plus he hadn't wanted to scare her. But then he'd been the one who was scared.

He'd seen the man jump her.

And the only thing he'd been able to think was *I won't be able to get to her in time*. Unbelievably, he was shaking slightly and he could see that her own calm was starting to disintegrate as shock settled in.

When Molly moved her hand back to her head, Wade's eyes narrowed. "Your head hurt?"

"A little. I must have hit it when I fell…."

He shifted closer and gently ran his fingers along her skull, wincing when he felt a sizable lump near her left temple. But she wasn't bleeding and her eyes looked clear. "How many fingers am I holding up?"

"Three."

Gently, he helped her to her feet, but kept a supporting arm under her elbow.

A squawk rang out, followed by soft thuds.

"Oh my Lord! Gator!" Molly exclaimed.

Huh? "Excuse me?"

"Gator. My parrot. His cage—"

That's right. She'd been holding something as she'd walked. From where he'd been, he hadn't been able to make out what it was, but…Her gaze flickered frantically around her, and Wade started checking behind the nearby cars. Before he got to the third one, he heard more scrapes and flutters. A second later, he saw the cage with the parrot inside. He took a step toward it, freezing when it screeched, "Bastard!"

He heard a moan behind him and turned.

Molly was there with a hand over her mouth.

He cocked an amused brow.

Unbelievably, when she lowered her hand, she was smiling a chagrined smile. "I called him a bastard. The man who attacked me…Now who knows how long Gator will be saying it."

"But you'll be around to hear him say it," he pointed out softly. "That's all that matters. Here, let me get the cage for you." He picked it up and gently righted it.

"Bastard." *Squawk*. "Bastard."

He laughed, the parrot's words managing to relieve some of the tension he was feeling. "Guess he's got my number." He handed her the cage and she shushed the bird, sticking her fingers through the wires so she could gently caress his feathers.

"It's okay, buddy. You're okay," Molly crooned. The bird instantly head-butted her fingers and calmed down.

Wade stared in amazement. "I didn't know parrots were so affectionate."

"You'd be surprised. Gator's got a mouth on him, but he's definitely a lover, not a fighter."

"Lucky guy."

The instant the words popped out of his mouth, the air became supercharged. The spark of awareness that had previously lit her eyes flamed out of control, and he felt an answering warmth spread throughout his body.

He shook his head and tried to concentrate on the fact she still looked slightly pale and traumatized. Then he didn't even have to try. Her body vibrated with fine tremors and he heard her breath hitching.

"Molly," he said gently. Taking the cage from her, he set it on the ground then placed his hands on her shoulders to turn her.

"I'm okay," she breathed out, but her stalwart expression crumpled and a tear leaked out of her eye.

"Oh, baby girl," he said. "Shhh. It's okay. You're okay."

Her fingers grasped at his uniform, and suddenly her face was buried in his neck and her body plastered up against his. He hissed at the way his body automatically reacted to her, hardening and preparing for what it thought would be a huge slice of heaven. He tried to shift himself to the side so he didn't alarm her with his erection, but she simply burrowed deeper into him.

He held her and stroked her hair for several long minutes, until she pulled back. He tried to smile as he swiped her tears away with his thumb.

Need pressed down on him. It wasn't professional and it wasn't politically correct, but he wanted to kiss her. They were both shaking, their bodies thrumming with the need to affirm she was whole and healthy in the most basic way possible. His gaze latched onto her

mouth and her eyes widened, not in alarm but desire.
She licked her lips. Inwardly, he groaned, wanting to
chase her little pink tongue with his own. Hell, he didn't
want to just chase it. He wanted to catch it, rub it, devour it. Devour her. Instead, he forced himself to draw
back. He was acutely aware of the bruised swelling
near her eye. Once again, rage filled him, and he didn't
doubt that if he had her attacker here, he'd be tempted
to exercise a little police brutality on him. Of course,
he wouldn't. At least, he hoped he wouldn't.

"You okay now?" he said, his voice crisper than he
intended, because even thinking the words *police brutality* had him shaken. He wasn't that type of guy. Didn't
have an anger-management problem. But with her, when
he remembered watching the man's fist striking her
face…He reined in his spiraling emotions with iron-
willed control, knowing he needed to keep things cool
and calm, if only for her sake.

It was as if his gaining control gave her the ability
to do so, as well. She blinked and her face cleared. She
moved away from him, and he frowned at the feeling of
loss he experienced. He wasn't sure why he was having
such a strong reaction to her. She was pretty, but he'd
dated and bedded much more beautiful women. What
was it about this sweet, dark-haired yank that made him
want to sweep her up and shelter her away?

His eyes flickered to the office behind her. "We need
to have you checked out. You said there's medical staff
inside, right?"

She shook her head before wincing and raising her
hand to her temple again. "No. I mean, yes, there's medical staff here, but I'm fine. I—"

Like hell she was. But he could tell immediately she

was going to be stubborn about this. "We need to take photographs of your injuries," he pointed out. "For the report."

"Report?"

"Crime report. Incident report. About the attack."

"Oh." She sighed and looked at him pleadingly. "I'm so tired. I really, really just want to go home. I've worked almost twenty-four hours straight. Can't we just—I don't know—can't I come in and have pictures taken tomorrow? Talk to you then? The bruises from where he hit me will be more visible by then anyway."

He hesitated, but then shook his head. "I'm sorry, but I can't let you go without getting checked out first."

She sighed. "Okay. But I'll have to bring Gator with me."

"Of course," he said, and picked up the parrot cage.

Twenty minutes later, after conducting an exam and taking pictures, a doctor reassured them that she'd be fine. He did, however, recommend her getting a ride home.

Wade nodded. "I can give you a lift."

"No, that's okay," Molly rushed out. "I've already called my friend Nina."

Nina, Wade thought. The name coupled with their location probably wasn't coincidence. "Would you be talking about Nina Whitaker, by any chance?"

"Yes. You know her?"

He nodded. "Nina interned here several months back."

Molly's lips pressed together. "That's right. Shall I tell her you said hello?" Though the question was polite, he thought he saw a spark of jealousy in her gaze. Wishful thinking?

"Sure," he said. "But before she gets here, I'd like to ask you a couple more questions. You up for that?"

She sighed, her exhaustion magnified by the swelling and bruises on her face, but she gamely nodded. "Ask away."

"You told me he said your name. Do you know anyone who might want to hurt you? Ex-boyfriends? Anyone bothering you at work or the gym?"

"No. Well, I was dating someone a while back who didn't like it when I broke up with him."

Amazing how much it bothered him that she'd been dating someone. Anyone. Amazing how satisfied it made him feel that she'd broken it off. "How long ago?" He pulled out his pen and notepad.

"Six weeks."

"What do you mean, he didn't like it? Did he get violent?"

"He grabbed me pretty roughly. But he didn't hit me."

His jaw clenched. "What's his name?"

To his surprise, she looked away, her expression turning stony. "I'd rather not say. He isn't the type of person to wear a ski mask and jump me in a dark parking lot, and I don't want to be accused of causing problems for him."

"No one's above the law, Molly."

She turned back to him. "I know that, but you talked about your grandfather's delicate social position, and this person has his own status to worry about. I have to live here, and I don't want to make accusations and cause problems unnecessarily. I told you, it's not him."

He stared at her. When it came to ruling out a violent suspect, he didn't give a rat's ass about social po-

sitioning. But she'd been through a lot and this wasn't
the last conversation he planned on having with her.
"We'll get back to him later. Now, how about anyone
else?" he asked, with his pen poised above his notepad.

"I was carjacked in L.A. a few years ago. I testified
at the guy's trial and he wasn't really happy with me.
Made a few threats. But he should still be in prison."

Dear Lord, he thought, trying to visualize her being
held at gunpoint. She must have been terrified. He jotted down notes. "What's his name?"

"Luther Jones."

"How about at work? You get a lot of phone calls
from strangers, but you told me your real first name.
Do you give it to your callers?"

"When someone asks, yes."

"So the man who attacked you could have been anyone who called?"

"It's possible, I suppose. Someone unhappy with
what I said."

"Or maybe even someone happy," he pointed out.

Her face screwed up with confusion. "What do you
mean?"

"You've got a great bedside manner, even on the
phone. Could be someone took a liking to you and
wanted to make the connection more personal than
professional."

"That would be a strange way of asking me out."

"It's certainly not the way I'd go about it."

Her eyes widened and she flushed. But it wasn't just
embarrassment he saw on her face. He saw interest
there, too. The same interest he felt coursing through
him, demanding he find out if her lips were as soft and
lush as they looked. But now wasn't the time....

"Sorry," he said. "I'm getting ahead of myself." He gave her a hint of a smile before wiping his expression clean. "So any weird calls that indicate someone has a personal interest in you?"

"I can't remember anything specific. I even take notes, and I would have kept them if I was concerned, so... No, absolutely not."

"You sound sure," he said.

"Oh, I'm certain."

His brows raised. "Nothing a little out of the ordinary?"

"People have called asking if we remove bugs that the government implants in citizens' brains," she said dryly. "There's plenty out of the ordinary with my job."

"I guess that's true. I should know, with my grandfather hunting imaginary ducks."

She smiled slightly—a sweet, humorous, gentle smile—and he forced himself to put his pen and paper away.

Okay, he'd satisfied himself that she was going to be okay and she had a reliable ride home. His backup had radioed in, and unfortunately, Molly's attacker had gotten away. He really needed to get back on patrol. But first... He reached into his front uniform pocket, pulled out his card and scribbled on the back of it. "Here's my card with my personal cell phone number. You call me if you need anything."

She glanced at the card and bit her lip. "The number. It's the same."

"Excuse me?"

"When you called me earlier. About your grandfather. You used your cell phone."

The right side of his mouth tipped up. "That's right. Very observant."

"I try to be. And I'm normally really good with voices. The guy who attacked me, he was disguising his voice, otherwise I might be able to give you a better lead."

"It's okay. But if you remember anything else—"

"Sambuca," she exclaimed. "His breath, it smelled like sambuca!"

"Isn't that an Italian liqueur?"

"Yes! My grandparents loved it. They used it in their coffee instead of sweetener. They called it *caffè corretto*." She smiled at the memory, her expression bittersweet. "Corrected coffee."

"They're gone now?" he asked gently.

"Yes. Gator belonged to them."

He nodded. "So, sambuca. Right. That's a unique detail. I've never actually tasted it before."

"It tastes and smells like licorice. Black licorice."

"All right. I'll keep that in mind. Right now, I'm going to talk to the night guard. Take a look at security tapes. Then I'm going to drive around and see if I can catch sight of our perp. You be sure to call me if you need anything. Otherwise…"

She paused and looked at him. "Otherwise?"

He swallowed hard and took a step back. "I'll see you later. So you can meet my granddaddy. Are we still on for that? I'd understand if you're calling in sick…."

She shook her head, then licked her lips, leaving a sheen of moisture he wanted to trace with his finger.

"I'm not altering my life for some psycho who hides out in parking lots. I'll see you later tonight."

He smiled. "Tonight. Until then, remember what I said before, too, darlin'. Sweet dreams."

CHAPTER THREE

"Yippee ki-yay."

Still groggy from sleep, Molly gradually grew aware of Gator's squawking in between the incessant buzz of her alarm clock. Sunlight filtered through her fluttering lids and she groaned. She would have grabbed a pillow to block out the noise, but even in her sleep-deprived state she was careful. Besides, instinctively she knew she wasn't alone. Even now, a male had his face buried in her neck.

And judging by the smooth, hard surface butting against her, he was happy to see her.

Gator's beak rasped lightly against her skin as he once again lifted it to chime, "Yippee ki-yay."

"Yeah, yeah," she said. "The first movie was great, but then what happened? Bruce is due another blockbuster, don't you think?"

Gator squawked in agreement. When she was home, she rarely kept him in his cage, but it was at night that he particularly liked his perch and freedom to roam about.

With a groan, she opened her eyes all the way and reached out to smooth Gator's feathers. "I'm glad you're feeling better, buddy. At least one of us is." She sat up and immediately winced. Her left eye felt as if it was on fire. She widened and narrowed her eyes, trying to get rid of the proverbial cobwebs until she could read the digital clock next to her bed. Eleven a.m.

Groaning again, Molly got up, put on her favorite robe, then brushed her teeth while examining the massive shiner under her left eye. She'd have to pile on the makeup and then maybe, just maybe, it wouldn't look as if she'd been in a street brawl. As a favor to Nina, she was attending a charitable gala at the Magnolia Plantation before work. The plantation and surrounding gardens were an elegant and popular setting for some of the area's most upscale events. Heaven forbid she show up looking like she'd gone nine rounds in the ring with—

A loud knock on her front door made her jump.

The first thing she felt was fear.

Last night, her attacker had known her name. Maybe he knew where she lived. Maybe he was at her door right now.

The next thing she felt was rage.

Because of her abusive father, she'd spent most of her childhood living in fear, until her grandparents had taken her in. When she'd finally gotten out on her own, she'd sworn never to live in fear again. To never let a man dictate how she lived her life. She could still hardly believe her mother had stayed with her father despite his abuse. Molly had been a child then. Now Molly was nearly thirty, and damned if she would let a stranger shake her foundation so ruthlessly.

She searched for some kind of weapon when another knock sounded.

"Molly, it's Officer Wade King."

Her anger morphed into intense curiosity. Why was hot Officer King knocking on her door? And why was she feeling such delight because of it?

Ruthlessly, she pushed the feeling away. Stepping toward the door, she called, "How'd you find me?"

"I got your personal information for my report, remember?"

She gnawed at her lip with indecision. While every cell in her body demanded she let this man into her house, she hesitated.

Gator squawked, then flew into the room and landed on her shoulder. Automatically, she braced her arm out so he could trail down to perch on her forearm. At the feeling of his weight, her anxiety diminished slightly. But not completely.

She'd heard stories about assaults being committed by cops. Or people pretending to be cops. But she doubted Wade King had hijacked a patrol car, police uniform and all the other accoutrements she'd seen on him last night in an elaborate attempt to…what? Save her and then attack her in her home in broad daylight?

But she still didn't open her door.

"Molly, why don't you call the police station and ask them about me?"

She jerked and, even though she felt slightly foolish, she walked to the phone and did as he said. A few minutes later, the dispatcher confirmed that Officer Wade King had called in and warned them to expect a call from a Ms. Molly Peterson, and that he was currently at her house. Slowly, still balancing Gator on her arm, she opened the door.

"My little friend," Gator squawked.

Wade's eyes crinkled in a way that made her insides clench just the way they had the first time she'd heard his voice. "At least he's not calling me a bastard today."

He was out of his uniform and dressed casually

in jeans and a short-sleeved polo shirt. Thick biceps stretched the openings of the sleeves, and she was once again struck by how handsome he was. There was a slight furrow between his brows. "I know you worked late. I'm sorry to show up here so early. I was just…"

The silence hung in the air as the possibilities went through her mind: he'd just been in the neighborhood. Or he'd just been in a hurry to finish his report and had additional questions.…

"I was just worried about you." He cleared his throat. "I wanted to make sure you were all right."

She sucked in a breath.

"Sorry to show up unannounced." He shrugged, then seemed unsure what to say next.

"You're out of uniform." Immediately, she felt foolish for pointing out the obvious, but she couldn't get out of her head that he was worried about her. Was that in a protect-and-serve kind of way or something altogether different?

He looked down at his clothes and battered cowboy boots and smiled. "I got off shift a little while ago, but I was thinking about you. Wondering how you are. Truth is, I could have waited to see you later tonight, but I didn't want to be distracted when I brought my grandfather in. I hope that's okay."

It felt more than okay, but she couldn't say that, of course. "That's fine." She pulled the door open wide and gestured with her hand. "Please come inside."

He walked in and looked around.

She tried to view the carriage house from his eyes. Looking at him dressed so casually, he didn't appear to be the grandson of a socially prominent man. But he'd said as much on the phone yesterday. Also, because she hadn't been able to sleep, she'd researched him on the internet. To say his family was affluent was definitely an understatement.

The King family was renowned in Charleston.

He was from old money. Lots of old money. His family home looked like something out of *Gone with the Wind.*

Someone like that, she'd thought, would be the type to lord his privileged background over others. That's why, when he stepped inside her home, she waited to see the thinly disguised disdain in his gaze. Or, at the very least, some trace of arrogance. Instead, all she saw was appreciation for the cozy touches she'd added to the carriage house. And an endearing awkwardness that almost made her think he was feeling shy around her.

But that was impossible, wasn't it? The guy was all charm and testosterone. Why would he be shy around *her*?

"How are you feeling?" he asked, and took a step closer to her.

A step too close, obviously, for Gator suddenly shouted out, "Bastard."

They both stared at each other a second before bursting into mutual laughter.

"Maybe I didn't need to check on you. Looks like you've got your own personal bodyguard right here. May I?" He extended a finger while cocking his brow.

"Uh, well, I don't mind, but Gator's a little skittish around strangers under the best of circumstances and—"

But Wade was already working that magic voice of his, rubbing Gator with his finger, soothing and crooning and cajoling Gator to come to him. And to Molly's shock, the parrot actually did. For several seconds, he perched on Wade's arm, head tilted, staring at him inquisitively before suddenly shouting, "Yippee ki yay," and then flying onto Molly's shoulder.

She petted him with the crook of her finger. "Anyway, as you can see, I'm fine. We're fine. But I appreciate you checking."

He nodded, but his gaze darkened as he focused on her face. In his other hand, he held up a digital camera. "You made a good point about your injuries being more visible with time. I thought I'd take a few more pictures. Do you mind?"

"No. That's fine."

Nodding, he stepped closer, focused his camera on her and took several shots. At one point, he pushed back a strand of her hair and lightly traced the arch of her cheekbone with his fingertips. "That looks like it hurts."

"It's a little sore, but not too bad," she whispered.

His gaze lowered to her mouth before he stepped back again. He took several photos of her face and palms, then said, "Do you have any other injuries that have only now showed themselves? Other than those I can see, I mean?"

She tugged at her robe lapel. "No. Nothing."

To his credit, he managed not to look disappointed. "All right, then. If you're sure you're okay, I'll be going. But please be extra careful. And if anything happens to make you uncomfortable, you still have my phone number, don't you?"

"Yes. I do." Relief swept through her at the knowledge that this tension between them would finally be over. But she felt disappointed, too. His face and especially that voice were hard to resist.

"Great."

"Great," she echoed.

"I'll see you tonight."

She suddenly remembered the appointment with his grandfather and felt a jolt inside her. At least she'd have some time to recover before she'd see him again. "Yes, tonight."

He stopped at the door and turned around. "Unless…This isn't exactly kosher. I'll be upfront about that. You're a crime victim and I was the responding officer. I'm glad I was there, but it complicates things in terms of—" He shook his head. "Sorry, I'm babbling. What I mean is, despite the fact it's not something I'd normally do, I'm hoping I can interest you in some coffee before tonight?"

She was tempted. Very tempted. But then she remembered everything she'd read about him on the internet. "No. I appreciate the offer, but I'm not interested." She lifted her chin, hoping the action would give more credence to her reply.

He stared at her for several seconds. "Are you romantically involved with someone, Molly?"

She swallowed hard. Shook her head. "No, I'm not. But I don't think that's—"

"No means no, and you turning me down won't affect the way I handle your case, I promise you that, but I feel a spark between us. Something worth investigating. I'm pretty sure you feel it, too."

Wow, talk about getting to the heart of the matter. Was he always so straightforward? Despite herself, she found his manner quite refreshing. And alluring. Which was dangerous. Hadn't her experience with men taught her anything? "You're wrong," she forced herself to say.

She didn't clarify whether she was denying the spark or the something worth investigating. "Here, I'll show you out."

But he didn't move. "Look, I know you don't owe me any explanations, but did I—did I do anything to make you uncomfortable? To make you fear me?" He looked genuinely concerned. In a flash, she remembered feeling his hard body against hers last night and how he'd politely tried to hide his physical reaction from her. She'd appreciated his discretion even as she'd felt a tingling response at the knowledge that he was attracted to her. As attracted as she was to him.

She bit her lip. How could she explain she didn't want to open herself up to being hurt by a man again without actually explaining… "No. It's just, I'm just— I'm happy with my life the way it is. I'm not looking to complicate things."

He pursed his lips, stared at her as if he was mulling her words over in his head, then smiled. "Well good. Because neither am I."

Was that another spurt of disappointment she felt? "Good, then it's settled. No complications for either of us."

"Yes, it's settled," he said easily. Too easily.

For a second, she was suspicious.

He stepped out onto the porch and turned back to her. "But one thing, Molly. I've found that sometimes things that seem like complications turn out to be blessings. So please don't write me off yet. Not until you figure out which one I am."

CHAPTER FOUR

WADE KNEW A skittish female when he saw one.

And Molly Peterson was definitely skittish.

With good reason. Case in point, the attack she'd suffered the night before. But he had a feeling there was something else at play. Something in her past that was the more likely cause. He could tell by the precise way she carried herself and her manner of interacting that she was an independent spirit. There was also the fact that she'd fought back against her attacker, and that she'd obviously had some self-defense training. She didn't trust easily, yet she had a big heart. And a courageous one. She'd have to in order to do the kind of work she did. He could tell it was more than just a job to her—she actually cared about people she'd never even met.

He admired that. It had taken him far too long to drum up the courage to leave his father's law firm and do what he truly wanted to in life. That's why he was in his mid-thirties and just beginning his law-enforcement career. Police work was too blue collar for a family as pedigreed as the Charleston Kings. At least, that's what his father had always said. And what Wade had always believed. Until he'd lost his grandmother, and his grandfather had become determined to encourage his grandson to do what made him happy instead of doing only what people expected him to.

Listening to his grandpa Paul was the best decision Wade had ever made. Even the more mundane aspects of police work interested him, and he had a personal goal to make detective within the next few years.

"We going hunting, Wade?" his grandfather asked now.

Wade turned to look at his grandfather, who sat beside him. He really didn't understand the whole hunting thing. Except for his obsession with that topic, his grandfather seemed fully functional. Cognizant. Even so, despite the fact Grandpa Paul was a guest at the gala this evening, Wade had tried convincing him to skip it. Grandpa Paul, now spiffed up in his custom tuxedo, had insisted. The event raised funds for the SPCA, his grandmother's favorite charity, and his grandfather was on the board of directors. In truth, his absence would probably have caused more gossip than a little eccentric talk about duck hunting. Wade would just have to stick close by. They'd make a quick appearance, then get home to change before he took Grandpa Paul to see Molly.

"Wade? I asked if we're going hunting."

"Not yet, Grandpa. First we're going to the party at the Magnolia Plantation, remember? After that… Well, I have a lady friend I want you to meet."

"That so?" Grandpa Paul muttered. "And who's this friend you're talking about?"

Wade grinned. "You remember the girl I told you about? The one I met yesterday and want your opinion on?"

"Ah, that's right. You've always had a keen eye for the girls, Wade. I'm sure she'll be wonderful."

Wade couldn't argue with him. He already thought Molly was pretty wonderful, and he hardly knew anything about her. He wanted to know more.

The car slowed, and the partition between the driver and the passenger sections of the limo lowered. "We're here, Mr. Wade. Would you like me to pull around the front or the back?"

He looked at his grandfather, who was staring out the window. "The front tonight, Samuel. Two Kings wearing their tuxes? We might as well give the ladies a thrill and make a production of it, right?"

Samuel chuckled. "Yes. Plus your father will be pleased."

"You know I'm always looking to please my father, Samuel."

Samuel just shook his head and laughed.

Before the driver could step out and open his door, Wade opened it himself and helped his grandfather out of the limo. Grandpa Paul looked good. His tall frame was straight and robust. His coloring healthy. His silver hair distinguished and styled. But then he mentioned those ducks and… Wade winced. He truly hoped the psych evaluation Molly conducted later tonight ended with hopeful news. His grandpa was one of his favorite people, and to think he might lose him, if only mentally, made him sick.

Governor Charles Whitaker greeted them as soon as they walked in the lavishly decorated plantation foyer. "Good evening, Paul. Wade. So lovely to see you here."

"Good to see you, too, sir."

"I believe you've met my daughter, Nina."

Wade nodded and shook the hand of the pretty blonde standing next to the governor. She was as classy and beautiful as ever. It still threw him a little that she was Molly's friend. Not because Molly wasn't worthy of Nina's friendship, but because Wade had once thought himself romantically interested in Nina. They'd exchanged a few flirtatious conversations and he'd considered asking her out not too long ago. Things had changed since he'd met a certain spitfire brunette yank. While he still appreciated Nina's beauty on an objective level, he had zero interest in pursuing her. Instead he had his sights on her friend.

To his shock, said friend suddenly materialized in front of him.

"Molly?"

Her eyes widened and her "Wade?" was confirmation enough that he wasn't hallucinating. Even so, his brain struggled to reconcile the image in front of him with the woman he'd talked to earlier. That woman had been bare-faced and in a robe, the bruises on her face stark in the morning light. This woman was made up to the nines, her lips glossy, her eyes heavily lined and her bruises almost fully disguised under her foundation and blush. She was wearing a simple, body-hugging blue gown that managed to be both modest and incredibly sexy.

His first thought was he was happy to see her. His next thought was he'd be even happier to see her out of her gorgeous dress and back in her simple robe. Or better yet, unclothed altogether.

Nina looked back and forth between them before she smiled. "Molly, I didn't realize you and Wade had met."

"We haven't. I mean," she said, blushing, "we only

met today." She looked at Nina pointedly. "Er, last night."

"Oh. Ohhhhh," Nina said, her eyes widening.

Obviously, despite Wade telling her that he knew Nina, Molly hadn't mentioned him to her friend. Was it because of his grandfather and his request for discretion? Whatever the reason, it made his warm feelings for Molly grow even warmer.

Next to him, his grandfather cleared his throat. "Where are your manners, Wade? I'd like to be introduced to your lady friend."

Wade jerked. "I apologize. Molly, this is my grandfather, Paul King."

She smiled, and the expression lit up her face like sunshine on a cold winter's day. "Mr. King. It's a pleasure to meet you. Wade has spoken very highly of you."

The caring way she spoke to his grandfather made him swell with joy.

"The pleasure's all mine, ma'am," Grandpa Paul said, as he reached for Molly's gloved hand and lifted it to his lips.

He could tell his grandfather spoke the truth. Approval emanated from every pore. Wade had to work hard not to stare at how delicious Molly looked, not to acknowledge how damn jealous he felt that his grandfather had gotten to kiss even the back of her gloved hand.

"Ah, there's Tyrone, Wade," his grandfather said. "Talking with your father."

Wade nodded reluctantly. "If you'll excuse us," he said to Molly, "My grandfather wanted to find an old friend of his straightaway."

"Of course. Have a wonderful time," Molly said.

"I'm hoping so," Wade said under his breath. Not

many women surprised him, but she had, showing up at an event like this. And the way she'd gone from simple beauty to glamorous, like flipping a switch? He couldn't wait to find out what other surprises she had in store for him.

"WELL, WELL, WELL. You've certainly been keeping some hot secrets, haven't you?" Nina murmured. Molly's friend looked like a million bucks, literally. Like Wade, she came from old money. People at the clinic couldn't believe Nina had chosen to intern there instead of at some high-profile, ritzy research hospital.

"No. Not at all," Molly rushed to reassure her. "I don't know what you mean."

"Please, Molly. You're trying to conceal it, but it's written all over your face." Her friend arched her brow. "You and Wade King?"

She tried to make her face unreadable, to hide how anxious being that close to him made her. "Me and Wade King what?"

"I'd heard he quit his father's law firm and is dabbling with a new career." Nina sipped her Chardonnay. "So he's your police officer, huh?"

"Don't say it like that," she said, even as her stomach heated at the thought of him being hers. "He's the patrol officer I told you about. The one who stopped that man who attacked me."

Nina shivered suddenly, pulling Molly in for a hug. "Thank God Wade was there. I mean, I know you've learned to take care of yourself, but it sounds like the guy was much bigger and stronger than you. How are your hands?"

Molly looked down at the white gloves covering her

abraded palms. "They're doing okay. But I might have to leave in a little bit."

"You just got here. You can't abandon me yet, no matter how nervous Officer Wade King makes you."

"He doesn't make me nervous."

"He would if you could see how he's looking at you right now. He looks positively…hungry, darling, despite all the waiters carrying around smoked salmon, braised beef and caviar."

Automatically, Molly turned in the direction that Nina was looking. Sure enough, Wade was standing with his grandfather and two other men, one who resembled Wade so much he could only be his father, but his attention was on Molly. His cheeks were flushed, his eyes lit with an intense glow. She suddenly couldn't breathe. She heard a buzzing noise in her ears and was barely able to make out Nina's next words.

"In fact, you're looking pretty starved yourself, Molly. Come on, let's get you what you need." Nina tucked her arm into the crook of Molly's and led her toward Wade.

Just then a dark-haired, handsome man came up just behind Wade. Recognizing him, Molly gasped. She pulled her arm away from Nina's and walked in the other direction.

"I SEE YOU'VE got your eye on Nina again," Wade's father, Thomas King, said. "That's good. Despite her philanthropic little hobby at the local clinic, she'd make an appropriate match for you."

Wade barely refrained from rolling his eyes. To his father, an appropriate match had nothing to do with love, common respect or shared interests, but pedigree and political clout. Until Molly had mentioned Nina the night before, Wade had forgotten Nina had interned at the clinic. Even if he hadn't, he wouldn't have taken his concerns about his grandfather to her. He liked her, but he didn't know her well enough to know if he could trust her with sensitive information like that. Yet he wholeheartedly trusted Molly, a woman he'd only recently come to know. He knew she'd be discreet.

Even if he wasn't being so himself.

Hell, discreet was the last thing he was being.

With the way he was looking at Molly, he might as well club her over the head and drag her into the nearest bedroom. He couldn't seem to help himself. That's exactly how primal he was feeling. His attraction to her was unbelievably strong, and it was only his duty to his grandfather that was keeping him from doing something about it.

Because despite her wariness, he knew she was attracted to him too.

She kept sneaking little glances at him, and he wanted to answer the curiosity in her gaze with more than just words, but again, this was neither the time nor the place. Soon, he thought, he'd have to explore his connection to the little yank more thoroughly.

Quite thoroughly.

"Can you believe Nina invited that little bitch here?"

At the venomous words, Wade frowned. He turned to the speaker, Elliott Grange, the governor's nephew, who was standing just behind him.

"Elliott," Grandpa Paul snapped. "Language."

"I'm sorry, Paul, but Nina's friend is a gold digger on the prowl. I should know. She was trying to dig her claws into me a few months ago before I finally had to ditch her."

Wade stared at Elliott. He'd never liked the man, and he immediately recognized his words for what they were—sour grapes. There was more to it than that, though. Elliott looked positively dangerous as he glared at Molly.

Wade sized him up. He was about the same height as the man who'd attacked Molly in the parking lot. Despite the anger and suspicion swirling through him, Wade grabbed two glasses of champagne from a passing waiter and handed one to Elliott. He caught his grandfather's gaze, and Grandpa Paul winked before turning away to speak with Thomas.

Damn, looked like his Grandpa was his usual sharp self. Wade was relieved as he turned to Elliott.

"So who is she? And how come I've never heard of her?" Wade asked.

Elliott snorted. "Maybe because you do everything you can to avoid coming to these types of functions. I'm surprised you're here now. Molly Peterson's an old college friend of Nina's, recently moved to Charleston after her grandparents died. They were in the movie business in Hollywood before moving south."

He said "movie business" with a distinct sneer. Cocky little shit. Like he'd accomplished anything besides learning how to spend his father's money and bossing around people whose respect he hadn't yet earned.

"She's pretty," Wade said, tossing out the bait.

"She's okay. Nina's a whole helluva lot more beautiful. But the bitch has nerve, thinking I'd want anything to do with her."

"You tell her that?" Wade asked.

"I sure did."

Elliott must be the guy Molly had dumped. No wonder Molly had been reluctant to go out with Wade. With his comment about his grandfather being of a certain social stature and needing to exercise discretion, she probably assumed he was no better than Elliott. That annoyed him a little. Not enough to make him give up on the pull between them, but it irked him. Oh, maybe on the phone she would make that kind of assumption, but they'd met face-to-face. She'd seen for herself that he worked the streets, in a job as blue collar as anyone's. He'd have hoped she'd give him the benefit of the doubt, but it looked like Little Miss Independent needed a lesson in not judging others just as much as Elliott did.

Well, maybe not quite as much.

"You're such a prick, Elliott," Wade said, leaving the other man staring at him openmouthed. "You always have been and you always will be."

"What's wrong with you, Wade? You got a thing for that little—"

"Don't," he drawled. "You'll regret it." He stared at Elliott for several seconds, daring the man to defy him. He didn't. "Someone attacked Miss Peterson yesterday outside her office. You can bet, no matter what their background, I'm going to find out who it was and I'm going to make that person really sorry."

Elliott sputtered. "What? I didn't—I wouldn't. Are you crazy? I was on a date last night—*all night*—with someone much more deserving of my time and attention. If you don't believe me, I'll give you her name and number and you can call her."

"You do that, because I'll be checking into it. By the way…do you like licorice?"

"Licorice? What kind of question is that?"

"Just a question. Someone was telling me about a drink. Coffee and sambuca. It's supposed to taste like licorice. You ever try it?"

"I've had sambuca neat. I found it disgusting," he sneered. "Your friend must have horrible taste."

"Right. Like I said. You're a prick. And I'd lay off the sambuca for a while."

Elliott's scowl was turning uglier by the second. "I just told you—"

"Excuse me, I need to speak with my grandfather." Wade turned, walked to his grandfather and waited politely until the older man finished his conversation and turned to him. "We going hunting, Wade?"

Thomas frowned. "What's he talking about?"

"It's a private joke, Dad. Grandpa, would you like to talk to my friend, Ms. Peterson, some more?"

"Ms. Peterson?" his father said, but Wade and his grandfather ignored him.

"Don't mind if I do. She seemed perfectly delightful. Reminded me of my sweet Pearl, may she rest in peace."

"Wonderful. Let's go."

He saw Molly slip onto the patio and led his grandfather toward her.

CHAPTER FIVE

MOLLY TOOK IN the sight of the garden grounds. It was gorgeous and reminded her of the greenhouses in California her grandparents had taken her to when she was little. She glanced at her watch, literally ticking down every second until she could leave. Nina was her best friend and didn't enjoy these things any more than she did, otherwise she'd never have come. But a promise was a promise and—

"Molly." The smooth and sexy male voice came from behind her. "Are you enjoying yourself? It's sure beautiful out here."

She turned and saw Wade and his grandfather coming toward her. She smiled. "Yes, it certainly is."

His father called out to him from inside. "Wade, can you please come here. There's someone important I want to introduce you to."

The implication being that he didn't think Molly was important. Wade gritted his teeth. "I apologize for my father's rudeness. Would you excuse me for just a minute? Grandpa, do you want to come with me or—"

"We can chat a little while you're gone," Molly said. "That is, if you'd like," she said as she looked at Paul, who smiled.

"I'd be delighted, young lady."

"I'll be right back," Wade said, his expression grim

as he stalked toward his father. By the way they spoke, Molly could tell Wade wasn't afraid to get into it with his father no matter where they were.

She was growing more fond of him every time she saw him. Could he really be what he'd presented himself to be? A kind, charming man who adored his grandfather. A cop devoted to protecting and serving others. Even his inability to completely ignore his rude father indicated he was a man with a high degree of integrity. But past experience had taught her that first impressions could be deceiving.

"I adore my grandson, but my son sometimes acts like a bag of wind. Lizzy saw something in him, though, and once in a while Thomas reminds me why. I try to remember that. I apologize for his rudeness."

"Lizzy is Wade's mother?"

"She was. She's gone now, just like my Pearl." He looked wistful, and she automatically thought of Boyd and the young wife he'd lost. It hurt to lose those you loved. She knew that from experience, even if the only loved ones she'd lost were her own grandparents. That was painful enough, and she couldn't imagine losing a spouse who was supposed to be with you when you were old and wrinkly.

Her eyes instinctively sought out Wade. He put his life on the line every time he went to work. She barely knew him and the idea that he could get gunned down, that his vibrant life force could be extinguished, made her sad.

"Are you ready to go duck hunting, Molly?"

She jolted at Paul's words. She studied him intently, but his eyes were clear. "Um— Right now?"

"I've got the hunting dogs waiting for us. As soon as Wade returns, we can be on our way."

She gave an exaggerated grimace and took his arm, leading him away from the elderly couple that was walking toward them. "To tell you the truth, sir, I'm not that fond of hunting. I'm quite squeamish about it, actually. Especially since I inherited my grandfather's parrot and became friends with the little guy."

"A parrot?" Paul looked intrigued.

"Yes. He belonged to my grandfather. His name is Gator and he quotes lines from action-movie heroes. He's even starred in a couple of movies himself."

"How delightful. I'd have loved to meet him if I weren't going duck hunting."

She tilted her head. "Perhaps I can arrange for you to meet him later tonight. After your hunt, if you like."

"Yes, that would be wonderful."

"I'll arrange for it with Wade?"

"Yes. Please do." He squinted, deepening the wrinkles around his eyes, and took a good look at her. "You've got stunning eyes, my dear. Reminds me a little of my Pearl. She had fire in her eyes, too."

"Me? Fire?" She put a hand to her chest. "Well, Paul…nobody's ever said that to me before."

"I know fire when I see it." He nodded, clearly in his own world. "Wish I weren't going duck hunting so soon. It would've been nice to spend more time with you."

His eyes were still clear, but something was obviously off. "We're on for tonight, though. Don't forget."

He nodded again. "Wouldn't miss it."

Wade returned then.

Her belly flipped, but she simply smiled. "Wade, I need to be going to work, but your grandfather mentioned the, uh, duck hunting. He said he could stop by the clinic to meet Gator before he goes, though."

Concern immediately flashed across Wade's face.

Automatically, she placed a hand on his forearm, trying to reassure him. She felt his muscles tighten before the jolt of electricity zipped up her arm. She dropped her hand.

"Do you think you can be there by nine?"

He glanced at his watch. "Yes. You'll be there?"

He looked so uncertain and worried about his grandfather.

It melted her heart and made her long to comfort the strong male in front of her. Both of them. "Yes. I'll be there." She turned to Paul. "Until then, sir."

Grandpa Paul picked up her hand and kissed it. She turned to Wade. This time, he kissed her gloved hand as well. Before he released her, she went with instinct and stepped forward to hug him. He jerked in surprise, but she held on and patted his back. "It's going to be okay," she whispered. "We'll find out what's going on. I promise."

He held himself stiff for a second, then nodded and gently kissed her below her ear. She stifled a gasp at the flames of heat that swept through her, and drew back.

He stared at her. Nodded his head. And whispered, "Thank you, Molly."

CHAPTER SIX

AN HOUR LATER, they left the gala and Wade used his own car to take his grandfather straight to the medical clinic. It was the best situation, really. Anyone who might care where his grandfather was was already at the gala, so that lessened their chances of being "found out."

The parking lot of the medical clinic was even emptier than it had been last night, but Wade saw Molly's small white hatchback. Something inside him fluttered with anticipation as he parked his car beside hers, then walked his grandfather into the building. They passed by Danny McKinney, the guard who'd been on his rounds when Molly had been attacked. The same one who'd provided Wade with the security tape from last night, the same security tape that showed him squat. Tonight, the sullen-faced young man directed him to an office a few hallways down.

As they walked, Wade remembered the convenience store on the other side of the parking lot. If it had a security system and cameras set up, it's possible they'd caught a glimpse of Molly's attacker. He made a mental note to find out.

When they entered her office, Molly was sitting by herself and talking on the phone. She'd changed into casual clothes and was sitting behind a small glass partition, the fluorescent lighting making the bruises on her face stand out far more than they had earlier.

She looked up at him, smiled politely and pointed a finger in an "I'll be with you in just a minute" gesture.

But one thing she also did was blush, a pretty, feminine shade of pink that had him immediately wanting to take off her clothes and see if her skin was that pretty all over her body. He just bet it would be.

"Good taste continues to run in our family," his granddad said. "She's a pretty one. Seems smart, too."

"Yes."

"And kind."

"Yes."

"She brave?"

Wade thought of the way she'd fought off her attacker last night. The way she'd tried so hard to hold it together afterward. The way she'd refused to let him in her house the next morning until she'd called the station and confirmed who he was.

"Definitely. But she's already turned me down."

His grandpa's eyes narrowed as if he were trying to figure out what he meant.

"I invited her for coffee earlier today and she politely declined."

Instead of looking disappointed, his grandfather looked amused. "You've got King blood running through your veins, so I'm sure you won't let a little thing like that stop you."

Wade had never really talked about women with his grandfather, so he didn't know how to answer that. He was right, of course, but still.

When his granddad didn't say anything else, Wade turned to him. "Well?"

"Well what? I said you had great taste. I'm just wondering why you're still sitting here with me when she's off the phone."

Wade stood as she approached them, a smile on her face and Gator perched on her shoulder. "Hello, Wade. Sir. It's so nice to see you again."

She nodded her head at Grandpa Paul, who beamed.

"Pleasure to see you again, ma'am. Thank you for making time for my grandson to come calling. He's certainly smitten with you."

She looked at Wade and gave a nervous laugh when he didn't refute the statement.

"Uhm." She coughed. "If I don't answer, calls will be forwarded to another hotline. So I have time to see Paul now."

"That duck's a mighty fine specimen, Molly. You bag it yourself?"

Wade frowned, his pleasure at seeing Molly dissipating at his grandfather's continued hallucinations. "Grandpa—"

"It's okay, Wade. Paul, this is Gator, my parrot. Do you remember me telling you about him? He—"

"I'll be back." *Squawk.* "I'll be back."

She looked relieved, and Wade winked, knowing she was glad Gator hadn't yelled out, "Bastard."

"That bird does a mighty fine Arnold impersonation." He waited a beat. "You told me he quotes action-movie heroes, remember?"

"That's right, Paul. I did! Would you like to come in the back room with us and keep us company? I'd love to get to know you a bit more. Wade said you haven't been feeling all that well lately, but that you've been a bit…happier since you've started duck hunting?"

Grandpa Paul winked at Wade. "So, we're here to discuss the duck hunting." His brows furrowed. "My wife didn't really approve of duck hunting...."

"Your wife? That would be Pearl, right?"

"She's passed." Grandpa Paul looked at Wade and, for the first time, worry pinched his face. "Hasn't she, Wade? But I could swear I was just talking to her the other day."

"Grandma's been gone three years, Grandpa."

"Well, yes. Of course she has. Not a day goes by that I don't miss her," he said to Molly.

Molly nodded. "I understand. I recently lost my grandparents and I miss them terribly. Gator does, too. So, would you like to come back into my office, Paul? I'd just like to ask you some questions and then I have a lab tech here who wants to do a few tests. Is that okay?"

She looked at Grandpa Paul first, then at Wade.

Wade nodded. "I trust you, if you think it's necessary."

"I think it could help us rule out some things."

"Okay. Grandpa Paul?"

"If it'll make you feel better, sure. And I'd love to spend more time with you, little lady."

Wade watched as the two of them walked back into Molly's office.

"IT'S NOT SERIOUS," Molly told Wade thirty minutes later. "But he has a UTI."

Wade frowned. "Excuse me?"

"A urinary tract infection. I know it sounds weird, but on rare occasions UTIs can cause psychological disturbances like the kind he's been suffering. We believe his hallucinations were coming and going as his body fought off the infection."

"Seriously?"

"Yes. The doctors are prescribing him antibiotics right now. You should note a gradual improvement, and then hopefully his desire to duck hunt will be gone completely."

"Thank God. Thank you."

"You're very welcome. He's wonderful. I can see why you care so much about him."

"Can I see him now?"

"I think he's just getting dressed, so you might want to wait a couple of minutes."

"You didn't leave Gator with—"

"Uhm, no. I put Gator back in his cage. I figured it would be best until your grandfather was completely better."

"There's no one waiting for you? On a call, I mean?"

"No. It's been a pretty slow evening."

"In that case, can I have another hug?"

Her eyes widened, but she looked far from displeased. "Excuse me?"

"Earlier, you hugged me, and I wasn't in a state of mind to fully take advantage of it. But now that you've told me my grandfather is going to be okay, I'd like to give it another try."

She looked around, but they were the only ones in the medical office.

He didn't push her, and perhaps that's what prompted her to step up and hug him. This time, he wrapped his arms around her and hugged her back.

When he pulled away, they were both gasping for air. From a single hug. Jesus.

"What time do you get off work?"

"I have a twelve-hour shift. Then—then I'm off for the rest of the week. Why?"

"Because after I get my granddad settled in, I want to see you."

"I want to see you, too."

"No, I mean I want to *see you*. After your shift. I know that you were reluctant to make things personal between us. And as I already said, it's complicated with me being the cop that saw your assault. So if you're not interested, just say it one more time, Molly. Just know that I am interested. More than interested. I want you. I want to take you out and I want to take you to bed. Not necessarily in that order, but I can take it as slow as you need me to. Just tell me what you want. Because what happens between us now is completely up to you."

MOLLY KNEW IF she said yes she'd be agreeing to a heck of a lot more than a polite social call. She could see it in his eyes. In the quiver of his lips. In the way he clenched and unclenched his fists, as if fighting the need to touch her.

"I'm single, Molly. I'm healthy. I'm trustworthy. I know this is crazy, but say yes," he urged. "Please. But only because you want to. Because you want me as much as I want you."

She licked her lips. Watched his gaze follow the movement. Then whispered, "I'm all those things, too, but you're right, this is crazy." She held her breath. Then, before disappointment could mar his expression, she said, "I want to see you, too. And I don't want you to go slow. Not if—not if you really want more. Because I want it, too."

He took a deep breath and nodded. "I'll be back at
the end of your shift to drive you home."

"You don't have to do that. I have my car."

"I want to. Then I want you to rest. Catch up on your
sleep. Because once we're together, I plan on keeping
you awake for a long time."

CHAPTER SEVEN

DEAR LORD, she thought, as she drove home after her shift, Wade King's headlights in her rearview mirror. What am I doing? This isn't me. I don't have sex with hot men I barely even know, no matter how single, healthy, trustworthy and...well, *hot*...they are.

But Molly didn't kid herself.

That's what she and Wade were going to do. Eventually. But apparently only after she slept enough to be well rested for the upcoming festivities.

True to his word, he'd picked her up after her shift and escorted her to her car.

After arriving at her house, he silently walked her to her front door, where he took the key from her shaking hands and unlocked it.

She turned to him. "Thank you for seeing me home. Are—are you sure you don't want to come in now?"

He shook his head. "I have to take care of a few things. But I'll be back." He smiled and she knew he was thinking of Gator. "Just...think of me while I'm gone, okay?"

He lowered his head and kissed her. It was nothing like a first-kiss type of kiss.

It was deep. And long.

Intimate in a way that shouldn't be possible.

His tongue skillfully swept inside her mouth, intoxicatingly certain of its welcome. It made her think of how thoroughly he'd take her in other ways.

If there'd been any doubt as to his intentions, his kiss decimated it.

He wouldn't be coming over later for coffee or conversation. Oh, they'd likely get around to both those things, too, either initially or after they did the deed, but he was going to take her. Make love to her. With Wade, she didn't doubt the experience was going to be raunchy and divine. Multilayered and intense.

Hot. Sweaty. I'm-aching-and-only-you-can-fill-the-void sex.

After two years of going without, Molly Peterson was going all-in.

And she'd never looked forward to anything more.

Hours later, with Gator in his covered cage, she answered the door to let Wade inside. To her surprise, even as nervous and excited as she'd been about seeing Wade again, she'd actually fallen asleep. She was now well rested, showered and dressed in a simple T-shirt and jeans. If she'd been more daring, she'd have put on the sexy teddy she'd bought several years ago and never worn, but she hadn't. She'd have felt silly, for one. And two, she knew Wade didn't need the visual stimulus.

There was no doubt in her mind that he wanted her just as she was.

Just as she wanted him.

His eyes took in her casual clothes and bare face as if she was a beauty queen.

"Hi," she said lamely.

"Hi, darlin'," he said softly.

"I, uh—do you think you can—can kiss me?" she

rushed out. "Because that's all I've been thinking or dreaming about since you left."

His eyes widened and his jaw clenched. He cupped her face with his big hands and lowered his mouth to hers.

THEY'D ONLY KISSED once before, but the feeling of his lips meeting hers was a lot like coming home, though this home was one she'd only ever dreamed of owning. His tongue tangled with hers in a frantic rush of need and heat. In response, she opened her mouth wider, pulled him closer and pressed herself into him in the hope he'd never let her go. And he didn't. He cradled her against him even as he swept his hands down her body, exploring the soft give of her curves while pressing her against his own hard planes and muscles.

When his hands crept under her T-shirt to touch her bare back, she gasped and pushed her chest into his, trying to ease the throbbing ache in her nipples. He immediately ripped his mouth away from hers and sucked in several breaths. At the same time, he placed his hands at her waist and gently pushed her back despite the way she automatically resisted.

"I have to—I need to—" He kissed his way down her neck and gently cupped her breasts. She hissed in pleasure and arched into his touch. "You feel so good," he said.

"You *make* me feel so good," she corrected.

She felt him smile against her throat. "I'm going to make you feel a whole lot better."

She laughed, liking how naturally the sound came out of her. "Promise?"

He pulled back to stare at her, and for a brief second

she wondered if she'd said the wrong thing. But then he grinned. "I absolutely promise," he said. "And I think you'd feel a whole lot better if you took off some clothes. As in all of them."

"Oh, do you now?" she teased. "Is it that I'd feel better, or you could *feel me* better?"

His eyes darkened and he slipped his hands underneath her shirt to cup her breasts through her bra. He drew maddening circles around her nipples but never quite touched them.

"Both," he rasped out.

She grabbed his wrists and directed his movements so that he rubbed against the tight points aching for his touch. "Both," she echoed with a sigh.

He eased her shirt over her head and admired her pink lacy bra for all of three seconds before unhooking the front clasp and pushing the material away. Immediately, he covered her breasts with his big palms and rubbed her nipples again. His touch was electrifying.

When she whimpered, his dazed eyes met hers. He kissed her again, then trailed his lips down her neck until he latched onto one nipple. He sucked gently before increasing the pressure. She relished the sharp sensations for several minutes, but when his hand tried to insert itself between her thighs, she pulled away.

"Don't you think you'll feel better without your clothes, too?" she asked.

"So long as I get to touch and taste you, I'm feeling great."

"But I want my turn," she said with a mock pout.

Gaze fastened to her lips, he flushed slightly, then backed away to begin ripping off his clothes.

"Fine. But I hope we agree I'm not done with my turn yet."

"Oh, I'm not about to argue with you there," she said and reached for her own pants. In seconds, they were naked. Stunned, she ogled his fit, sinewy body. But he didn't let her look for long. He swept her into the cradle of his arms and cocked a brow. "Bedroom or somewhere else?"

"How about bedroom first, then everywhere else next?"

He laughed. "Remember you said that when you're ready to cry uncle."

"Uncle?" she said with dramatically rounded eyes. "That must be another one of those southern terms I'm not familiar with."

"Gotta love you yanks," he said before he hightailed it to her bedroom, where he tossed her on the bed. Even before she stopped bouncing, he was braced over her.

"Right now, just concentrate on loving one yank," she murmured. Her hands clutched his thick biceps, and her eyes trailed down his big, beautiful body. When her gaze returned to his face, she smiled and kissed the underside of his jaw, then leaned down to kiss each of his shoulders.

"Come back up here," he growled.

She eagerly obeyed and kissed his mouth, then groaned when his hand slipped between her thighs. Almost instantly, her hand found his hard shaft and he groaned, as well.

"Wow," she said.

"Yeah," he choked out. "You can say that again."

"So you like…this?"

"Your hand wrapped around me? What's not to like? Do you like this?"

He ran his fingers through her moist cleft and circled her with his thumb.

"Your fingers on me? I love—love it," she gasped.

"Good," he whispered. He slowly penetrated her with a single finger. "How about this?"

She squeezed her eyes shut and pressed her lips together, but didn't respond.

"Molly? Do you like this? Am I hurting you?"

"Yes. I mean, I like it. You're not hurting me. But I—I don't think I'll be able to talk much longer."

When she tightened her fingers around him and swirled her thumb over his wet tip, he shuddered. "Me either," he said. "S'okay. This is one case where I definitely prefer action to words." He added another finger, then curled each of them so he stimulated a pleasure point inside her.

She cried out. "Wade. Oh God, that feels so good! Please—please don't stop."

"I'm not going to stop, darlin'. We're just beginning."

True to his word, he lavished attention on her entire body, then gave her the same opportunity to learn his. When they were shaking and breathing hard and sweating and unable to hold back any longer, he slid on a condom, settled himself in the cradle of her thighs and slowly pushed himself inside her. He didn't stop until he was embedded to the hilt, groaning at the way her internal muscles milked him.

He pulled back and pushed in. Back, then in. Over and over again, he used his body to entice and entrance hers, and when she finally fell over the edge, he swallowed her cries of pleasure in another deep kiss. Only then did he let himself go.

And even then she didn't cry uncle.

Not for a good long time.

WADE COULDN'T REMEMBER a time when he'd been happier.

Except maybe when he'd actually been in Molly's arms. Inside her body.

Damn, that was probably going to become his favorite place in the whole entire world.

They'd spent hours in bed together. Learning each other. And everything he'd learned about her had told him she was someone he could love. For a lifetime. He'd hated having to leave her, but he'd needed to check in with his grandfather and finish up some reports at work. Now he had the next two days off with nothing but time to spend with her. First, however, he had one more stop.

He drove to Molly's medical clinic but parked in front of the adjacent convenience store. Although the security tapes from the clinic's cameras had been useless, the business adjacent to clinic, a little twenty-four-hour market, had video surveillance that might have captured Molly's assailant lurking around or cutting through the property on his way to her. When Wade entered the market, the cashier, a middle-aged woman with a smoker's voice, told him he'd have to come back in the morning when the manager was there.

Wade pulled out his business card and handed it to her. "Would you have your manager call me in the morning as soon as he comes in?"

"Sure," she said.

Wade turned to leave when his eye caught the racks

of candy and gum next to the front counter. He turned back. "You happen to sell licorice here? Or a fancy licorice-flavored liqueur called sambuca?"

"Nope. Nothing like that. Just the gum. And someone already bought me out several days ago."

Wade froze. "Gum? There's a licorice-flavored gum?"

"Yeah. It's hard to get. Called Black Jack. Like the card game, you know."

"Sure. And you said someone bought you out? Someone you know?"

"I don't know him. He's just a regular customer. I tell him when I get in my shipments and he buys up the lot."

"You know his name?"

"Danny. His name's Danny. He's a guard at the medical clinic next door."

CHAPTER EIGHT

WHEN SHE WOKE, Molly's body still thrummed with the excess pleasure Wade had heaped on her, yet she instantly mourned his absence from her bed. There was a rose from her garden and a note next to her on the pillow.

Raising herself on her elbow, she picked up the rose, inhaled its sweet scent and then read the note. "I'll be back. W."

She laughed. Instinctively, she knew Wade was teasing her with the famous movie line, once again using his familiarity with Gator as an inside joke. She got out of bed, used the bathroom, then let Gator out of his cage. Next, she retrieved a small vase from the kitchen, filled it with water and placed Wade's rose inside it. She set the vase next to her bed, then climbed back in and under the covers to wait for Wade.

They had an inside joke, she thought as she stared dreamily at the rose.

Despite their short acquaintance, she actually knew some important stuff about him. That he was a wonderful grandson. A dedicated cop. That he was a generous lover. That he shivered when she kissed a spot on his right shoulder blade and trailed her fingers down his thigh to—

She shivered, then sank deeper into her sheets, thinking about Wade until she started to drift off again.

"Bastard." *Squawk.* "Bastard."

Molly jerked fully awake at Gator's squawks. Was Wade back already?

"Bastard. Bastard."

Frowning, Molly slipped out of bed. Gator never repeated himself like that. His voice sounded panicked, almost as it had on the night she'd been attacked in the parking lot and had dropped his cage.

"Bastard."

This time, Molly understood.

Gator was warning her.

Someone was in the house with them, and she was pretty sure it wasn't Wade.

WADE WENT STRAIGHT from the market to Molly's clinic. However, Danny McKinney wasn't on duty, so he tried calling Molly. She didn't pick up. Considering where he'd left her, that had his panic spiking. It escalated out of control when he pulled into her driveway and saw the bicycle discarded on the sidewalk in front of her house.

As he got out of his car, his heart thundered with fear. In the house, the lights were still off. One high-pitched scream after another blasted through the windows. Wade pulled out his gun and ran to the front door. Simultaneously, he radioed in to the station and called for backup.

When he got inside, he could hear crashes and thumps coming from the bedroom. Gator's cage was empty. When Wade barreled into the bedroom, Gator was attacking a man lying prone on the floor. The screams he'd heard were not only the bird's and Molly's, but the intruder's.

Gator bit the man's face even as his body bounced and shook on the floor. A naked Molly stood over the man, her face filled with both horror and determination. In her hand, she held a Taser and the prongs were still embedded in the body of Danny McKinney, the guard from the medical clinic and the man who'd dared to threaten her in her own home.

"Holy shit, Molly. Are you okay?"

Her eyes were slightly dazed as she stared at him. She nodded. "I got your rose," she said weakly.

SEVERAL WEEKS LATER, Molly woke to a game of hide-and-seek.

Only, she wasn't the one hiding or seeking.

"Where's Gator? Where'd Gator go?"

Wade's crooning voice drifted into Molly's bedroom from the living room. Three seconds later, she smiled when she heard the flap of Gator's wings and his squawking reply, "Here I am!"

It had taken less than three days for Wade to teach Gator that one. The two had become fast friends. And she and Wade...

Stretching, she rolled over and buried her face in a pillow—Wade's pillow—and inhaled his wonderful scent. It was just one of the things she loved about having him stay with her. Of course, she also loved his kindness and affection, his playfulness with Gator, his strength and intelligence, his devotion to his family, and the way he pleasured her and completely relished the pleasure she gave him in return. In short, she'd fallen in love with him. The whole package. And for a second, that scared her.

In such a short time, he'd come to mean so much to her. Granted, the first few days of their acquaintance had been intense, even after Danny McKinney had been arrested and locked up. Apparently he'd recently broken up with his girlfriend and his only consolation had been fantasies about Molly. He'd sworn he'd had no intention of hurting Molly, that he'd just wanted her to talk to him and give him a chance, but Molly and Wade had both known that, despite his lies or delusions, he would have done far worse than punch her in the face if he'd been given the chance. Of course, thanks to the three of them—Gator, Molly and Wade—Danny was in jail and finally getting some psychiatric help even as he dealt with the legal ramifications of his actions.

Wade walked into the bedroom. He was bare chested, with soft gray pants hanging low on his waist and Gator propped on his arm. "Hey. You're awake," he said with a smile. "Perfect."

She sat up and tugged the sheets up around her. "Perfect for what?" she said.

"Perfect for me. I've been missing you."

She cocked a teasing brow. "Really? Sounded like you and Gator were doing just fine without me."

"Surviving without you," he corrected. "Isn't that right, Gator?" he crooned.

Squawk. "Say hello to my little friend," Gator called.

Molly laughed with delight. "You taught him to say the whole thing."

"It just took a few more viewings before he got it right. I have a few other movies in mind for him, too. Do you mind? Me teaching him new tricks?"

Her eyes narrowed. "What other new tricks have you taught him?"

Wade shrugged, then pursed his lips and made kissing sounds. Gator immediately placed his beak against Wade's cheek. "Thanks, little guy," he said. "Now, it's time for the adults to have some private time."

"Hmm. And what's this private time for?" she called as he walked Gator into the other room.

When he came back, he shut the door behind him.

His serious expression wiped the smile off her face. "Wade. What's wrong?"

"Shhh. Nothing's wrong, darlin'. In fact, everything's great. I told Grandpa Paul we'd stop by for brunch today. Does that sound good to you?"

"Of course. I love your grandfather and I'm so glad he's doing better. No relapses, right?"

"No relapses. And he loves you, too. You and Gator. Why, he told me flat out I'd be a fool to ever let you go."

She swallowed loudly. "And what do you think?" she whispered.

"I think my granddad's just about one of the smartest men I know."

She wondered if her face reflected the sheer happiness she was feeling. "Just *one* of the smartest?"

"Yup." He sat beside her on the bed and cradled her cheek in his palm.

She closed her eyes, relishing his touch. "And who's the smartest?"

"Why, the man who got you this, of course." He shifted even as her eyes sprang open.

Slowly, he brought his hand out from behind his back. In it, he clasped a small ring box. He opened it up, revealing a simple but gorgeous diamond engagement ring. Molly's breath caught and all she could think was *Am I dreaming?*

But Wade took her hand, knelt beside the bed and said, "Molly Peterson, I know we've only known each other a short time, but I can't think of any woman, let alone any yank, I'll ever love more. Nor one I'll ever want to spend the rest of my life with. Will you marry me?"

Molly gazed at him. She thought about her parents' marriage. Her own bad luck with men. The differences in their background and social status. How people would think she was insane for rushing into marriage when she and Wade hadn't known each other long at all. But she knew everything about him that mattered. He wasn't perfect, but he was good. He loved fiercely and loyally. He had honor and humor and, despite coming from money, he worked hard and tried to help those less fortunate than him. He'd even understood her desire to visit Danny McKinney and get him some private help.

That told her a lot.

It told her she wasn't dreaming.

It told her Wade was her dream come true.

After she'd said yes and after he'd placed the ring on her finger and after he'd wiped her tears and his own away and started to make love to her, she dimly heard Gator from the other room.

"Make my day," he called. *Squawk.* "Make my day."

He already has, Molly thought. And together they'd make every other day count, too.

* * * * *

VIRNA DEPAUL was an English major in college and, despite a passion for Shakespeare, Broadway musicals, and romance novels, somehow ended up with a law degree. For ten years, she was a criminal prosecutor for the state of CA. Now, she's thrilled to be writing stories about complex individuals (fully human or not) who are willing to overcome incredible odds for love.

A national bestselling author, Virna's blessed to write for Harlequin HQN and Harlequin Romantic Suspense. Virna also writes paranormal romantic suspense, including her Para-Ops series. All of her books encourage individuals to "brave the darkness and discover the light." She loves to hear from readers at www.virnadepaul.com.

Look for the newest book in Virna's Special Investigations Group series, *Shades of Passion*, coming soon from Harlequin HQN!

DOG TAGS

Catherine Mann

To the selfless heroes and heroines who work at the Panhandle Animal Welfare Society in Fort Walton Beach, Florida. Thank you for your tireless work to help the neglected, abandoned and abused animals that come into your care. It's an honor to know each and every one of you.

CHAPTER ONE

TECH SERGEANT BRODY Ward unlatched the gate to the white picket fence, more than ready to see his girl. After a twelve-month deployment to Kuwait, he'd been away from Penny for far too long.

But he knew without question she would be waiting for him.

The Florida sun hammered down on his head, his flight suit sticking to his back. A loadmaster on an AC-130, he hadn't even bothered to change out of his uniform after they'd landed at Hurlburt Field. He'd sped through in-processing and driven his old truck straight across Fort Walton Beach until he'd arrived at the waterside duplex.

And then he saw her. Sitting on the front porch of the yellow stucco cottage. Waiting for him.

"Penny," he called out, his heart already squeezing tight.

In a flash, she raced down the stone walkway. Long hair streaked behind her.

Kneeling, he held out his arms.

His Border collie loped faster, barking, and barking some more. *Penny.* Named for the copper streaks in her white fur that rippled as she ran to him.

Finally, a sense of coming home hit him as hard as his fifty-pound dog slamming full-on against his chest.

"How's my girl?" He buried his face in the soft fur along her neck. "Did you miss me? Because I sure missed you like crazy."

Penny's barking shifted to more of a whimper talk that seemed to say, *I missed you like crazy, too. Where have you been? Skype sucks because I can't sniff you or lick your face.*

Although she was more than making up for that now.

Laughing, Brody wiped the dog slobber off his chin onto her fur. Thank God she was okay and healthy. Most important, she was back with him. This deployment had almost cost him Penny forever. He swallowed hard and scratched her ears.

When he'd flown out a year ago, he'd thought Penny was safe and cared for with his dad and his stepmom. He'd left plenty of money in an account to pay for dog food and any possible vet visits. He'd been sad to leave his pet, but his stepmom had assured him they would look after Penny.

He should have known better than to trust his old man.

A month into the deployment, an emergency message had come through from county animal control. Penny had been picked up as a stray, thin and matted, her coat full of sandspurs. His dog's microchip had enabled the shelter to contact Brody.

Straightening out the mess from across the globe via sketchy cell phone calls and email had been tough as hell, but he'd refused to give up. His dad had insisted Penny was too much trouble and refused to spring her from the shelter. Animal control made it clear his father had been doing a crappy job caring for Penny anyway, and they were considering cruelty charges for neglect.

His dad had never been the most dependable, but his father's new wife had seemed trustworthy.

Fury had been futile. In his limited time for calls, he had to focus on securing a safe place for his dog to stay for the remaining eleven months of the deployment. There wasn't any other family to call, since his mother lived in a no-pets apartment across the country. He'd broken up with his girlfriend two months before flying out. All his friends were deployed to Kuwait with him.

He'd been at his wits' end, calling dog-sitting businesses, willing to hock his truck if he'd needed to, since his dad had already spent all the cash.

Then the shelter had mentioned a possibility.

They had a handful of volunteers willing to foster long term for deployed service members. The list filled up fast. But they'd given him a name to try—Leah Russell.

His own personal godsend.

She'd come highly recommended, ran her own gourmet dog food bakery. She'd agreed and had taken in his dog for eleven months. He owed Leah Russell a debt he could never repay. She'd cared for Penny, sending him photos and video updates. She'd even set up Skype sessions so Penny could see his face and hear his voice.

Then he'd heard *Leah*'s husky voice. Seen *her* beautiful face. And wow. Just wow.

Today, he would meet her in the flesh for the first time.

Brody looked up from Penny to the duplex, searching for Leah. Was she somewhere across the simply manicured lawn? Standing in a window? Hanging out on the porch?

The creak of a chain caught his attention and he realized she sat on the porch swing. At least he thought it was her. Late-afternoon shadows grew longer, which accounted for why he hadn't seen her right away.

Standing, he took a step toward her. "Leah?"

"Welcome back, Brody. You're early." She sounded like Marilyn Monroe with a southern accent, even sultrier without the filter of computer technology. "I didn't expect you for another half hour."

"Is it okay that I'm here now?" He hadn't been able to wait to see Penny.

To see *Leah*. In person, rather than in computer HD.

Intellectually, he knew he was just some cause to her. Support our troops. A part of the patriotic wave to lift a warrior's spirits. So he'd tried not to make too much of her emails and care packages. Still, he'd found himself anticipating those Skype sessions more and more.

Could the connection he'd felt have been his hyped-up imagination, spurred by battle fatigue and the need to connect with home? His feet grew roots on the flagstone walkway. Leah stayed in the shadows, the swing creaking.

"Of course it's okay that you're here now." Her voice carried on the salty breeze rustling the palm trees. "Penny has been watching for you every day."

Moving forward, Brody walked the last few feet to the house, his hand still resting on Penny's head. His eyes adjusted to the shaded dimness of the porch, to the sunset and shadows. Leah's caramel-blond hair shone as she swung into and out of the light.

At the top of the four steps, he finally saw her clearly. And more than wow. The reality of having her close took his breath away.

She wore jeans and layered tank tops that hugged

her curves. Her long, lean legs were tucked to the side. She had the sort of soft, pale beauty that made a man go all protective, especially when he already had twelve months of battle mind-set testosterone pumping through his veins.

He locked in on the deep blue of her eyes, noticing the flecks of green that hadn't been evident online. "I can't thank you enough for taking such great care of Penny."

She waved away his words with a slim hand. "Brody, anything I did is minor in comparison to your sacrifice this past year. I'm just happy to help in my own small way."

"You made my time away less stressful, and as far as I'm concerned, that's no small thing."

"Penny's such a good girl, it was easy. I even took her with me to work."

Leah's tank top bore the logo for the Three Pups and a Pony pet-food shop stamped across it—across her breasts. His mouth damn near watered.

What was she saying just now?

Oh, right. Something about his dog, who was currently plastered against his leg.

"You're joking about taking her to work with you, right?" Brody dropped into the wicker chair near the swing, stroking Penny's neck. "I know she's a great dog—the best—but 'easy to handle' isn't a phrase I would use."

Although his dog was sure behaving right now.

"She just needs to be worn out and kept busy." Long feather earrings played peekaboo in Leah's shoulder-length hair. "She's a working breed."

"You understand dogs."

Her plump lips curved into a smile. "Penny's not my first foster for the shelter. And I gain insights from clients at the shop." She smiled, her cheekbones as high as any model's. "Then too, I have my own dog."

"Monty. Your golden retriever." Monty had made his fair share of appearances in the photos and on Skype. "Where is he?"

"In the house." As if on cue, paws thudded on the window behind her. A long, golden nose pressed against the pane. "I was just spending a little alone time with Penny before I have to say goodbye to her."

Goodbye? Whoa. Wait.

"Who says this has to be goodbye? I know this started out as you just helping another deployed service member. But you and I spent a lot of time getting to know each other over the past eleven months. Talking, laughing, hanging out. That doesn't have to stop just because I'm back in the States."

Friends, right? He was going with that. For now.

Which meant there was nothing wrong with a friendly invitation to supper, even though his body's reaction to the sight of her was more than a "just friends" kind of thing.

He held those thoughts in check, though. Because, damn it all, he wasn't just some horny guy looking for any woman once the landing gear touched down on U.S. soil. This was Leah—and she truly was a friend. They'd spent eleven months talking about everything from family dramas to favorite college sports teams— FSU for her, LSU for him. Music—country for both of them. Their common love of animals.

Their favorite meals—seafood.

"Leah, I'd like to take you to supper, to thank you

for saving my ass. For saving Penny. Or we could go for a day on the beach, Jet Skis and skimboarding. You name it."

If not for Leah, Penny could very well have ended up being euthanized due to shelter overcrowding.

More green flecks shone in Leah's blue eyes. "You sent money every month for Penny's care and vet visits. You don't owe me a thing."

He'd wanted to send more, but his dad's stunt had cost him, big-time. "There's no way to repay what you've done for me. But I would like to try."

"Okay, then." She looked away, picking along the side seam on her jeans leg, fidgeting. "Maybe sometime we can go out to eat."

"Sometime?" He was getting shut down and he didn't understand why. He couldn't have totally read her wrong for nearly a year. Their camaraderie, their banter had been real. He had the printed-out proof. "I'd like to go tonight, but I should shower first. I've only eaten god-awful boxed in-flight meals since we took off."

"Don't you have anyone else you would rather hang out with?" She chewed her bottom lip nervously.

Was she wondering if he'd been truthful with her? Could she think he'd just used her and was looking for an easy hookup?

He leaned forward, elbows on his knees. "Leah, you know everything about me."

"Everyone has secrets." Her smile tightened.

"Not me. I'm an open book with you." Other than telling her just how deep his feelings for her went. But he needed to be sure it wasn't all an illusion. He wanted to be careful—and sure —for both their sakes. "Do you really think I'm going to be heading over for a welcome-home dinner with my jackass old man who damn near killed my dog with neglect?"

Sympathy warmed her eyes. "I guess not."

He pushed back the anger at his father and tried to lighten the mood. "If you're worried I'm secretly a psycho or a guy looking to get lucky, parade me in front of family and friends before we go. You share the duplex with your mother, don't you?"

"You already know that."

Her mom had been widowed a year ago, so they'd bought the duplex and the bakery business together. "Right, because we do know everything about each other. It's like we've been—" Dating? "—getting to know each other, intensely. We emailed more than I wrote in all of high school. We talked a helluva lot, too. And now I'm grateful to have the chance to speak to you face-to-face."

To know, finally, that she smelled of lemons and home.

She placed her hand on his, twining their fingers together on top of Penny's head. "Those emails, Facebook messages and Skype sessions were high points in my week. I worried about you being over there, and I'm so very glad you made it home."

Someone cared if he made it back. This woman, who he hadn't met in person until today but who knew so much about him, cared more than his own family. And it wasn't as though she needed anything from him. She had her mom and a business, with a wide circle of friends.

Still, he saw that connection in her eyes again. Leah was looking at him, and finally, they were touching. His skin heated where her hand rested on his. Electricity shot through him, and he wanted to gather her in his arms to find out what she tasted like.

After eleven months of "dating," he wasn't exactly rushing things. He wasn't some inexperienced teen. He was twenty-eight years old, a combat vet who'd served three rotations overseas. And no pen-pal letter from others on those earlier tours had come close to developing into what he'd experienced with Leah.

He was halfway in love with her, and he needed to figure out if he was going to fall the rest of the way.

He slid his thumb around to caress the inside of her wrist. "So? Are we on for dinner tonight?"

Her smile faded and her pulse sped up under his thumb. "There are a couple of things I should tell you first, things I, uh, failed to mention."

Everyone has secrets.

Her words from earlier detonated in his brain like an unexpected roadside bomb.

Ah crap. This was the point where she would tell him she really had a husband and two kids tucked away in that duplex. That all those Skype sessions had been nothing more than a cyberaffair.

Damn it, the thought made his gut roil. He'd seen too many friends lied to and cheated on while they were deployed. Her uneasy shifting on the swing only spiked his anxiety.

Brody pulled his hand away, leaning back in the wicker chair, bracing himself. "What's the problem?"

"Not a problem, exactly. Just…something about me you don't know." She motioned behind her to the metal ramp he hadn't noticed earlier. "That wheelchair over there? It's not my mother's. It's mine."

CHAPTER TWO

LEAH WAITED FOR the inevitable awkwardness to descend.

She really should have told Brody about her paralysis before now. But five minutes into their initial Skype session, she'd realized he didn't know she couldn't walk. The shelter director hadn't told him. For the first time in the two years since she'd been struck by a car while jogging she could…well…not run, exactly. But she could talk to a man without her wheelchair or crutches between them.

Sure, she knew there were good guys out there. Her fiancé had stayed with her all the way through her recovery from surgery. At first, she'd even believed he still loved her. He probably would have been with her now out of pity, out of obligation, if she hadn't broken up with him once she'd detected the panicked, trapped look seeping into his eyes.

And she was certain that, given enough time, even a good guy like Brody would want to leave, too.

She shook off the memories of that heartbreak and focused on the present—focused on the tall, dark and hunky man in front of her. Brody radiated muscle-bound strength and athleticism with more warmth than the glowing red sunset. His tan-colored flight suit stretched across shoulders an NFL linebacker would kill to possess.

Although, more than anything, her fingers itched to smooth the exhaustion from the corners of his brown eyes, that kind of tenderness made her nervous.

Brody was here as a friend, saying thanks for taking care of his beloved dog. Their conversations may have been flirtatious at times, but only lightly so, never, never overtly sexual. She'd been careful of that, especially after noticing the heart-tugging way he cared for his pet. He really was a good guy who didn't deserve being led on about her intentions while he'd been overseas. So then why had she been so scared to tell her "friend" everything?

She looked into his charcoal-dark eyes and found... Empathy. Compassion. And a flash of hurt hidden so far behind the rest she might have missed it.

Then he blinked away all emotion. "You're in a wheelchair? Did you injure yourself? Break something?"

"My spine," she answered dryly. "Two years ago. Monty's my service dog."

She'd lost so much in an instant. She'd been in her final semester of culinary school, then her whole life changed.

"I didn't know." He scrubbed his stubbled jaw.

"I didn't tell you."

"Neither did the animal shelter."

She bristled. "Would you have said no to my offer to help if you'd known?"

"Of course not."

"Because I *am* completely capable of caring for your dog and my own."

"Whoa." He held up his hands. "I'm not arguing with you. You've obviously done a great job with Penny. She's actually better behaved than when I left. I can't believe how quietly she's sitting now rather than knocking me over. I'm truly thankful."

Her defensiveness deflated. She could manage, but no doubt, everything was tougher. She used a wheelchair sometimes, but she could also use the metal crutches that she'd tucked under the blanket beside her. Thank God she'd come out here early, just in case he arrived ahead of schedule, so she could arrange herself and give herself time to ease into explaining. She'd wanted just a few final moments to enjoy being with him before she told him.

A few more moments to pretend the past two years hadn't happened.

"Sorry. I didn't mean to get defensive. I'm still... adjusting to the changes in my life." To the way people saw her differently.

"Looks to me like you're adjusting damn well."

"Thanks, but, uh...I was a marathon runner before the accident." She found herself falling right back into their easy way of sharing things. Except by telling him this, she knew it was more of a test. She kept her eyes locked on his. Watching. Reading every nuance. "A drunk driver hit me when I was out for a morning jog. It was an incomplete break at the L-2. That's lower down on the spine. The doctors say I'm lucky because I still have some sensation below the waist."

"'Lucky' can be a relative term when so much has been taken from a person."

She appreciated his insight, the way he said the very thing she felt guilty about voicing when others in the physical-therapy office couldn't move their arms or were missing limbs. Many of them were military veterans that had made her think about and worry for Brody.

"I'm alive. With so many losing their lives overseas, I do realize how easily that drunk driver could have killed me."

He reached for her hand again—no hesitation, just the straightforward man she'd known for eleven months. "Leah, you should have told me."

The rasp of his calloused fingertips teased along her oversensitive palm, then the inside of her wrist. His hand eclipsed hers. His touch darn near engulfed her as her nerves pulled tight and focused on that one spot. Since the sensation in her legs had dulled, it was as if her other senses were doubled.

Right now, more like tripled.

No doubt she'd been attracted to him. Good God, he was serious eye candy. Funny to talk to. Intelligent to correspond with. Now to discover that the feel of his skin against hers could send lightning strikes through her? Her body was on sensual overload.

She'd dated a couple of guys after leaving the hospital. She knew she could still be turned on, have sex, even reach completion with some extra work and creativity. But what she felt now in this simple hand-holding surpassed anything she'd experienced before or after her accident. She needed to get her head together fast and figure out what to do next.

Gulping down the urge to just kiss him, and to hell with risking her heart, she said, "You're right. I should have explained everything. I'm sorry if I hurt you."

He nodded tightly, still holding her hand. Other than that, he didn't move, just clasped her fingers and looked

into her eyes as if he couldn't get enough of seeing her
in person. The same way she couldn't get enough of
looking at him, taking in all the details that even the
best pixilation couldn't capture.

Like the way his close-cropped hair curled just a hint
with perspiration. Or how she now knew he used Dial
soap and had a crisp sprinkle of hair along his wrists.

No telling how long she would have just stared at him
if Penny hadn't nuzzled their hands, eager for some of
that attention, too.

"So, Leah, are you still interested in dinner tonight?
I know of a couple of places that allow pets if you're
eating outside."

Dinner, tonight, with Brody. God, it was tempting to
actually give it a try. Penny barked. In agreement? Or
disapproval? Monty pawed harder at the window, as if
he wanted out to join them.

Of course, he went nuts when the mailman was outside. Or when anybody approached the house—

Oh crap.

How could she have forgotten the second thing she
hadn't told Brody? Her stupid, stupid plan to give herself distance from him and the very real possibility that
he could break her heart?

"I'm going to have to pass on dinner." She grabbed
Penny's leash from beside her on the swing and thrust
it at Brody. "You need to leave."

He squeezed her hand once. "Are you sure about
that?"

"Very sure," she answered, already inwardly wincing. "Turn around. That guy in the Jeep behind your
truck? That's Chet. He's my date."

"Date?"

Brody went still. Really still. Regret stabbed through her. She'd been so sure that when he saw her, when he realized she was paralyzed, he would be ready to run. So she'd set up a safety net for her pride. She'd agreed to go with one of the shop's customers to his firehouse cookout.

Brody's hand slid from hers and she clenched her fist to keep from reaching for him. He took the leash from her other hand. This was supposed to be his homecoming, and she'd been thinking only of herself, of her pride. She chewed her bottom lip as the Jeep door slammed. Time was short.

Brody shook his head. "This Chet guy is a new relationship, if it's even that."

"I'm that transparent, huh?" she whispered, praying Chet wouldn't hear their conversation over the bullfrogs and distant waves.

"I've been looking in your eyes for the past eleven months," he said matter-of-factly while clipping Penny's pink leash to her collar. "You may not have told me about your injury, but I do know the interest, the chemistry between us was—is—real. Don't bother denying it."

Standing, Brody looped Penny's leash around his hand. "That Chet dude may be your date, but there's no ring on your finger. So I'm serving notice. I don't give up easily."

BRODY OFFICIALLY HATED Chet and he'd never even met the guy before he'd picked Leah up for their "date." The lucky bastard had gotten to spend the evening with her while Brody hung out here on her porch swing like a sap, waiting for her to come home. He reminded himself to take heart. Her eyes, her speeding pulse earlier had made it clear who she was interested in—and it wasn't Chet.

Once the guy had arrived, Brody had made tracks out. He'd gotten his point across to Leah that they would need to talk more. That he wasn't going to pretend the connection between them didn't exist. He figured he had a limited amount of time to accomplish a boatload of things. He'd gone home to his small houseboat— freshly out of dry dock. He'd showered, fed Penny, fed himself and returned to Leah's.

Now he waited for her on the front porch. Fresh jeans and an LSU T-shirt felt strange after a year in a uniform. Strange, but good. Monty had come through the open doggy door to join Penny, lying across Brody's feet. Sitting here on a porch swing with potted plants and a couple of dogs, he had a sense of hominess he'd never experienced in a lifetime of being shuttled between his mom and dad. Neither of them had wanted to be parents, but they'd housed him, fed him. They'd done their duty.

He'd expected his dad to do at least that much for Penny. Maybe a part of him had even hoped for more from his father. Period. He toed the porch swing into motion, letting the night wrap around him and ease his still-simmering anger at his old man.

The screen door on the other side of the duplex squeaked and Brody sat up straighter. Leah's mother, Kay, poked her head outside. "Brody Ward? Oh my God, welcome back, warrior man. It's good to see you here on U.S. soil."

She stepped the rest of the way outside, a glass of tea in her hand. He'd met Kay briefly in a couple of the

Skype sessions. She wore knee-length exercise pants and a long T-shirt. Her hair was blond like her daughter's, but lightening with hints of gray. They shared the same athletic frame, except Kay stood on both feet. A sense of what Leah had lost washed over him.

Kay strolled from her side of the porch to Leah's, resting a knee on the wicker chair.

"Sorry to have missed welcoming you home earlier." She placed the glass of tea on the end table by the swing. "I was holding down the fort at the store so Leah could take the afternoon off to meet you here."

"I wouldn't have minded coming to the shop to pick up Penny."

"I believe Leah preferred a place without interruption so you could enjoy your reunion with your dog." She smiled sadly. "And so she could tell you about her accident."

Yet she'd set up a date to put an end to the meeting… in case it hadn't gone well? To give herself a pride-saving out if he'd turned out to be the kind of jerk put off by her paralysis? Instead of easing his frustration, that merely ramped it higher. Apparently, she didn't know him as well as he'd thought—just as he didn't know everything about her.

"Mrs. Russell—"

"I've told you before, call me Kay. You make me feel old, as if being a widow doesn't make me feel older already." Kay couldn't be more than around fifty. Leah was twenty-six.

Since he intended to get to know Leah better, he was best off not alienating her mom. "All right, Kay, then. Do you mind if I wait here for Leah to finish up her, uh, date?"

"A date? Her favor for a friend, you mean," Kay said, confirming Brody's impression about the outing.

He breathed a sigh of relief. "Leah's not seeing anyone else?"

"Not since she broke up with her fiancé a little over a year ago."

Fiancé? Crap. More secrets. There was a story there but he didn't know how far he could push Kay for confidences. And honest to God, he would prefer that Leah started telling him these important details herself. So he settled for, "Thanks for letting me know this Chet guy isn't someone I need to worry about."

"You bet. I'm happy to see she didn't chase you off." She shoved away from the chair. "Well, I'm going to turn in. I've got an early morning baking at the shop. There's a big shelter fundraiser at the park behind Three Pups and a Pony tomorrow." She paused, smiling. "It really is good to have you home safely."

The door swished closed after her.

Leaning, he scratched both dogs' heads. He wondered why Leah hadn't taken her service dog with her, but that was just another question he would ask her.

Soon, apparently, since Chet's Jeep was pulling up now at—he glanced at his watch—only 9:37. An early night. A very good sign.

He was surprised at how fluidly she moved from the Jeep to the sidewalk using her crutches. Given the way she was currently refusing to let Chet escort her to the door, the date definitely hadn't turned into a great romantic outing.

Ooh-rah.

Since she had now officially sent Chet on his way, the Jeep rumbling down the street, things would be considerably less awkward. Because he couldn't deny the truth. He wanted more than Leah's friendship.

Brody cleared his throat. "That was some passionate good-night handshake."

"Oh my God! You startled me," she gasped, and nearly lost her balance on the crutches. Monty loped down the porch and stopped alongside her, wide chocolate eyes alert.

Brody kept his seat on the porch swing. She had it under control, and he suspected, given her prickly pride earlier, she would be more upset if he treated her like a fragile flower.

He stretched his arms along the back of the swing to keep himself from launching into action, hoping like hell that Monty was as well trained as he thought. "I could hold your hand again and you can compare me with him if you need to. But given the way you didn't even watch Chet drive away, I'm thinking it's no contest."

"Don't be a smart-ass." She worked her way up the flagstone walkway. The crutches made for slow going, but she was adept, strong, not even winded.

And unmistakably self-conscious. So he kept his eyes level with hers and simply took in the way her loose hair caught the moonlight.

"But I'm a wise smart-ass. Or would that be a smart wiseass?" He shrugged, deciding there was no better time than now to shift the tone of their relationship. "Regardless, there's nothing developing between you and that guy. Which makes him a damn fool because you look smokin' hot tonight."

He let his eyes skim downward, lingering for just an

instant on curves that called to his hands for a helluva lot more than support.

"Are you kidding?" She managed the two steps, then slid into the wide wicker chair. She set her crutches aside. "I'm wearing jeans and a tank top. I went to a barbecue, so I smell like smoke."

"We can talk about how you look in that tank top if you really want."

She crossed her arms over her breasts. "Don't you need to go home? Decompress after your long trip?"

"I'm doing exactly what I've planned for months."

"Which is?"

"I'm hitting on you."

Her eyes narrowed. "Ahhhh, because you haven't been with a woman for a year and you figure I must be so desperate you won't have to work for it."

His smile faded. Anger snapped through him. "Don't insult me or yourself."

Sighing hard, she studied him, wariness radiating off her in waves. "What's going on? Why are you back here tonight?"

"Do you really even have to ask that?" He shifted from the swing to sit on the arm of her wicker chair. He tucked a knuckle under her chin. "I've spent months wanting to be face-to-face with you, to confirm what I already know deep in my gut."

Her throat moved in a slow swallow, but she didn't pull away. "And that is?"

"That kissing you will be damn mind-blowing." He lowered his mouth to hers.

He waited an instant for a protest....

Her lips parted under his. She grabbed his shirt in her fist and tugged him closer, pressed their mouths more firmly into a sensual seam. Hell yeah. His tongue swept her mouth. She tasted like honey barbecue and sweet tea. Although the way she kissed him back was anything but sweet. She was passion and some bite, as edgy and hungry as he was.

He stroked the nape of her neck, his thumbs brushing just under her ears. The purr in her throat, the way her head fell back, stoked his own desire higher. Her passionate response and sensitivity to his touch encouraged him.

The need to be closer pulsed through him. His hands glided down to cup her shoulders. He ached to touch more of her, but that would have to wait. Now wasn't the time to rush. He finally had a no-kidding chance to be with her, and he refused to ruin that. He wanted more than a quick welcome-home lay.

He *wanted* Leah Russell—in his bed and in his life. He'd been planning how to romance her for months. Her paralysis complicated things, without question, but not in the way she might think. He wasn't put off by the issue—only taken aback that she hadn't told him.

"Go out on a date with me tomorrow."

"I have to work." She gripped his shoulders, holding him close.

"You also have to eat."

"So?" She panted in hot gusts against his chest.

His hands roved along her back. "Dinner."

"No dinner date." She kissed the hollow at the base of his neck.

He sketched his mouth over the top of her head. "Then lunch. At the park behind your store."

She tipped her face up to look at him, her eyes sad, not angry. "I said no date—"

"Picnic. Lunch. Low-key."

He kissed away her "no" and then pulled back. Before temptation could root him here, he left, jogging down the walkway with Penny trotting alongside. For the first time in a year, he looked forward to something besides checking his email and logging onto Skype.

CHAPTER THREE

LEAH PRESSED THE cookie cutter along a slab of dough for peanut butter treats shaped like dog bones, palm trees, squirrels and hearts. Once they were baked and cooled, she would frost them. Because she would be here in the store all day long. She wasn't going anywhere—most especially not out to lunch with a man who kissed like sin.

She was certain he'd only been acting on impulse, caught up in the rush of homecoming. He couldn't have been thinking straight. The phone would ring any time now with his excuse. A *polite* excuse, of course, because he was a nice guy. She knew and accepted he'd just been lonely while he was overseas.

All morning long, she'd told herself that, even if Brody showed up at the shop for lunch, she would turn him down again. And she would be polite too, because she was a nice person as well. She didn't want to be witchy about it.

She'd held firm to her plans even as she'd picked out her favorite pink jeans with a whispery babydoll top— totally the wrong thing to wear for baking all morning. Now she was stuck wrapped in the biggest apron. Perspiring. Alternating between watching the front door and listening for the phone.

She peeled up cookies, transferring them onto a bak-

ing sheet and planning how she would politely tell him
no when he showed up or control her disappointment
if he called—

The chimes over the door jingled.

In walked Brody with Penny and a small cooler.

She tore a doughy heart in two. Damn it, damn it,
damn it, her stomach tumbled and a fresh batch of
sparks showered through her.

Her fist clenched around the cool dough and she
couldn't even try to look away from the man candy in
front of her. She'd thought last night that a computer
screen couldn't come close to doing justice to Brody
Ward in the flesh—and he'd been mighty damn hot
on the monitor in his uniform and survival gear. But
in the full-out daylight, he was heart-stoppingly *male*.

Some guys seemed to deflate without the uniform.
Brody, however, was still every bit larger than life, no
matter what he wore.

His hemp sandals slapped the concrete floor as he
made his way around displays. Penny sniffed a row of
metal canisters full of all-natural chew strips and bones.
Brody's eyes roved her shop, from the wall of leashes
and collars, to stacked dog beds and bags of food, all
carefully chosen to stay within the budget they'd set.
She and her mother had worked hard to build their business in a tough economy. Thankfully, people had soon
realized a quality product made for a healthier pet, saving vet bills in the long run. It certainly hadn't hurt
business that their customers enjoyed the social scene—
mingling in the park out back. The shelter fundraiser
going on today was generating a steady flow of extra
traffic.

But her eyes stayed locked on Brody. His perfectly

sculpted mouth curled into a smile. She started to smile back in spite of herself.

Except…Huh? He was looking past her.

"Kay," Brody called out, walking right by Leah. "I brought you lunch."

Leah turned her chair around as Brody kept sauntering to the back of the store, toward her mom.

Holy cow, he had a nice butt. Why hadn't she noticed that last night? His board shorts rode his narrow hips. His T-shirt stretched tautly along his shoulders, but stayed loose at his waist.

Her fists clenched on the wheels. No question, she wanted to explore that hard, honed body as thoroughly as she'd explored his thoughts for the past eleven months. "You brought lunch for my mother?"

He looked over his shoulder. "You said no when I asked you last night."

Except he hadn't sounded like he believed her then.

Her fists unfurled with the delicious realization that he was flirting. "You're playing with me."

His eyes twinkled. "I *want* to play with you. But you have to want it, too."

A customer by the doggy–ice cream freezer covered her grin—almost.

Leah wheeled closer. Monty's nails clicked on the floor as he followed.

"Brody," she whispered between her teeth, "not in front of the shoppers. Okay?"

He leaned one hip against the counter, so sensually at ease in his skin, it heated the store ten degrees. "Does that mean you'll take your lunch break outside with me?"

"I thought you had lunch for my mom," she teased right back.

"I do." He set the cooler on the counter by the cash register and a bucket of dog bandannas. "I figure I owe her lunch if I'm going to take you away for a long break."

He pulled out a paper sack and offered it to her mother, who wasn't missing a second of the exchange as she put the finishing touches of yogurt icing on a granola birthday cake for a Great Dane turning one today.

Kay set aside the frosting gun and took the lunch sack. "What's in here, warrior man?"

"Crab-cake sandwiches." Brody closed the cooler again. "I was craving them like crazy for the last couple of months of the deployment."

Her mom peeked inside the bag. "That beats the hell out of the PBJ I packed for myself this morning. And crab cakes are Leah's favorite."

Although he already knew that. She'd told him in a Skype session, late one night when she'd set her alarm to wake up to talk to him because of the time difference. He'd had the computer to himself, most everyone else out on missions. The flight doc had temporarily grounded him until he got over some kind of deep sinus infection that would have burst his eardrums in flight. Her house had been quiet and they'd talked and talked. She'd known he was lonely and that when he got home things would change. Would end. Still, she couldn't stop herself from waking up for those calls, looking for the emails, keeping her phone connected to the internet so she would see when he was online.

The more she learned about him, the more she liked him. A lot.

She'd worked damn hard not to feel sorry for herself over the accident. But right now, she wanted so badly to stand up out of the chair and hook her arm in his, walk by his side to that park. Or dare him to race her, and give him a good run for his money.

That kiss last night had felt real. Intense. Honest. Could she trust him? Trust that? Chances were strong that he would lose interest now that he was home—even if she wasn't in this chair.

But having her hopes dashed would hurt even more now than if his emails had dwindled while he was overseas. She couldn't deny that. Her heart, her emotions were still raw from all that had happened to her, and he'd stepped into her life at a time when she was particularly vulnerable.

That was difficult to admit, especially for a woman who'd always prided herself on being as tough as nails. A marathon girl who never gave up.

She was still strong. Still resilient. But not quite as fearless.

Yet an old part of that hardiness pushed through and she found herself pulling off her apron. "You better have more than two of those sandwiches left, or you're going hungry."

THE SIGHT OF Leah in hot-pink jeans and a shirt that shimmered over her breasts just about drove Brody to his knees. Then he cleared his brain enough to register what she'd said. He'd won. She would have lunch with him.

He resisted the urge to pump his fist in victory. Best to keep it low-key and get her outside before she changed her mind.

She wheeled beside him along the walkway. He would have offered to push, but the defiant tip of her chin as she'd set herself in motion warned him off. He'd settled for opening the back door—a gentlemanly thing to do regardless. He'd also made absolutely sure the traffic was clear or stopped before they crossed the narrow street to the waterside park.

Seeing her in the wheelchair today knocked him off balance again, but he'd done his best not to show it. It wasn't the wheelchair itself, actually, but he was still reconciling the fact that she'd kept the information from him for the past eleven months.

However, it didn't piss him off enough to leave. He needed to know if the intriguing woman he'd met on-line really existed. Or was that a lie, too? A persona she'd put on for amusement?

That pinched his pride—and deeper.

He adjusted his hold on the two leashes and the cooler.

The park was packed with people and other dogs. Signs declared it was the shelter adoption event Kay had told him about, with a mobile vet unit set up doing discount rabies vaccinations and microchips. Nearly everyone waved at Leah—and those who didn't stared at the two of them with outright curiosity.

A lady wearing a polo shirt with the shelter's logo strode over to them quickly. "Leah, Penny," she said, running her hand along the collie. "And is this Penny's 'dad'? I'm Tasha, the—"

Brody took her hand. "The shelter director. I can't thank you enough for helping me find a foster home for Penny."

"Our pleasure to see things work out so happily for

this sweet girl." She ruffled Penny's ears and smiled at Leah. "I've got to run. We're slammed, which is good, but I just wanted to say hello and welcome home."

Turning away, she left them to their picnic.

He set the cooler down on a park bench. "You're a popular lady."

"This is my circle. My turf, so to speak." Stopping, she set the brakes. "What else did you miss while you were overseas? Other than food?"

Sex? Definitely not a polite answer. He looped the dog leashes around the end of the bench. "Simple stuff, mostly. Watching football in my recliner. Coaching a Little League team."

She winced.

Damn.

She had to miss sports. Hadn't she said she was a runner?

He passed her a sandwich and tried again. "I missed fishing."

Her eyes lit up. "You fish? How did we not talk about that before? Seems like we spoke of everything else."

"How could we not have talked about it when I live on a houseboat?" He opened two sodas and took out another sandwich for himself, more focused on watching her face and remembering the feel of her mouth, her hands.

"I guess we do still have some surprises to learn about each other after all."

He suspected she could surprise him for a long time…indefinitely. "Tell me more about what kind of fishing you like."

"From the dock or deep sea. Either one." She'd already polished off half her sandwich. She hadn't been kidding about liking seafood. "I have a freezer full of catches."

"Well, my freezer is very empty. What do you say we go fishing together tomorrow, since the shop's closed on Sundays?" He waited for her answer and didn't even try to deny that hearing her say yes was important to him.

She finished the rest of her sandwich before answering. "Fishing. You and I?"

"I'm on mandatory vacation after my deployment. They make us take time off to give us a chance to decompress. I can't think of a better way to do that than fishing and hanging out with you."

The wind lifted her caramel-blond ponytail, her eyes so wary. He wanted the unreserved, computer Leah back. Damn it, she hadn't been a figment of his imagination.

"Brody, surely you have friends or family to see, someone other than me."

"My buddies are all going on vacation with their families. And if I had any relatives worth visiting, do you think I would have had to resort to asking a stranger to watch my dog?"

The shutters fell away from her eyes in a flash. Her hand rested on his arm. "That had to hurt when your dad didn't come through for you."

"It pissed me off."

She ducked her head toward him, the wind blowing her ponytail lightly against his neck. "Lots of people mask hurt with anger."

His defenses went up. "Therapy is free for veterans, so I don't need to get it from my friends."

"My apologies." She straightened.

Already he missed the feel of her hair brushing him,

making him imagine what it would be like to have her hair tangled up in his hands while he kissed her again.

While he made love to her for the first time.

"Leah, I don't want your apologies or sympathy."

"What do you want from me?"

His hand slid behind her neck. "This."

To hell with restraint today. He slanted his mouth over hers.

A KISS IN the park was safe. Right? It couldn't get out of control with so many people around.

Leah rested her hand against Brody's chest, the well-washed cotton warmed from his body, his heartbeat speeding up under her fingertips. That heat spread through her all too quickly, even as their mouths stayed closed, the press of his lips to hers carrying a different sort of intimacy. The kind that relayed a growing familiarity in connecting anytime. Anywhere.

Suddenly the kiss didn't feel so safe after all. Taking things to this level could be infinitely more dangerous than an impulsive, out-of-control moment.

She eased back an inch, her breath and heart racing. "Why did you do that?"

"Because I wanted to kiss you again," he said simply. "I've thought about it since the first time we Skyped. You were so earnest about giving me the opportunity to talk to Penny—and you had her show off the new trick you'd taught her. She even had that silly bow on her head."

Her fingers drew circles on his chest, taking in the flex of muscles under her touch. "It wasn't silly."

"We can agree to disagree." He kissed the tip of her

nose and sat back on the bench, taking his Coke from on top of the cooler.

"Disagree about the bow."

"Okay, the bow. But that's not the point here. Did that little side road in the conversation give you enough time to think about whether or not we're going to spend the day fishing tomorrow?"

"Brody—"

"Stop right there." He pressed a finger to her mouth.

"Stop what?" Her lips tingled from his kiss and the light tracing of his fingertip. She nipped him. "I haven't said anything."

His pupils widened with awareness. Arousal. "Yet. I can see you're about to say no, and that's not the right answer."

"Do tell why you get to decide my answers." She crossed her arms under her oversensitive breasts.

"Your response tells me you enjoy it when we kiss. A lot." He grinned unrepentantly. "So do I, in case you were wondering."

"That's beside the point."

"That's *exactly* the point."

"Whatever flirtation we had while you were overseas was just that, a flirtation." Would she believe him if he argued? "It was your escape from the war."

His eyes went serious. "What was it for you?"

And in that moment, she realized she had the power to hurt him as much as he could hurt her. She quit worrying about protecting her heart and spoke with total honesty. "Those times we spoke online, the Skype sessions…"

"Skype dates."

"Okay, I'll concede to them being cyberdates."

"*Monogamous* cyberdates."

How could their conversation have turned so intimate in a park full of people? The safety in knowing they couldn't take things further also led them to share more…as it had during the times online?

She swallowed hard and forged ahead. "Those times offered me an opportunity to walk again. Even if just in theory." She refused to cry, damn it. "But I'm back to reality now. This is like starting over getting to know you."

"I disagree." He sketched his fingers along her forehead, and her eyes slid closed before she could stop herself.

The roots of her hair absolutely tingled. "Brody…"

Was that husky moan hers?

His broad hand cupped her face until she looked at him again. "Leah, you can keep trying to brush me aside, but until you give me a good reason—one that has nothing to do with that wheelchair—then I'm not giving up. You want us to spend more time together, getting to know each other better? I'm very cool with that."

CHAPTER FOUR

THE GULF OF MEXICO stretched out in front of him for his day of fishing with Leah. He'd chosen to join the air force rather than the navy. He loved to fly. But that was his job.

This, the water, fishing, his houseboat offered his recreation. Enjoying a plateful of the day's catch, peace all around him. Today was even better than normal, having Leah at the table with him, their dogs asleep on the bow.

His houseboat wasn't large—only forty feet—but he'd never had much cause to stick around long. He had everything he needed in two small rooms. One with a sofa and kitchenette, the other with a double bed. Advanced technology made it easy to hook up his computer and TV for the ultimate man cave. He could also grill outside, and his one decadence? On the top deck, he had a hot tub on the upper command bridge.

They'd spent an easy afternoon out here fishing. Through the day, he'd monitored two rod holders, while she kept watch over one. Between them, they'd made a good dent in restocking his freezer, with enough red snapper left for supper.

He picked at the last of the grilled fillet on his plate, his taste buds still salivating over the unexpected blend of spices she'd chosen. "You really do know your fish."

She dropped another lemon into her ice water, stirring with a spoon for so long she had to be stalling or prepping her answer. "I was actually in culinary school before the accident."

His fork clattered against his plate. "You really have been holding out information about yourself."

"I told you I had baking skills, and I told you about my shop. You just assumed I was only a master at dog-treat cooking." She winced. "Although I can see how I encouraged the misconception. Should I apologize again?"

He reached for his sweet tea, laying off the booze tonight. He needed to keep a clear head. "Do you want to apologize?"

As she stared into her glass, her eyes took on a distant look. "Not really. The past eleven months, talking to you, the freedom to just…be.… That was amazing." She glanced up at him with a half-sad smile. "If I'd mentioned culinary school, I would have had to mention not finishing, which would have led to questions about why I left."

"Then it wasn't an act." He swirled the ice in his glass, sounds of the night wrapping around him. Waves lapped against the side of the boat. A fish plopped in the distance. "You weren't pretending, just leaving this out."

"Like letting you believe I could hop up out of the computer chair?"

Her braced shoulders shouted bravado, but he saw the apology in her eyes for not being straight with him from the start. While it wouldn't have changed things if he'd had the full scoop, she'd had no way of knowing that then. He could understand her reasons for holding back.

He propped his feet on the bench across from him. "Tell me about culinary school now."

She sipped her water before speaking. "After my surgery, I got Monty."

The golden retriever lifted his head at the sound of his name, looked to her, but she made some gesture and Monty settled back to rest. The night was so quiet in their secluded cove, there wasn't anything to disrupt them.

"Your service dog," Brody said, nodding toward their dogs still napping on the bow of the boat.

"What can I say? People don't like animal fur in their food, and there wasn't a hairnet big enough to cover him."

He wouldn't have considered that. He'd just always assumed service dogs were accepted everywhere, by law. "I'm sure there must have been a way around that...."

"If Monty wasn't welcome, I didn't want to be there." She glanced back at her service dog again, deep affection lighting her blue eyes like reflected stars. "I'm happy in my job now. Animal fur is a given at Three Pups and a Pony. I could take both Monty and Penny."

"That's why she behaves better now. That's a bonus I hadn't expected in the fostering gig."

A wry smile played at her lips. "I had to teach her a few manners first. But she and Monty both are great helpers."

"You're more amazing than I even realized."

"Damn right, I am." Her eyes went pensive and she toyed with a gold hoop earring. "This is the strangest first date I've ever had."

"I wouldn't call this a first date." He felt closer to

Leah than he had to anyone in his life, except maybe his crew. But then what he felt for Leah was very different. "Seems to me like we've been going out for months, the old-fashioned way. We talked while eating meals. Granted, I was eating an MRE in Kuwait, and you were having supper at your place in front of the computer. But we talked, got to know each other. Honest to God, you know more about me than anyone else. Still…learning about your paralysis makes me wonder about other things we discussed."

She leaned forward on her elbows, closer, even though they were totally alone out here. "Everything I told you about me, my life, was all true, right up to two years ago. That was my life before I was hit by the car."

"What about after?" God knew, he felt every war deployment changed him. Had her personal battle changed her? Had she reconciled the before and after?

"I'm still the same person on the inside." A long sigh shuddered through her. Her hands fell to her knees, squeezing hard. "It's the outside that won't cooperate. But I'm trying. Trying to find ways to fill those holes in my life left by the things I can't do anymore. Things like running. So I swim instead, go fishing."

"And taking in foster dogs? Is that new?"

"Actually, my family has always fostered shelter animals, just like I told you in our Skype chats." Twirling a fork on the table, she stared back at him with sad, wise eyes. "Now, why don't you ask what you're really wondering about the accident."

"What would that be?" Yeah, he had a suspicion of where she was headed, but he wouldn't risk being wrong. She needed to be the one to bring up how much she *did* feel below the waist. It wasn't automatically his or anyone else's right to ask.

"You want to know what everyone does. How bad was the accident? How much can I feel?" She set the fork aside, her entire attention focused on him. "Can I still have sex?"

He stayed silent, waiting, letting her take the lead on this, even though, yes, he wanted to know. For her, so that if he was ever lucky enough to have any chance of intimacy with her, he wanted to do, to *be* what she needed. But first, he had to know she was okay in other ways—like in the head. She'd been in a life-changing, traumatic accident, not something that could just be shrugged off in a second.

"Brody?" she urged, the lull of waves the only other sound.

"Just tell me what *you* want me to know."

"Diplomatic answer. You're such a good guy," she said in a way that he wasn't sure was an endorsement or accusation. "If you say we've been 'dating' for eleven months, then it's not strange for us to have this conversation." The gentle lap of the water filled the gaping pause. "Well, are you going to say something?"

"I'm not sure you're going to want to hear what I'm thinking."

"Oh, uhm, why not?"

Time to step up to the plate for her. He shifted from across the table to sit beside her, scavenging for the right words. "You're talking about sex and I'm still processing that someone I care about was hurt, badly." He slid an arm around her shoulders. "Sure it happened two years ago, but I just learned about it yesterday. If I want details, it's because I care about you, not because I'm trying to decide if we can have sex or not."

Because, honest to God, he already knew the answer to that.

She sat stiffly beside him. "Remember when I told you my SCI—spinal cord injury—occurred at the L-2? It's an incomplete versus complete. Complete means loss of use and sensation." She rattled off the details in a flat voice, studying her fingernails. "Since mine is incomplete, I still experience some sensation and even a minor degree of muscle control. I'm able to use crutches, just not for a long time. And I can still achieve an orgasm."

He placed his hand over hers, covering her fingernails until she had to look at him. "Leah, it's okay. While I want to know what happened, you don't need to share, uh, more than you're, uh, comfortable with telling."

Once her eyes met his again, her body relaxed against his side. "You said this wasn't a first date." She skimmed her knuckles along his jaw. "So why are you blushing?"

"I'm not blushing." He frowned even though his face felt warm. Had to be her touch. "Badass warriors do not blush."

She laughed. "Right. Whatever."

He let himself smile with her because the shadows were gone from her eyes. "Damn straight."

Glancing at him slyly out of the corner of her eyes, she said, "You're not a virgin, are you?"

He choked on a laugh, then laughed again, harder, until they both sagged back on the bench at the table. This was the Leah he knew, the easy camaraderie, the ability to make him smile even in the middle of hellish times. Now he realized she'd understood more about pain and stress than he'd known then. His hand gripped her shoulder more firmly, tucking her against his side as if he could somehow insulate her from any more of life's harsher whims.

She flipped her hand to link her fingers with his, but her eyes shifted back to her nails. "I've had sex since the accident. I needed to know if I still could. And I can. So don't think this is a ploy for a pity lay."

His eyebrows shot up. "Leah? Leah," he insisted until she looked at him. "Just so you know, I haven't had sex with anyone since we started talking eleven months ago. It's not just because I was deployed. There are women over there, too."

"No one since we met?"

"Nobody. You fill my mind until there's no room for anyone else." And God, wasn't that the truth? Saying it was tougher than he'd expected, pushing the words up his tightening throat. "I'm not rushing or pushing for anything tonight, but you should know I want more from you than friendship."

"What if I had told you something different tonight? What if I'd said I feel absolutely nothing below my waist?"

Would that have made a difference for him? Hell no. But he knew she needed the right words to convince her. "Don't all the how-to-please-a-woman articles say most sexual pleasure happens in a woman's head? That it's about taking time and creating the mood?"

"You read articles on how to please a woman?"

He tapped her forehead, her nose. Her lips. "You're losing focus here."

"What is the focus?" she whispered against his fingertip, her lips brushing him.

Arousing him.

He cupped her face, threading his fingers into her silken hair. "There's a lot more to having amazing sex than part *A* fits into slot *B*."

"Oh really?" She angled her face into his hand, nipping the flesh base of his thumb. "And what else would that be?"

His pulse skyrocketed—along with the possibilities for tonight. "Are you asking me to have sex with you?"

Her hand fell to rest on his chest, her mouth a whisper away from his. "Since this is far from our first date, then perhaps it's time for us to take things to the next level."

He wanted to shout, "Hell yes!" but he also wanted to be sure she meant what she said. He started to speak.

She shook her head. "This is where you kiss me again." Her fingers twisted in his shirt and she tugged him closer. "Or maybe I'll just kiss you."

ABOUT TEN SECONDS into the most explosive lip-lock of her life, Leah decided to take this further. All the way, in fact. She didn't know if she and Brody had a future, but she would always regret it if she didn't have a "now" with him.

Here on his boat anchored in a secluded cove, they had a pocket of time away from the world. She didn't know if he was still riding an adrenaline rush from being in combat, but she was certain he felt more for her than gratitude.

Very. Sure.

Her hand slid lower between them, dipping just a

hint into the waistband of his board shorts and skimming over bare, hot skin.

His abs flexed along her fingertips and he growled against her mouth, "So you truly are propositioning me."

"Do you *want* to be propositioned by me?" She leaned closer against him, her breasts achy with the need to be touched and explored by this man.

"Leah," he groaned into her mouth, his voice husky with unmistakable need, "I've wanted to be with you for months."

She couldn't help asking, had to know.… "And now that things will be different than you imagined when you were thinking of this for those months?"

Inching back, he held her with his narrowed, sexy gaze as firmly as his hands palmed her between her shoulder blades. "Are you asking if I had dreams about you? If while I was in the shower, I thought about you…"

Confidence and fire seared her. "So I have been the object of your fantasies."

"Yes, ma'am." His brown eyes went molten-black.

"Those fantasies will need to be adjusted," she said, regretting for the first time that she hadn't told him earlier.

"I like creativity." He claimed her mouth again, his hands sliding lower as he stood, taking her with him.

Monty lifted his head from his nap and barked once.

"Stay, it's okay, boy," Leah commanded before shifting her attention back to the warmth of pure man against her.

Brody held her against him, his arms under her bottom so her feet were just off the ground. She kept her arms looped around his neck as he walked across the deck. Somehow she knew he wouldn't drop her. In his arms, she was safe.

Yet safe had never felt so deliciously dangerous. "Where are we going?"

"Up to the top, to the hot tub." He brushed his mouth along her cheek before nuzzling her ear, his five o'clock shadow rasping gently. "Is that cool by you?"

He would have to carry her the rest of the way. He was asking for more than that, actually. He was asking for her openness. He was asking for her trust. Maybe he needed that because she hadn't told him everything before. She hesitated for an instant.

He nibbled her earlobe. "Or we can stay here."

"No, it's okay. Really…" She savored the scent of the salty air clinging to him. "You want to carry me up there, which is a romantic thing, something a lover would do."

"Except it's different for you." He backed her against the table until she could sit on the edge.

"Yes, I just want us to be equal in this, and I can't get up those stairs by myself."

"Then we decide together," he said so blessedly simply. "Do we head for the bed? Or upstairs in the hot tub?" He grinned roguishly. "Hell, in the kitchen's fine by me. I'm good with anywhere as long as you're there. So you choose and I'm one hundred percent on board."

His sincerity couldn't be missed any more than the heat in his eyes. And right now, she wanted it all—the man and the romanticism.

"Carry me upstairs."

"Yes, ma'am." He swept her up against his chest with ease, an arm around her shoulders, the other hooked under her knees.

Wind rolled in from the ocean, tugging harder at her hair the higher they climbed. As much as she wished she could take these steps on her own, being in his arms felt right, too. And she couldn't deny how amazing it was to be here. Closer and closer to the stars.

Before she could blink, he plunged them both into the hot tub—fully dressed. The warmth swallowed her.

"Are you crazy?" Laughing, she leaned back in the corner, water sluicing just under her shoulders.

He knelt in front of her, swirling jets frothing around him. "Pretty much, and it's all your fault, lady."

The steam in his eyes equaled the heat billowing up from the water. Words evaporated into the windswept air as well, as she let herself sink into the moment. She let herself be swept away by the music of the ocean, the low hum of the tub's jet and their breathing.

Her dress billowed, filling with water. But more important, his T-shirt plastered to his chest, his dog tags visible through the wet fabric. He might as well have been bare. Every cut and ripple of his honed chest waited a few inches away. Steam rolled up around them, between them, and she reached through it to touch him, outlining the definition with her fingertips.

She flattened her palm to his chest, and his low growl of approval vibrated against her skin.

"Nice," she purred right back at him. "And I suspect it's going to get even better."

"You can bet on it."

Holding her eyes with his steady gaze, he untied the strings of her dress along one shoulder, tugging slowly until the dress drooped and exposed the edge of her strapless bra. Thank goodness she'd chosen pretty pink.

Maybe because she'd been hoping for just this?

He stroked along her collarbone to slip the other knot free. The bodice of her dress floated away from her. She reached behind herself and unhooked her bra. A flick of her wrist sent it sailing, then landing on the deck in a slap of wet lace.

His breath hissed in a low, appreciative sigh and he palmed her breasts, cradling the weight until her nipples were just visible above the waterline. The night air brushed her skin a second before his mouth closed over one taut peak. Laving. And sipping.

The hot-tub jets throbbed against her, massaging her until the tug of his mouth, the stroke of his hands and the swirling pulsation stoked her need higher, hotter. And he took his time. God, she loved how he didn't rush exploring her body, lingering at any hint of a breathy gasp.

He was the man she'd known for the past eleven months, the caring guy who protected everyone, from people in another country to his beloved pet at home. Except she wasn't thinking mushy, sentimental thoughts now. Her mind, her body focused on the aching need to take this to completion.

Her fingers bunched the hem of his T-shirt, peeling it up until he had to stop touching and tasting her. She made fast work of tugging the shirt off his body and...

"Damn," she said softly, reverently. "Just damn."

"That's supposed to be my line."

She smiled, but couldn't look away. She'd spent more than her fair share of time in gyms. His body couldn't be built from free weights alone. His dog tags hung from his neck, between perfectly sculpted pecs. She scratched a fingernail down the chain, slowly, then traced along one flat nipple, then the other. His throat moved in a long swallow.

A rush of feminine power surged through her. Her fingers walked lower. Lower still. Until her hands went to the fastening on his board shorts.

He covered her hand with his. "Wait, just a second."

Standing, he tugged his dripping wallet from his back pocket. He pulled out a condom and tossed the wallet aside before stepping out of his shorts and boxers. Then she couldn't even think, much less speak.

He rolled the condom on before sinking back into the hot tub. Lifting her, he shifted their positions until he sat in the corner, settling her to face him. She straddled him. Her arms looped around his neck and she stared into the eyes of the man she'd come to know over the past months, the deep brown gaze of Brody. Her friend. About to become more...

What had seemed so complicated became beautifully simple as he cradled her hips and lowered her onto his erection. Apparently he had thought this through, figuring out the way they could be together, and that touched her. Touched her as lusciously as the way their bodies fit, the moonlight and the rush of water. The rocking of the boat partnered with the buoyancy inside the hot tub to roll her body against his. All of it worked together to give her a sense of power and equality she hadn't expected to find.

His hands, his mouth roved from her back to her hair until her nails sunk into his shoulders. She'd hoped for good. This was so much more.

Arching closer, she gripped the edge of the hot tub, lifting and lowering herself. Taking control for the first time since her accident. Feeling aggressive and sensual and...*feeling*.

Pleasure gathered in her breasts, in her belly, between her legs. She didn't know if the sensation was just so intense or phantom, but she didn't care, because it felt so damn good she didn't want to overthink. He seemed to understand about touching her everywhere, keeping the steady flow of bliss pulsing through her.

Even kissing him turned her inside out, with the bold sweep of his tongue and spicy hint of their supper together. The scent of chlorine and salt air mixed with the perfume of their perspiration-slicked bodies blending. The smells and tastes multiplied through her, overwhelming her until...

Her orgasm crashed through her. Hard and unexpected in its intensity. She bit her bottom lip but her moans pushed through anyway until she let them roll as free as the aftershocks shimmering all the way to the roots of her hair.

His arms clamped around her, tighter, his head falling to rest on her shoulder as he shuddered against her with his own release. Which sent a fresh flash through her. She held strong to Brody, the dampness of the night binding them until she couldn't tell the difference between the steam and her tears.

She couldn't hide from the truth or tell herself this was just a friends-with-benefits kind of moment. This night, being with Brody, all of it was special. And no question, special was so scary she didn't know if she could handle it if he turned away. Or worse yet, if he stayed with her out of obligation, the way her fiancé had tried to do.

Her chest tightened with a sense of claustrophobia.

She needed space and time to test what they were feeling for each other, to be sure she wasn't setting herself up for another heartbreak. Because she knew without question, Brody had the power to hurt her battered heart far more than her fiancé ever had.

CHAPTER FIVE

Having Leah next to him in bed, the way they'd been together, was as damn close to perfect as he'd ever experienced. The sex, the connection between them had been one of a kind. He knew that. She'd affirmed it with her words and reaction. After the hot tub, he'd brought her down to the cabin, where they'd made love twice more.

And while all the sex had been incredible, something had changed when they'd left the hot tub.... In the cabin, she'd been more intense, silent. Afterward, she'd turned away and gone to sleep.

Weren't women supposed to be into cuddling and chitchat? Instead, he was awake and staring at the way her hair looked splayed across his pillow. Testing the feel of a lock between his fingers. Falling the rest of the way in love with a woman who'd pulled away from him.

And he didn't understand what had set her off.

Their time here on the boat was limited, the sun already starting to rise. She would have to leave for work soon. Right after she'd fallen asleep, he'd driven the boat back to the dock and tied it off so she could sleep right up until the last second. He'd even taken the dogs for a quick run before turning in for a couple hours' sleep. Now she would have to head out to the shop soon.

She'd worked hard to build the business with her

mom. Maybe Leah was worried about a relationship with him, a military guy. He should have thought to pay more attention to discussions about her store. He thought back to a Facebook messaging conversation they'd once had about her starting up the place. He'd wanted to know why there was a pony in the name when it was a dog bakery. She'd told him she always wanted a horse and the alliteration sounded cool.

His cell phone rang on the bedside table. He snatched it up before it could wake Leah. He thumbed it on and stepped outside.

"Son?"

Damn it. His father. He should have checked caller ID. He was already on edge from trying to figure out why Leah had closed down on him. A call from his father was the last thing he needed to deal with now.

"Yeah, Dad, it's me." Head tipped back, he looked up at the sky that had offered him an escape from his home life through a job in the air force. "What's up?"

"I'm just calling to welcome you home."

"Thanks." Penny nuzzled his hand. Anger blasted through him as he thought of how his father had abandoned her. "What do you want, Dad?"

"Just what I said," his father continued as if nothing was wrong. As if he hadn't dropped the ball on the only thing Brody had ever asked of him. "Is there anything wrong with wanting to speak to my son?"

"It's pretty early." He leaned a hip against the railing, the rest of the dock only just coming to life. "If you really want to talk, we can set up a time to meet for a burger."

"Sure, yeah, right," his dad said. "As long as you can pick up the tab. I'm a little short of cash—"

Brody bit back a curse. "Of course you are."

"Hey now, no need to be disrespectful."

"How much money are you calling to ask for?"

"It's just a loan since you've got deployment money." When Brody didn't bother answering, his father continued, "Are you still pissed at me over the misunderstanding with your dog? I'm sorry about that. I ran low on cash, so I couldn't take Penny to the groomer."

The anger built until it overflowed. "You think I'm angry because you skipped getting my dog bathed? Even you aren't that dense. You didn't feed Penny. You refused to drive your cold, hard ass across town to pick her up after you let her run loose on the streets."

"I made a mistake." His father rambled on in a breezy tone as if this was no big deal, for God's sake. "One time, son, and I'm sorry about that. It all worked out in the end, just like I knew it would."

"One time?" He couldn't let this slide. He couldn't just shoot the breeze and eat burgers with his dad as if nothing was wrong. Being with Leah had his defenses down, wall blasted through. "Like the way you only forgot to hire a babysitter for me every now and then?"

"You were old enough to take care of yourself. Your ma left me in a jam when *she* walked out," his father ranted bitterly. "This is *her* fault."

"I was eight years old." And right now he felt like crap for imagining for even a second his dad could have reformed.

"If you think I'm such a crappy human being, why did you leave your almighty precious dog with me in the first place?"

"Because your new wife seemed reliable." And there hadn't been any other options. Because he'd cut himself off from any kind of real relationship so entirely, he had no one in his life to count on. Leah was probably smart to pull away from him. "Forget about it. Thanks for the call. Goodbye, Dad."

And this time, he meant it.

Penny nuzzled his hand again, her wide brown eyes calming, sympathetic. His dog had given him far more than his parents had, and he'd let her down.

A sound from the cabin snagged his attention and he realized that Leah was moving around with her crutches, Monty's nails clicking on the floor.

He tamped down his anger and stepped into the cabin, seeing the one step down with new eyes as he thought of Leah having to maneuver it with her crutches.

Yanking open the fridge, he pulled out eggs and milk. "I'll get something going for breakfast whenever you're ready."

He tossed his cell phone on the counter.

"Who called?" She settled onto the sofa, setting her crutches to the side.

"Sorry to wake you," he said, sidestepping the question.

"It's okay. We should probably take the dogs out anyway."

"They had a break on the shore when I drove the boat back to the pier. I let them swim a little." He'd been trying to get his head on right again.

"I bet they loved that." She shoved her tangled blond hair from her face and she looked so damn right in his home, in his life, he would do anything to keep her here, even when he knew he should let her go.

"They did."

She angled her head to the side. "Something's wrong."

"No, nothing." He glanced at the phone, thought about how many nights as a kid he'd wished for a regular home. He'd wanted a family, a big, extended family that lived and worked together, as Leah and Kay managed to do. And then everything gelled in his head, what he wanted for himself and why Leah must be pulling away. She saw him as rootless. She saw the way he didn't connect with people, and she must be worried.

He knew now what he needed to do to keep Leah. "I just…I can't pretend this is only a friendship hookup. Leah, I want you to marry me."

A PROPOSAL?

Leah felt as though her world had been rocked, and for once the off balance feeling had nothing to do with her legs. She'd been trying to figure out how to keep the relationship simpler, to give herself time to be sure Brody wasn't staying out of a sense of obligation.

Now he had made things unimaginably more complicated.

Although, even if his proposal was ill advised and a by-product of heaven only knew where, she couldn't just throw it back in his face. She measured her words. "Brody, this is so out of the blue, I have to wonder if you really mean it."

"Is it all that crazy to think I could have fallen for you over the past few months?"

"Are you asking because we had sex? Because you think I'm a needy woman in a wheelchair?"

"No. No. And hell no. You're the last woman anyone would call needy." He started to turn back to the counter of food. "Forget I said anything."

"Brody…" God, she wished she could just go to him

easily, rest her head on the back of his shoulder. Simple things in life that others took for granted. "I'm not saying no or yes. Just wondering why you asked."

"Like I said, forget about it." His hand fell to rest on top of the cell phone.

"Who were you talking to?"

He looked back over his shoulder sharply. "That's irrelevant."

"I don't think so."

His head dropped. "It was my old man, wanting to welcome me home with his hand out for cash."

In a heartbreaking flash, it all made sense. Brody was hurting, aching to have someone in his life. She thought of the stories he'd shared with her about his parents, and so many things fell into place. She ached all the way to her fingernails for him, and for herself too, because now she was more certain than ever that their affair couldn't go any further.

Leah reached out a hand to him. "Your parents let you down again and again. You deserve a simple relationship in your life, an easy give-and-take."

His shoulders lifted with a hefty sigh. "Doesn't everyone?"

"Brody? Look at me, please." She waited until he turned to face her before she continued. "I can see how our relationship would have seemed simple—emails, Facebook messages, Skype. Yes, we have a lot in common and I can't lie that there's a connection between us."

Even now her body hummed with awareness and a desire to be with him again. "Oh God, Brody, can't you see a relationship with me will be anything but easy? It's not just my legs. It's about everything else I lost. My life has been turned upside down. I'm functioning, yes, but I'm not okay about this." The bitter words poured out of her even when she refused to release the bottled tears. "I can't be what you need me to be."

And she couldn't bear to see the disappointment in his eyes once he realized that. Finding that look in her former fiancé's eyes had been the most painful thing she'd ever experienced, and she hadn't loved him half as much as she loved Brody.

He dropped to his knees in front of her and took her hands in his. "How are you so certain you know what I need?"

"Because I care about you, too. I love you, Brody. I see you and see your needs in a way that others haven't." Each word, each truth tore her apart inside and solidified her resolve. "Because I understand that, I…I can't be what you need."

A tic started in the corner of his eye. "Is this a morning-after kiss-off?"

"No, not at all…just a wake-up." She squeezed his hands. "We both helped each other through a difficult year and now it's time to move on."

"That's bull." The tic increased.

"Don't make this even more awkward." She tugged her hands from his. "Last night was a beautiful tribute to the friendship we shared this past year, but that's all it can be."

His face closed off from her, freezing until even the tic couldn't push through.

"Fine then. You don't have to worry about me making things 'awkward' anymore." He rose slowly, backing away. "I'm going to take the dogs for a walk. Then I'll drive you home once you're dressed."

She watched his broad shoulders as he left, heard him call for the dogs, and already she missed him. But she had to hold strong for him. She refused to be another person who would let him down.

And she damn sure wouldn't let another man try to stay with her out of obligation.

BRODY GAVE LEAH a week to calm down.

He gave himself a week to get past the pain of having been turned down flat.

As he parked his truck in front of her shop, he willed his heart to pump at a normal pace. The pain wasn't gone, but it had finally dulled enough for him to realize he'd moved too fast. He'd been a dumb ass in pushing her out of some knee-jerk reaction to his father's call. He'd rushed her out of a need to hold tight to the happiness he'd found in Leah's arms. Because if he'd learned anything as a kid? He'd figured out fast happiness was kind of like food in the fridge.

There wasn't much to go around and it spoiled fast.

But Leah wasn't that way, and he should have known that from the start. He shouldn't have let past garbage cloud his view of the present. Of the amazing gift that had landed in his life.

Leah.

He needed to back up and do this right. She deserved to be romanced. Not rushed.

He hooked the leash to Penny's collar and stepped out of his truck, his eyes locked on the front door to Three Pups and a Pony. He thought about how she'd always wanted a pony. She would probably enjoy horse-back riding.

If he hadn't been such a dimwitted jerk, he would

have thought about that right away rather than having the idea come to him halfway through his week of self-imposed seclusion. He refused to think the chance with Leah had been lost.

Leash in one hand and bag for Leah hooked in his other, he pushed through the shop door, bells jingling. The shop was bustling with customers, something he was beginning to realize was the norm here. Her mother was behind the cash register ringing up an order for a guy holding a Pomeranian under each arm. Kay waved and pointed toward the back of the shop, shooting Brody a wink as he walked by.

He found Leah in the kitchen, pounding the hell out of a mound of brown dough. Love for this complex, steely-sexy woman filled him. He knew the feeling wouldn't fade and intended to wait however long she needed.

He gave himself a moment to just look at Leah, the woman who'd absolutely stolen his heart. Her honey-gold hair was tugged back in a high ponytail, leaving her neck and flushed cheeks exposed, making him ache to kiss her. Her canvas apron covered curves he now knew fully, every luscious inch stamped indelibly in his memory.

Monty nudged her elbow. She looked up sharply, her eyes colliding with his. A flash of joy shone before she quickly masked it. "Brody?"

"I hope you're not imagining the dough is my head."

She wiped her hands on the apron. "What are you doing here?"

"You wouldn't return my calls." He stepped into the kitchen, pulling the door closed behind him to give them privacy.

And she didn't object.

"You only phoned twice. And it was this morning."

Ah, he saw some frustration in her face. Good. He unhooked Penny's leash and let her walk over to Monty. "I thought you needed space. I didn't want to be a stalker."

"You're hardly that."

He reached into the bag and pulled out a bouquet of wildflowers. "I brought you flowers." He set them in front of her with a flourish. "And candy." He placed a box of truffles by the flowers. "And a pony."

"A pony?"

He set a purple My Little Pony on the counter with the rest of his offerings. "I would have brought you the real deal, but I didn't want to go overboard. This, the flowers, all of it is a symbol, though."

Her fingers gravitated to the curling mane on the toy horse. "A symbol for what?"

"My intent to romance you and take my time." He stroked the top of her hand lightly, taking heart when she didn't pull away. "Yes, we got to know each other in those conversations, but I didn't have the opportunity to give you a first, second, third and thirtieth date. You deserve the romance, to feel adored."

And God knew, he did adore this woman.

Her fingers fisted around the purple pony. "What about the things I said on the boat? What if those thirty dates aren't everything you expected?"

He'd been so mesmerized by her strength, he'd overlooked her own vulnerabilities. He was the one who'd failed here. She'd been right about him idealizing things. Now he needed to be real. For her. For them.

Lifting her hand, he risked a kiss on her wrist. "Our

time on the boat was pretty damn amazing—and I don't just mean the hot tub. Fishing. Dinner. Being with you is everything." He squeezed her hand. "Except, wait, I'm rushing you again. So let me back up. I want more dinners. A movie. Horseback riding for real. Can we do that?"

"Horseback riding?" She sat up straighter, her eyes lighting with unmistakable excitement.

"I spoke with the shelter director—Tasha—the lady who helped with Penny. She told me they have some horses in their care now. They need volunteers to work with them, the same way volunteers help with the dogs. I told her to count me in." And he had to admit, he was stoked about the notion.

"You're fostering a horse? Where?"

"Tough to do on a houseboat." Right now probably wasn't the time to tell her he'd started house shopping. That fell into the category of pressuring her. "But they need help at the shelter, too. I thought we could go riding after you get off work. Unless there's something you would rather do."

"What if it turns out my body doesn't cooperate with horseback riding?" Her eyes filled with tears. "And in case you're wondering, the pony thing is becoming a metaphor. What if I fail at a real relationship? It's so much easier to dream about something. Dreams stay perfect."

Damn, she was so special she was breaking his heart. "I don't want perfection."

"You deserve perfection." She reached up to cup his face in her hands.

"So do you." He skimmed her hair back with his

knuckles. "But I'm afraid you're stuck with me, and I'm far from perfect."

She swayed toward him and that was all the encouragement he needed. He scooped her up into his arms and shifted them both into a chair at the table, Leah in his lap. She looped her arms around his neck and leaned right into the kiss he knew couldn't go too far with a store full of customers.

She nipped his bottom lip. "I think you're amazing."

"Then why are you dumping me?"

"You really want to try this?" She threaded her fingers through his hair. "With me?"

"Yes, Leah, I really do. You are without question the most amazing woman I have ever met. I've been waiting my whole life to meet someone like you. After the way I grew up, I do not take for granted how rare, how special it is to find a person as genuinely good as you."

"Wow," her eyes filled with tears again, "that was… beautiful."

"I meant it."

"And what you said on the boat, the part about having fallen for me, about wanting to get married?"

"I'm not going to apologize for saying that, only for saying it too soon. But hey, my lips are sealed on the subject of love and marriage until you're ready."

"What if I were to unseal your lips? What if I were to kiss you, tell you I love you too, and then kiss you again…." She wriggled closer, her breasts pressing against his chest. "Could you be persuaded to tell me how much you love me? Could we make some plans for the future?"

"I believe you could convince me to do just about anything."

She inched back, but only far enough to pull off her apron. "What do you say we leave, so we can get started on that date and put your theory to the test?"

"I say yes." Standing, he held Leah in his arms, their dogs at his side.

God, it was good to finally be home.

* * * * *

USA Today bestselling author and RITA Award-winner **CATHERINE MANN** lives in the Florida panhandle with her flyboy husband, their four children, three dogs and one cat (who thinks he's a dog). The Mann family has fostered more than fifty puppies and special-needs dogs for their local Humane Society, where Catherine serves on the board of directors. For more information on Catherine Mann, her work and her adventures in pet fostering, she can be found online at:

Website: http://catherinemann.com

Facebook:

http://www.facebook.com/CatherineMannAuthor

Twitter: http://twitter.com/#!/CatherineMann1

And look for the latest in Catherine's edgy Alpha Brotherhood series, *Playing for Keeps*, coming soon from Harlequin Desire!

MANE HAVEN

Jules Bennett

CHAPTER ONE

THERE WAS NO way this place would be cleaned up before Mr. High and Mighty arrived. Of course, if the farm weren't in tip-top shape, perhaps he'd decide that there was too much work to be put into such a rundown house in a small, no-name town, even if the stables were halfway decent. She could only pray he would take a slight glance and, repulsed at what he saw, head off to any other town, to flip those old, glamorous homes she'd seen featured in magazines.

But that was a long shot, and Allison Barrett had no right to think any of this place was hers. And that's what hurt the most. When Charlie Wymer had passed on only a month ago, he'd not left the "estate," such as it was, to her as she'd hoped, dreamed. He'd left it to his only living relative, Mr. Jake Anderson.

And Jake was due any day to see about fixing up the house, putting it on the market, selling it off and going back to his big life of making money and renovating homes just to make a profit, and to hell with everyone else.

Allison jammed her pitchfork into another pile of hay, trying to clean out all the manure. As she flung it over her shoulder, a burst of laughter escaped, echoing in the stable. She'd love to see Charlie's nephew try mucking a stall, just once. The image brought a bright light onto her dim mood. She doubted he even knew the difference between a quarter horse and a Thoroughbred, a colt or a filly.

Tears pricked her eyes as she thought of the horses that she and Charlie had rescued over the years. Any money they'd received from donations had gone to keeping the animals safe and fed and nursed back to health. Unfortunately, not all of them made it. The loss never got any easier; if anything, the guilt of not being able to save the animal wedged deeper into her heart each time.

Allison shoved the pitchfork back into the pile and gave another fling over her shoulder.

"What the hell?"

Allison jerked around, shocked at the stranger standing just feet behind her. She'd been so caught up in her fantasy of a big-city hotshot flinging crap, she'd completely blocked out reality and obviously hadn't heard anyone sneak up.

Though by the looks of the man standing just feet from her, this had to be the long-lost nephew. The snazzy jeans, sans rips and tears, the shiny black loafers and a long-sleeved, tight black tee that hugged wide shoulders and well-defined biceps made it pretty obvious.

Even if she hadn't seen his pic plastered over every home-improvement magazine, she'd know this man was certainly not from Langston, North Carolina.

And while his choice of wardrobe made him stick out in these parts like a proverbial sore thumb, it was the pile of crap on his cheek and shoulder that drew her attention and had her smirking.

Southern hospitality at its finest.

His index finger made a swipe across his jaw, flinging a small, dark blob to the straw-covered concrete. "Tell me this isn't what I think it is."

"That depends on whether you think it's horse manure." She wanted to laugh, but didn't feel this was the appropriate time. Later, though. For now she'd take a mental picture so she could enjoy the amusing image once she was alone. "And you are?"

Though she already knew, she wanted to hear him say it.

"Jake Anderson." With careful movements, he tugged the tee from his jeans and, despite the chilling temps, pulled it over his head, careful not to smear any more across his face than necessary. Turning his shirt inside out, he wiped his face. "Is this how you treat all your guests?"

Oh, no. He did not just take his shirt off as if he didn't have a clue of the effect his perfect body had.

Great, now instead of laughing later at his stunned expression, she'd be fantasizing about how abs like that would feel under her fingertips.

If he was trying to distract her, it was working. But only for a moment. Seeing a man's chest had never before rendered her speechless; no need to let a spurt of immaturity overtake the moment. She had her head on straight, and if he wanted to fight dirty, she was game. "Only guests who threaten my home," she said with a sweet smile, leaning on her pitchfork. "There's a sink over in the corner if you'd like to wash the rest of manure off. I'm sure there's a spare shirt in the tack room."

He eyed her another minute as if he wanted to say more, and she had no doubt he did, but he kept his mouth shut and marched to the sink. Smart man.

Her hands and insides may have been shaking, but there was no way she was going down without a fight. This farm was the only thing that had saved her from a childhood of pain—a childhood nobody should ever have been subjected to—and she'd be damned if she would let an outsider take it away.

She went into the tack room, grabbed a spare shirt that belonged to Tucker, her only worker, and headed back out to her unwanted guest.

If Jake Anderson thought she'd pack her bags, and her horses, and leave without a word, he had another think coming. Her own father may not have taught her how to stand up for herself—he could barely stand up himself…literally—but Charlie had taught her that and so much more. She owed everything to the man who'd stepped up to rescue her when she'd needed it most. And choosing another path when life threw a fork in the road would certainly just be a slap in the face of his memory.

Allison clutched the old, plaid flannel shirt and kept her eye on Jake while he washed off. He draped his shirt over the edge of the sink, grabbed some paper towels and dried himself. Once he'd pitched the sheets into the trash, he stalked back. And yes, a man who looked that sexy, that predator-like, stalked. He probably turned on the charm, threw a dimpled smile—and yes, there were dimples, two of them—and thought he could have any woman do anything he suggested. Too bad she was immune to charm and dimples.

Well, she wanted to be immune to them. She could still appreciate the man's exterior, but that didn't mean she had to like the cold heart that lurked inside.

"I need to speak to the person who runs these stables now," he told her, settling his hands on narrow, denim-clad hips.

She thrust the shirt at him. "Here, put this on."

He shrugged into the shirt and, wouldn't you know, his magnificent pecs kept it from buttoning all the way up. Fan-flippin'-tastic.

Allison shoved a stray hair that had escaped her ponytail behind her ear. "You're here to sell, right? What exactly do you expect me to do with all the horses we're nursing back to health? What about the ones who are pending adoption or the dogs I've recently taken in? Where do you expect all of us to go?"

The litter of puppies had been abandoned in a box at the end of her long drive. People in this tiny town knew she was a sucker for strays…having practically been one herself.

Jake raised his eyes to the ceiling and sighed. "Can I just speak to the stable hand? I'll take up my business with him."

Allison smirked. She could so use this to her advantage, but she'd never been one for playing games. "There is no *him* in charge," she told him, swallowing the lump of remorse that crept up anytime she thought of Charlie. "Since your uncle passed, I'm the manager, stable hand, proprietor and anything else that falls under the umbrella of those titles. How can I help you?"

Jake stared at the raven-haired beauty with a chip on her shoulder. Oh, yeah, she knew exactly why he was here and she wasn't into playing games. Which was good, because he didn't have time for them either…and he'd lost his sense of humor somewhere back, about the same time his ex-wife had left with barely a note after depleting their joint bank account.

He offered her a smile anyway, knowing charm usually worked. "You have an obvious advantage over me, as it seems you know who I am."

Almost as if mocking him, she smirked. "The prodigal nephew? Yeah, I've heard all about you from Charlie."

She turned to finish working in the stall—mucking it, or whatever the hell that was called. Obviously she didn't have enough manners to supply her name. At least she'd offered a shirt, even if it was too small.

"And you are?" he asked, not bothering to hide the irritation in his tone.

"Allison," she said, as she continued to dig her pitchfork into the straw.

He stepped back, not wanting another manure episode.

"Unless you're here to offer condolences, which it's a little late for, I don't really want to hear what you have to say."

This bitterness obviously stemmed from fear, but Jake wasn't here to make friends. He'd come to his estranged uncle's farm to renovate and sell the place that had been willed to him, and quickly return home to Florida to get back to work on the set of condos he'd recently purchased. That was going to turn a big profit and make him a nice home right there on the beach in Miami. Now, that was a lifestyle he'd gladly run to.

"If you could turn around and talk to me, that would be helpful," he told her. "I apologize for the impression you have of me, but I assure you I'm not an ogre out to take advantage of you or your horses."

She spun around, planting her pitchfork firmly beside her. Jake had the sinking feeling she'd like to use that weapon of choice on him, but he wasn't one to scare easy, especially when facing a little sprite of a woman. But her temper was flaring—that much was evident. Whatever she had to say, he might as well let her, so he could move on with his plans.

"Let me ask you this." She rested one hand on her tool, one on her round hip. "Do you intend to sell this property?"

"Yes."

"Is there anything I can say or do to change your mind?"

"No."

Her eyes narrowed. "Then this conversation is over."

Before she could turn back around and ignore him, he reached for her arm and held her in place. "This farm is legally mine, so I'd think you would want to work with me on this."

Her eyes went from his hand on her arm to his face. "If I can't change your mind, how is it we're supposed to work together? Your uncle slaved over this farm for nearly two decades, and I started here fifteen years ago. We've built something here, and you think I'm just going to go along with you selling it? This is my life."

The hitch in her voice got to him.

"Listen, I think we got off on the wrong foot, and obviously you have the worst impression of me." He slid his hands in his pockets, trying to seem less intimidating. "I'm staying at the bed-and-breakfast off Route 4. Let me clean up and this evening we can talk. I can come back around six."

Those mesmerizing green eyes, still narrowed, held so much hurt and anger. "Fine, but you won't change my mind. Renovating and selling this place will never be okay with me."

"Who told you I would renovate it?" he asked, though the house itself was falling apart and in major need of some repairs, and those were indeed his exact plans.

"That's all Charlie talked about," she told him. "His amazing nephew who flipped houses. You were featured in two magazines and on TV once. I know all about what you do and why you're here. You have nothing personal invested in this farm, in these poor animals. So, are you gonna lie to my face and tell me you're not planning on gutting my home and turning it over for a profit?"

He'd never lied to a woman and he didn't intend to start now. "I'll see you at six."

CHAPTER TWO

"STUPID, STUPID."

Allison muttered under her breath at her pathetic attempt to straighten the house before Mr. House Flipper arrived. After vacuuming, fluffing the throw pillows on the couch and lighting a baked-apple candle, she looked around the open floor-plan of the old farmhouse and sighed. She didn't know why she wanted to make a good impression.

No, she did know why. She wanted him to see that someone lived here, someone cared for this place whether it was falling down or not.

She glanced at the pictures displayed on the mantel above the fireplace. So many of her with Charlie, of Charlie with horses, one of her riding the horse Charlie had given her when she'd come to work for him when she was only twelve. A tender age when her life could've gone down a number of paths, but Charlie had made sure she stayed on the one that would take her in the right direction—which was more credit than she could give her junkie father.

Biting her lip, as if that would hold the tears and anger at bay, Allison recalled how timid she'd been around the animals. When she'd realized they were hurting and abandoned just as she was, she'd known this farm was the exact place where she was needed.

Fate had landed her on the doorstep of Mane Haven, and she'd die before she let some long-lost relative fix it up, sell it off and profit from the fact that he'd turned away horses who needed medical care and love.

"What were you thinking?" she whispered to a picture of Charlie, his arm around a beautiful brown mare, taken just before she'd been adopted. "You had to have known this would happen."

And perhaps that was what stung the most. She'd have given anything for this land, the house and the stables to be willed to her. But he'd left her possession of eleven horses, his ten-year-old truck, the trailers used to haul the animals and a lump sum he'd saved in a bank account she'd known nothing about. The amount wasn't huge, but hopefully enough for a down payment if she ended up having to buy the house.

Unfortunately, if she was able to take out a loan, she'd also have to get a job outside the home, and work during the day when Tucker was available to stay at Mane Haven.

If she had her way, Jake would just go away and let her use the money for much-needed renovations, like the water heater, the buckled kitchen floor with chipped linoleum, the slight leak she'd recently discovered in her bedroom closet from the old roof. And that didn't count all the cosmetic things she'd like to do to the outside of the old farmhouse.

She was certainly thankful for all she'd been left, but more for the fact Charlie had taken her in when she'd had no one else who cared whether she received her next meal. She just couldn't believe Charlie would work twenty years building a reputable home for abused horses and then will it to a virtual stranger…family member or not.

Before she could travel too far down the path of worry and confusion, the front doorbell chimed.

And so did an idea in her head. If Jake wanted to fix up the house, then who was she to stop him? She'd actually hand him a to-do list and let him have at it. Then she'd pray the money she had in the bank would indeed cover the cost of a down payment.

Allison ran a hand through her hair, cursing herself for not pulling it up and out of her way after her shower. She crossed the living area and turned the squeaky knob on the old mahogany door, a little more eager to get this meeting started than she had been a few moments ago.

"Mr. Anderson," she greeted. "Come on in."

"Here's your shirt. Thanks."

She took the shirt he'd borrowed earlier, knowing she'd never get that image out of her head. Flannel had never looked so good.

He stepped over the worn threshold. "Call me Jake."

But that would imply something more personal, and she intended to keep this all business. He would fix her house, she would buy it and they'd go their separate ways, living happily ever after…or however that warped fairy tale went.

She set the shirt in the basket on the staircase and gestured toward the old floral sofa in the center of the open living area. "Please, have a seat."

Jake moved past he, and the scent he left in his path was hypnotic. He'd donned a dark gray, long-sleeved tee that did amazing things to his ripped muscles.

If he was trying to appeal to her as a woman, he was doing a good job, but she had to keep on track here. This house, the horses, they were her life. Her home. She'd never felt secure anywhere until she'd come here. She couldn't afford to lose the only real home she'd ever known. And Jake was going to make it livable again.

"Let me start by saying that the fact Charlie left this farm to me is quite a shock." Jake sat on the edge of the sofa, elbows resting on his knees. "I met him years ago when I was maybe five. He and my mother had a falling-out. The fault, she admitted, was her own and they never rekindled their relationship. I know Charlie was a good man, but he was still an uncle I knew very little about. I regret that now."

Allison sat on the other end of the couch. She had no intention of interrupting Jake. Who knew what she could find out about this family? Charlie had always been so tight-lipped about his sister, Jake's mother. But he'd always mailed Jake letters, Christmas presents, only to have everything go unanswered.

"My mother passed away three years ago," Jake went on. "She rarely mentioned Charlie, and I know it was because she was ashamed of the way she'd shut him out of her life so long ago. She wouldn't forgive herself. She had a tendency to ignore problems instead of facing them head-on. Confrontation certainly wasn't her strong suit."

Total opposite of her brother Charlie, Allison thought.

She cleared her throat, because talking about Charlie in the past tense still caused that ache to spread through her. She still expected him to burst through the back door, swiping the damp sweat from his wrinkled forehead with the old red bandanna that could always be found dangling from his back pocket. She longed to hear that robust laugh he was known for resonate through the old, two-story house. She wished she could have just one more of so many things. A smile, a pat on her shoulder, a kind word. Anything.

"Old family business is none of my concern, and there's three sides to every story—his side, her side and the truth." She turned to look Jake in the eye, intent on keeping her depressing thoughts from slipping into this conversation and taking control of her emotions. "And you're not the only one in shock from the will."

He held her gaze as an uncomfortable silence settled into the room. She didn't want him here. Didn't want him looking at past memories and trying to find a place where he could fit in with Charlie or this farm.

No, there was nothing here for Jake other than the repairs. Unfortunately, he didn't agree and probably already saw dollar signs. That was all well and good, so long as he accepted her offer when all was said and done. She refused to allow this property to be sold to some hoity-toity rancher with prize-winning purebreds.

And Allison would do everything in her power to keep this house, this farm and, most important, these animals from getting into the wrong hands.

She sighed, resigned to the fact she'd have to at least make some sort of friendship with this guy. That whole "keep your enemies closer" quote kept resounding through her head. Besides, if she played her cards right, turned on charm of her own, perhaps he'd have a soft spot when it came time to sell.

On a sigh, she attempted to smooth her hair back off her face. "Listen—"

"Miss Barrett." Tucker, their part-time worker and the only employee they had left on the farm, other than the on-call vet, stood just inside the back door to the kitchen, off the living room. "You may want to come to the barn. I think Jezabel is in labor. She's pacing all over the place."

Allison ran past Jake and Tucker. Many horses on the farm had been in labor, but this particular horse was her baby. Jezabel had come to Mane Haven already pregnant and malnourished, but Allison had seen the scars on her and knew she'd been abused as well.

Just the thought, the image, made Allison sick to her stomach. But at least Jez was safe now and hopefully would birth a healthy foal. Allison had prayed for months that Jezabel wasn't too malnourished at the start of her pregnancy to provide enough nutrients to her baby.

"Did you call Doc Warner?" she called over her shoulder, knowing Tucker would be right on her heels.

"I did," Tuck confirmed. "He'll be here as soon as he can. He was giving shots over at the Millers' farm."

Allison had been around enough births to know that this could take a while, but still, she wanted to be with Jezabel. The poor horse, like all the others, had never known love until coming to Mane Haven. In a sense, all these amazing animals were her family—especially with Charlie gone.

A shrink would so have a field day with her thought process.

Allison reached the stables and moved to the stall where Jez now lay on her side. Those large chocolate eyes staring, as if asking why this was happening. The miracle of life was a beautiful thing, but Allison hated seeing any animal in pain. And even though she'd known this moment was coming—all the signs had been there—she was scared to death of how the foal would come out. Surely Jez had been here long enough for Allison to have nursed her, and in turn the foal, to health.

"Let's see if we can dim some of these lights," Allison told Tucker.

"Why?" Jake asked.

Allison threw a glance over her shoulder, crouched down to Jez. "You still here?"

"I'm not leaving."

He stood with his arms crossed over his chest as if daring her to say otherwise.

On a sigh, she turned back to the mare and stroked her mane. "We dim the lights during the birth because most horses don't like the bright lights. They need to be relaxed as possible. She's stopped pacing, so hopefully this process will go quick and soon we'll have a healthy foal and a happy mommy."

The lights dimmed, leaving only a soft glow from the back of the stall and the sunset streaming through the open stable. She couldn't concentrate on entertaining Mr. Big City; all she cared about was her mare and the unborn foal.

"Might as well go back to your B and B." She didn't turn to look at Jake this time—he'd know she was talking to him. "This takes hours and will probably last well into the night. We can talk tomorrow."

Footsteps shuffled over hay and concrete. "I'm staying," he repeated in a low, powerful tone.

Shivers crept up her spine and she didn't take the time to consider why. She didn't have the energy to deal with him right now, and keeping Jezabel as comfortable as possible was her top priority.

"Um…Miss Barrett," Tucker said. "I'll just go out front and wait on the doc."

Jake squatted down beside her. "What can I do?" he asked.

Get out of her personal space? Stop clouding her judgment with that intoxicating cologne that made her want to inch closer and inhale a good breath of man, and remember she was a healthy, young, single woman? Let her have her farm, her life the way she'd always wanted? Fix up her house and out of the goodness of his heart just give it back to her?

The requests were endless and utterly selfish on her part.

"Seriously, go back to your room." She dared glance over, knowing she'd see a handsome man completely out of his element here in the dirty, smelly stable where she felt so at home. "This can be scary to see for the first time, not to mention very, very messy."

Jake studied the woman who obviously cared so much about these animals, this farm. There was no denying Mane Haven was her life. In their two brief meetings, he could see the compassion, the determination rolling off her. But the dark circles beneath her eyes, the old, worn jeans and tattered flannel shirt she wore indicated she also put everything and everyone's needs above her own. He had serious doubts that she could afford to purchase the house, but he really needed to find a way to make this work. He had a man who wanted first look at it, but that didn't mean he had to sell it to him. Allison belonged here.

He'd never let his heart guide him on a business venture before, so why was he letting it overtake his plans now?

"I don't scare easily," he told her, holding her gaze.

She quirked a brow. "Neither do I."

A smile formed before he could stop it. How could he not admire a woman who fought for what she wanted? And there was no way he was leaving now. Especially since this was his property. He wanted to stay and see what his uncle had left him.

And he was starting to get a better understanding of why Charlie had left him the farm. Allison needed someone. Whether she wanted to admit it or not, she couldn't do this on her own. Best keep that thought to himself.

"Let's put our differences aside while you tell me what I can do to help," he told her.

"There's nothing any of us can really do," she replied, stroking the mare's shiny chestnut coat. "It's always best to let the mother deliver on her own, but I want the vet here because of Jezabel's history."

Jake eased a little closer, still unsure how his presence would be perceived…by Allison or the mare.

"How did she come to live here?" he asked, suddenly more curious than he had been this morning.

Perhaps it was the atmosphere, perhaps it was the fact that this property was all his now, or perhaps it had something to do with digging deeper to discover the woman behind the hurting eyes and caring ways with the animals. All he knew was that he wanted to know more…about everything.

"She's a Standardbred."

Jake wasn't even going to pretend he knew types of horses or anything about caring for them. But what he did want was to hear Allison talk about Jezabel. When she spoke of the animals, her eyes softened, a hint of a smile formed on her unpainted lips, and the gentle tone of her voice stirred something deep within him.

"Forgive my lack of knowledge," he told her. "Tell me about Standardbred horses."

He wanted to keep her distracted, keep her focused on something other than her obvious fear for the unborn foal.

"A Standardbred horse mostly does harness racing. Jez wasn't winning, she wasn't bringing in enough money, and she was sold. Unfortunately, she was sold to a farm that has since been shut down for neglect and cruelty to animals."

Even though Jake didn't know much about horses, he couldn't imagine the mind-set of any human being neglecting a helpless animal simply because they weren't bringing in a paycheck. What kind of sick person thought like that?

As he glanced around to the other horses in their stalls, he had a sinking feeling he wasn't going to like any backstory he heard about the vulnerable animals. He also figured he wouldn't like Allison's backstory, if he ever got that out of her.

"By the time we got her, she was pregnant, malnourished, and I instantly fell in love." Allison turned to face him once again, unshed tears shimmering in her eyes. "I fall in love with all of them, but she just touched my heart."

Allison laughed, swiping at her damp cheeks with her palms. "And I have no idea why I just told you all of that."

To be honest, he didn't either, considering he'd asked about the breed of the horse, but now that he'd gotten another glimpse inside Allison Barrett, he was all the more intrigued by her own past. He didn't need a PhD in psychology to know she had just as dark a history as these neglected horses. And that unspoken truth hit him in the gut and squeezed his heart more than he liked.

"I've been told I'm pretty easy to talk to," he replied, reaching over to stroke the mare's silky coat. "So what's your story?"

Those watery eyes turned to slits. "Are you going to fix this place up and sell it?"

"Yes."

"Then my story is irrelevant to you."

The steel behind her words was obviously the material she used in her line of defense. How many times had she had to erect that instant wall? She didn't want to let an outsider into her world, that much was obvious. But if he'd come here under different conditions, would she be so cold? Jake knew her bitterness stemmed from fear—most anger did— but how could she already hate him so, when none of this was technically his fault?

He certainly hadn't wanted to take time from his remodeling of the condo in Florida to come to some small farm-town that was barely a speck on the map, just to discover a job he thought would be a cakewalk was going to be, in fact, months of work.

He should know by now, in his line of work, things were never what they seemed on the outside. There were always layers and layers of wear and tear. And in that aspect, he'd learned the houses he fixed up were much like people. If everything was loved and cared for in the proper way, it could thrive for years.

Unfortunately, his ex-wife hadn't received that memo on life.

But that was the distant past and he was here now,

and there was a two-story, old farmhouse in desperate need of some major cosmetic renovations. Unfortunately, he had no doubt the interior had more problems than just peeling wallpaper. Hopefully Allison would let him have a thorough walk-through to make notes and see for himself exactly what he was dealing with.

"Doc just pulled in," Tucker called from the stable doors.

Allison simply nodded, not taking her eyes off the mare.

Jake didn't want to make Allison angrier, so he stood off to the side when the vet came in. He'd wait out here as long as she did. What else did he have to do? Besides, now that he knew the horse's history, he wanted to see just how the foal would turn out.

And Jake had a sinking feeling that, if he stuck around too long, he'd get pulled deeper and deeper into this world he knew nothing about. But knowing nothing and feeling nothing were two completely separate things.

CHAPTER THREE

AFTER ONLY A few hours of sleep, Allison threw on her heavy flannel coat, shoved her socked feet into her rubber boots and made her way out to the stables. The grass was slick with heavy frost, and the low fog settled over the acres of land.

She breathed in the crisp morning air and smiled. Sunday was her favorite day of the week. Since Tucker mostly volunteered his time, Allison insisted he take Sundays off to spend with his family. On Sunday she had the entire day alone with her horses. Most people would think she had no life, the way she spent every waking moment in a stable talking, exercising and grooming the once-neglected animals. She didn't really care what people thought of her—they hadn't walked in her shoes for even one step, so what did they know?

Life was so much more than appearances, flashy lifestyles and one-upping so-called friends. Superficial people had never meant much to Allison. Perhaps that's why she found herself alone again. Other than Charlie, she'd yet to find someone to give her unconditional love.

Love. Allison knew, better than most people, that love mattered more than anything. If there was love, the stability, trust and compassion followed. Unfortunately, love had been missing from not only her life, but the lives of the eleven, now twelve, horses she owned.

After she let the five bundles of fur out of the tack room so they could roam free and get their puppy energy spent, she moved to the stall where Jezabel and her new foal lay. The bond of a mother and child always made Allison's heart clench. If only her own mother had lived, perhaps her life would've turned out different. The few pictures she owned of her mother showed how much the woman had loved Allison. The love was evident in her eyes and in the hugs captured on film.

"Hey, sweetheart." Allison stroked the mare's nose, laughing as Jez nudged her hand when she stopped. "I know, I know. You're in need of some extra lovin' today. You had a big night."

It wasn't until Doc Warner reassured her that the foal was perfectly fine that Allison had allowed herself to go in to bed, but she'd only slept about three hours. She had to see for herself that Charlie was okay.

And she hadn't even needed to think twice for a name when the foal had come out a male.

"I thought I'd find you here."

Allison whipped her head around to see Jake standing in the open doorway that led to the stable. The rising sun breaking through the fog sent an angelic glow all around him. Ironic, considering she certainly didn't feel that he was a saint.

The puppies were jumping around him, trying to get his attention. He squatted down, rubbing the tops of each of their little heads.

"What are you doing here?" she asked, coming to her feet, brushing the hay from her jeans and resisting the urge to fiddle with the messy hair she'd haphazardly pulled into a topknot.

Since when did she worry over her appearance in the stable?

Jake stood, too, and moved on into the stable, making her aware that once again they were alone, and once again she couldn't deny that this man was beyond attractive. Why couldn't Charlie have had a nephew who was an obese slob—or better yet, a niece? Another woman would've certainly been easier to handle.

"I had a feeling you'd want to be near the baby horse—"

"Foal," she interrupted.

"Sorry." He grinned, shoving his hands in his pockets. "Still not sure on the lingo to use around here. Anyway, I wanted to come by when I was positive we wouldn't be interrupted."

Fear slid through her, gripping her heart. Was he going to tell her the potential buyer had decided to purchase without seeing the property? Was he going to tell her that she needed to start packing and finding homes for the animals sooner rather than later?

She needed to be strong. She certainly hadn't conquered her past only to fall on her face when she was just getting everything she'd ever wanted.

"Actually, Tucker is off today, so we're alone," she told him.

"Perfect, because I have a lot to discuss." He turned and started to head toward the door. "Let's go inside the house and talk."

Allison stared at his retreating back. Seriously? He was just going to come here, order her around and expect her to follow?

A burst of laughter spilled out and Allison sank back down to her knees next to Jezabel. If he wanted to go on into the house, more power to him. The place was his anyway, so it wasn't like she could stop him, but she certainly wasn't going to jump at his command. Oh, she had no doubt many women did just that when those dimples and sparkly grin were flashed, but Allison liked to think she wasn't that shallow.

"I think I'll just stay right here," she said in defiance, holding out a sugar cube for Jezabel.

Jake Anderson may think he was running the show since he'd discovered his inheritance, but Allison was not going down without a fight. She only hoped that it wouldn't get ugly and she wouldn't cave and become a crying, blubbering mess when she had to face reality and leave. Confrontation had never been her strong suit, but she refused to give up everything she loved, everything she'd ever known.

JAKE STARED OUT the wide kitchen window toward the stables, not a bit surprised that the defiant, lovely Miss Barrett kept him waiting. He admired the fact that she wasn't some wilting flower that shriveled up at the first sign of cold weather.

As he glanced around the kitchen, he took a number of mental notes on all the repairs that needed to be done. The ceiling had dark spots from water, but he already knew the shingles were falling off and needed replacing. Since the kitchen jutted out from the rest of the house, there was no second floor over it. He assumed the second-story bedrooms also had dark spots, but he highly doubted Allison would care for him traipsing through the house uninvited…especially into her bedroom. He'd quickly deduced she was a private person.

Jake used his time alone to get a closer look at what

he would need to do before he could actually start on the cosmetic side of sprucing up this old farmhouse.

It didn't take long to see that the rusty old pipes beneath the kitchen sink would also need to be replaced. And more than likely the entire kitchen would have to be gutted, because he had no doubt there were mold and mildew beneath the cracked linoleum.

"What are you doing?"

Jake eased his head out of the cabinet, rose to his full height and smiled. "Just checking out the plumbing."

Allison's anger radiated from her as she stood in the doorway, hands on her rounded hips. The screen slammed as she stepped further into the room.

"And is that what you plan on starting with?" she asked.

Part of Jake wanted to rise to his reputation for not backing down in getting what he wanted. But the side that was captivated by this intriguing woman had him closing the gap between them. Fiery passion in women never failed to turn him on, but his emotions had sure picked a hell of a time to come to the surface.

"I'm not the enemy, Allison." He stepped close enough, forcing her to tilt her head back to look him in the eye. "I have an obligation."

Her eyes held his as moisture gathered in them. Damn. He certainly didn't want to upset her, and normally tears did nothing to his hardened heart, thanks to his ex, but something about Allison's did. He just had a bad feeling this woman had shed too many over the years.

"And what is that obligation?" she asked. "Make the only home I've ever known something grand and flawless and sell it to the highest bidder? Did you ever think that not everything can be saved, can be made new again?"

Jake studied her face, the defiant tilt of her chin, the unshed tears. He took a slight step back, not wanting to be the overbearing, intimidating man she seemed to think he was.

"Who hurt you, Allison?" he whispered.

When she only stared, he reached a hand toward her cheek, but she jerked away from his touch.

"This is not about me," she told him, turning her back completely to him. "This is about the horses who count on me to keep them safe, to find them a loving home. I can't do that if I'm forced to move."

Jake ran a hand through his hair, frustrated that he couldn't get her to open up. But there was one person she had obviously trusted.

"Did Charlie know your history?" he asked. "Did he know this pain you keep hidden inside?"

Allison turned once again to face him, her eyes red, her cheeks tear-tracked. "He knew everything about me."

"I don't see why we can't work together on this."

The corners of her mouth tipped slightly into a hint of a smile. "Work together? Really? Well, in that case, I have an entire list of things that need done around here."

She skirted around him and gave a tug on what appeared to be a junk drawer. Pulling out a folded paper, she handed it to him.

"Every time something went wrong, I wrote it down," she told him. "There should be enough work there to keep you busy for months."

She was certainly eager to let him help now. Interesting. Perhaps she just wanted to keep him busy for a while until she could figure out a game plan, or perhaps she had some ulterior motive.

No matter what the lovely Miss Allison was thinking, or plotting, this place was his and he intended on fixing it up whether she agreed or not.

He glanced down at the list, and indeed there were plenty of projects listed, but most of them were minor. The largest projects were the roof and the kitchen.

How had Charlie let this house fall into such a shambles?

"I have some money to fix the house, but it's not near enough to do what all needs done. I was going to replace the roof in a couple months when it gets a bit warmer."

The roof needed replacing now, but he'd take care of that and keep his thoughts to himself. He also wasn't taking her money for the repairs.

After reviewing the list, he glanced up to see her biting her bottom lip. Nerves were obviously getting to her. Well, if he were in her shoes, he'd be nervous and a bit scared, too. And for some reason he decided to open his mouth before thinking things through.

"I'd like you to help me," he blurted out.

He hadn't planned on this, had never taken on another person while doing renovations, but he realized she needed to be close to this project. She needed the closure in case she ended up having to move, and perhaps he needed to prove to her that he wasn't the bad guy, that he could be on her side.

"I want you to help me make the changes," he told her, amused when her eyes widened and she took a step back as if in shock. "You know this place better than anyone, and I'd like a woman's touch."

"You've got to be out of your ever-lovin' mind." She

propped her hands on her denim-clad hips once more. "Do you honestly think I'd help pick out things for my house, a house I love, just so you can sell it?"

"I want you to be happy with the changes I'm going to make."

He would never understand how an idea could sound great to a guy and totally anger a woman. Just one of the little mysteries of life. And if this were a cartoon, Allison would have the whistle above her head with steam erupting from it.

"I'll never be happy with this entire situation," she all but yelled, throwing her arms wide. "I've just learned this house is no longer my home, and I have twelve horses that will need to find homes. That's thirteen beings you're putting out just so you can make a buck off a man you never even knew."

"Then what do you suggest I do?" he asked, mimicking her move by placing his own hands on his hips. "You're more than welcome to make an offer, but I should warn you, the man I have interested in the property has made a sizable offer."

Allison took another step back, bumping into the cheap, crackled countertop. "You're serious? He hasn't even seen the place."

Jake knew he should've kept that part to himself. He really was trying to find a way to let Allison keep the house.

"I haven't agreed to anything," Jake repeated. "He wants to take a look at the place when I finish."

Allison shoved a wayward curl from her forehead and nodded. "Well, then you better get to work."

She turned on her booted heel and walked out the

back door. She eased the screen door back in place, as opposed to letting it slam the way a person who was mad would do. Which only proved to him she wasn't mad…she was hurt, and he'd done it to her.

Jake slammed his hand onto the splintered wood table and cursed. This was not the way he had planned to earn a living—making perfectly happy people find another place to stay.

No, his career stemmed from his wife walking out on him, leaving him with no money and little more than a shack. Luckily he was good with his hands and had fixed up the place and sold it. Thus had begun the cycle of buying and selling.

Unfortunately, he'd put Allison and her horses in a tough position, and he didn't blame her at all for the hatred she must be feeling for him right now.

He didn't want her out in the stables crying, but at the same time he also knew when to leave a woman alone with her thoughts.

What he could do was show her he had a softer side, a compassionate side. He needed her to know where he came from, then maybe she'd see he wasn't some big-city guy destined to ruin her life.

And maybe he could still find a way to let her stay here, but he'd keep that bit of information to himself for now. He didn't want to get her hopes up, in case it turned out he had to sell. He just had to see how much he had invested in the house. This was still business, and he had to make a wise investment.

But his heart, yet again, seemed to be guiding his choices. He had a feeling that, by the end of this renovation process, he'd just give the house, property and all, to her without asking for a dime.

If only she knew the power she already held over him.

CHAPTER FOUR

ALLISON POURED BOWLS of food for her new puppies and quickly stepped out of the way before the five fur babies tripped her.

She laughed as their tiny little bodies all wriggled into one bowl and totally ignored the others she'd put out.

Keeping them in the stables' tack room during the night seemed to be working out, but she so wanted to take them inside and cuddle with them. Charlie had always told her that dogs needed to be tough first, then you could spoil them rotten. She'd needed good dogs to keep outside, and when this litter had been dumped at the end of her drive, she'd known God himself had sent that box, answering her prayer.

As the dogs feasted on their morning chow, Allison turned to check on Jezabel and her foal when the slam of a car door caught her attention. She stepped out of the stables to see Jake getting something from the bed of his truck.

Mercy, but the man did look good in a pair of jeans. Oh, Lord, he was getting his tools. She didn't need to stand around and watch him strap the tool belt on; she had no doubt he looked just lovely in it as well.

And just because she was appreciating the scenery

didn't mean she was any happier about the inevitable outcome.

"Morning," she called to him. "You're here early."

With tool belt beautifully in place on his hips, Jake hoisted up his toolbox and sauntered over to her. "Thought I'd get started. I'll be inside working in your kitchen. I've got two guys coming tomorrow or the next day to help me get going on that roof. We're putting up metal because it will last longer than shingles."

"In the cold?"

With a one-shoulder shrug, he smiled. "It's either cold or hot. I'm used to both elements, and we want to get it replaced before all the spring rain comes."

She pulled her flannel coat tighter around her waist and crossed her arms. "Have you had breakfast? I made some biscuits this morning and there's some homemade jam."

"Is this a peace offering, or did you poison the jam?" he asked with a crooked grin.

Allison laughed. "I promise it's the same batch I just ate from. Come on inside and I'll get you some coffee to go with it."

Jake fell into step beside her, and Allison couldn't help but breathe in the crisp, cool morning air, combined with the clean scent of freshly showered man.

No, he wasn't the enemy, as he'd reminded her yesterday, but the situation still sucked. She'd tossed and turned all night thinking of all the reasons she should hate him, but couldn't really come up with one. This was his house now, and technically he could tell her to pack and be gone five minutes ago, but he'd asked for her help and never once told her when she'd have to leave.

Perhaps he was a gentleman and there was no reason for her to be rude. Besides, this was Charlie's last living relative, and because she respected and loved Charlie, she knew treating his nephew properly was the right thing to do.

Just as she reached for the screen door, Jake stepped around her and held it open for her.

"You made breakfast—I can at least get the door."

My, my. Chivalry certainly was alive and well and living in the fine body of Mr. Jake Anderson.

He set his toolbox in the corner near the basement door and moved over to the table, taking the tool belt off and laying it on an empty chair.

"Is there anything I can do?" he asked.

"Just have a seat."

The last man she'd fed in this kitchen had been Charlie. And while she'd been on dates and had a couple of boyfriends over the years, she'd never invited a man into this house. Jake's presence seemed to take over the spacious kitchen, but Allison kept busy and readied the coffee and a plate of biscuits in an attempt to keep her shaky hands occupied.

"Cute puppies, by the way," he told her as she placed the plate in front of him.

"Aren't they, though? They were dropped off a few weeks ago in a cardboard box at the end of the driveway." Allison slid the pot from the coffeemaker and poured a mug. "I'd been meaning to get a dog or two to keep outside, but these just literally landed in my lap."

When she reached across the old, scarred table and set the mug down, Jake grabbed her wrist. "Sit with me."

His strong yet gentle touch sent tremors, one chasing after the other, up her arm and through her body, instantly warming her from the late-winter chill.

She took a seat across from him and reached for a napkin from the holder, sliding it toward him.

"I've been thinking," she said, picking at the marred tabletop. "This is your house now, and you're paying for a room at the B and B. If anything, I should be there and you should be here."

He swallowed a bite, took a sip of coffee and eased back in the creaky wooden chair. "Do you honestly think I'm going to ask you to leave?"

"No, but I also don't think it's fair that you're paying for a place. There's a finished basement, with a bathroom, that you could stay in. There are also three other bedrooms upstairs. This house is huge, and it's just me."

"Are you inviting me to stay here while I work?" he asked.

When the words came from his mouth they sounded much sexier than when the initial thought had sprung into her head.

"Yes." She nodded. "It's the right thing to do."

"You don't know me." He sipped his coffee again. "Do you normally invite strangers into your home?"

"I moved in here when I was sixteen, and other than me and Charlie, no one has ever stayed here."

He studied her face, and suddenly Allison wished she could omit the last two minutes of conversation. To say the silence was uncomfortable and awkward was a vast understatement.

"I'll stay in the basement," he told her. "That way we won't bump into each other, except in the kitchen. Deal?"

A bit of relief settled over her. "Deal."

"I'll only go upstairs when I need to work, which won't be for a while." He came to his feet. "Which reminds me, I'm going to need to take a look around up there so I can get an idea of what needs done. I may see things that aren't on your list."

She rose, too, taking his empty plate and putting it in the sink. "Come on up now. Other than the small leak in my closet, there's not too much going on up there."

Once they were upstairs, she showed him to the bedrooms and stood in the doorway as he glanced over every nook and cranny. The windows, the ceilings, the spare bathroom.

"And this is my room." She gestured to the door at the end of the hall. "Don't mind all the clothes. I had to take everything out of the closet."

He moved to her walk-in closet and pulled the string overhead to light up the small space.

"Your ceiling is sagging in the corner," he told her. "That will have to be replaced. And let's hope there's no mold in there, but I wouldn't count on it."

Great. Just what she needed.

She leaned against the tall post at the end of her king-size canopy bed. "Just do what you need to do. I can sleep in another room if I need to."

He moved from the closet, clicking the light off and closing the door. "I'll let you know. Like I said, it won't be for a while."

Allison wrapped her hand around the post, the reality settling deep that she may not be able to cover the cost of the house with her account and a loan. This home had been her sanctuary, her own haven when she'd needed it most. How would she honor Charlie's memory if she couldn't keep this farm going?

"Hey." Jake stepped in front of her, bending slightly to look her in the eye. "You okay?"

"This is just a little overwhelming for me. I should warn you now, I'll have some of these moments." She rested her head against her hand on the pole. "I just miss Charlie. I miss knowing I have security and some stability in my life. He's the only person who ever provided that."

Jake couldn't stand the forlorn look on her face, the sadness lacing her voice. Without thinking, he cupped her cheek with his palm.

"It's normal to be upset, Allison. I don't expect you to think this situation is okay. Did Charlie ever mention that he was leaving the house to someone other than you?"

He didn't think he was imagining her nestling her face against his palm; he actually liked knowing she felt comfortable with him.

"He never discussed his will," she told him. "I had no idea this would happen until the will was read."

Jake smoothed the hair off her forehead and stroked a finger down her cheek. He had no right to keep touching her, but he couldn't force himself to move away.

"I figure he wanted to leave this place to you because he was always so impressed by your work. He'd boast about you being his nephew to his friends whenever he saw you in a magazine or on a home-improvement show. And I hate to admit it, but I think he still worried about me running the farm alone."

"How did you come to work for him and live here?" Jake asked.

Her eyes darted back up to his, a smile spreading across her delicate face. "He saved my life. The short story is my mother died suddenly when I was five, my father drank and used drugs like it was his job, and half the time he forgot he had a child to raise. He won a horse in a bet, and after we'd had it about a month, Charlie came around and offered to buy it from us."

Jake took Allison's hands, urging her to sit on the edge of the bed, then took a seat beside her.

"I was so upset the horse was leaving," she went on, fidgeting with her short, unpainted nails. "I knew there was no way we could care for it when we barely had enough food for ourselves. But Charlie promised I could come see the horse every day. He said he'd even come get me and bring me home afterwards."

Jake's heart warmed at this telling description of the man who was his uncle—a man obviously used to rescuing things.

"I thought he was just saying that. I mean, I'd heard so many broken promises in my life."

"How old were you when all this happened?" Jake asked.

"Twelve."

Again Jake took both her hands in his, squeezing for reassurance. "Go on."

"Basically, he made good on his promise and before I knew it, I was helping him on the farm every day after school. When I was sixteen, I ended up moving in with Charlie, because I was old enough to know my father was never going to do anything for me, and he didn't care that I was leaving so long as he kept getting my mother's social security check in my name. I never wanted the money, I wanted..."

"Love," Jake finished. "And Charlie provided that."

Allison smiled, looking him in the eye and nodding.

As glad as he was that she'd trusted him with this much, he sensed there was more to her story, the longer version, and he intended to uncover it.

"You're a remarkable woman, Allison."

She laughed, looking down to their joined hands. "I don't know about that, but I do what I need to in order to get by. I will say, I must've been a strong little girl to survive living with my father."

Jake loathed the man and he'd never even met him. How could anyone neglect a child, especially one's own?

"I'd love to learn about your horses," he told her, surprised that he meant it. "I don't know much, but I see they mean the world to you, and I'd like to know more."

She jerked her gaze back to his. "Really?"

That glimpse of happiness he saw in her eyes had him acting before he could even process what he was about to do.

He framed her face with his hands and tilted her head, just enough for his mouth to fit over hers. And when she melted against his chest, her fingers curled into his jacket, Jake knew he hadn't made a mistake in acting on his feelings.

Her soft sighs and gentle moan made him wish they could make use of this bed they were sitting on, but he had to be realistic. But Jake had a feeling she hadn't had many relationships and he didn't want to confuse her or let lust make a major decision that they may regret later. For her sake, and his, he needed to tread lightly so she wasn't hurt even more.

Not to mention, she'd probably had very little tenderness thrown her way by men other than Charlie. Jake knew Allison was special, and he intended to treat her accordingly.

Easing back, he smiled when it took her eyelids a moment to rise.

"Well," she said, leaning weakly against the post on her bed. "I would've shown you the horses without the kiss, but if you can kiss me that good, I'll let you ride one."

Jake laughed even as his heart clenched. Great, she was as vulnerable as a newborn kitten, had a sense of humor he admired and had forged a core of steel despite what life had thrown at her. He was in so much trouble.

CHAPTER FIVE

ALLISON COULDN'T BELIEVE the speed with which Jake worked. His two employees had come, replaced the roof and helped gut the kitchen. The subfloor was replaced, and Jake was currently working on the pipes. The two workers had already gone back to Florida—not that she could blame them—and she and Jake were alone once again.

And not one word had been mentioned of the kiss they'd shared in her bedroom a week ago. Nor had another kiss been attempted.

Even though he'd moved into her basement. She barely knew he was there. He'd remained true to his word of staying out of her way. But why? Most men would've so taken advantage of such an opportunity.

Had she been a bad kisser? Too much tongue? Not enough? Halitosis? Granted, she wasn't the most experienced woman, but she knew how to kiss. Or so she'd always thought.

As Allison led Max, the Arabian horse that was getting adopted this week, around the oval ring, she tried to stay focused on his exercise, but her thoughts kept drifting back to the gentle way Jake had touched her. He'd touched her, kissed her as if he actually…cared. The kiss they'd shared hadn't been just a stepping stone to sex, as most men might have assumed. He hadn't pressured her or made her uncomfortable.

As frustrated and irritated as she was, she couldn't fault him for being a pure gentleman. Damn him.

She led the gelding around for another loop, hating that she'd be saying goodbye, but thrilled that he was going to a good home. Adopting horses out was always bittersweet.

"Allison."

At Jake's voice, she turned. Unfortunately, just as she did so, Jake walked into the ring right behind Max and got a hoof straight to the abdomen.

With a grunt of pain, Jake doubled over, wrapping his arms around his waist.

"Jake!" Allison hooked Max's lead rope around the post on the ring and went to Jake. "Are you all right?"

He sucked in air and nodded. "Got…the…wind… knocked…out."

Allison wrapped an arm around his shoulders and guided him out of the ring and into the stables, where he could sit on an old wooden bench.

"You never learned the rule not to walk behind a horse, did you?" she asked, once he was seated and breathing without struggling for gulps of air.

"I've never been around horses in my life," he told her, rubbing his stomach. "Mercy, that mare packs a punch."

"That's not a mare," she told him. "Mares are female horses. That was a gelding, a male horse that's been neutered."

Jake smiled, looking her in the eye. "No wonder he's pissed off, then. He's horny."

When she laughed, he did too, only to stop short with a wince.

"Let me look," she offered, going toward the zipper on his jacket.

"I'm fine." He waved her hand away and took a deep breath. "See? I've got the air back in my lungs."

"That may be, but you probably have a hoof print on your abs, too. Can I check to see if you're okay?"

"I knew you wanted me out of my clothes," he joked with a wink. "All you had to do was ask."

Heat consumed her even though the temp outside was in the low fifties. The fact that he was joking with a pained smile on his face didn't lessen the fact that he was absolutely right. God help her, she did want him out of his clothes. Now what? It wasn't as if she was some sexy siren. She played with horses all day, wore flannels, tattered jeans and worn boots. Her hair mainly stayed in a knot on top of her head and she wore no makeup. Oh, yeah. She was quite the catch.

"Allison?"

She jerked her attention back to him, only to find that he wasn't smirking anymore and the heat that had spread through her now looked back at her from cobalt-blue eyes.

"Don't look at me like that," she murmured, going for the zipper once again.

His hands covered hers. "And how am I looking at you?"

Allison closed her eyes, not sure what to say, how to act. It had been so long since she'd been intimate with a man or even on a date, she was definitely out of her league here.

"Just let me look," she whispered.

"You can…just as soon as you look in my eyes."

She shifted her gaze to meet his and her breath caught. He'd inched his face closer, heavy-lidded eyes focused on her mouth.

"I'm fine," he told her. "Sore, but fine. I've been through worse."

Allison knew he'd have a huge mark and it would hurt for days, but a man like Jake would never complain, nor would he let it slow his pace in working on her house…his house.

She cleared her throat and looked around the stables. "Maybe we should go over some basics, since you're going to be here for a while, and if you need to talk to me during daylight hours, you'll most likely find me in here."

He rubbed his hand over his abs and laughed with the slightest hitch in his breath. "That might be a good idea."

A bit of nostalgia spread through her as she remembered when Charlie had led her through the stables to give her the do's and don'ts of horses, as well as to educate her on all the basics. The information had been so overwhelming at first, but now she didn't even have to think about how to groom or walk the animals. Everything was second nature.

She went over the boring basics of keeping the stalls clean, and how their environment needed to stay as sanitary as possible to keep the horses healthy.

"What's this big guy's name?" Jake asked, reaching out to rub the nose of a very affectionate horse.

Allison dipped into her pocket for a sugar cube and handed it to Jake. "Here, you'll be his best friend."

When Jake stretched the cube toward the horse's

mouth, Allison was pleased. Most people were reluctant around horses at first. The size could be intimidating.

"This is Sam," she told him, rubbing Sam's mane. "He's a Tennessee walking horse. He actually came to us along with Clyde and Annabelle." She turned to point to the two other Tennessee walking horses, in the next two stalls. "They were on a farm when the owner had to file bankruptcy. They weren't neglected, but a bit malnourished simply because the owner kept trying to hang on to his land without selling, but it just got to be too much for him. We were lucky to get these three at a small price."

Jake moved to the other stalls, and Allison found his questions on the horses and their history very comforting. He wasn't asking just to appease her. He genuinely wanted to know, and her heart swelled at the possibility that he might be growing to like this place more and more. Perhaps he wouldn't sell it.

One could always hope.

"Hey, I didn't think to ask." She turned to look at him as he hooked his arms over the wood stall gate. Their faces were close—too close for her to concentrate on rational thoughts. "Why were you coming to find me in the first place?"

He flashed those two dimples once again. And once again, there went her mind. Completely blank.

"I wanted to take you out to dinner."

Allison jerked back. "Dinner? But…why?"

Shaking his head, he laughed. "If you don't know, then I'm really doing this wrong."

"Doing what?"

"Asking you out. I was going to use the excuse that your kitchen is still torn up and you're probably tired of sandwiches and chips." He smoothed a wayward curl from her forehead, tucking it behind her ear. "But I can't lie to you. I'd like to take you out because you fascinate me and I want to get to know you."

Allison shot to her feet and went back outside to get Max. Once she'd led him back into his stall, she fed him a sugar cube and returned to the bench where Jake still waited for an answer. She didn't sit, didn't trust herself to.

"We can't go out," she told him. "Why would we? I mean, you're only here another month or two. It's not like anything could come of a date."

In that slow, panther-like way she'd come to appreciate from him, he got to his feet and closed the gap between them.

"Tell me you haven't thought about that kiss." He ran his hands up over her fleece jacket and settled them on her shoulders as he stepped in closer. "Tell me when you think of it, you don't start thinking beyond that kiss."

She looked him in the eye, knowing she could never lie to him. "I've thought of little else," she conceded.

"Good. I take comfort in knowing I wasn't alone with the fantasy."

Her heart lurched, her belly tingled and every part of her wanted him to kiss her again. Oh, please, just one more time, to see if it was just as magical, just as toe curling.

At the same time her heart soared with excitement, reality and common sense slapped her in the face.

"I'm not naive enough to believe that you're attracted to someone who smells like horses, someone whose dressiest outfit consists of jeans with no holes."

He ran a fingertip down her cheek. "Perhaps I'm attracted to the woman beneath all of that. And the fact that you aren't all made up, you're just...you, makes me even more attracted."

Jake stared into the eyes of the woman who'd seen more in her lifetime than she probably should've. And he had no doubt she was scarred so deep on the inside, she might never be able to let herself feel or love without hesitation and worry.

"I don't own lipstick," she blurted out. "I don't even own a nice dress."

He laughed, framing her face with his hands. "And you think a dress and makeup would make you more appealing?"

When she shrugged, Jake leaned down, capturing her lips once again in a brief, tender kiss.

"I'm not concerned with the wrapping on the package, Allison. Though I have to say, you are beautiful without being fake." He forced her to look at him before he continued. "I'm intrigued by the woman who's hell-bent on nurturing every animal back to health and making sure they have good homes. I'm fascinated by the woman who is so guarded around people that it's obvious she's scared to let anyone in. But most of all, I'm completely miserable because I haven't been able to get her out of my mind and I want more."

Jake couldn't believe he'd shared his feelings, but now that he had, he was relieved. Perhaps now that he'd shown her his vulnerable side, she'd be able to open up as well and not feel the need to keep her own feelings so close to her heart.

"I don't know what to say," she whispered. "No one has ever been intrigued by me before."

And that statement right there solidified his thoughts.

No one, other than Charlie, had ever put her first. No wonder she was always looking out for others. She'd never learned to take care of herself first.

"Call Tucker and see if he can come out for the rest of the day," Jake told her.

Allison blinked. "Actually, he'll be here soon. Why do you need him?"

"You're taking a break," he told her. "You're going inside, getting ready, and I'll be taking you to dinner. Tucker can handle grooming, exercising or whatever else needs doing, can't he?"

Allison tilted her head as if the idea were preposterous. "I can't go out to dinner, Jake. Sam is leaving in two days, and I want to make sure he's perfectly groomed before he leaves. Besides, I'm still watching over Charlie."

Jake dropped his hands. "You're making excuses. The foal is fine, the vet has reassured you every day since his birth, and Tucker is more than capable of doing anything you need for Sam. So, what else do you think is standing in your way of a nice evening out?"

As she worried her bottom lip with her teeth, Jake stood and waited. Yet again, fear guided her choices. He didn't want her to think too far ahead. Didn't want her to find more reasons not to let someone into her life.

The sound of tires crunching over gravel was literally music to his ears.

"Perfect," he said, moving toward the opening of the stable. "Sounds like your relief just arrived. Tell you what. You take an hour and work with Tucker and Sam while I go inside and work on the kitchen sink. Then I'll go shower myself and pick you up at five. Sound good?"

The look on her face was priceless, but he just steam-rolled right over her before she could speak.

"Great. I'll see you then."

He walked from the stable, stopping in front of Tucker.

"I'm taking Allison out for dinner. I assume you can do what needs to be done here without her?"

Tucker glanced over Jake's shoulder toward the stable, then back to Jake. "It's about time," Tucker proclaimed. "I've been telling that girl to go have some fun, and I'm glad a man's finally making her get off this farm. I'd be thrilled to take care of the animals."

As Jake went in the back door of the old farmhouse, he couldn't help but smile. At least one person was in his corner, and before the end of the night, Allison would see what she'd been missing.

Only thing he worried about was that he'd see what he'd been missing, too. How he could have gotten so far entangled in Allison's web of vulnerability was beyond him, but there it was. The cold, hard truth was that he was beyond smitten, or any other silly word. He was starting to really care for her, and he wanted to take this, whatever this was between them, to the next level. He wanted her to open up, to talk to him so he could understand what he was dealing with.

He realized he wanted to heal her, make her smile more and show her that love was the greatest feeling.

Strange for him even to consider that, when his own marriage had ended on such a sour note, but Allison was nothing at all like his ex.

And perhaps that's why he was so intrigued and fascinated by her. And why he was so determined to make her see that this chemistry they had sparking between them wasn't going away anytime soon.

CHAPTER SIX

"How's your stomach?" Allison asked, as they walked in the back door leading to the kitchen.

Jake held the screen door open and followed her in. "I'm stuffed from dinner, but if you're talking about the kick I took from Sam, I'll be fine."

When she flipped the kitchen light on, she stepped around the sawhorses set up in the middle of the room. Renovations may have been coming along fast, but the mess and inconvenience always made it seem longer.

She walked into the living room and hung her coat and purse on the hall tree in the foyer.

"Thanks for dinner," she told him, shaking her hair over her shoulders. "I'm glad you got me out of the house."

"Don't you mean dragged?" he joked, coming into the spacious room and taking a seat on the sofa.

"I wasn't dragged!" She laughed, taking a seat beside him. "I went of my own will. I'll admit there was some persuasion on your part, though."

Jake loved seeing her smile, loved watching that light sparkle in her eyes. If he had his say, he'd be seeing that beautiful face long after his work here was done. But no need to scare her. It was time to ease his way deeper into her life. Someone as fragile and vulnerable as Allison definitely required baby steps, though she'd probably throw horse crap at him again for suggesting such a thing.

She sank into the cushions and sighed. With her head tilted back and her eyes closed, she muttered, "I really should go check on the puppies."

Jake took in the sight of her. Though she'd put on a green sweater that did amazing things to the curves she'd kept hidden, and had donned a touch of makeup, she still looked physically exhausted.

"I'll go check on them. Wait right here and don't move."

He grabbed his coat and ran out the back door. Once he made sure the dogs were safe in the tack room for the night, complete with food and water in their bowls, he rubbed their little furry heads and closed the door. He even checked on the horses he'd come to love. Funny how just a month ago he'd known nothing about them, but now watching Allison work with them, care for them as if they were children, he found himself not so eager to return to Florida, where a condominium awaited him.

For a guy who'd loved the beach life, it was hard to believe that horses and a certain raven-haired beauty seemed so much more appealing.

His boots crunched over the gravel as he made his way back to the house. He assumed he'd find Allison asleep on the couch, but when he entered, he found her running the vacuum. Seriously?

"What are you doing?" he yelled over the humming of the sweeper.

Okay, that was a dumb question, but the fact that she was cleaning was even dumber.

She tapped the switch with her foot, sending the

room into silence. "I haven't cleaned in here for a while, and all the dust from the remodeling was driving me nuts."

"You just can't relax, can you?" he asked, walking over to take the vacuum from her hand.

"I'm not good with staying still," she told him with a grin. "I never have been. If things need doing, I can't just sit and pretend they'll get done on their own."

He shoved the sweeper into the corner and came back, taking her hands in his. "But the dust and any other chores will still be there after you take some time for yourself."

"I wouldn't know how." Those emerald-green eyes came up to meet his. "Do you know what it's like to not know where your next meal will come from? Or if your heat will get kicked off because your junkie father forgot to pay the bills?"

Oh, Lord. She was ready to open up. Jake had waited for this moment, but now that it presented itself, he wasn't so sure he was ready to hear it. But he would listen, because he was finding himself falling a little harder for Allison each day, and he'd be damned if couldn't man up when she needed him most.

He tugged her over to the couch, tucking her into his side with his arm around her. "No, I have no clue what that's like," he whispered against her ear.

"If I didn't find something to cook for us, if I didn't write the checks and put the bills in the mail, who knows what would've happened.

"My father couldn't hold a job for longer than a week or two, because he'd either steal or be too hungover to show up for his shift. If we didn't have the money coming in from my mother's social security, I don't know how we would've survived."

Jake gritted his teeth. How the hell did a father, a supposed man, allow a young girl to take care of him? Jake wanted to find the jerk and pummel him.

"I remember one time, my dad told me to call a friend to come get me because he was going to kill himself." Allison sat up, looking into Jake's eyes. "I almost wanted him to. Is that terrible? I mean, at that time I was ten and I had lived for five years like this and I just wanted to go live with anyone else. I wanted to know what it was like to have a roof over my head, food in the kitchen and no fear of having the heat shut off. I wanted someone else to give me security, but at the same time I felt guilty, because if I left, who would take care of my dad?"

Jake wiped the lone tear streaking down her cheek. "Even though that loser completely neglected you, you were still determined to save your family. Don't even try to convince me you're not remarkable, Allison. I know better."

She blew out a breath and smiled. "I don't know about that, but I do know that I'd lost my mother, and even though my father was a deadbeat, I didn't want to lose him, too. I mean, he was really all I had left. That was the only life I knew."

Allison shook her head and came to her feet, forcing his hands to fall to the cushion. He watched her pace to the window and wondered how long she'd battled this inner war with herself.

"You were lucky when Charlie came along, then," he told her rigid back. "I wish I'd known him beyond when I was a kid."

Allison threw a smile over her shoulder. "I can't even begin to express how proud he was of you."

That wedge that had driven his mother and uncle apart only made his heart ache for the love and bond that was stolen from him.

Jake stood and crossed the scarred floor. "I'm glad you two had each other. I'm a firm believer that paths cross in life just when we need someone most."

When he placed his hands on her shoulders to turn her fully around, it wasn't tense muscles he felt, but soft, relaxed woman.

"Do you believe that, Allison?" he murmured, as he leaned in closer to those lips that mocked him.

"Right now I'll believe anything if it means you're going to kiss me," she said, smiling.

How could a man turn down an invitation like that?

Enveloping her in his arms, Jake leaned down and kissed her. Arching her backward, he completely overpowered her. He didn't want to be so demanding, but he couldn't stop himself from taking control any more than he could stop his myriad feelings where this woman was concerned.

She clutched his shirt, moaning, as he deepened the kiss and ran a hand down to the small of her back, his fingers slipping just inside the waistband of her jeans.

"Take me upstairs," she murmured against his lips.

"We can go to my room," he told her.

She eased back, looking him in the eyes. "No. I've never had a man in my bedroom, and I want it to be you."

Jake was utterly humbled at the fact that she'd not only opened up enough to trust him, but that she'd invited him to her bed. They could've been naked and on the couch at this point, but she wanted to bring him just another level deeper into her world.

And he wasn't about to turn her down.

He led the way up the stairs, stopping several times to kiss and undress her. By the time they reached her room at the end of the hall, Allison was down to a sheer purple bra and matching panties.

"And you thought your wardrobe was boring," he joked as he started work on his own shirt removal.

Allison laughed, reaching to assist him. "Just because I'm farm girl on the exterior doesn't mean I can't be a little more feminine on the inside."

He tossed his shirt into the corner and toed off his shoes. "Thank God for that."

Allison watched as Jake finished undressing, and she was doing a little thanking God herself. Mercy sakes, she'd seen him without his shirt before, on that first day when she'd smacked his face with horse manure, but now that she knew this man was in her bedroom, wanting to make love to her, she could appreciate the package all the more.

Rippling muscles covered by taut, tanned skin clearly showcased that this man hadn't gained his drool-worthy body in some gym with the AC running. No, those glorious pecs and well-defined abs were evidence of all the hard work he did for a living.

She was so glad she'd put on her prettiest bra and panty set tonight.

"I have a confession," she told him, stepping back to admire him as he stood wearing only a pair of black boxer briefs. "When we left tonight, I was hoping we'd end up back here, just like this."

As he stalked toward her, her heart quickened. She bumped into the bed and fell back.

"Oh, yeah," he said, looming over her. "I've been hoping we'd end up just like this since you flung crap in my face."

Allison laughed. "You're so lying."

"Do you really want to discuss this now?" he asked, bracing his hands on either side of her head and sliding one firm thigh up onto the bed beside her heated body.

"I don't want to discuss anything."

Allison barely got her answer out before Jake descended on her, wrapping her in his strong, warm embrace. They rolled over the mattress, throw pillows sliding to the floor, underwear quickly discarded.

And from somewhere, she didn't know and didn't care where, Jake produced a condom. As he hovered above her and she looked up into his eyes, she wanted to remember this moment forever. She wanted to always remember this feeling of passion, desire and…love.

God, how could she already love him when she'd known him less than two months?

As he slid into her, he kissed her. Slow, soft motions, as if to keep the moment from slipping away. He wasn't just making love, he was cherishing her.

And that's how she knew she could love this man. He'd taken his time with her. He'd let her invite him into her bedroom, instead of seducing his way in there as most men would do.

As Allison dug her nails into his back, her body hummed and demanded more. She arched her back, breaking the kiss.

"That's it, sweetheart," he murmured. "I've got you."

Allison let the overwhelming sensations claim her.

Jake kissed her neck, her breasts, as wave after wave of pleasure consumed her, and just as she was coming down, his body tensed, his eyes locked onto hers and he, too, relinquished control of his body.

As their bodies stopped trembling, Allison pulled the covers up around them, silently asking him to stay. When he tucked her against his side and kissed her forehead, she knew she'd done it. She'd gone and fallen head over dirty work boots in love with him.

And he was more than likely going to not only sell her house, but leave and go back to the life he knew—a life she would be no part of.

CHAPTER SEVEN

JAKE WASN'T A shrink, but he did know when something wasn't right. He and Allison had made love two nights ago. He'd even spent the night in her bed and made love to her again that next morning. And now she was acting as though nothing had happened.

She hadn't once tried to kiss him or even cop a feel. Nor was she at the other end of the spectrum, pouting and sulking as some women did because they didn't know how to approach a man after sleeping with him.

No, Allison was right, smack-dab in the center and not giving him any type of vibe.

And he was starting to get a bit pissed about it. Just once he'd like her to show some emotion, voice how she felt instead of going about this daily routine she'd bottlenecked herself into. He'd love for her to just cut loose and have a yelling fit. She kept all her feelings so guarded, he knew it was just a matter of time before everything bubbled to the surface and exploded.

Now that the plumbing and the sink were installed and the laminate wood floor was partially down, Jake decided to take a break and head out to the stables, where she'd been keeping herself more and more lately.

As he walked, he noticed a full-size truck and trailer pulling out of the drive. His gaze drifted to where Allison stood with one hand shielding her eyes from the sun, the other holding her jacket closed around her waist.

As he got closer, he realized she'd been crying…and then he remembered.

"Was that Sam?" he asked.

She nodded. "Yeah. He's officially got a new home. You should've seen the little girl's face when she found out the horse was for her."

Damn. Had he known she'd been out here dealing with all this, he would've put that kitchen floor on hold.

"I'm sorry," he told her, knowing there were no words to ease her hurt.

"Oh, you'd think I'd be used to this," she declared, waving an arm and turning to go back into the stable. "I'm thrilled Sam has a new home, and I'm even more excited the little girl's mom and dad were able to give such a great present to her. She was so happy, Jake. It's just…"

With her back to him, she stopped, dropped her head in her hands and sobbed. The gut-wrenching sounds tugged at his heart as he moved around her and pulled her into his arms. Her body shook, her hands clutched at his shirt and tears soaked through the material.

There was no need to say the words aloud. They both knew Allison saw herself in that little girl's eyes. Allison saw the child she'd wanted to be, but fate had had different plans for her. As if saying goodbye to the horse weren't hard enough.

After several minutes, Allison eased back with a pink nose and red-rimmed eyes. Tear tracks streaked down her creamy skin, and he wished like hell he could make her life so happy she'd never have to cry again.

"I'm sorry," she told him, wiping her nose with the

back of her hand. "I'm an ugly crier, but I couldn't help it. You just happened along at the wrong time."

He lifted her chin with his index finger and thumb, staring straight into those beautiful eyes. "Actually, I think I came along at the right time."

Her swift intake of breath told him she knew he wasn't referring only to seeing her cry over the adoption.

"You can't mean that, Jake." She stepped back, avoiding his grasp. "Don't say things just because we slept together."

"Do I strike you as someone who would speak in niceties just because I slept with you? Allison, quit putting up this wall so you won't get hurt." Anger coursed through him, fueling his words before he could really think. "You're missing out on life because you're moving away from people who care for you. You're deliberately pushing me away by avoiding me."

She rolled her eyes and stalked by him. "I'm not avoiding you."

Jake started to reach for her when Tucker walked in. "Hey, Jake."

"Tuck, could you leave us for a bit?"

Tucker looked from Allison to Jake, as if he wasn't sure what he should do or who he should take orders from.

"Uh, sure," the elderly man answered. "I've got to run into town to the feed store anyway. I'll be a while."

Once they were alone again, Jake marched over to the tack room, where Allison had disappeared. She was squatting down feeding the puppies.

"Damn it, will you stand up and look at me?"

Allison came to her feet, turned and laced her fingers together in front of her. "What? Do you want me to argue? I know I put up walls, Jake. You're not telling me anything new. I have to. Don't you see? Everyone I've ever loved has left me in some form or another. I can't afford to get close to people. You don't know what it's like."

Jake moved forward, taking her by the shoulders and giving her a gentle shake. "Don't I? You aren't the only one who's lost people they loved, Allison. My mother died, I had an uncle I didn't know and my wife walked out on me. You're not the only one who's known loss, but building this bubble around yourself won't keep hurt from seeping in. So you might as well take down this defense and knock this chip off your shoulder and let people into your life. People who want to care for you, comfort you. Love you."

Allison's heart stopped. She literally held her breath for fear that she'd throw off the intensity of the conversation if she so much as exhaled. What if she hadn't heard right? What if she'd just mistaken what he meant?

Jake dropped his hands and stepped back. "Forget it. I shouldn't have said anything. I need to get back to work."

He stalked off, leaving her standing in utter shock in the tack room while five little fur babies jumped at her legs. As if her whole life hadn't just taken a major turn, she bent back down and finished feeding the dogs. She needed to come to grips with what had just happened.

Jake...loved her? No, impossible. He couldn't love her. He pitied her, which was the dead last thing she wanted from anybody.

Damn, why did she have to get involved with him? She'd known this would happen. She'd known once he heard her history he'd want to play the white knight. Well, that was another fairy tale she'd never believed in.

But she couldn't stand the thought of hurting Jake's feelings, so she found herself stalking toward the house after him.

When she entered the back door, he was standing over the sawhorses measuring another piece of laminate flooring.

"Go back outside," Jake told her without turning around. "I'm not in the mood for an argument."

Heart beating hard against her chest, Allison moved closer. She stood on the other side of the sawhorses and waited until he looked up at her.

"Did you mean it?" she whispered, scared to hope, but finding it impossible not to.

His eyes searched her face, the muscle ticking in his jaw. "Yes."

Closing her eyes on an exhale, Allison smiled. "How do you know?" she asked, looking at him again.

Jake rested his hands on the piece of flooring and leaned forward. "How do I know I love you? It should be simple, but since I came here, that word has stopped being part of my vocabulary. I thought I could do some repairs, sell the house to my potential buyer and be back in Florida within a couple months."

He shoved off the wood and raked both hands through his hair. "But the second I saw your compassion for these horses and learned all you had overcome, I was amazed. Your determination, your passion, the way you throw every fiber of your being into all you do, made me realize I've never met anyone like you. I've never met someone who makes me want to be a better person, who makes me think of her every waking second."

Allison came around the work area and gazed up into his eyes. "You almost sound upset by the fact."

"I am," he admitted, resting his hands on her shoulders. "I'm upset because I want to beat down that damn wall you've put around your heart. I want you to give me a chance, give us a chance."

Allison brought her hands up to hold on to his wrists. "That wall has been crumbling since you kissed me."

Jake stared for only a moment before easing down to capture her lips. "Tell me you'll give this a chance."

Fear gripped her at the same time emotions overtook her, and tears pricked her eyes. "Where? You're going back to Florida and I don't know where I'll be."

"Stay right here," he told her. "I'll be right back."

What? They were in the middle of a life-altering conversation and he needed…what? An intermission?

He dug into his toolbox, produced a small sack and went out the back door.

O-kay.

She watched out the window above the kitchen sink. Before long, Jake, along with all five of her fur babies, came out of the stables. When Jake stepped back into the house, the dogs came with him.

"Jake—" she started, but he cut her off with his hand.

"I know you don't want to get them used to being in the house, but trust me."

She looked at the puppies, who were growing into their fat paws more each day.

Jake turned to the dogs. "Stay. Sit."

Much to her surprise, each dog obeyed.

"How did you do that?" she asked.

Jake threw a charming smile over his shoulder. "I've been working with them a little."

A little? She glanced down to the dogs and noticed something flashing on their necks.

"Are they wearing collars?" she asked.

Jake picked up one puppy, examined the collar and dog tag, and held it out to her. "Read it."

Intrigued, she fingered the gold, bone-shaped tag. "Will," she read aloud.

He put the dog down and picked up another, examining its tag before thrusting it at her.

"You," she read.

Another dog was in her face just as fast.

She eyed the tag, saw the word and whispered, "Marry."

Another white bundle of fur appeared in her blurry vision.

"Me," she croaked.

He lifted the last puppy to her and she lifted its tag. "Allison."

With a hiccup, cry, laugh combo—God, she was a hot mess—she looked down at the obedient dogs and back to Jake, who stood with hope in his eyes.

"I don't have a ring," he said apologetically. "I only had the tags made yesterday and wanted to keep them until I thought you were ready for the question. I guess I couldn't wait."

Allison swiped at her damp cheeks. "What about your buyer?"

Jake shrugged. "I already told him the house was off the market."

Shock had Allison taking a step back. "You're kidding. When did you tell him?"

"A few days ago. I knew I couldn't sell this farm. These horses need this land, need you. I need you."

"Are you sure you'll be content with living on a farm?" she asked. "This couldn't be further from what you're used to, and I'm pretty set in my ways."

Jake stepped forward, wrapping his arms around her waist and lifting her off the ground. "I better be included in those set ways, Allison, because I'm not going anywhere. You're going to teach me all about these horses, because I want to help rescue them and care for them with you."

Allison wrapped her arms around his neck and kissed his cheeks, his forehead, his lips. "I love you, Jake. You'll be awesome with the horses."

"Is that a yes?" he asked.

Allison kissed him again, squeezing him tight. "Definitely."

"I do have one condition," he told her, face void of all laughter.

"What?"

"Swear to me right now you won't fling manure at me again."

Allison laughed, squeezing him tighter still. "I can't guarantee that. What if you make me mad?"

He kissed her hard, deep. "I have better ways to blow off steam."

* * * * *

National bestselling author **JULES BENNETT** is no stranger to going after her dreams. Before fulfilling her goal of becoming a published author, Jules became a salon owner at the age of 21 and published her first novel at 27. She lives in the Midwest with her high school sweetheart husband and their two young girls.

When Jules isn't writing or spending time with her family, she enjoys working out and talking to the fictitious people in her head. She loves to hear from readers and can be found on Twitter or through her Facebook Fan-Page. You can also stay up to date on new releases, sign up for her newsletter or contact her through her website www.julesbennett.com. Check out Jules's latest release, *Behind Palace Doors*, available now from Harlequin Desire!

REQUEST YOUR FREE BOOKS!

2 FREE NOVELS
FROM THE ROMANCE COLLECTION
PLUS 2 FREE GIFTS!

YES! Please send me 2 FREE novels from the Romance Collection and my 2 FREE gifts (gifts are worth about $10). After receiving them, if I don't wish to receive any more books, I can return the shipping statement marked "cancel." If I don't cancel, I will receive 4 brand-new novels every month and be billed just $5.99 per book in the U.S. or $6.49 per book in Canada. That's a savings of at least 25% off the cover price. It's quite a bargain! Shipping and handling is just 50¢ per book in the U.S. and 75¢ per book in Canada.* I understand that accepting the 2 free books and gifts places me under no obligation to buy anything. I can always return a shipment and cancel at any time. Even if I never buy another book, the two free books and gifts are mine to keep forever.

194/394 MDN FVU7

Name	
	(PLEASE PRINT)

Address	Apt. #

City	State/Prov.	Zip/Postal Code

Signature (if under 18, a parent or guardian must sign)

Mail to the Harlequin® Reader Service:
IN U.S.A.: P.O. Box 1867, Buffalo, NY 14240-1867
IN CANADA: P.O. Box 609, Fort Erie, Ontario L2A 5X3

Want to try two free books from another line?
Call 1-800-873-8635 or visit www.ReaderService.com.

* Terms and prices subject to change without notice. Prices do not include applicable taxes. Sales tax applicable in N.Y. Canadian residents will be charged applicable taxes. Offer not valid in Quebec. This offer is limited to one order per household. Not valid for current subscribers to the Romance Collection or the Romance/Suspense Collection. All orders subject to credit approval. Credit or debit balances in a customer's account(s) may be offset by any other outstanding balance owed by or to the customer. Please allow 4 to 6 weeks for delivery. Offer available while quantities last.

Your Privacy—The Harlequin® Reader Service is committed to protecting your privacy. Our Privacy Policy is available online at www.ReaderService.com or upon request from the Harlequin Reader Service.

We make a portion of our mailing list available to reputable third parties that offer products we believe may interest you. If you prefer that we not exchange your name with third parties, or if you wish to clarify or modify your communication preferences, please visit us at www.ReaderService.com/consumerchoice or write to us at Harlequin Reader Service Preference Service, P.O. Box 9062, Buffalo, NY 14269. Include your complete name and address.

ROM13